Please
ake the   name

First published in Great Britain in November 2002
by Benchmark Press,
Little Hatherden, Near Andover, SP11 OHY.

A CIP catalogue for this book is available from the British
Library.
ISBN: 0-9537674-3-4

Cover by John Sage, Andover.

Printed and bound in Great Britain by Antony Rowe Limited,
Bumper's Farm Industrial Estate, Chippenham, Wiltshire, SN14
6LH.

STEVE AND THE INTELLECTUALS

GUY   WILSON

BY THE SAME AUTHOR:

NOVELS

The Industrialists   (Dent)

A Touch of the Lemming   (Bles)

The Ardour of the Crowd   (Chatto & Windus)

A Healthy Contempt   (Images)

The Art Thieves   (Rampant Horse)

The Carthaginian Hoard   (Harold, Martin & Redfern)

Second Time Round   (Benchmark Press)

SHORT STORIES

The Three Vital Moments of Benjamin Ellashaye   (Chatto & Windus)

Collected Short Stories   (Benchmark Press)

Brought up in Devon, Guy Wilson was educated at Marlborough College and Gonville and Caius College, Cambridge. After a stint in the Royal Marine Commandos and a statutory attempt at being a schoolmaster, he determined to be a novelist. He and his wife, Angela, set off to Spain on a motorbike. This was the start of an adventurous and precarious existence. They spent three years in Spain, two in Algeria, three in Italy and one in Paris, supplementing literary income by starting and running English language schools. Then they found themselves in charge of Padworth, the international sixth-form college for girls, which they ran for twelve years. The Wilsons now live in Hampshire.

FOR ANGELA

Chateau Lamartine
Vigny-les-Pins
Alpes Maritimes

'Dear Steve,

For some reason I've been thinking of the past quite a lot lately - and of course the past includes you, so I've been remembering you, too.

Today I had an idea. I am actually in Paris writing this but I'm about to have some leave from my job here and shall be at the Château for a month. It's ages since you were with us, why don't you take an extended break from all your important goings-on in England and come out to see how we've progressed? I remember that you're something of a painter - among your other attributes. We might get Hortense Beerbohmer, our extremely gifted artist, to give you some help. And your wife - Jubilee is her name, isn't it? - there would be plenty for her to do if she were interested. I do pottery and enamel work. Maybe she'd like to try her hand at one of those - or at one of Liz's many activities, indoors and out!

Even if you just want to have a lazy time and do nothing creative, there is plenty to entertain you. Long lovely walks, and we are a particularly exciting community at the moment with two top brains, one of them a fine historian who has us all on our toes.

It's a bit primitive, I know, but the sun makes up for everything and Alfonso has made some improvements since you were here. Do write and say you'll come.

Love, June.'

Steve had selected the letter from the day's mail out of curiosity - because of the French stamp and the familiar handwriting, which he couldn't place for a moment. But when after reading a couple of lines he glanced up at the address and then to June's name at the bottom, he half-skipped the rest. He put the letter back in the envelope and stuffed it into the side pocket of his new Saville Row suit. He said nothing to Jubilee, who was frying something delicious for their supper in the new kitchen he had recently had entirely re-modelled and re-equipped for her.

Like a practised card-player he rapidly sorted through the other mail. There it was. He drew out what he was looking for, threw the other envelopes on the table, and slit it with his powerful little finger. The job was in the bag, he saw, the debenture bank wanted him up there tomorrow. It could be a grand or two sauntering in his direction. He smiled to himself. 'Worth the bus-ticket,' as Ma used to say in Kentish Town days.

He took off his jacket and got down to the rest of the mail. Half way down the pile, which included cheques, also half way down the neat double whisky Jubilee had brought him, his ebullient and naturally generous nature ignited suddenly. What was all this money for but to spend on Jubilee? Swallowing the rest of the liquid at a swoop, he bounded into the kitchen.

'Jubee honeychile, how's'bout a noo roo-bee stone to put on dem my-dee pretty digits of yours? I'ken 'fford it.'

Reading-born Jubilee, whose English was impeccable, didn't in the least mind Steve's implied joke about her racial origins, which from time to time he teasingly indulged in - sometimes she teased him back by calling him 'white trash'- but at this moment she didn't participate. She smiled but answered distinctly. 'I don't want any more rings, thank you, Steve. There's no room left on my fingers.'

'A holiday then? What do you say to a safari holiday this time? Something completely new.'

Jubilee took her time. She had put on a very becoming red dress protected by a pink apron with crinkled edges, and was in the act of serving a first course of langoustines fried in garlic butter to be eaten with the fresh rolls she had baked. When he had sat down at the pine corner area where they ate most of their meals, and when she had heaped three-quarters of the browned crustaceans on to Steve's plate and liberally spooned the liquid

2

over them, she put her bare brown arm affectionately round his shoulders and kissed the ham-coloured space on top of his head.

'If *you* wish, Steve. But it doesn't seem to have registered with you yet that I really have everything I want and am perfectly content. You don't have to buy me any more things to make me happy. I *am* totally happy. With you, I'd be happy living in a hut in a forest.'

How romantic Jubilee was, Steve thought, how un-grasping and totally unlike another, not-to-be-named. What a stroke of luck to find a girl like her in the jungle of existence and to find she returned his love. But in a part of his consciousness to which he didn't have daily access, her remark left a mild disturbance. Women were different from men of course, but that anyone of either sex could say they were 'perfectly happy', and mean it on any but a momentary basis, had to be a worrying concept. Didn't you have to work for, pay for, content? Could one truthfully believe otherwise? A worse thought glinted. What if Jubilee really didn't want the things he strove to give her?

He dismissed such silliness. Of course she appreciated what he gave her. It was just that she was an immensely sweet and beautiful girl and was thinking of his pocket. That was why he had married her, amid a silent company of raised white middle-class eyebrows. She was a girl among a million.

The next morning he recalled this sensible judgement with even greater certainty as his Rover effortlessly pulled ahead of two nose-to-tail juggernauts exceeding the speed limit in the northbound middle lane of the M.1. He had overtaken a few juggernauts in his time in more senses than one, he thought. Reaching for the stereo button he rejected three stations pumping the usual tattoo, and settled for - Beethoven was it? Beethoven, Brahms, one of them. OK, stirring stuff. Keeping time, he beat his small but muscular fist on the steering wheel, like a speaker making points.

The doomed business was a brick works specialising in hand-made bricks. Driving through the impressive wrought-iron gates, Steve began to get the message already. With an all-embracing glance he took in these gates, a beautifully-built curving brick

3

wall on either side of them, immaculate grass, and flower-beds sporting an ambiguous piece of modern sculpture, a modern brick-and-glass office block and, behind, the mess of brickyard outhouses, what looked like a kiln, and, beyond these, high-rise towers of unsold bricks.   One fork-lift was in operation - presumably adding to the stockpiles - but at least half a dozen green-overalled men were sitting around smoking under a roofed-in area.   As he parked, a girl and a woman, their arms akimbo, emerged from the office block and teetered across the yard with a social air.   Stand-easy time?   One presumed, but was it much different from the rest of the day?

Steve had more thoughts-in-advance as he entered the building. He had known hostility to his appearances - rudeness, even once or twice physical menace.   Here, so far at least, there was no such thing.   The girl on the desk, a dark-haired beauty with a skin like an eggshell, obviously didn't expect him and seemed totally at ease.

'Can I help you at all?' she said in a singsong way, coming up from a magazine and re-positioning a flower in a vase at her side, apparently amiss.   She viewed first his briefcase, then his clothing as if these constituted evidence relevant to her.

'Mr Addicot?' she repeated amiably when he had supplied his name.   'Oh yes?   And who is it you were wanting to see?   Sales is it perhaps?'   She cast another look at the brief case, as if it were likely to be full of samples.

He resisted the temptation to say, 'It's sales all right.   I'm selling your job.'   'Mr Hunter-Smith,' he said instead.

There was no escort, no security, just a direction from the girl to the ultra-modern lift, which still smelt new, and the words 'you should find him on the first floor at the end of the corridor on the right.   He *is* in.'

A pleasing accessibility you might say. Derek Hornby Hunter-Smith *was* exactly in the place forecast, in an exceedingly plush office equipped with a pale blue carpet, a vast desk with a tooled-leather top, and an amount of jungle-green vegetation.   A man in a white coat was meticulously cleaning the leaves of one of these plants.

Hunter-Smith was on the phone.   Lolling in a high-backed

swivel chair, he had one leg doubled underneath him. The other, stretched forward, was toeing the handle of one of the desk drawers. He wasn't wearing a suit, but grey flannels, a sports jacket of a pronounced pattern, a checked shirt and a yellow tie with a motif of horses' heads. He took no notice of Steve's entry. Steve became an enforced witness to the remainder of the telephone conversation.

'Well, that's encouraging,' Hunter-Smith said as he finished his call. 'Five hundred more copings, instant delivery to Lady Glastonbury. More like her and we'll be out of the wood.'

Steve introduced himself.

Apparently no notice was taken of this. 'These banks get windy at the first adversity,' Hunter-Smith continued as if the two of them were everyday acquaintances and Steve had just breezed in for a chat. 'It's true things aren't moving with quite the speed we'd hoped. But that's to be expected with a high-class product like ours. A couple of really big orders, and we're there. I had an enquiry from a big city firm of architects the other day. One windfall like that . . . The crucial thing is that when we do start on the big orders there'll be no delay. The stuff's ready out there. That's why I've never stopped production. You must always think big. That's what father always said. "Look after the pounds and the pence'll look after themselves . . ."'

Steve felt this was enough fooling. Though not invited to do so he had by now sat down opposite the loquacious director and placed his brief case on top of the desk. 'Will you ask this gentleman to leave the room?' he interrupted. This, as he had intended, left something of a vacuum.

'Herbert?' murmured Hunter-Smith, as if the leaf-cleanser were a trusted co-director.

Steve's eyes levelled in Herbert's direction proved more effective than Hunter-Smith's mention of his name. Folding the cloth neatly over the side of the pail and leaving both items, the man withdrew and with some presence of mind closed the door after him.

'I don't think you've quite grasped the situation,' Steve said. 'As you've been informed in writing by recorded delivery, you are no longer in charge of your business, I am. Indeed it's no longer your business.   I'm here as official receiver appointed by your debenture-holder to dispose of what assets remain to the best advantage, and to distribute the proceeds, costs having been retained, to your creditors.'

Steve didn't like this approach but it was necessary if he wasn't to waste more time and money than was necessary.

Another of Steve's dislikes was for categories, categories being commodities better belonging to administrators and bureaucrats whom his calling made him regard as obstacles in life.   But it was difficult not to file Hunter-Smith in one.

Public school - Stowe, he was informed very early in the apologia which followed, as if this in itself inoculated him against misfortune - the son of a very successful industrialist (brass fitments), it seemed he had knocked about a great deal for the twenty years or so adulthood had vouchsafed him before his widowed father died.   A yacht based in Ibiza was mentioned, a racing car.   It was only when on the father's decease the company was sold and the spoils divided with a sister that a more promising outlook ensued.   Hunter-Smith had always wanted to do something worthwhile, he confessed, it was just that brass-fitments hadn't seemed quite his thing.   He had always shared with the Prince of Wales, however, an interest in the aesthetics of architecture.   With father's capital available, he felt the time had come for the realisation of his dream.   He would be joining those elite few who were helping to provide the raw materials for a new urban splendour which would slowly replace the thoughtless barbarisms of the recent past.

Steve truncated this redundant autobiography as soon as he could, and got down to work.   He decided to set himself up in the waiting room on the ground floor, ordered the books to be brought down to him and had the door key found so that he wouldn't be disturbed.   Half the morning was enough to have most of the jigsaw in place.   Hunter-Smith had bought the yard and the kilns very cheaply, but the building and its environs ('so necessary to attract the right sort of client') the huge amount spent on the most expensive kind of fork-lifts, three huge lorries, two new cars, and above all the labour force - large enough to build a pyramid manually - had absorbed far too much of the capital too quickly. Practically nothing had been spent on the sales side, only large amounts on showy and probably ineffective publicity, which included a brick wall at the Chelsea Flower Show, and a no doubt beautifully constructed brick kiosk for publicity at Badminton.

Steve knew he would have to be brutal. He began at the top. He went up to Hunter-Smith's office again. He rather hoped at this juncture the man would be angry. He usually found this easier to deal with. 'I'm sorry, Hunter-Smith, but there's nothing I can do,' he said at once. 'You're bankrupt. I shall begin by releasing your entire staff except for two fork-lift men (who, hopefully, can also drive the lorries) a secretary, and the night-watchman. Everyone will get what is owing to them, and redundancy. I'll then set about disposing of the stock. As I'll need the telephone and the fax-machine and may well have to receive clients, I'll use this office. I'd like to make a start right away. Maybe you'd like to move out of here any personal belongings, then gather together your staff to break the news to them? If you prefer, I'll do the latter.'

The displaced director had been standing by the window when Steve entered, staring down at the gardener watering the rose-beds. He said nothing immediately after Steve had spoken, but returned to the presidential chair and sat in it. He leant forward, laid one arm on either side of the large blotter, and adjusted its position.

'I was just off to Bermuda for a couple of weeks,' he murmured, 'I need a break.'

It was then Steve noticed Hunter-Smith's head was shaking quite pronouncedly as if he'd had an onset of delirium tremens, and his naturally pale skin had gone a pastel shade paler. Steve had an instinctive wish to amputate expenditure, but a practical thought combined happily with the more humanitarian impulse this abject sight aroused in him. A condemned man was entitled to a last request, surely, and it would neatly dispose of him.

'Why don't you do just that?' he said. 'A week, anyway. I can probably incorporate the air-fare at least into winding up expenses.'

Hunter-Smith knew the truth.   He had known it all the time. They finished with a brief discussion about the white sands, the beautiful shells, and the deep-sea fishing available in this tropical paradise.

Hunter-Smith chose not to address his ex-employees himself. A few minutes later Steve saw the Jaguar turning through the sumptuous gates - almost certainly for the last time.   He asked one of the office staff how the loudspeaker system worked and delivered an abrupt message to the entire premises.   Ten minutes later, standing on a fork-lift palette in the yard, he gave it to the assembled staff in a few words.   He told them who he was, then explained that the company they had worked for no longer existed.   He explained the pay arrangements, and said that if they would be good enough to call at eight the next morning they would be able to collect their P.45.s and what was owing to them. He was sorry, but beyond this there was nothing he could do. He then hurried back to the office, turning his back on the frightened, angry conversations which would no doubt break out.

The next morning, when the queue outside the accounts office had dwindled and finally dispersed, he got cracking.   It was always unpleasant until this happened, like waiting until a funeral is over.   He chose to assist him the middle-aged woman in the accounts office.   She had secretarial skills, did not mind using them, and he could tell from her face that she knew very well long ago all this had been coming and that, whatever other illusions she might have, she had none about her ex-boss.   When it was just her and himself, with the telephone put through to the office and nowhere else, he felt a surge of optimism and energy as he contemplated the deployment of his know-how.   He got through to a big builder he knew in Essex.   As a kite, he offered five thousand of the best bricks at half-price.

A receiver becomes an expert in pauses.   It's an emperor's clothes situation.   People unskilled in the art imagine that when silent they are fully clothed. It is not the case.   When the builder said, after a long pause which he firmly believed denoted indecision, 'well, I suppose if you're pushed, Steve, and the bricks are as you describe them, I could take a few off your hands,' he imagined Steve would think he was bestowing a favour. Steve knew it wasn't a favour at all. He was confirmed in his diagnosis when the next man he spoke to said much the same thing - to a three-quarter price offer.

By eleven, a very large builder in the vicinity had called him. He had heard news of the bankruptcy on a local radio newscast. One of the two people he had phoned first phoned again to increase the favour they were granting. When they heard there would be a fifty per cent escalation in the price for an additional order, their charity stretched to the most commendable heights. They still took the bricks. By the time Mrs Honeywell, flexing fingers which had been well exercised on the computer keyboard, suggested he might like her to go down the road to obtain sandwiches from the pub, Steve was on the outskirts of a new idea. While she was out, he switched off the phone, put a biro between his teeth, and tilted back reflectively in the large chair.

'Mrs Honeywell, we have a new situation,' he declared on her return. While the woman placed change on the desk, then unpacked two neat bundles of sandwiches, he put to her what the new situation was. Almost certainly the business had been underselling itself. The demand for high quality bricks was obviously there if you looked in the right places. They shouldn't be selling stock, they should be putting the whole business on the market as a single enterprise with a potentially prosperous profile.

Having a well-balanced attitude to life and a finely-tuned sensitivity to correct priorities, Mrs Honeywell's attention was largely being spent on the apportionment of food at this moment and on the question of whether Mr Addicot preferred an egg and cress mixture or straight ham or one of each. She had dared to presume he liked mustard, she added. But that did not mean her business instincts were other than temporarily detained.

'I always thought so,' she pronounced as they embarked on the food, 'and did on several occasions venture to point this out to the powers-that-were.'

'Point out what?' asked Steve, whose thoughts had run on a bit from the ex-Director's shortcomings.

'Why, that our bricks were under priced and that insufficient attention was being paid to sales.'

Steve had the footnotal thought that if Mrs Honeywell had been running the business he probably wouldn't be sitting here.

In view of the distance from home, reluctantly Steve had to stay in a hotel, just going back for the weekend.   On the Friday evening of the second week he felt well satisfied as he drove. Three-quarters of the stock was sold for an average price in excess of Hunter-Smith's philanthropic levels. The proceeds had paid most of the pressing debts.   The sale was also now as good as sewn up. He'd already had three tentative offers for the business, and had gazumped one of them. It was now a question of clinching the deal and creaming his spoils. He calculated his remuneration - very substantial, he found.   About this he felt no guilt.   It was more than probable that before long at least some of the people he had dismissed would be back in their old posts, albeit with rather more to do than hitherto.   A good idea would be receiving its just reward, and the economy of the country a corresponding benefit.

As it was early he decided he ought to stop off at Ma's bungalow, which was on the way.   He had bought this dwelling for her five years ago in the nearest big town to the village where he and Jubilee lived.   He had wanted to build her a house on their land but she wouldn't have it.

'I can't talk to cows and geese,' she complained, 'and your Jubilee doesn't want me hobbling about all day.   If I've got to leave Kentish' - which had been her continued habitat after her husband's decease - 'I want some humans round me for God's sake.'

There were a number of humans around her, streets-full of bungalows like hers, clambering up and down the hills that surrounded the area of office blocks emerging from a blue haze below.   Representing no doubt some marine nostalgia of the developer or of the town official responsible, the streets had names reminiscent not of industry but of the more popular stretches of the British coastline.   There was Scarborough Terrace, Brighton Grove, and - a Celtic touch - Pwllheli Drive. Ma's road was called Shingle Way.   Steve had humorously suggested that Ma should call her house Pebble Cottage, but Ma hadn't been taken with the idea. Being a traditionalist and not sympathetic towards her son's wilder flights of imagination, she preferred the '53' already inscribed on the gate, the '3' a little drawn back from the '5' like a female tango dancer leaning backwards from her partner.

Each bungalow had a car parked in front of it. Not as large a variety as Steve's, but new looking. There was the odd banger, but most vehicles represented their owners' success in life. Two were being cleaned energetically when Steve arrived. He was pleased to see it, also the spanking condition of the houses, each with a different coloured front door. He had to criticise Ma's door a bit. She'd had the very subtle shade of apricot she inherited covered with a treacly brown. 'Doors should be brown,' she said definitively when he made the mildest of comments on this choice. There were also no flowers in the small patch of garden between the street and the building as was the case with all the adjacent dwellings, the only adornment an old basin which Mrs Addicot refused to move despite requests from her neighbours. She kept a plug in it, and when it didn't rain topped up the level of water. Local dogs on their daily rounds made a point of visiting it to slake their thirsts

'Oh it's you,' said Ma as Steve appeared round the back. There had been no answer to his knock. 'I wondered if you'd be dropping in.' She was sitting upright in her canvas chair, ankle-deep in un-mown grass, enjoying the evening sunshine.

Steve kissed his mother on the white expanse of forehead that lay beneath a hairstyle reminiscent of a nineteen-twenties schoolgirl. Light brown - the shade more precisely of light-tan boot-polish - the texture coarse like thread - it was cropped all round at a uniform height, parted at the side, and held in position by a large tortoiseshell slide.

'Time you had that firm in to cut the lawn, Ma,' he said, bringing down a second seat from the small balcony. 'You'll have tigers roaming this jungle soon. I'll get on to them - the firm, I mean, not the tigers.'

The old woman seemed to ignore the offer and the joke as an irrelevance. 'Well,' she said, running her eye down the newly-tailored dark suit, 'we do seem pleased with ourselves today,

11

don't we?   Business good, is it?   Lots more lovely money coming in?'   Her eye finished on the parcel Steve had absent-mindedly put beside his chair.   The state of the grass and hedges had momentarily made him forget it.

'Oh yes - for you,' he said, giving it to her, 'your favourites.'

She took the parcel on her knees which, by outward pressure not unlike the mechanism of the canvas-seated chair, spread a horizontal platform of black skirt between them.   She picked rather half-heartedly for a moment at the knot of saffron-coloured string, then gave it up and broke it robustly with her thumb.   She laid back the paper, lifted the lid of the box and was confronted with a rectangle of dark chocolates, each one surmounted by a violet.   Two marauding plump fingers violated the symmetry and her cheek was already bulging as she handed him the box.   'You know my weaknesses, Steve,' she said.

Steve became reflective.   He hooked his arm over the back of the chair.   'Yes, I have as it happens had a very remunerative week,' he said.   He paused.   'We'll be off for a holiday soon to celebrate.'

'Oh yes?   What's it to be this time?   Timbuctoo?'

'You have the right continent.   Safari, I thought.   Kenya - that sort of area.'

'You'll get your tigers there all right.'

'Kenya, that is, if . . .'

'And elephants.   You might get yourself a tusk or two.   Good for rheumatism, they say.   Or is it love?'

'You're thinking of rhinoceros tusks, Ma.   No, what I was saying was . . .'

'No, I'm not thinking of rhinoceros.   It's elephants - aphrodisiacs, that's what they call them.   "Afro", you see, from Africa, that's how they get the name.   Though you'd better watch your step.   They seem to be shooting the poachers now, not the animals.'

'. . .Though what I was going to say was I'm not so sure Jubilee's as keen as I am.'

Steve really didn't know why this sentence came out of his mouth.   Had Jubilee expressed any discontent at the idea of stalking large animals in the tropics?   Had he even entertained the idea before this that she might not?   He couldn't remember either was the case.   But perhaps fortunately his remark fell on deaf ears.   A second cavity had appeared in the tray of chocolates and a loud smacking of the lips was indicating Mrs Addicot Senior's renewed enjoyment.   Her attention had also been diverted.   She began to talk of the man next door.

'Goddam him, he's started up that sprinkling thing again,' she said, launching a hostile glance over the hedge.   'We'll have it all evening now, fizzing away.   It comes over my hedge, too.   I got soaked to the skin the other night.   People ought to be more considerate.'

There must have been some recording and play back mechanism in Ma's brain, however.   As he said goodbye to her, she said, 'You take her, she'll enjoy it when she gets there.'   It was only when he was overtaking the pink ice-cream van and its attendant young buyers further down the street that Steve realised what she had meant.

From her desk in the open plan office on the fourteenth floor, June Aguas de Villanova (née Smith and known as Mademoiselle Smith at work) looked down on the Seine, which was like a green length of rope snaked at her feet.   On either side of the river sped two endless lines of traffic.   The huge room around her was in a ferment as people were packing up and leaving for the week end. Several colleagues came hurriedly to wish her a happy holiday. Quite suddenly no one was there.   Two cleaning women in white overalls appeared with their hoovers and began stacking chairs on the desks.

June watched a Bâteau Mouche turning in midstream, loaded with sightseers.   The hazy evening sun visited in turn several of its many glass panels so that they became momentarily plates of gold.   A huge commercial barge, low in the water and flying the German flag, pushed heavily upstream.   June forgot her worry for a few seconds.   Tomorrow evening she and Alfonso would be back at the Château, where they belonged, for four whole weeks. Something could be worked out, she was sure.   They had always got over difficulties before.   Her telephone gave a short assertive ring.

'*Mademoiselle Smith?   Monsieur Doorn vous attend.*'

She picked up her summer coat, her furled umbrella, and her brief case.   On her way to the lifts she said '*Bonsoir madame*' in turn to each of the cleaning women, and received their vigorous replies.   She pressed the 'up' button.

She could remember only a handful of occasions during her twenty years with the firm when she had been to the top floor. Doorn, the new director, she had met only once at a social function.   She had told him, oddly, about the Château and how it had always been a secondary ambition of hers to give shelter and the right atmosphere to a group of talented thinkers and artists. She remembered he had been intrigued, also by the fact that her husband was an artist who worked in metal.   He himself, he had said, went in for a bit of 'tinkling' on the piano when he could find the time.   When he retired, he said, he had a fond hope of taking up music seriously. Perhaps she would admit him to her Château, he had added humorously.

As the lift whisked her upwards, she clutched at the small hope that it would be something to do with the Château Doorn wanted to talk to her about. He would have seen her name on the summer leave list and had something personal to say to her perhaps. She flirted fancifully with the idea that he might wish to involve the company with her project with a donation from the charities fund. Heaven knew, they could do with one just now. On the other hand it might just be that on the eve of her month's leave he wanted to give her an encouraging pat on the back for her long devoted service in the personnel department of the company. People were saying Doorn had a personal touch.

The lift gave a little jolt and the heavy metal door rumbled open. She found herself in quite a different atmosphere from downstairs. What was it - the deeper pile of the carpet, the faint odour of expensive perfume, a certain quality in the silence, the extra mature chic of Doorn's secretary who was advancing to meet her down a corridor of polished light-coloured wood?

Doorn rose from a large paperless desk. Alone upon it were a small vase of scarlet rosebuds and a photograph in a leather frame of a woman and three children. Two of the latter were mounted on ponies. His smile and outstretched hand confirmed the humanity suggested by the snapshot.

'Miss Smith, how nice to see you,' he said in perfect English with just a becoming trace of a Dutch accent. 'I think we'll sit ourselves over here, shall we?' They repaired towards two comfortable-looking modern armchairs, and to her considerable surprise he offered her an aperitif. She asked for a *campari*, a bottle of which she saw in the glass-fronted cabinet.

How young he was, she thought as he served the drink, to be managing director of a huge petroleum concern like theirs. And how nice that he could be so relaxed and human. He had said for example 'sit ourselves' not 'sit' - which she knew was deliberately idiomatic phraseology, not a foreigner's mistake, and he began to talk in an easy way which suggested the meeting was for a purely social exchange.

When they had chatted for about five minutes, he went silent all of a sudden and began to massage his hand. 'Miss Smith,' he said, 'you're aware, I'm sure, that we've had a severe problem of over-employment and that it was one of my most unpleasant tasks when taking over my job to do something about this?'

'Er - yes,' she said, 'it was painful for a lot of people. Those of us who survived considered ourselves lucky.'

He coughed. 'Quite so.' He spoke more slowly. 'But the fact is a new survey is telling me we haven't yet slimmed down quite enough.'

Her hearing was severed as if she had jumped into water. She was in a new element, she felt her body weightless, and had the notion that if she tried to stand up her limbs wouldn't comply.

She didn't hear any more, and didn't emerge from this state of amnesia until she found herself downstairs. Pushing blindly at the swing door in the main entrance, she found she had twirled herself back into the hall. Half stumbling, and finding herself observed with anxiety by one of the night security staff, it struck her then what had taken place. In a space of minutes, after twenty years of unremitting work, she had been dismissed with what Doorn had called a 'lump sum' and with the present balance of the pension fund she and the company had paid into and which she wouldn't receive until she was sixty. If her own income had become inadequate to defray the expenses of the Château, how much less would the proceeds from the investment of such a small sum? The Château now would be out of the question. She would have to sell the remainder of the lease in order to live. It was the end of her dream.

She didn't have the courage to tell Alfonso at once. As she emerged from the suburban station building, she saw his huge shaggy figure leaning against the large battered car on the further side of the station park. He was rolling a cigarette, but at the same time, she knew, keeping an anxious eye on the gate. He saw her, waved briefly, and ran the paper along his tongue. She knew he was pleased to see her as he always was at the end of the day, and was only pretending to be nonchalant. The realisation deepened her gloom and brought on a renewed crisis of emotion, which she had to fight to overcome.

As he drove her through the familiar streets and chatted in his amiable way about his achievement in the forge that day, she was just able to imagine that what had happened to her at this age of forty did not matter in the least. Alfonso would support them now. The ending of her employment would force him to do something or other to earn money. Heavens, he had skills enough. She would set him up in something with the capital sum she had just been awarded. They would relieve themselves of the heavy expenses of their Paris dwelling, and live in the Château. Wasn't that what they wanted? Perhaps they should have done it ages ago.

But before they reached home she knew it was a hopeless idea. Even if Alfonso would agree to a part-time job which took him away from his real work, which he wouldn't, he would never earn what her job had brought in.

Alfonso had baked them a fine mackerel he had selected in the market. She told him when they were half way through the meal. She said it dully, without emphasis, while he was thumbing through some metallurgical catalogue he had on the wall-seat beside him.

He didn't seem to register at once. He turned over a page before he looked up. '*Muy bien*,' he said then, taking it as the most imaginable event in the world. He blew out his cheeks as he began to think about it. 'So, we live in Château. *Mucho mejor*. I have my *guapissima* all day - and eat big e-lunches.' He gave a bray of laughter, his fine white teeth showing splendidly between his black beard and black moustachios.

In bed later, she cried out. 'Don't you see, Alfonso, we'll have to sell the Château lease to live?'

He didn't understand. 'Sell Château? Of course we not sell Château. We e-live in Château, make e-love, eat and work in Château. *Para siempre.*'

He began to kiss her, then to make love. At first she couldn't respond, she felt too despondent. Then as always he set her on fire, and she finished giving back to him passionately. They slept deeply.

The alarm clock shrilled into the grey silence of the summer dawn.   June's first thought was of Steve Addicot and the letter she had written.   She immediately felt guilty.   She had thought at the time she wrote it that her wish to invite him had been entirely spontaneous in the way she had described.   But had it been? Hadn't she even then had at the back of her mind the idea that in some way she didn't define Steve, a rich man and an expert on money, might somehow provide her with a solution to those money problems of the Château which had existed even before last night's events?   Even if she hadn't had this idea, in the new totally critical situation created by her redundancy, wouldn't people at the Château be bound to think her invitation had an ulterior motive?   She felt her cheeks flushing at the shame of the idea.

This was nonsense, she told herself.   It was highly unlikely that Steve would accept her invitation, and if by any chance he did she would have to write again and put him off.   Nobody would know she had written.   Her mind fastened onto the graver matter at hand.   How on earth was she going to tell them all?

She and Alfonso started early on their way south and were through the tunnels and environs of Paris before the daily wrestle of traffic began.   As the sun rose and began to colour the old grey houses with a rosier hue, Fernando turned the ageing Mercedes onto the *autoroute*.   With two stops and if not hindered by other cars or a breakdown, he would drive them at an average speed of a hundred and twenty kilometres an hour.   They would arrive in the late afternoon.

3

Jubilee liked to wake first. She usually did, especially in summer when the sun rose so early. When she opened her eyes she knew the golden light would already be shining across the garden and the green cornfield beside it. It was streaming through their window.

She thought a little about sunshine on this particular morning, about how it was always there. At night it was there on the other side of the world, like someone you were fond of who had gone out and would be back. If you closed the curtains it would politely withdraw, but then when you reopened them it would instantly flood in again and occupy every corner of the room as if that were its natural right. Even when it was grey and wet it was there above the clouds, waiting.

Then she listened to birds. There was a blackbird, which she knew would be sitting on the topmost branch of the silver tree growing in the middle of the lawn, whose leaves rustled when there was a wind. The swallows were awake under the eaves outside the window, whispering excitedly. She couldn't see them from the bed, but she imagined one breaking away like something coming unstuck and racing in a crazy circle over the garden with a rapid flimsy flight. She smelt the aroma of damp mown grass.

She looked at Steve, still asleep, his head turned towards her. This was the main reason why she liked to wake first. His face was so different at this time, clear, boyish, just as it was when she first saw him in the supermarket store where she had worked four years ago. When his eyes opened, they blinked and looked lost for a moment. Then, when he saw her bending over him, he would smile in quite a different way from most other times. He hadn't yet put on the day and what other people said and how he thought they thought of him. She sometimes tried to conjure this look during the day, but she could never quite recreate it as it was. On this particular morning - which, unknown to her, was to be the beginning of so much - it was more fleeting than usual.

'What time is it?' he said, waking suddenly, already peeling back the bedclothes on his side. He felt for his spectacles, pulled the flexible metal shanks behind his ears with both hands as he always did, and peered at the clock. 'Oh, not too bad, but I'll have to get a move on.'

While he had his shower, she went down in her dressing gown to start breakfast. The clean white surfaces of her kitchen awaited her. Secretly, she hadn't wanted all these beautiful new contrivances. There had been a drawer in her old wooden dresser for example, which wouldn't open unless you knew exactly the angle to set before exerting strength on the handles. She missed it. You could open these drawers with your little finger, so truly did they glide for you. She preferred her old gas stove, the blue-green flares, the merry little 'pop' as you ignited them, the deeper more resonant 'plump' of the oven which denoted the more serious purpose to which it was put.

But she was getting used to her new possessions. She was learning that they could be just as obedient under her charge. The glassy hot-points of her new electric stove showed no visible change when you turned them on but the heat broadened soon enough. Contentedly, she watched her two knobs of butter chase each other round the pan as she reached for the plate of sliced kidneys. In the grill above, the bacon was already spitting, the toast browning in the machine. The coffee pot gave its first pulse and brown liquid dashed against the glass. The subtle odours of her breakfast began to twist, mingle and spread through the house. She imagined Steve catching a whiff of them as he dried himself on the big woolly towel she had put out fresh yesterday, and being pleased.

He was away by a quarter to seven. As usual she stood by the door watching the car back from the wooden garage, its exhaust pipe steaming. It turned to make the angle to set off down the drive. This was the moment when they blew each other kisses, but the car door opened and he got out. She thought he'd forgotten something and made way for him to go inside. But he seized her round the waist and kissed her. 'Another two weeks and I'll be free,' he said. 'I'm taking on no more work for a month. We'll *have* that safari holiday.' This was the only reason he had come back, just to say this. She was pleased, not so much because of the idea of the holiday, which they had already talked about, but because he had got out of the car like that when she would have expected his mind to be fastened on to his day's work.

She waited by the door until the sound of the car had gone altogether. This was a kind of discipline of hers. It was like seeing him off on an aeroplane at the airport, as she had several times. She went up to the observation terrace when she had said goodbye to him on these occasions and waited to see him take off. She would stand there until the cloud swallowed the plane or the last glint of silver had gone from the skies. It had to be the same with the car, a kind of talisman that he would come back. Only when the total silence had settled did she allow her concentration to relax. Closing the door, she then felt the friendly spirits who kept her company during the day come out from their corners. She began her tasks.

When she had cleared the kitchen she went up to the bedroom to make the bed, put away clothes and tidy. When she was hanging up the suit Steve wore yesterday, as usual she went through the pockets. He was always mislaying his possessions and being distressed by their loss. It pleased her to be able to produce them for him like a conjuror. She found a letter still inside its envelope, which had a French stamp. Their address was handwritten.

Her first thought was that he hadn't read it. He had put it into his pocket and forgotten it. Then she saw that the envelope had been split open. She propped it up against the mirror on the dressing table to remind her to take it downstairs and put it on the hall-table. He would see it with the other letters when he came home. It was as she was doing this that she was tempted to read it. Steve, she knew, got very few personal letters. Those he did receive she always recognised by the handwriting or the postmark. She didn't like the idea of reading a letter he hadn't shown her. She pulled the letter sufficiently clear of the envelope to read the sender's address. 'Château Lamartine,' she read, 'Vigny-les-Pins.'

She pushed it back. Why on earth was her blood pumping, and why was she feeling breathless? She turned the letter over and, upside down, pulled out the sheet again. She caught the words at the bottom, 'Love, June.'

She was horrified at herself and put the letter down. Obviously, there was some quite simple explanation. She wished she hadn't looked at it at all. But she couldn't stop herself from pondering. It was addressed to their home. She hadn't noticed it in yesterday's mail, but it must have been there among the business envelopes, which she never bothered to scrutinise. There was no doubt he must have opened it yesterday evening. He had just put it in his pocket and said nothing to her about it.

It was ten o'clock, almost time for her real day to start, a succession of delights in store, but she could think of nothing but this letter. Who was June? Steve had never mentioned her as far as she could recall. By the time she had made Matthew, their gardener, a cup of coffee and had one herself with him, she knew she was going to have to read the letter because that was the only way she could stop the silliest thoughts coming to her.

She went back into the hall and in a gingerly way, as if it were in some way contaminated, pulled the letter entirely free of the envelope. As she read, she ignited with joy and relief. It was nothing serious at all, only a wonderfully exciting offer. A holiday in a French Château with what sounded like some kind of a colony of clever, gifted, perhaps famous people. How different, and intriguing. She had never been to France. How could Steve possibly have kept such a thing to himself? Did he imagine she would prefer a safari holiday? Surely they must go?

With such a delightful prospect ahead of her, it wasn't at all difficult now to start what she had planned for the day. She gained the summer-house where she was going to spend several hours today, there being no shopping to do. She was glad to see Matthew had moved from the flower bed and was nowhere in sight. She liked having Matthew about, but preferred to feel completely alone when she was working. She drew back all the sliding windows so that the stale imprisoned air could be replenished and sweetened and so the full summer hum of the garden could reach her. Without allowing herself to look at any of them she took the pictures out of the envelope which they sent her through the post and drawing-pinned the first of them on to the wooden board she had standing ready on the easel. She liked to look at the pictures before she read anything about them and the questions they wanted her to answer. Then she lay back on the upholstered seat. For a moment she kept her head still turned away and savoured the view she had under the jutting edge of thatched roof - the mowed lines of the lawn, an outbreak of scarlet poppies in one of the beds, and behind them the house settling now into the drowse of midday. On a flower nearby she watched a Red Admiral settle. It spread its wings, absorbing the warmth, then suddenly was off again, jinking away. She closed her eyes so she could appreciate the enormousness of the insect noise at large around her.

A memory of her school days came up on the screen of her mind, as if a slide was being shown. She saw the huge classroom, the layered rows of yellow benches stretching back behind her. The teacher, one of the lady teachers she admired, was wanting to tell them about Queen Elizabeth I and her feelings about religion. She had brought in some postcards of people and events, which she was going to show them on the overhead projector to illustrate what she said. Jubilee remembered only one of these - a terrible one of a man being put on the rack to make him confess to something - for as usual the lesson soon broke up into noise and unruliness. Some boys, and the girls who went with them, were creating some not very nice disturbance at the back of the room. She never did discover what the Queen thought about God and the Church.

To expunge this involuntary image she reopened her eyes, knowing they would alight straight on to the picture. She recognised it. It was called 'The Birth of Venus.' Venus, she recalled, was the goddess of love and was born of the sea, which accounted for her position in the picture on a shell floating on the sea. She remembered that the artist's name was Botticelli, which meant 'Little Barrel' because he was short and tubby, that he was Italian and lived in the fifteenth century.

She loved the scene, as she always had, and she would have known it was by the same artist who had painted another picture she'd had a few weeks ago. This one showed three clothed females in a row and was called 'The Spring.' In view of this, it was like a second meeting with someone one already knew. She began to reflect about the picture. She realised that if it hadn't been for Botticelli she would have imagined Venus quite differently. She would have thought that the face of someone who was responsible for so important a thing as love would have been older and more important-looking. She was surprised and excited to see this beautiful young woman with such lovely thick golden hair, so modest with her downcast eyes and with the curved gracefulness of her body. The discovery of her youth, together with the other notable things about the picture - the sea, the creatures in it, the lovely sunlight which seemed miraculously everywhere, and the pretty sea-shell in which Venus was standing - made her feel almost as if she, too, were standing on that shell floating on the sea.

Later she took up the art history book by Gombrich, which the Open University had asked her to buy, and opened it where her vellum marker was. At twelve she would have to get lunch for Matthew, but she knew that she wouldn't worry about her own. She could go on all day, finish the recommended passages in the book, then begin to think about the questions they had asked her.

4

It was known by one at least of the inhabitants of the Château Lamartine that June and Alfonso Aguas de Villanova had returned as expected from Paris. The entomologist, Frederick Hapsburg-Trench was the occupant of the accommodation in the north-west tower, the only one of four which had a roof and was habitable. This room commanded a good view down two sides of the building. At supper the couple's non-appearance had been noted, but soon afterwards Frederick, working at a table in his window, saw June drawing the curtains in her room.

Frederick knew that June was a warm and highly sociable individual, that she was always pleased to return to her rural seat for the long week ends and leaves which punctuated her admirable earning activities in the capital - on which they all depended. He knew also that she always did a round of everyone on these homecoming occasions, whatever the hour. However, he read nothing menacing into this failure of routine. He assumed the traffic had been bad on the *autoroute* and that she was particularly fatigued, a view confirmed to him when very soon after it had gone on the light went off again and the curtains were redrawn. He returned with some disappointment to the reading from which he would have welcomed a break. Among several books he had obtained through the local lending system was a work by a Second Empire French author on the possibility of some Vandal influence in Midi place names from their brief stay in the region on their way through Spain to North Africa. It was a plodding work.

Early the following morning, other members of the community were also ignorant of June's predicament as they went about their daily tasks - for example the Lady Elizabeth Elder-Fynes.

At nine o'clock, Liz as she was known, emerged from one of the Château's several outhouses in her wine-coloured corduroy dressing gown. Under each arm she carried a bundle of hay. Round her neck on a strap hung a huge radio, its aerial pulled out to its extremity. It was repeat-broadcasting an episode from 'The

Archers.' As this programme was coming from England and as she was in the south of France, there was a good deal of pyrotechnic crackling. In its fight to retain coherence the transmission was also being assaulted from several French stations and one from German-speaking Switzerland. On her way to the stables, Liz had to put down one of the bundles to fend off these intruders with an adjustment to the tuning.

Inside the stables, reception deteriorated further. There was a crescendo of noise like that of a battlefield, overcome finally by a Gallic voice fervently describing in French the social properties of a deodorant. Liz sat on a bench and wrestled with the controls with both her hands. But when at last she recovered her exiled fiction it was only to hear the familiar notes of the sign-off tune. 'Blast you, you bloody Frogs,' she said aloud. She beat the top of the wireless with a clenched fist and switched it off.

She recovered quickly from her annoyance. 'Darlings,' she said, rising, her voice having quite a different tone. She addressed a pair of donkeys who, having less interest than their mistress in British radio fiction, had lifted their heads over the half-door and were eyeing the hay with as much animation as donkeys can show. She went into the stall with the food and, while the animals fed, positioned herself between the lowered heads and spread her arms lovingly over the two bony grey shoulders.

When she had mucked out the animals and changed their water, she went to 'The Patch.' This was a considerable area between crumbling walls, which she had cultivated. On one side she had sweet corn. She had planted this crop along the crests of shallow ridges, mattocked up so as to leave trenches between the rows. She went first to these, placed the plastic hose into the trench furthest from the wall and went to turn the tap on. As there was a slight slope, the water would run down the row. When it reached the bottom she would switch the hose to the next one.

There had been no rain for a month to replenish the natural underground reservoir which provided for the Château, consequently the issue from the tap was grudging. Each trench would take a good half-hour, and she felt guilty taking the water, even though she knew everyone would stop scoffing at her efforts and eat with relish when the produce was ripe. She went to feel one of the cobs which were beginning to form. Peeling back the outer envelope of leaves and parting the curtain of green whiskers, she saw that the grain was still white and meagre.

She went next to her three English peach trees, which were espaliered along the south-facing wall. She had grafted cuttings brought from home on to Midi stock, maintaining that English peaches are the best in Europe and that it is only the English climate which doesn't always cooperate with them. This was their sixth year. Last year there had been two delicious fruits - even Damon had agreed on their quality after consuming his rationed segment. At the present time she had several dozen ripening nicely.

'Goddam you,' she exclaimed again, as she began her inspection.

The tree she was examining was alive with earwigs. Paying a rapid visit to the other two trees she found they were in the same predicament. And there was no doubt at all what the earwigs were making for. Some had already found their targets. Several peaches had been pierced and had little globes of a black glutinous substance in their navels.

She went back to the stable, got one of the old brushes she used for grooming the donkeys, and spent more than an hour cleansing the trees of these abominable pests. Sweeping them to the ground she trod on them. They seemed to have a prehensile urge to live. Even when their bodies were half-crushed, remaining legs and feelers continued to function.

By now the sun was heaving itself into the sky and the temperature was rising. A corduroy dressing gown is not ideal clothing for horticulture in the Mediterranean climate, and she couldn't remove it as she had only scanty clothing underneath. Her whole body was bathed in sweat. It was then she made a discovery. She had imagined the earwigs were attacking from the ground, moving up the trunk and branches. After a rest in the shade, she went back for a last look at the trees. There seemed as many earwigs as when she had started. She realised - they were not coming up from below at all, they were hatching from eggs laid in the trees, probably in the fruit itself. However many she killed, there would be more. The slaughter was useless.

Just at this moment she realised the hose had stopped. In her preoccupation with the earwigs she had forgotten the irrigation of the maize. The water supply must have dried up some time ago. The yellow earth was marginally damp not even as far as half way down the first channel. She sat down on a stone and burst into tears.

It was not only the community which seemed to have gone rotten. Nature itself conspired. Nature did not want them here, it was clear - a group of quarrelsome hard-up exiles. In the end nature would have its way, as it always did. The Château would be empty again and the remorseless tide of plant and animal life would overcome it.

A few minutes later, when she had recovered a little, she looked up and observed the unchanged, motionless landscape of pines, thorn-bush and light-grey rocks stretching in all directions, which was so massively indifferent to her emotion. In the distance the unremitting shape of the Mont des Lézards was already blue and beginning to shimmer in the haze. She wavered on the edge of another failure of courage, then stoutly rallied.

'Goddam it,' she declared for the third and last time that morning - though the exclamation this time carried a much different meaning. What she meant to communicate was not annoyance, but that she, for one, wouldn't give in to inanimate forces, and that she had an idea how to defeat the earwigs. The Château depended on her for her auxiliary supply of foodstuffs. One did not bow to minor adversity.

While Liz engaged with the forces of nature, elsewhere in the Château another not untypical drama was being played out.

Hortense Beerbohmer, an aspiring artist of *la nouvelle onde* - a category she had invented for herself - with her husband Paul, a self-exiled American who possessed some means, occupied two rooms in a prime central position on the first floor in the front of the building.

There were of course any number of empty rooms for June's community to chose from. Most inmates, with the cost of furnishing in mind, chose to occupy only one room, and one of modest size. But thanks to Paul Beerbohmer's savings from a previous American employment, the couple were able to make sense of the lavish dimensions of their selected living space. Both their sitting room and bedroom had the same rose-coloured wall-to-wall carpet over the parquet, from large quoit-like rings hung four pairs of voluminous if old damask curtains of an attractively faded strawberry colour, and the widely-striped pink paper of Pompadour design did justice to the dimensions of the walls. The sitting room was lavishly furnished with a chintz-covered suite, and it contained a white baby grand piano. The bedroom had a brass four-poster bed, made up with its full complement of linen sheets, blankets and a dainty white coverlet. There was a huge white eighteenth century dressing table, which Pompadour might not have rejected on a country progress, several handsome ornate mirrors which were part of a built-in wardrobe, and two ample antique armchairs Hortense had purchased and claimed were also Louis Quinze. Damon Raspin, the bachelor historian in the community, had scornfully rejected this claim within her hearing. They were primitively made copies, Damon had said with that authority no one in the community except Hortense would dispute, late nineteenth century at best and as provincial as their new French owner.

Unlike her husband, who saw no reason to rise early, Hortense had been up since seven. She had been at work in her studio on the third floor of the building for two hours. She had then gone down to the basement kitchen to make herself some breakfast. It was here that she made a discovery she certainly saw as *pas convenant.*

She was forced to share the large refectory table with Frederick Hapsburg-Trench. This unpleasantness would normally have been weathered by silence - at least on her part. She considered she had quite a formidable brand of silence, which even Frederick found it difficult to intrude on. But it was soon clear Frederick, with a look of unusual consternation on his saturnine features, considered himself in possession of some 'news'.

'You've heard?' he said, after a few moments of *dégoutant,* audible mug sipping - he held the receptacle in both hands as if he were an animal drinking at a trough. She did not interrupt her decorous spreading of apricot jam on the bread. 'June's got the sack.'

'*Que dites-vous?*'   Her head had come up, and her question, though hostile, had slipped through her defences before she could censor it.

'I've just talked to Alfonso.   After all these years Juney's got the boot from the oil company.   Cost-cutting or something. Alfonso thinks it'll all work out somehow, but how can it?   If June's lost her job we're all finished.'

'You 'ave spoken to June?'

'Not yet.   I suspect she's hiding.'   Hortense withdrew.   Quite enough had already been exchanged with Frederick.   Alfonso must have got it wrong, the Mexican idiot, and trust Frederick to seize on any tidbit.   She made an impatient gesture with her shoulders.   'Apparently they're going to sell the lease on their Paris house,' Frederick added.

Freed of Frederick's company in which, out of sheer disgust, it was necessary to discount anything he said, Hortense had second thoughts.   Was it possible?   Was such a disaster possible just as her profoundest, most creative dreams to date were on the point of realisation?   She had to concede it *was* possible.   In which case there was only one solution.   She did not return to the studio, but instead to her rooms.

Paul's motionless shape was still in bed.   '*Comme tu es indolent,*' she said forcefully.   '*Tu ne te rendes conte?*   It-is-nine-o'clock-already.   Rise up, 'ave you no tasks?'   She seized the sheet and ripped it from his face.   'If you will not rise up, *tu écouteras,*' she said.   'I 'ave just heard June 'as the sack.   She will no more pay money for us.   We must pay.   Those who cannot pay must leave the Château.   I cannot leave my work on Lézards. I work there today, probably *jusqu'a crépuscule.*   You will pay June today, a big sum, whatever is *nécessaire.*   When I am returned I do not wish to find courage is lacking to you.   My work must not be interrupted at this moment *critique.*   Paul, you are attending me?'

It appeared Paul was not attending her.   He was about to disappear again under the bedclothes.   Hortense made a lunge, attempting again to seize the sheet.   But Paul with equal alacrity had it well tethered from within at the level of his throat.   For a moment, locked in a stalemate of strength, they were face to face.

'Perhaps,' said Paul, '*you*'d like to pay her something if you're so keen. I'm not giving another dollar more than a fair rent. I've given enough, even if the place folds.'

Hortense reached a certain crisis within herself. Her Gallic temperament suggested to her a crescendo of rage, perhaps physical violence. But Paul, despite his small stature was remarkably strong. The further Gallic characteristic of realism came into play, then another of even more decisive force.

She relinquished the sheet, and made a disdainful dismissive grimace. Would she live a moment longer, she thought rhetorically, with this prime example of slothful American manhood, with this puerile intransigence and vulgarity, this pretence at the artistic life, if it were not necessary for the highest motive nameable? Of course not - especially when there was such an exciting alternative awaiting her if only she had the courage to grasp it.

On the tide of her emotion she went to sit on the stool in front of the dressing table. She began to weave her long golden hair, which had been hanging loose, into a labyrinth of tight coils on top of her head. When she had completed this extensive operation, she tied a piece of bright cerise chiffon round her neck, then stood up to better adjudge the effect in one of the long mirrors.

She didn't seem to Paul displeased at what she saw. Paul had now sat up against the pillows leaning his neat head with its central parting and well-trimmed goatee beard comfortably against the padded bed-head. He viewed the display with amusement. Turning to one side, Hortense thrust forward her bust, ran her thumbs under the snakeskin belt which tethered her quite slender waist, then kneaded her palms with an inward-pressing downward motion over the upper part of her hips whose convex contour was displayed so faithfully by her mock tiger-skin trousers. She tilted a fraction further upwards the upstanding collar of her white shirt and with both hands renewed the setting of the chiffon and threw one of the loose ends over her shoulder.

'Styling up for your day in the studio?' he said.

'I am not working more in the studio. I change my mind. I

go to Lézards.'

'I see.'

'I need - to observe the morning light.'

'And for that you need to put on a pink chiffon scarf and plait your hair?'

From the cupboard she collected her easel, her portfolio, her wooden paint-box, and a haversack - with an afterthought a drawing-block - and left the room.

She went first to the kitchen again, thankfully empty now. From a huge home-baked loaf the size of a small suitcase she cut four slices, and made two sandwiches with a quantity of goat's cheese she took from the fridge. She filled an old plastic bottle with water, packed these into the haversack, and returned upstairs. Tripping lightly across the cracked but still beautiful black and white flagstones of the hall from which twisted upwards a fine mahogany staircase with a wrought-iron balustrade, she skipped down the crumbling steps which led from the door on to the weed-grown drive, and made for the outhouses. If only, she thought, if only courage could bring her what she deserved, why would she care about any worldly entanglements such as money.

Hearing one of the donkeys bray she tried the stable first. She found the donkeys unaccompanied, so went next to the greenhouses. They were similarly deserted. This left 'The Patch.' As she turned through the gap in the wall her pulses accelerated. Liz was standing by the fruit trees at the far end. '*Mais qu'est-ce-que tu fais, ma chérie?*'

She was used to the delightful eccentricities of this strongly handsome daughter of an English marquis, but whatever Liz was doing now would surely take some explanation? There was no answer to her first call. Liz had apparently sawn a number of narrow strips of wood, each about two centimetres across and of varying lengths. She had placed them in different positions against branches of the peach trees so that their lower ends rested on the ground about a metre from the wall. They were standing in plastic cartons of varying sizes. Each carton contained a quantity of water on whose surface were a number of concentric black rings. Liz held a jar in one hand and with a spoon in the other was daubing the ramps at intervals with what appeared to be very small quantities of jam.

'I think I've got the little varmints this time,' she said. 'Those plastic cups contain disinfectant.'

Hortense did not know the English word 'varmints' but she guessed it must mean earwigs, several of which appeared to be embarking on journeys down the baited ramps. Hortense released an example of what she considered to be one of her most attractive features, an arpeggio of rapid youthful laughter. '*Chère Liz, comme tu es drôle,*' she said. 'I adore your lovely English ideas. What a *génie* you are.'

Liz didn't share this ardour. She was still busy daubing. 'I was afraid they preferred peaches to apricot jam but it's clear they don't. I think my fruit will be saved - which we shall need if things are as bad as June says.'

There was nothing Hortense could do except wait until the operation was completed. She had to join the mood of seriousness which Liz was engendering and jettison her own output of that suggestion of gay abandon with which she hoped to make her invitation, knowing as she did how Liz, despite her being English, could be hooked by sudden enthusiasms. By the time she at last had space for a change of subject she knew she had lost most of the initiative.

'*Bien,* now you are killing your "varmints" you are free to do what I pro-pose. I go 'alf way to Lézards today, where there is a stream. You must absolutely come. I give you another drawing *instruction*, and we swim. I 'ave with me all the things we need - and food. What do you say?'

Liz frowned. Hortense had to admit she didn't admire Liz quite so much when she frowned. She had a large very plump healthy-looking face, with that complexion the English are famous for, but the bunching of the skin on the forehead gave it a prognothacious look. The long brow seemed almost to bulge forward.

'Oh no, not today,' she said. 'I've this to attend to. Here, hold this for me.' Hortense found herself holding the spoon and the pot of jam while Liz looked for stones to wedge the ramps and the death traps more securely.

She entertained the hope for some minutes that if she helped with this work there might still be a chance. She'd had vivid thoughts of their picnic. She had been so sure it was the moment, with Damon so more than usually engrossed in his work these days.   But the more she tried to help, the more she knew her plans wouldn't be realised.   You could always tell with Liz. When her mind was clamped onto something, nothing would move her from it.

She realised she would be painting alone today.

5

On leaving his mother's bungalow, Steve was eager to return to Jubilee, but he decided he had something to do first. He took the road into town, and in a few minutes was sitting in their local travel agent's.

'I think I have just the sort of thing you'll like,' said blue-skirted Jennifer as she got up and went on forage among the shelves of prospectuses behind her.

In the seats next to Steve's an elderly couple were discussing with another blue-uniformed girl a journey up the Nile. He heard words like Aswan and Abu-Simbel and Karnak being thrown about with the ease of beach balls. On his other side two young girls were tasting the glamorous possibilities of the Greek Islands.

Jennifer returned with the two booklets, one of which had a huge tusked male elephant on the cover, in lesser perspective a pride of lions and for good measure a herd of very vigilant-looking antelope. 'These are in my opinion the finest safari holidays on the market, Mr Addicot,' she said.

Steve had no doubt that, if Jennifer said so, they would be. He had dealt with her before and never been disappointed. She knew his standards. He would probably have booked there and then if she hadn't added more. 'Well, I expect you'll want to take the brochures home and discuss them at leisure with Mrs Addicot.'

He had planned a fait accompli, but somewhat reluctantly, he supposed Jennifer was right. On his way through the automatic glass doors he even wondered if she was not being mildly intuitive. Was it possible she sensed Jubilee's judgement might be different from his?

On the drive out to their rustic home, Steve found himself concentrating with particular intensity on Jubilee, from whom he had been severed for several days. He recalled her gentle and playful voice, her easy supple movements, the softness of her flesh. He conjured aspects of their love-making. Did she have the same yearning for him? She said so when he asked, and he thought she did, but he knew also that Jubilee was a great deal more rooted in whatever she was doing in the moment than he was. She never seemed to live in anticipation of future events, as he was prone to do. It seemed to him sometimes that, whereas he was always on the way somewhere, she had arrived. Once again he had an uninvited mental visitation from his first wife. He couldn't stop her naming herself on this occasion. 'Gloria, my name was Gloria,' she reminded him with cynical glee. 'You won't forget me in a hurry.'

She also recalled for him the exact circumstances in which she had left him. He came home one evening, an evening just such as this, and she was gone. No note, nothing. She had taken all her own possessions and many of his, as well as a lot of his money which he had foolishly put in her name. He had to employ an agency to find she had gone back to the States with an American serviceman she had met and had apparently been seeing for some weeks.

Disturbed by this involuntary memory, not for the first time he had the ridiculous dread that the same might happen with Jubilee. She was ten years younger than he was. As he breasted the last hill and the motionless house came into view below, he was beset by another fear. Something could have happened to her. He didn't like leaving her alone, and had sometimes suggested she might like to invite someone to stay when he was away for long periods, but she had always adamantly refused. If he wasn't there, she preferred being alone, she said. He garaged the car, didn't stop to close the doors, and called her name in the hall. Thankfully, he heard her answer at once from the kitchen.

She was rolling pastry. He bounded forward to kiss her. She held her hands sideways, one holding the rolling pin. 'I'll get flour on your suit,' she warned.

He wouldn't have minded if she had. Didn't she realise he wanted her to feel the same instantaneous relief and joy he felt at being together again? But his silly fears dissipated. He chided himself. 'I'm an impatient ass,' he thought, 'and Jubilee is deliciously sensible. She's cooking. You can't leave pastry in the middle.'

Throwing down the travel brochures on to one of the working tops, he lifted himself up beside them and tucked his hands under his haunches. He had been going to talk about the brickworks sale as a lead in, but he was too impatient. 'Dropped in to see Jennifer in town,' he said in a rush.

'Jennifer?'

'The nice girl in the travel agent's.' He nodded towards the brochures. She edged a lock of black hair from her eye with her wrist as she gave a quick sideways glance, then returned to the pastry. 'This safari trip looks breathtaking.' She gave the dough a squeeze with one hand and began to roll it out. 'You mean you don't want to go, Jubee?'

'It sounds lovely,' she said.

'But you'd rather not go - is that it?' He waited in suspense, watching the elastic substance spreading and thinning on the plastic surface. Her movements were over-energetic.

'I'd love to go,' she said in too small a voice.

He couldn't understand what seemed to be the abrupt change in her mood. He was sure she wasn't that much against the holiday. Disappointed, he went into the hall to collect the week's mail from the table. To one side, propped against the brass dolphin, was June's letter, which he had completely forgotten. Jubilee must have found it somewhere. Could her odd behaviour be something to do with that? He went back at once into the kitchen holding the letter. To her surprise she ran to him.

'I didn't mean to read your letter. I don't know why I did it,' she said in distress.

He clasped her to him. Now the flour was getting on his suit all right. 'But, I don't understand. I don't mind you reading my letters, Jubee, you know that. Why shouldn't you read my letters?'

'I shouldn't have. I've no right to, if you don't want to show it to me.'

'But I didn't not want . . .'

'You put the letter in your pocket and didn't say anything about it to me. I should have left it there.'

It occurred to Steve with dawning joy the point he might have been missing. 'Jubilee darling,' he said, pulling away from her and holding her by both her arms. 'June is an old school-friend. About ten years ago I went out to see her and her Mexican husband Fernando in this crummy Château they have in the south

37

of France.   They run a kind of colony for penniless artists and intellectuals.   Quite honestly it's a dump.   June's well meaning, but there's no proper sanitation, there are no carpets, when it rains the roof leaks.   The place is running with animals, some invited, some not - including rodents.   And all they do is sit round talking a lot of twaddle all day.   To be truthful I was glad to leave. That's the reason I put the letter in my pocket and forgot about it.'

Jubilee's face had miraculously brightened.   'But it sounds wonderful, Steve,' she said.   'Artists, and talk, and sun . . .'

'You wouldn't like it really, you know.'

'I could read, and take some pictures and books to study.   And you *could* do some painting again, as June mentioned.   You haven't done any for ages.   Oh, do let's go.   It sounds a beautiful place.   I've never been to France.'

To humour her and because he was relieved that the cause of her distress was so unimportant, he agreed to a couple of days on the way to Nairobi.   The deviation to Nice would probably cost him the advantage of a package deal price, but he could afford it, couldn't he?

He didn't allow himself to dwell on his certainty that Fernando would have done little in the ten years to stem the natural decay that history was busy with.   The point was it made Jubilee happy, and because of that it made him happy, too.   When she saw what it was really like she would be as pleased as he would be to move on.

6.

From time to time, when he reached critical phases of the massive historical work on which he was embarked, Dr Damon Raspin had let it be known that he wished to be left in total silence at meals, at which he sat a little apart from the others, usually reading with bowed head.

The arrangement had not been totally proof against the froth of human intercourse. Sometimes, with no malice intended, people forgot and addressed remarks to him. Paul Beerbohmer had come to lunch one day with the inside pocket of his jacket bulging with the manuscript of another of his long essays on musical notation. Artlessly, he had sat next to Damon, then started talking about it to Frederick Hapsburg-Trench across the table, knowing Damon's concentration would be pierced and hoping he would in some way offer to read his work, as he had its predecessors. To shut him up Damon had finally held out his hand sideways to gather the rubbish.

Hortense's interferences were malicious. Malice came naturally to Hortense, particularly against Damon whom she considered the obstacle to the requiting of her passion. During his mealtime silences, she spent a good deal of her energy loudly introducing views which she knew were anathema to him.

Damon's work had reached an even more critical point than on these earlier occasions. He was about to write up the results of several months' research whose fine detail he must keep in his mind. He needed to muster all his powers and sustain them at a high level. He was determined that this time his need for hermetic privacy wouldn't be assaulted in these irritating ways. He thought he knew how this could be effected. He would eat his food in the kitchen away from the others, and he would not this time rely on random goodwill. His act should be formalised. On the very day of June's return from Paris and of the dismal news which came with her, he decided he would take a formalised *vow* of silence and asked Frederick Hapsburg-Trench to be his acolyte.

What is different about a publicly stated vow? The answer, Damon thought, lay surely in the deeply superstitious nature of the human race. Vows are a part of our oldest and most deeply embedded instinct. How are the vows of the most closed orders of monks and nuns, for example, regarded by those who affect to despise such self-denial? They can be mocked, trivialised, explained in terms of sexual or economic cowardice, but are these no more than rationalisations of an awe that survives all attempt to expunge it? When Hortense knew that his intention had been *sanctified*, even her robust malevolence would surely falter, as would Paul's masochistic need for intellectual flagellation.

Frederick Hapsburg-Trench could be impressive when formality of this sort was called for. At supper that same evening when everyone except June and Damon were present, he stood up, cleared his throat meaningfully, commanded silence by his bearing, and announced that that afternoon, in the chapel, he'd had the honour of being the witness to a solemn oath taken by a member of their community - significantly absent, as he pointed out. He made a considerable oration, outlining how communal life, of necessity, here and there impinged on personal liberty, but stressing how sovereign in this fellowship of high artistic and intellectual endeavour was the right of the individual to pursue his or her talents as was seen fittest. He was certain, he said, that everyone would exercise the utmost rigour in respecting Damon's vow, which would be operative from this moment until his task was complete.

Damon had realised all along that the greatest difficulty would be with Liz, with whom he co-habited. On the last occasion, he had exempted her from the ban during the hours of darkness. He didn't feel he should this time, but the matter hadn't been discussed. To have done so, Damon felt, would have been to descend to a banality their relationship excluded.

The room Damon and Elizabeth occupied was on the north side of the Château which, like the kitchen, was on the basement level. As its two barred windows looked on to the deep ditch that was once a moat, and as above them rose the semi-derelict drawbridge permanently in the lowered position, the room was dark - Damon had chosen it for this reason, there was less distraction through its two windows. It contained an untidy miscellany of objects. On one whole side were amateurly erected bookshelves, which were tightly filled floor to ceiling with Damon's books, his only possessions apart from a few well used clothes and writing materials. A makeshift farmyard ladder rested at one end. There was a double mattress on the floor, covered with bedclothes, some simple wooden chairs, two armchairs, a solid table, and several chests and cupboards whose tops were largely occupied by trays of plants and by retorts filled with different coloured liquids on their way to becoming wine. In a corner, standing on a trestle, stood an electric cooker with two rings, whose enamel was chipped and rusted through. There was a square metal tray with a handle, used, it seemed, for making toast on one of the electric rings, a huge frying-pan as black as a witch, and several blackened saucepans. In one of the window bays was another plainer table where Damon worked.

The Lady Elisabeth Elder-Fines, an expert in the field of animals and horticulture, could surely in no sense be categorised as an intellectual. Elisabeth herself, though not given to abstract definitions, would certainly not have seen herself in this way. It might be thought unexpected therefore - as it was from time to time among the more gossip-inclined inmates of the Château Lamartine - that a person of her very pragmatic parts should have wished to pair with a man of Damon's exceptional erudition.

The question is interesting, but for the moment must be left aside in favour of one easier to explain - why Damon was attracted to Elisabeth. Undoubtedly, as his own clear mind had diagnosed, among the qualities which drew him was this very practicality. Damon was not impractical himself, in fact his talents had a Leonardo da Vinci scope, but Liz's expertise surpassed his. More important, with Liz it was not just that she could do things, that she spent her life doing things and talking about doing things, it was that this activity amounted by implication to philosophy. It expressed her unshakeable certainty in life and her position in it. This was something Damon had never been sure of. His background hadn't endowed him with a great deal of certainty. The intense activity of his mind daily presented him with fresh material for doubt. In short Liz was a rock, an anchor. To add a third metaphor, she was the airfield from which he flew his globe-embracing sorties.

Damon wasn't a snob, but undoubtedly Liz's peerage had something to do with his admiration. Not the title itself, a newer peerage probably wouldn't have done. Newer peerages, even inherited ones which have survived two or three generations, wear their distinctions, like their coronets, as objects that have been placed on their heads by others. Because they are embellishments, attachments, *awards,* they connote by their very nature that they are detachable. The aristocracy, bred through centuries not decades, often of older lineage than royal dynasties, is another matter. A title such as Liz's is not so much inherited as inherent. Liz's smallest act - and her life was a miscellany of small acts - was endowed with a historical majesty and legitimacy. Her very lifting of a forefinger was *de jure* not *de facto*. Like the early Stuarts she reigned by divine right, the law was a lion under her throne. This was what had become indispensable to Dr Damon Raspin.

After supper on the first day of his vow, Liz returned to their room where Damon was just finishing his day's writing. Damon was apprehensive. During the day he had hardly seen Liz, who had been hard at work on her various horticultural ploys. They had had no occasion for speech and he was sure Liz would respect his wish for silence when in the company of the others. But in the evening, when they were alone together, it was another matter. How, he thought, was Liz going to behave? Would she assume she would have a dispensation from the embargo, as last time?

It seemed so. While he was at the top of the ladder searching for a book on the top shelves, she began to set up her distaff below, part of the equipment she used for making woollen

42

clothes. Simultaneously she launched into the topic of the Château's finances, which had received such a blow that day with June's return and her revelation.

'In my own mind I am clear,' she said, 'we are all going to have to turn to. There's no reason why we should not be self-sufficient if everyone pulls their weight. There will have to be further austerities of course, and I shall set about a massive increase in production from my farm. Feudal services will be demanded from everyone, each donating part of the day to the common weal.'

Damon found the book he intended to read that evening and began to leaf through it, still mounted on the ladder. Surely she would soon notice his lack of comment? In the margin of his consciousness he registered a quickening of his pulses.

There was no slackening in the flow of Liz's speech. Accompanying her words, she began now to peddle her spinning wheel, deftly pulling the grey strands to one side and winding them on to the ball. Any moment she would ask his opinion on the burning topic. If she did, he would have to cede, he thought.

Then suddenly he realised a fact - she wasn't going to stop talking. That is to say, she wouldn't stop until she had exhausted her thoughts. At that point she would simply say no more *and expect no answer.* This was how it was going to be. As always in their relationship, the matter had been resolved at a decently sub-conscious level. There would be no need for the banality of an exchange. She would continue to talk to him like this in the evenings when they were alone - or not, as she chose - but she would expect nothing from him. She wouldn't even insist he listened. Could a better example be found of her massive phlegm and stability?

Entirely happy at this outcome, on the following morning he rose as usual, with Liz, at six. They went out separately to the pump in the stable yard to wash. He had calculated that his income, derived from a small legacy two thirds of which he gave to June, did not stretch to coffee on more than three mornings a week, consequently he drank a glass of water for breakfast together with one of Liz's wholemeal rolls, made yesterday from gleanings she had harvested from a nearby field then pounded into flour with an ancient mortar and pestle. The rolls had, apart from her effort, cost nothing but a quantity of milk and a segment of butter whose value he would debit to himself in his accounts. The bread had been baked in the range oven in the kitchen, which burnt wood culled from the surrounds of the Château. When Liz went out he was free to get down to work.

Settling at his table, he made minute but exact preparations for his plunge into his task. First he rearranged in good symmetry the some half a dozen books he had assembled at hand. Then he squared an ancient leather blotter in front of him with the edge of the table and adjusted the block of paper on which he was about to write. He took from the drawer an old-fashioned nib, pen, and a bottle of ink. He removed the screw top from the inkbottle and placed it underneath so as to deepen the declining quantity of ink. Finally, he dipped the nib.

Damon's major study was 'The Eastern Question', that compendium of enormously widespread political problems which arose out of the slow decay of the Ottoman Empire in Europe during the nineteenth and early twentieth centuries. Eschewing several tempting offers of posts in European universities, he had been working at it now for over five years. The sizeable piece he would be starting today (sizeable, but a small part of the total work) was already mapped in his mind. It concerned the sexual obsession of a Grand Vizier with a girl in the harem at the time of the Convention of Olmütz, which in his submission had a crucial bearing on the eventual outbreak of hostilities in the Crimea in 1854. To form the view he was expressing he had read about a dozen books, several of which were written in Turkish, a language which, with others, he had mastered. Six hours later with only one break of a few minutes in which he ate another of Liz's rolls, this time with the addition of some salami and a slice of water-melon, he put down the pen, covered the last page of what he had written with a sheet of blotting paper, and swept his fist across it.

Damon's vow allowed for a small deviation, not as far as his own speech was concerned but, as with Liz, in terms of physical exercise and of human companionship. He had been aware for some half an hour that Frederick Hapsburg-Trench was lurking outside. Ever anxious for an excuse to escape from his own studies, Frederick was early as usual. He had appeared before for a minute or more, pretending to examine the bole of the walnut tree, which grew on the far side of the moat. Not getting a response, he had gone off. Now he was back, sitting with legs dangling on the decaying boards of the lowered drawbridge. With the crafty skill with which he could notice such small incidents, he was well aware that Damon had at last looked up. As he did so, Frederick looked pointedly at his watch.

Damon smiled faintly as he returned to his work. 'You can bloody well wait, you crooked idle bugger,' he thought. But with still lowered head he lightly tapped the window once to indicate he was coming.

Frederick, a thirty year old bachelor, five years older than his friend, and who with his mane of grey hair and cadaverous features resembled Mephistopheles, was also a scholar - as has been noted - of the labyrinthine subject of place names. The first exchange between the friends was not concerned, however, with either this or The Eastern Question.

'I'm virtually sure our hope is extinguished,' Frederick said, as he led them off on their afternoon walk. Damon could indicate a great deal with his eyebrows, which Frederick was watching, but they remained inactive. 'I do use my ears, you know. I overheard them talking.' They walked several paces. Frederick waited. Some acknowledgement was due, surely, for his opening remark, a nod, a movement of the eyebrow. As none came, he had to continue. 'It's all very well your taking such a lofty view. If Paul doesn't cough up, who will? I can't, you can't, Alfonso can't, nobody can. June has no other source of income than her ex-job as far as I know. It's a crisis. I think the least you can do is acknowledge the fact. Your private income, unsupported by the reasonably priced accommodation here, would be as useless to sustain you as would be the meagre trickle mother allows me from my

45

inheritance. What will become of our work?'

An even longer silence followed this gloomy question. In the even greater silence of the sullen overheated landscape they could hear the noise their feet made on the rough track they were following, and the increased tempo of their breath. What was Frederick hoping for - that in some way his friend would communicate at least some diminution of his philosophical stance, some acknowledgement of a shared unease? If he was, he was disappointed. He was left with the one crumb of hope he had gleaned that morning. June had invited a guest to the Château, an old school friend. He had heard her mentioning this to Liz and asking her if she thought she should put him off in the circumstances. He mentioned this now. 'This friend is an accountant,' Frederick announced, 'as such, he is likely to be well endowed. It is, I suppose, a factor worth noting if nothing more.'

He turned to his friend and saw - not the sign of decent optimism which would be appropriate - only an ironic grin. If this rich visitor were to come, would not he, Frederick, then know just how to exploit such a situation - this is what seemed implied. Frederick took quick offence. His demonic features clouded even more darkly. 'I sometimes think, Raspin, that you do not keep an entirely sane grip on life,' he said. 'High-minded aloofness can be taken too far. Fortunately there are still some of us with feet on the ground. Anyway, this personage may not come. It is only an invitation. I gather as yet there has been no reply.'

The two-hour walk continued - from then on with no further speech from Frederick, and certainly none from Damon.

7

Outside the arrival terminal of Nice Airport, Steve and Jubilee sat in their hired Renault car, their luggage stowed in the boot. Steve, in the driving seat, was trying out the various buttons and gadgets. He finished by wiggling the gear leaver and twisting the ignition key.

Jubilee was very excited. In a sleeveless primrose-coloured cotton dress and yellow sandals with a matching wide-brimmed hat, she looked stunningly pretty. In her hand she held the French phrase book she had already used to good effect. '*Où sont les voitures à louer?*' she had asked a male official, her finger on the page. The man had obligingly taken them right to the car-hire booth and, when Jubilee had thanked him, disclaimed lengthily the value of his service. She was now busily looking up a sign she had observed - '*Attention. Tenez le droit.*'

'Watch out. Keep to the right,' she proclaimed, 'you have to keep to the right here, Steve.'

'You can rely on the dear old Frogs to do everything back to front,' Steve said as he carefully set the car in motion.

Moving from the shadow of the building the heat struck them again, as it had when they got out of the plane. They crossed a river, and a crescendo of cicada noise assaulted them through the open windows of the car. Sunshine twinkled on the metal of innumerable other cars. Here and there they had glimpses of the sea, which was of a more vivid and translucent blue than Jubilee could have imagined. Beside the road there were fruit stalls, one with a mountain of large green melons - a few sliced like open mouths to show you their blood-red flesh - another of peaches packed into tilted trays. Jubilee was kept busy looking up French phrases, which jumped at them to right and left on a continuous avenue of hoardings. These advertised petrols, sun-lotions, perfume, beach wear, fruit drinks. She used her language-aid like someone visiting a museum full of highly valuable objects, catalogue in hand.

They got on to a motorway, travelled some distance, then turned off northwards on to a lesser road which left the thronged coastal area and finally began to climb a deep valley mounting inexorably into dry rocky hills clothed with pines. On both sides the cicadas throbbed continuously. Sometimes, Jubilee observed, usually as they were taking corners, the intermittent pulsing merged excitingly into a one-pitched scream. Once they stopped to allow Jubilee to look at a lizard she had noticed on a rock. While she did so, Steve looked at the dial which gave the kilometres, then at his watch, and said they would be there in about another hour.

Steve couldn't remember the intricacies of the route from his last visit, and they had to ask the way twice. The torrent of explanation which was triggered by the words 'Château Lamartine' and 'Vigny-les-Pins' overwhelmed the few phrases they were learning or remembered from school, and they didn't gain much from the instructions. But by trial and error they found the place at last.

There seemed no formal entrance or drive. The unmade road which ambled on upwards through unvarying pine woods didn't seem very promising, until without warning it debouched suddenly into a wider weedy area which had traces of gravel. There before them was an imposing three-storey building of grey stone with a short flight of steps leading up to the front door.

'Oh how crumbly and utterly beautiful,' exclaimed Jubilee in awe. She immediately began to search for something. On the two front corners of the building there were stout ruined turrets without roofs, like broken hollow molars, but there unmistakeably on the third side, visible to them at an angle, she found what she was looking for, the tower with the pointed slate roof which June had mentioned in her second letter. 'There, there it is,' she said, pointing. 'It *is* just like a witch's hat, just as June described it, Steve. That's where you stayed before.'

When Steve had drawn up at the front door she got out and walked to a stone balustrade on the far side of a strip of untended browned grass. She looked out over the wide panorama stretched before her. It was apparent to her that the Château was built on a long ledge of white rock. The semi-wooded country sloped away from the foot of the ridge, then mounted again in the middle-distance towards a huge slab of a treeless mountain jutting up into a sky of chalky-blue haze like the upturned bows of a sinking ship.

Almost unable to contain the surge of delight she felt, she turned her back to the balustrade and looked along the unkempt terrace which ran the length of the house on this, its sunnier side. Once apparently there had been long oval flowerbeds. The beds were now almost indistinguishable from what remained of the grass, which in this climate would require constant watering to flourish. There were a few meagre floribunda red roses still struggling for survival amid the variety of grasses and wild flowers which choked them and which at this time of year had mostly gone to seed. She looked up at the house. Apart from some red curtains in two big windows on the first floor there was no evidence of habitation. Her gaze ranged back over the wide unkempt area into which the drive debouched, and beyond it. There were two hens scavenging in the direction of some outhouses, otherwise the place was silent and seemingly deserted. 'Oh Steve, it's so lovely,' she exclaimed.

Steve was getting the suitcases out of the car. She rejoined him to help and, together, they ascended the steps which led to the front entrance. Beside the open double door there was an old-fashioned rusted bell-pull. Jubilee was going to pull it when Steve noticed with a chuckle that the wire was severed. They went inside into an unfurnished hall, floored with uneven black and white tiles and sporting a fine staircase which wound up to a landing. Where a chandelier should have been, hung a single unshaded electric light bulb. The only sound was made by a frantic insect caught in a web somewhere.

'They're mad enough to have packed up and gone without telling anyone,' Steve said. He put a hand to his mouth and nautically twice shouted, 'Ahoy there.' Un-nautically, the Château slept on without response.

They heard footsteps outside, approaching through the trees on the far side of the drive. 'Ah,' Steve said, going back to the door, 'an inmate after all perhaps.'

The approaching male inmate, if such he was, materialised, looking extremely English. As if to defy the weather, he wore heavy-looking whipcord trousers and a check shirt of the lumberjack variety. He was making for the front door, eyes fastened on the ground in front of him. 'Hallo, we're the Addicots,' Steve stated cheerfully from the top of the steps. Jubilee gave her warmest smile.

The man climbed the steps two at a time, ignored the hand Steve thrust in his direction, and swept past them with no sign of even having observed their presence. He disappeared through a door on the far side of the hall. Silence re-closed.

Steve flushed with annoyance, but Jubilee laughed and clapped her hands together. 'I'm sure it's the intellectual June spoke about,' she said. 'He was probably thinking about something frightfully important and didn't even take in we're here. Oh Steve, how gloriously eccentric. I'm so glad we came. I know it's going to be wonderful. I've already fallen in love with the place.'

June Aguas de Villanova remembered it was her turn to cook this evening. She had been busy all day in the studio on batik work, trying to forget the heavy cloud which hung over them all. People, especially Liz, had been wonderful. Liz had promised various 'emergency measures'. But she hadn't yet had the courage to tell them it was no longer a question of a few hundred pounds of savings which had to be made. She hadn't told them that very soon she wouldn't be able to afford the outgoings, above all the rent without which their tenure would be ended. She had never told them she was a tenant, they thought she owned the Château.

She thought again of the meal she was responsible for and looked at her watch. It had stopped just after midday - the battery must have run out. But the angle of the sun told her it must be getting towards four. Never mind, there was plenty of time to get to the village and buy food. She slipped out of her overall and went downstairs. She wouldn't take the car, she thought, but find her bicycle.

As she stepped on to the hall landing, she froze in horror. There below was Steve and a young woman who must be Jubilee sitting on two large suitcases. Surely it was tomorrow they were coming? Just then Jubilee looked up, saw her, and smiled. The smile was warm and friendly, but this did not diminish her dismay. She ran down. 'Steve, I'm terribly sorry,' she said. 'I thought . . .'

'No matter,' Steve said, rising, 'we've been absorbing the atmosphere.'

'You should have found someone, or called.' She embraced Steve nervously. There was a fumble because he thought one cheek was enough. She was already questioning her decision to invite him and then, when the letter came, her failure to cancel the invitation. As well as her other misgivings, how could Steve possibly enjoy a place like this now he was so prosperous and no doubt accustomed to luxury? But Jubilee at least didn't seem at all dismayed.

'I love it here already,' she said at once when they had finished touching cheeks, 'what a fabulous place to live.'

June had to think fast. She had already decided there was only one solution to the problem of a room. She had spoken to Alfonso and he'd had no objection. But thinking the Addicots were due tomorrow she'd made no preparations as yet. Stupidly, she took them up to their room right away. As she went round on a harvest of scattered clothing and began to clear two drawers and some hanging space by throwing her things into a suitcase, Steve guessed.

'But look here, June, this is obviously your room. You can't move out for us. Surely there must be dozens of empty rooms we could use?'

'None of them is furnished.'

'I see, then why don't we find ourselves a hotel? There must be something nearby.'

In the midst of her blush June became almost clipped. 'No, we don't mind at all, it's fixed. It's just that I . . . muddled the dates.' She concentrated on Jubilee, telling her the amenities at her disposal. She took her into the all-marble bathroom and showed her how the shower did work but that it was temperamental and needed approaching with respect and some guile. Also the toilet . . .

Fortunately the girl didn't seem at all embarrassed and took everything at face value. As soon as she could, June set off on her way to the village and left them to settle in.

June told the Addicots that to welcome them she was going to ask everyone 'to dress up a bit', and that she 'supposed' they would be eating about eight. At five to eight the Addicots presented themselves in the room in which Steve remembered they had eaten on his last visit. It was a combination of a dining room and a lounge. Being on the south side of the house on the ground floor, it gave on to a paved terrace now very uneven, the flags much interleaved with weeds and desiccated moss.

The room hadn't changed much, Steve thought. It was if anything even more sparsely furnished. At the living room end, there were two armchairs of faded chintz, a torn *chaise-longue* of a deep purple colour with remnants of gilding on the legs and other visible woodwork, a piano stool, and a couple of mini wine-barrels surmounted by cushions which were obviously used to supplement the seating arrangements. On a huge baroque chest of drawers with a marble top of a pinkish colour - the only piece of any worth, Steve adjudged - stood a record player of some vintage. It was wired to two speakers, one of which was on the floor, the other on the mantelpiece beside an ornate French clock, which had stopped. There was a stack of long-play records beside the machine. At the dining room end, there was a substantial refectory table with six stout legs, and a number of wooden chairs scattered about in various asymmetrical positions. If this was where they were to eat it didn't seem any preparations had yet been made. The Addicots, who had followed June's instructions and changed for dinner, sat in the armchairs to await developments. Steve wore a white tropical suit with a gaudy tie, Jubilee a becoming print dress.

It was difficult to believe what June had told them - that there were seven people in the building. Since talking to her, they had heard a donkey bray, at five a factory siren had wailed distantly in the valley below, and above them now they could hear intermittently someone repeatedly playing the same arpeggio of chords on a piano. These chords seemed to presage a great deal more, though nothing further developed. Apart from these signs of life, there had been nothing.

'How amazing to think of them all here creating things,' said Jubilee. 'Didn't June say one of them is a composer? That must be him up there above us.' She lifted her head to a ceiling which had once been painted - apparently with a scene in heaven. There were cherubs. 'There he is again. Funny he keeps playing the same notes.'

'Steve giggled. 'Probably the only ones he can play.'

'A composer, an artist, a sculptor,' continued Jubilee, 'a historian and a . . . What was the word she said for the one who studies place names?'

'God knows,' said Steve.

'No wonder it's so quiet. They'd need it to be.'

Steve was having thoughts he decided not to express.

At ten past eight they heard rapid footsteps and brisk whistling in the hall. An amazing figure entered, quite smartly dressed in what at first glance one might have thought were the trousers of an evening dress suit, a white shirt, and a kind of cravat of a royal blue colour. Steve noticed that the trousers *were* those of an evening dress suit. He was carrying a large earthenware vase shaped like a Greek amphora and put it down on the floor near the table. He then made for Jubilee, held out his hand and, when she had proffered hers, bent to kiss it. 'Frederick Von Hapsburg-Trench. Very pleased to meet you, Mrs Addicot.' He marched to Steve, who had risen from his chair, and shook his hand with similar formality. 'Mr Addicot, welcome to Lamartine.' He broke off. 'Will you please forgive me for a few minutes? I have some small duties to perform.'

He withdrew, and within a matter of seconds returned with an old though fine and well ironed linen tablecloth. He threw it expertly over the table, adjusting its symmetry with the precision of a professional waiter. He drew a large double-decker canteen out of the baroque cupboard and from its green-baize lined interior took worn-looking but quite handsome silver. This he laid out on the tablecloth. There were, rather surprisingly, two silver pheasants in the cupboard, which were also placed strategically on the table, their positions finely attended to. He withdrew again and returned with an armful of evergreen leaves and a few dry looking but colourful wild flowers with very long stems. He placed the vase in the centre of the table and began to arrange the flowers in it with grave deliberation. The Addicots watched these movements with interest.

'You seem very expert at arranging flowers,' Jubilee said after a while. Frederick, she now registered, was extremely handsome in a demonic sort of way. He had a prolific mane of upstanding dark grey hair parted down the middle, a sallow skin, and very dark eyes, which seemed almost black. He had now renewed his whistling, though this time in a more subdued fashion almost under his breath. The tune was a hymn, Jubilee noticed - 'Onward Christian Soldiers' - endlessly repeated.

There was a long pause and she thought perhaps, as with the other man, they were going to be ignored again. But after re-positioning a waxy blue flower he had already moved twice, the hymn tune briefly stopped. 'If you don't mind frightfully, I think I'll just get this done, then I'll be completely at your service, Mrs Addicot. I find I do need to concentrate to achieve my best effects, and this, I gather *is* to be an occasion. If you'll permit me to say so, I begin to see why.'

While he worked, arrivals came suddenly thick and fast. A large lady in her middle forties of blooming health, who introduced herself as Liz appeared in a brown dress which might perhaps have been at an earlier point in history fashionable but as it was looked a little on the short side for a woman of her age. Likewise a dapper small man in a well cut blazer and spotted bow tie. He had a goatee beard in the centre of his chin, which at once made one think of that imagined bust of William Shakespeare which is always appearing in advertisements and on book tokens. He spoke in a grave voice with a discernible American accent, which was only just audible, and said his name was Paul Beerbohmer.

Paul brought with him two large plastic jugs filled with what proved to be red and white wine respectively. He also paid a visit to the cupboard under the record player, produced glasses, and began to ask people what they wanted. A very tall man with a Tennysonian black beard and a Spanish accent came in, also a very soignée-looking blonde lady in a pleated skirt, a see-through nylon blouse, and high heels - the only person of any distinction,

Steve thought. She spoke with a very pronounced French twang, and indeed - as if English could not for very long be trusted on its own - constantly reinforced her speech with French words and expressions.

Conversation flowed, so did the wine, and 'Frederick the Hapsburg', as Steve tacitly named him, had put on some very esoteric music which sounded like some sort of endless medieval chant such as you might expect to hear in a monastery. Smells of food reached their nostrils in a most appetizing way through the open door.

Everyone seemed to have immediately paired off as if they had all left their conversations in the middle when they were last together and wished to take them up at once. The one exception to this was Frederick. As he had promised, as soon as he had finished putting on the record and adjusted the volume and tone, he came up to Jubilee and led her to the mantelpiece, having stated that the antique clock - no, not functioning at the moment, he was afraid - was a most interesting piece and had a lurid history.

Steve had no objection. He was used to young men approaching Jubilee in this way. It was always happening at accountancy conferences he took her to. He didn't mind because he was as sure as he could be that Jubilee was impervious to anything that might lie beyond the conversational gambits made. She just took them at their face value.

Soon abandoning the French clock, clearly a gambit, Frederick began to question Jubilee about her interests in a way which suggested an intense wish to know everything about her. But it wasn't long before Jubilee had turned the tables on him. It was she who was asking the questions, and he who was outlining at length the scope of his own pursuits. Frederick wouldn't yet know that almost certainly Jubilee's fervent interest in him would be confined to wanting to know about his studies.

Steve himself fared less well as far as conversation was concerned. He was left alone sipping wine, until he found himself assaulted from behind in the most direct way. 'Steve Addicot?'

Turning, he found himself shaking hands with the woman he

now gathered was Paul Beerbohmer's wife, Hortense, who was indeed French. They exchanged some pleasantries, but Steve had at once the impression these were mere preliminaries. After a moment or two, in an almost simultaneous movement, she closed her mascara-ed eyes, tossed her well-coiffured head of plaited blonde hair and gave a lateral twitch to the upper part of her torso which was, admittedly, shapely enough to have attention called to it in this way.

'So - you are *expert comptable*?' she said.

'If that word means accountant, yes, for my sins I am.   I handle bankruptcies.'

'Bankruptcies?'

'Businesses, people, who've gone bust.'

'I am knowing the meaning of bankruptcy, Monsieur.'

'I see.   Sorry, I thought you sounded mystified by the word.'

'Not mystified, *curieuse*.   I'm curious to know why a man in your profession wants to come to a place like this.'

Steve gave a laugh.   'Oh, that's easily explained,' he said, 'Jubilee and I were invited.   I was once at school with June, you see.   I've visited here before, and in addition to that . . .'

'In addition to that?'

He found himself blushing.   'Well, when Jubilee heard about your set-up here she was *especially* interested to see it.   Jubilee is a person who is very drawn by books, art, that sort of thing, and is just starting out on an Open University course.   We're on our way to Africa as a matter of fact, a safari holiday, and it occurred to us we could . . .'

Hortense didn't seem to be listening.   She had closed her eyes again.   'I am asking myself if this is being, maybe, the only reason for your visit.   It is my impression that the attitude of money-people to the arts is being *ambigue*,' she announced. 'You are being able perhaps to inform me if this is so.   *D'un point de vue* money-people despise the arts, they think the arts are *un jou, une caprice*.   *D'autre part* there is an attraction to them. Have I reason?'

Too intense by half?   Steve had met people like this on his last visit here.   He kept it light.   'In my view it takes all sorts to make a world, Madame Beerbohmer.'

'Is that cliché your real opinion I wonder?   I am having to doubt it.   I am thinking it is much more likely that you, like all you capitalists, are despising artists.   For in what other way are you escaping your guilt?'

'Guilt?   What am I supposed to be guilty about?'

'Being such a *materialiste?*'

'You mean I'm a sort of guilt edged insecurity, is that it?'

The witticism was lost - even if it were linguistically registered, which had to be doubted.   'And to deal in bankruptcy,' Hortense went on, 'must make it *encore pire*.   How are you not being guilty to make money from the misfortunes of other persons?'

Apparently being serious was unavoidable - but this was at least a familiar charge.   He moved easily to a standard defence.   'Undertakers have also to live off the misfortunes of mankind, Madame Beerbohmer.   I venture to say most people nonetheless think their services are necessary.   And of course it isn't me who drives people to bankruptcy, it's themselves.   All I do is try to clean up the messes they've made.   Often I save jobs, restore good enterprises to their feet, retain employment.'

'Oh, you have comprehended me quite wrongly,' came the cool reply.   'I am not meaning to suggest that your kind of work is not *entièrement nécessaire*.   I was of course referring to the *point de vue personale*.   For it is not what you do that is important, but the effect of what you do on yourself.   *Vous n'êtes pas d'accord?*'

Steve found himself quite able to take this, too, in his stride.   'Well I don't know what accountancy has made me,' he said, grinning broadly, 'except one thing, and that is rich.   I have to confess I do rather like being rich - it's a weakness of mine.'

He was more than agreeable to continue the conversation with this lively, attractive, if intense lady, whose eyes were busy, he noticed, as she talked, with an examination of various parts of his physique.   But abruptly he found that for a shapely female front had been abruptly substituted a shapely female back, very largely visible to him through the nylon blouse.   He noticed there was a quite large black wen just peeping under the strap of her brassière.   It seemed to Steve it was like an enlarged punctuation mark - a

57

full stop, he thought ruefully.

It didn't greatly concern him. None of the people here except June and Alfonso had been here on his last visit, but the tenor of the conversation he'd just had was no different from others he had undergone then. On that first occasion he had at first been wounded by the barbs inserted into his flesh with such careless ease. Then he had learnt to regard them as little more than a sophisticated form of games playing. Probably also they were a defence mechanism against the lack of worldly success on the part of these indefatigable artists and intellectuals. The fatal thing was to take them seriously.

Seeking another contact, he stationed himself beside the stout woman, Liz, and his bearded host, Aguas de Villanova, who were in conversation. He listened to Liz talking at length about a goat whose milk-yielding abilities seemed to have failed temporarily. At any moment he expected to be included. He wasn't. Never mind, he thought. He had known what he would be in for. It was only two days, and if Jubilee enjoyed herself in this time why should he carp? He gave himself to sipping what was no doubt home made wine - not totally unacceptable - and to observing the company.

June arrived in a quite fashionable blue dress covered by a plastic apron. She carried a large tureen. Behind her traipsed the silent inmate the Addicots had already seen but not heard on their arrival, bearing a stack of hand-made ceramic soup bowls. June, it seemed, as she had been on their arrival, looked even more distracted. She was uncertain where to put the tureen until Frederick detached himself from Jubilee and stepped forward to take it from her. Having put it on the table in front of what would perhaps be her seat at the top, he then gallantly made to relieve her of her apron, which she seemed to have forgotten about. She rather irritably, Steve thought, pre-empted this operation by taking it off herself. The silent academic who had brought in the plates quietly withdrew, closing the door behind him. He was the only one who had not changed his clothes.

As June began to ladle onion soup out of the tureen, everyone sat themselves at the table. Steve, hanging back, was ignored. He was about to make his way to the far end of the table where there was a spare seat when June seemed to pull herself together and come to life. 'Here, Steve, you must sit next to me. Is no one looking after you? You and Jubilee are the guests of honour. Jubilee, you're happy where you are, are you? Paul, would you mind . . .' Paul, who had sat himself very positively on June's right, clearly did regret the change but obediently vacated the seat.

June asked Steve about his work, with none of the insinuations made by Hortense Beerbohmer. She made very nice remarks about Jubilee, whom she found 'so immediately friendly and charming.' She referred to their past association and to people they had both known. They shared knowledge on what had happened to some of these acquaintances. Steve revived his previous view of June, which had become somewhat faded in view of his rather marginal interest in her and by the gap of years, as a woman of undoubted goodness and sweetness, but with nothing very clearly in focus about her. A rather poetic simile occurred to him. She was like a hiveless bee, he thought, nipping from flower to flower, gathering honey, but with nowhere at all precise to take it to. If anything she was more distracted and distant than last time they had met. One thing about her, though, was very definite. She was a brilliant cook. The food, simple as it was, was delicious. Following the soup, after another visit to the kitchen by June they had a delicious *paella* in which both meat and fish were identifiable. After the main course they ate an excellent home made goat cheese. Apparently at least one goat was functioning properly. With the cheese went delicious bread, which June proclaimed was Frederick's creation. Finally there was a glorious melon at an apogee in terms of flavour and sweetness - also a product, it was said, of Lady Elizabeth's efforts. It was during the consumption of this latter item that Steve became aware of a disturbance at the far end of the table. Because of the wine, conversation had reached a crescendo. Suddenly it ceased. Everyone was looking towards June.

'*Ce n'est pas la verité, June - le Château, c'est loué?*' said Hortense, leaning forward in her seat.

June was serving Frederick on her left with a further slice of melon. She continued to do so. 'I asked you not to say that,

Alfonso,' she said quietly without looking at him, seated as he was facing her at the other end of the table. 'Yes,' she replied to Hortense, I rent the place. It's by far the biggest outgoing and of course inescapable.'

'So it's true, *ma chérie* - it's not only that those capitalist bastards in Paris have dismissed you but you are not *propriétaire* here?'

June smiled thinly. 'It's true, yes. Your great golden goose has miscarried at last.'

The note of bitterness which seemed to be contained in this remark surprised Steve. He had always imagined June enjoyed being the provider for these layabouts. Could it be otherwise? Had it become otherwise? Was she angry with them all for having taken her charity for so long? Or had he got it wrong? Was her bitterness just for the oil company for whom she had worked all these years? It was impossible at this moment to say. Either way, though it had no possible practical consequence, he had a not unpleasant sense of having strayed on to territory professionally familiar to him.

8

Repercussions from the dinner party rustled like thunder round the empty corridors of the Château Lamartine. Here and there they seemed to spend themselves with liberated booms, only to stumble on to further explosions which involved finally every inmate.

One of the loudest booms occurred in the rooms of the Beerbohmers. Disconsolate for private reasons as well as those stemming from June's misfortune, when he gained the sanctity of his apartment Paul went straight to the white baby piano in their sitting room. He thought of wrestling again with the variations of emotional intensity which can be conveyed by ankle control, head posture, stool height, above all by subtle alterations in the wrist angle - the foothills of a major work he planned on the purely physiological aspects of playing, with which he hoped to revolutionise concert performance. But he found tonight he had no stomach for it. Instead, eyes on the moulded ceiling, the keyboard illuminated by a single lamp, he tumbled into a piece by Gerschwin, one of the few cultural items he was able to salvage from a total rejection of his American past.

Jubilee, he was quite sure, was the most beautiful female he had ever met. Her face, turned to him as it once was during her enforced conversation with that ogre, Hapsburg-Trench, had been unbelievably understanding. He had given her a smile, one of the gravest in his repertoire, and she had with an electric spontaneity smiled back. He was sure this moment would turn out to be the most poignant of his life - he had photographed it indelibly. He knew that time and again he would take it out, as he was doing now for the first time, to analyse its content from every angle. If only she weren't married to that Englishman (surely greatly older than she?) who seemed to have gobbled whole the American materialist values he himself had so rigorously rejected, and if only Frederick Hapsburg-Trench hadn't, by getting in first, barged his own so much more sensitive courtship to one side and made that all-important opening move.

He was so absorbed he didn't hear Hortense come in. He got his fingers away from the keyboard only just in time to prevent their being severely bruised as she smashed the keyboard lid shut. 'Darn it, Hortense, that's overdoing the aggression a bit, isn't it?' he said.

"'Ave you spoken to June yet?"

From the piano top he took the large signet ring he never wore when playing and took his time screwing it back on to his little finger. While he did so Hortense swung away from him and went to sit purposefully in one of the chairs. 'You will do it tomorrow *sans faute*,' she said, crossing her legs. Pinching her skirt at the knee she let it fall, as if her statement concluded the matter. '*On ne se demande que la somme.*'

On this of all nights Paul didn't want a row. He tried to be patient. 'Hortense, I've already told you there are limits to what I can do. I'm not a rich man. I've already been more than generous with gifts and loans. There *must* be a limit. And now the situation is even more hopeless, it seems. One has to think a little of one's own interests.'

Hortense changed colour quite considerably. 'Our interests are that this place is continuing. To keep ourselves in Paris, or anywhere we would wish to be living, would be costing us a fortune compared with the money we pay 'ere - and that includes the few *maigre* sums you 'ave paid to June. You must *au moins* offer her *cent mille francs* to make a bridge until something is thought of. I cannot leave 'ere for at least another year. My whole development as an artist is *lié* with this landscape. To part with it now is being like . . .' She sought imagery severe enough to contain her emotion. 'Is being like the guillotine.'

Paul flushed. He reopened the keyboard lid and with one hand re-tinkled the theme of the piece he had been playing, with a higher wrist position. 'So *that*'s the story,' he said in an accent more American than it usually was. 'Now we have it, spoken plain at last. The great French ego discovered with its panties down when the lights went up.'

Hortense rose. 'You are a pathetic, vulgar Boston nobody.

Not only you are vulgar, you are not being an artist. All which you do is *analyser* the music of other people and pre-tend what you do is original. You are not more original than this Addicot.' She marched to the door into the bedroom, where she paused for the launch of a final missile. 'And why are you not shaving that absurd beard? Like the rest of you, *c'est un mensonge.*'

Paul knew what would happen and it happened. There was some opening and closing of closets, then she threw a sheet, a blanket and his nightshirt into the salon. She closed and locked the bedroom door.

He didn't mind, indeed welcomed, this domestic adjustment, which would leave him freer to think about Jubilee. He made up a bed for himself on the Louis Quinze sofa. In his closing thoughts for that day he visualised a number of secret venues in the grounds of the Château where he was meeting Jubilee. He thought of the softness of her brown limbs and of his hands running over them towards increasingly intimate destinations.

He woke, however, in a different frame of mind. Try as he could to re-conjure Jubilee and her young body, all he could think about was what Hortense had said about his work. She was wrong of course. He was on the brink of a major discovery. Hortense was jealous because her own painting had reached some creative impasse. But the thought of sitting at the piano that morning depressed him.

Breakfast was not a communal meal at Lamartine. All made their own way at different times to the roomy basement kitchen whose windows gave on to the moat like those of Liz's and Damon's room. Paul was the first down this morning.

He was pleased about this for more than one reason. Having more money than anyone here, he and Hortense could afford to have coffee every morning. When there were others present they always shared it, but it was nice not to have to for once. He riddled the never-extinguished embers of the nineteenth century wood-burning range, added more fuel, and eventually removed the hissing saucepan to pour its water into their own all-metal Neapolitan coffee maker. You filled the top half of the utensil with hot water, sunk into it a centre piece which contained the coffee in a compartment screwed on to its top, then, capping these two sections with the third which had a handle affixed, you turned over the ensemble to allow percolation to start.

While the machine released an appetising aroma, Paul took the large wholemeal loaf from the earthenware bin, cut himself two sizeable slices on the sideboard, and sat at the table with a plate, a knife, and a mug. The coffee finished its draining process. He poured, and was dunking the first piece of bread, when he heard footsteps. He was pleased to identify them as Alfonso's.

'Good timing, Fonsie,' he said, cheefully surrendering his solitude as the giant figure entered. 'I've just brewed.'

Alfonso went to the vast fridge, which was as tall as a sentry-box. It was a very early American model, which had a plaque above the door featuring the stars and stripes. Taking out a jug half full of goat's milk, he raised it distrustfully to his nostrils. '*Madonna*,' he remarked.

'Look,' Paul said, 'this coffee doesn't need that liquid cheese for God's sake.'

Grinning, Alfonso replaced the jug and, smelling strongly as usual of metal, sat opposite Paul with another mug unhooked from the dresser. He helped himself. Then, ripping Paul's second piece of bread in two, he took one half.

Paul was definitely feeling better. Being with Alfonso always improved his self-respect. For Alfonso wasn't just big in stature, there wasn't an ounce of superficiality in him. Unlike some on these premises, he was pure art. He lived and breathed it as if it were his element. Paul contrasted these amiable feelings with what had happened last night. He knew all of a sudden very clearly what he wanted to do this morning.

'Up on the dot, I see,' he said. 'The telescope again, is it? You've really been going at it night and day since you returned. Good phase? Must be up quite a bit since I last took a look.' Alfonso was chewing massively. He turned his head sideways, lowered it to the table and began a noisy lapping of the hot coffee. Paul trod carefully. 'Another few weeks perhaps . . .'

Alfonso waved bread in front of his face. 'Weeks?

Telescope ees *demasiado grande* - too much bloody big.'

'It's a big concept.'

'Too big - never finish.'

'You don't mean that.'

'I mean that.'

'You've just got to keep going, we all have to.' This was a wrong tack, Paul knew. Alfonso was usually joking, but not one hundred per cent of the time. If one happened upon a rare occasion when he was serious, an odd remark could throw him off course altogether. And apart from artistic considerations, which were of course paramount, it hadn't escaped Paul how important this sculpture was to the whole place. If it were completed and sold, it could save him from Hortense's goads, and all of them from bankruptcy. He plunged. 'Do you want a hand this morning?'

For an instant Alfonso looked as cross as he ever got. He shook his head. 'You have piano work.'

'As a matter of fact I've reached a phase of fermentation. I need something monotonous to do while the thing cooks up again. Really, if you've got something menial I'd be happy to help. Hump up the new delivery for you perhaps? It'd be my pleasure.'

The answer normally would have been no. Paul knew it. Fernie didn't like him on site when he was working. He didn't like anyone on site. But the lorry which had dumped a new load of steel rods on the wrong side of the house when no one was about was, he knew, a factor in his favour. The rods needed delivering to the site and probably up to the relevant platforms. He saw Alfonso wavering as he took this in.

'Is very heavy,' Alfonso said, weakening.

'I've told you, it doesn't faze me.'

Alfonso's eyes dropped to Paul's light-brown trousers and up again to his bow tie - the latter this morning of a dark brown velvet.

'You need change clothes.'

'I'll wear my boiler suit.'

The boiler suit was designed for work in a higher latitude. Though he wore only a vest and underpants under it, and though it was only seven-thirty in the morning, after two journeys Paul was sweating. The trouble was the length of the rods. The only way to carry them was to place your shoulder underneath their point of balance. But not only were they very heavy, as you moved, the rods moved up and down with a gait of their own which did not coincide with yours. You had the sensation of being wilfully bounced off the direction you intended. There was also a lateral momentum. When you made a corrective alteration of course, like a ship answering to a helm, you were swung away further than you intended. He hoped that Alfonso, already at work half way up the tower, wasn't observing his ungainly movements through one of the medieval slits which pierced the building at various points. On the next and subsequent journeys he would carry two not three rods.

Alfonso's work for that well-known United Nations Quango, the W.C.H.I.S.A.R. (The World Council for the Human Implications of Spacial and Astronomical Research) had been commissioned three years ago. The sculpture was to be sited on the immaculate lawns in front of the ultra-modern headquarters building near Versailles. Alfonso's idea was a huge skeletal representation of a telescope standing somewhat inclined from the vertical and pointing skywards as if an astronomer was in the act of observation. It was to be built in ingeniously curved, enlaced, and merging thin steel bars, kept rigid by four stronger bars, one at each quadrant.

W.C.H.I.S.A.R. owed its existence to the notion that astronomers and spaciologists were too busy and too single-minded to think of the human and practical implications of their discoveries and of their celestial journeys, and that a separate body was therefore necessary to do this invaluable work. Alfonso's idea was that adorning the telescope at various points inside - as if they were being observed by the astronomer's eye - would be solid shapes fashioned in light metals, representing different stellar bodies such as Mars, Saturn, and the Sun. He intended that these should be linked by means of very strong and rigid metallic 'ropes' (which would act also as props to the inclined telescope) to other figures positioned in a wide arc outside the base of the telescope. These would symbolise those purely terrestrial activities which the Quango wished to research and encourage. One of the interior shapes for instance, representing the round uneven surface of the Moon and made of a silvery alloy, was already in place half way up the telescope. This would be linked on the ground to a caricature of a ploughman and his plough, fashioned also in steel rods. One of the ploughman's hands would have left the handle of the plough to point upwards to the satellite. We were to divine from this that eventually the surface of the moon will be cultivated, that it will become a kitchen garden to the world's needs - this being a project already receiving the urgent attention of the World Council.

Since Alfonso's commission had been signed, there had been a further development in this matter. Lobbied by environmental movements, the Council was now grappling with the possibility of all of our industry being eventually so sited as well, thus relieving the earth of its smoky wens, and allowing its denizens to inhabit a veritable Eden of ozone-friendliness. Alfonso planned a second figure linked to the Moon, a representation of a blacksmith and his anvil. Likewise the model Sun (represented in a gold-coloured metal) would be linked to a model electricity pylon, W.C.H.I.S.A.R. already being at work on a more direct application of the Sun's energy to earthly needs via travelling space-stations. As well as those projects already under way, Alfonso saw no reason why others, not yet conceived, might not be added at a later date.

It had also been Alfonso's brainwave to carry out his construction inside one of the empty, semi-ruined Château towers, whose shape and height so closely paralleled those of the telescope. There were problems involved in this. He wished to retain the four wooden floors which were once rooms as work platforms, but of course they would impede the upward surge of the telescope. He found a brilliant solution. As necessary, he bored holes in the heavy planks in all places where the steel rods needed to pass through. When the sculpture was finished, the stages would be cut up and removed, ready for the apogee of Alfonso's plan, agreed to by the astounded but impressed representatives of the Quango. This would be the lifting of the telescope upwards by a helicopter and its delivery by air directly to the site.

There had been another problem to overcome, the sloping angle at which the telescope was to be erected - as Damon humorously pointed out, the tower at Pisa would from this point of view have been a better venue for the work than a vertical tower. But Alfonso had cunningly distributed the weight-load of the structure by cementing stout temporary stays into the side walls of the tower as it went up. This meant that the walls took the major part of the strain and not the one point of the tilted basal ring which touched the ground - the 'big toe' as Alfonso liked to call it. In a more lyrical mood one day he had spoken of the telescope as being like a delicate ballerina, gracefully poised on the point of one of her shoes, and firmly held at the waist by the embracing tower.

Alfonso's ingenuity had been further demonstrated by use of other amenities the tower offered. When delivered, the steel rods were some ten metres long. How were they to be brought inside? A crane would have delivered them through the open top of the tower. But there was no crane. Surely the slits in the walls could be used? They could be. It was thus Paul's task to post the top end of each rod into one of the slits, a third of the way up. As he fed the rod upwards Alfonso, mounted on the lowest of his circular platforms inside, drew it in and upwards, passing it through the floor above him by means of a larger hole he had made for this purpose. When the rod was completely clear of the slit he let it downwards vertically through another working hole he had made in the first floor stage flooring, until it reached the ground. The whole operation took the two men about an hour and a half.

Exhausted, but pleased with himself at having completed successfully a physical labour so unusual for him, Paul went into the tower and climbed the spiralling stone steps - blocks let into and protruding from the wall - to the first stage where Alfonso had been working in between the arrival of the rods.

As Paul sat watching Alfonso work under the bright arc lights he had installed at the Quango's expense, he marvelled anew at the amazing strength and confidence of the man. To have such a concept at all was inspiring enough, to be carrying it out was staggering. His head shielded behind a square mask, Alfonso was riveting two pieces of delicately fashioned steel. The blue flame of the acetylene lamp flickered ghoulishly as the acrid smoke rose. Paul remembered then what it was he had to say.

His resolve weakened. What was more important than art? Hortense had been thinking of herself of course, of her own work, when she had enjoined him to pay over more of his money. But he had to concede that in thinking of herself she was also involuntarily thinking of Alfonso, of himself, of the endeavours of all at Lamartine. Shouldn't he consider a further plunge into his pocket? But a hundred thousand out of already seriously depleted funds? That was a great number of dollars. Even if he got it back, in the interim he would lose the interest. And he had heard it said that Alfonso's contract awarded him six times that sum on completion.

Something had gone wrong for Alfonso, a piece of metal clattered to the floor. '*Coño,*' he bawled suddenly, throwing down the mask and his lamp. He strode to the nearest part of the wall, and slumped against it with a grunt. Taking a grimy handkerchief from his trouser pocket, he wiped his forehead. '*Mujer tan maldita,*' he said, looking upwards and shaking his fist, '*estoy finito con te. Fea,*' he added in a still louder voice.

Paul knew it wasn't a propitious moment, but it was now or never. He cleared his throat. 'Fernie, I've got something I've got to say to you,' he began.

Alfonso didn't seem to hear. He went on about the unruliness of steel rods which didn't do what he told them and which had a way of their own. Paul had to repeat what he had said.

'Eh?' said Alfonso.

'I've got something to say. Look, I'm really sorry about June's job.' Alfonso tossed a hand. 'Coming at this moment in your creation schedule it's really a blow. But, as I say, if you get this done this summer there's a chance, isn't there . . .'

'This summer? You mad?'

'Well soon. What I'm saying is, if you do that, it'll be all right, won't it?   There won't have to be any question of us all having to leave the Château?   That's why, if I can be of help . . .'

Alfonso was looking at him fiercely.   He screwed his eyes. 'What you trying say, Paul?'

This forced the issue frontally.   Paul blushed.   'What I'm saying is that much as I'd like to I can't cough up this time. You see . . .'

'Cough?   What cough?   What you talk about, Chriss sake?'

He gave up.   'I can't lend any more money,' he said lamely, and he felt his sentence had the banal thump of a hammer falling off the stage and hitting the ground below.

Alfonso's interest faded as he grasped what was being said. 'OK,' he said, 'so nobody ask you.'

'You mean you and June don't mind?   All of us do have to think of ourselves a bit from time to time, I know, but . . .'

'*De nada.   No hay que preocuparte.*'

Disappointingly, Alfonso's interest, so difficult to capture, had re-fastened itself on the point in the structure just above their head, which was the source of his difficulty.

Paul thought he should have been pleased.   He had done what he had decided to do.   He had got things off his chest. But he found he didn't feel pleased at all.   Only mean, and further belittled.

9

Early on the morning after the Addicots' arrival, Frederick Hapsburg-Trench was in his room at the top of the Château's one inhabited tower. Like the other three, the tower was a survivor of the fortified medieval building which had preceded the eighteenth century re-modelling and which lack of use over three centuries had caused to fall into decay. But a nineteenth century owner of the Château had decided to make the one tower habitable. Hence the serviceable pointed grey-slated roof, and the two windows which replaced the original slits in the upper part of the structure and gave light to Frederick's room. He was sitting in the deep bay which gave access to one of these windows.

Frederick was certainly not so ardent a scholar as Damon Raspin, but he was seldom totally idle. This morning a strong non-academic purpose inspired him, but as no action was immediately possible he was filling in time by writing a letter to his mother in England. He wrote carefully with a fountain pen in a fine hand which was nearer to calligraphy than ordinary script. The notepaper was a thick ochre-coloured sheet almost like vellum, which he had found at the back of an allegedly antique desk the Beerbohms had had delivered one afternoon when no one but himself was on hand. He had carried the piece up to the Beerbohms' quarters for them, and considered the paper a small reward for his services.

'*Dearest Mums,*' the letter read. '*I sincerely hope you are keeping well, taking regularly the infusion whose recipe and ingredients I sent you (culled I forgot to say by my own hand from our surrounding "maquis"). Since I found the recipe - quite by accident when chasing the derivation of a place-name - you will be interested to know I have come across an old gentleman in our village who also knows about it - and uses it, he says, with a totally beneficial effect. He has had no bronchial trouble whatsoever since the day he started the cure.*

'*Life here goes along smoothly. Daily, my social history of the Languedoc through its place-names gathers weight. But though I work night and day - and, yes, do sometimes ponder how long my own health will stand up to the strain - I cannot as yet quite see an end upon the horizon. But then, we are not Hapsburgs, are we, without knowing the price we pay for any great endeavour?*

'I say life goes smoothly, but I have to record that we are under a little pressure. June, our great inspiration and benefactress, has lost her job in Paris. It also transpires that she does not own this mansion, but rents it. That we shall find a collective solution to the problem I have no doubt. Indeed a great scheme is already afoot, unknown to June, in the mind of at least one of us who holds the well-being of the community most deeply at heart - modesty restricts me to telling only you that I am that person. But in the meantime there must inevitably be cuts to our life-style which, as you know from your visit here, is not lavish. We shall not complain, and tighten our belts steadfastly. But in addition to the very small allowance I at present enjoy, the detachment of a further <u>capital</u> sum from my ultimate inheritance would bring upon you not only my respect, blessing and gratitude, which you have already, but that also of my colleagues.

'Could you see your way, for example, to the release of the small sum of five thousand pounds?

'Kisses from your ever devoted son, Frederick.'

Completing the letter, Frederick folded it carefully, inserted it into the large envelope of the same material as the notepaper, and ran the gummed edge along his tongue. He wrote the Cornish address, then searched in his tin-full of French stamps which had escaped the franking attentions of the postal staff for one of appropriate value. He was attaching the stamp with paste when his eye was caught by movement in that window on the second floor half way down one of the two sides of the Château which were visible to him. He immediately snatched up the heavy and powerful field glasses he had at the ready – field glasses which had once rested in the hands of a German grand uncle at the Battle of Jutland - and gasped. The curtains had been drawn back. As he urgently rolled the serrated fine-adjustor, he heard the plumbing gulp in his own bathroom, which indicated use almost certainly in that part of the building. 'My God,' he said aloud.

His vision included the end of the bed. A part of his mind prayed that Jubilee would not appear. It would surely be too much, too soon, if she did? Yet every fibre of his body was strung to expect that she would do so, unclothed. When a garment - underclothing was it, or a flimsy nightdress?- appeared suddenly over the end of the bed, his anticipation reached a fever-pitch. He remained in this state for some fifteen minutes. Once there appeared to be leaping movements on one of the upper windowpanes, which must be some kind of a freak reflection. But nothing materialised.

Just when he was beginning to think the couple had left the room, Jubilee appeared - almost casually, it seemed to Frederick, as if to mock his prurient fever, full in the window, and fully clothed in the yellow dress she had arrived in yesterday. She stood, idly looking down. Steve then appeared behind her and took her round the waist. At this moment Frederick leapt back from the window, fearful they should see him, binoculars raised *in flagrante delicto.*

Yet, assaulted and under pressure as he was, Frederick's mind, as was so often the case, moved with a rapidity twice its usual not inconsiderable pace. He had planned to follow the Addicots down to the kitchen and assist in the provision of their breakfast while pretending to get his own, but an infinitely better idea now occurred to him. What was of paramount importance was to keep the Addicots isolated from the others for as long as possible. In the kitchen there was the risk of others being present. As he jumped up, his mephistophelean features moved into a smile. There was no more time to be lost.

Using the door which led into the main building from his tower, he was just in time with his knock at the Addicots' door. The door opened at once and it was plain they were both just on their way down to look for breakfast as June had instructed them to do.

'My sincere apologies,' said Frederick, bowing.

'Apologies?'

'For misjudging your rising time. After your long journey and the festivities last night I didn't imagine you'd wish for too early a start.'

As he had intended, there was a pleasing degree of mystification on the faces of both Addicots, though in Jubilee's case he was glad to note an element of incredulous humour showing as well. Did she see through his act? He took the notebook from his hip pocket and drew out the small pencil sheathed along its spine.

'I have been assigned the duties of breakfast waiter. Now what can I get for you? Bacon is a little difficult to come by at present - our local market is spasmodic, I fear. But - freshly-ground coffee of course, possibly eggs in some form from our estate, needless to say our own bread, which has been baked, I may add, by my own hand?'

Steve was recovering from his initial surprise. Frederick had noted last night that Steve was not someone who spent long being immobilised by surprise. 'But there's no need for you to go to this trouble,' he said, 'er, Frederick, isn't it? June said we were to go to the kitchen and help ourselves.'

'It's no trouble at all,' Frederick cut in quickly. 'In fact it's a positive pleasure. If you'd care to take a seat in our dining and common room, I'll be able to serve you in a matter of minutes.'

As he went down the stairs two at a time, the ramifications of his impetuous act were fed into his active brain and arranged into an orderly sequence of contingent planning. By the time he reached the kitchen this process was complete.

Quite a number of the difficulties were eliminated at once by the fact that the kitchen was at this moment empty. It took only a matter of seconds to place enough Beerbohm coffee into a plastic bag, slices of bread into another. Goat's milk was unthinkable, whatever state it was in. They would have to drink the coffee black. But he remembered just in time what he had observed from his room two days ago and stored for possible use. Liz had been returning from the direction of her hive with something in a brown paper parcel. In the normal way he wouldn't have exploited this knowledge, honour being involved where Liz was concerned. But this was an emergency. He fancied only he knew the whereabouts of the cache Liz had maintained inviolate now for two years. Only once before had he needed to take advantage of it.

It was a small cavity half way up the wall beside the row of long-disused bells. It was concealed behind an iron capping which had presumably once given access for repairs to the bell system. Standing on a chair, he opened it. There, sure enough, was the half-consumed honeycomb on a small plate. He took a modest portion and closed the capping. Liz would never notice on her next nocturnal prowl for additional food. Her intelligence agreeably lacked quantitative values.

With the eggs he was similarly fortunate. Liz's hens enjoyed an extensively liberated existence, but Liz was well versed in their laying habits, and Frederick, whose mind almost involuntarily registered anything which was presented to it, by frequent observations from his window knew well the route she took daily to collect the eggs. As far as he knew she hadn't yet made her morning round. He found three eggs in the second place he looked. Leaving one, he returned to his room.

Frederick had come near to selling the pieces of Viennese porcelain Mums had given him on her last visit - alas, in lieu of cash. Only the strong dynastic sentiment that coursed his veins had prevented him. It was after all a relic of the depleted family treasure. Today he was especially glad he hadn't yielded to temptation.

He had small cooking arrangements in his quarters, necessary when security or privacy was a factor. The meal he carried down on a Chinese tray - another heirloom - didn't have all the trimmings of a five star hotel repast, but it had style, he decided. Outside the living room he lifted the tray on to the upward-facing palm of his left hand. He found them outside on the crumbled terrace, sitting on the balustrade in the sun. Jubilee sprang to her feet as he appeared, delighted at what she saw.

'Oh Frederick,' she exclaimed, '*real* honey, and what darling little egg-cosies.' To Frederick's great alarm she placed one of her hands lightly on his arm. He had quickly to engage Steve in talk. He had remembered there was a card table inside. This, and two hard chairs, would make it possible for them to continue to enjoy the early morning sun.

While he was moving the furniture, Frederick had a second and even more exciting idea. Intermittently he had also been witnessing from his room this morning the interesting sight of Paul Beerbohmer carrying Alfonso's steel rods in a crabwise fashion towards another of the Château's towers. He suspected the job would be continuing for some time longer yet. Hortense on the other hand, he was sure had not yet left the building with her easel and paint-box. Brilliantly combining this information with the situation which now confronted him with the Addicots, a plan of quite masterly proportions presented itself, landing in his mind on all fours as it were. He hardly hesitated.

'Now, as to your day,' he said calmly, when he had them seated at the table, 'forgive me if I presume, but June did mention to us that you are an artist of some talent, Mr Addicot - lapsed somewhat, she led us to understand, owing to your business concerns - but an artist of potentiality nonetheless. She is most anxious that you should enjoy your short stay to the full - indeed, so are we all - and in view of this I took it upon myself last night to ask Hortense Beerbohmer, who as you know is our resident artist - an artist of acclaimed talent and originality - whether, if you were at all interested, she would take you with her today on her usual work-outing. She is painting at present in the direction of the Mont des Lézards, I believe, a major geographical feature of our region. Well, I'm most happy to tell you that she'd be delighted if you would agree to accompany her. Furthermore, again if you were willing, she undertakes to supply you with all the necessary equipment - sketchbook, pencils, etcetera. I did, I admit, press her a little on your behalf, and she also agrees to give you any benefit of her expertise you may wish to call on. Will you tell me at once if I've done the wrong thing?'

Steve blinked. 'I can't believe it,' he said. 'Hortense was

more or less telling me last night that I'm a capitalist philistine.'

'Ah,' said Frederick, drawing his head aside sagely and permitting a faint grin, 'you clearly don't know Hortense.'

'You mean she was pulling my leg?'

'Not pulling your leg, no. I've no doubt she thought she was being serious in what she said to you at the time she said it. But Hortense is a complex character. We have countless examples of her saying precisely the opposite of what she means, especially where art is concerned.'

Steve gave a little laugh. 'I don't think she said the opposite of anything to me. She put it in the clearest terms that she thinks accountancy a very low form of existence.'

'I assure you she's intrigued by you. She heard June say she thinks you are potentially a good artist. That's quite enough to arouse her interest. Anyway, to cut argument short, if what I say isn't true, what's your explanation for this offer she's made you?'

Steve looked at Jubilee. Jubilee was smiling broadly. 'Go on, Steve,' she said, 'you can't look a gift-horse. And you never know, you might turn out to be really good.'

'But what will you do, dear? You don't want to hang about an easel all day?'

'Don't worry about me. I'll find something to do. There's so much to explore here. Perhaps you'd show me around a bit, Frederick, if that wouldn't be interrupting your work too much.'

Frederick did not allow himself to dwell on this surely God-given windfall. There was still a great deal to be done and a great deal which could go wrong.

The relationship between Frederick and Hortense Beerbohmer could be described as an armed truce. Frederick knew that she despised him - the fact that he was impervious to the charms was enough in itself to make this a certainty. But he knew also that, being a snob, Hortense could not be totally unsusceptible to his name. Admittedly Hapsburg was only half of it, and it was unaccompanied by a title, but he had always kept a frigid correctitude in his manner towards her and this was not without effect, he thought. Her contempt was tentative somehow, conditional. He had always felt that, handled right, in an extremity he might be able to call upon a certain interest, even perhaps a sympathy.

Her door was ajar and he could see her in the room. He knocked and thrust forward his head in one movement. 'Hortense, are you there? Can I possibly detain you a moment?'

'Frederick? *Qu'est-ce-que tu y fais*? You see I am occupied.'

'He could see as a matter of fact that she wasn't occupied. She had been standing in front of a mirror looking at herself. 'It's a matter of some interest, I hope. It seems you have made a conquest with our new guest.'

'Addicot?'

'I've just been talking to him at breakfast. It's clear he thinks you're the most fascinating person he's met for some time.'

'If so, of what possible interest is this being to me?'

'That is a question I asked myself. However, I have a confession to make. In a moment of courtesy I found myself agreeing with a request of his. It appears he's been thinking about some points you put to him before dinner last night. To put it succinctly, he's come to the conclusion that you hit a number of nails on the head.'

'*Naturellement j'avais raison.*'

'Quite so. But there's more. The fact is he wants you to give him an art lesson today.'

'What?'

'An art lesson. He wanted me to intercede on his behalf and ask if you'd take him with you on your outing today. You are going out, aren't you?'

'I certainly am, but not, *je t'assure . . .*'

'I told him it was most unlikely you'd even consider it, that *any* accompaniment is upsetting to your concentration.'

'So?'

'So what, exactly, Hortense?'

'So if you think that, why are you coming to me?'

Frederick paused only fractionally. 'My reason was

initially, as I say, a knee-jerk reaction of simple courtesy to a visitor. But I have to say I did have another thought.'

'What thought?'

He risked all in the smile he composed. He intended it to be half way between the mischievous and the diabolical. 'I'm convinced he does find you extremely attractive,' he said. She remained silent. 'What I'm saying is that, in consequence - in the interests of art and of justice, perhaps in the interests of the honour of the Château - couldn't you somehow make use of the situation to put a cocky materialist in his place? You have the subtlety better than any of us to know how to do it.'

It was amusing to Frederick to see how this statement was received. Dull contemptuous puzzlement at first - what on earth was he driving at? But then the flash of recognition. She flushed, and turned away sharply.

For a moment the affair hung in the balance. '*Merde, c'est ennuyeux,* but I suppose I shall be taking the man if he insists,' she said then. 'I am being able certainly to show him he is knowing nothing about art. He probably thinks artists are drawing lines with a ruler.'

'That is very probable,' said Frederick. 'Shall I tell him he's to join you then?'

'At the drawbridge at nine. If he is not being there I shall not be waiting for him.'

Frederick adjudged a quick withdrawal was wise - before any second thoughts arrived.

On his way back to the Addicots he had a further thought. He went to the pay-phone concealed in an alcove in the hall and made a call.

He then gave himself to the untrammelled day with Jubilee which stretched before him.

10

The 'spare room' at the Château Lamartine deserved its name. It was on the best side of the house on the second floor, immediately above the Beerbohmers' apartment, but apart from the double mattress on the floor, a chest of drawers and a large old-fashioned wardrobe, it was bare. It was this room to which June and Alfonso repaired after so unselfishly yielding their own to their guests.

June had been woken by Alfonso getting up before sunrise, then dozed off again. She slept on a great deal later than she usually did. She was aware why. She hadn't been ready to face the day. Now sleep was no longer a defence. Through the open window she caught a whiff of the rosemary-scented air, then she heard a goat bleat and the sound of its bell. She had to fight back tears. Was it really true it was all over, that she would have to give up this lovely place and disperse all the creative activities of its occupants?

She made herself get up and put on her dressing gown, which had served as additional bed clothing. She went into the palatial marble-tiled bathroom - all the first and second floor rooms in the Château had palatial bathrooms - and looked at herself in the clouded mirror of the wash-basin. What a thin insubstantial figure appeared before her. Was it any wonder this person had been unable to realise a dream? She twisted the tarnished taps, which were stiff with non-use. There was a cough and a wheeze and after a few seconds a grudging supply of brownish water. She washed her face.

June's father had been a clergyman. In London days, when she went to the school Steve Addicot had briefly attended, she had gone along with the piety of the small unpretentious rectory. When you are young, what is is what is.

Most of the parishioners who came to the huge Victorian church were middle-class, but father had a great deal to do with quite poor people, too. Some of these came to the house and were closeted in father's study for a while, presumably talking to him about their problems. One was given a job at the rectory. He was supposed to keep the garden free of weeds, and did. But he also dug up a lot of plants which should have remained in the soil, and the experiment came to an end.

June remembered the day exactly when she went off religion. It was during Matins on Easter Sunday when she was twelve. As usual she was sitting with her mother in one of the middle pews, wearing the grey suit and matching panama hat which was her school uniform. Father was preaching the sermon in the pulpit. She never listened to the sermons, but it was nice to sit there with her own thoughts undisturbed. In the background, she was pleasantly conscious of father's voice, which was a very strong masterful one, and of all those people patiently listening to it.

'How do you know that for sure, Vicar?'

It was some moments before she realised these words had been spoken by someone else, not father, and that this someone else was female and standing up across the aisle from her. She remembered a purple dress down to her ankles and a lot of beads round her neck and in her hair. 'How do you *know* Christ rose from the dead?'

June realised that in the space of seconds what had been a gently slumbering congregation had become a highly volatile one and father's sermon had come to an abrupt halt. A rustle of horrified interest was sweeping across the nave-full of people. Heads turned, a chair squeaked on the stone floor, a few people whispered.

'How can we believe all this nowadays - when it was only hearsay two thousand years ago?' A man in a black suit sitting next to the woman got up and laid a hand on her arm, but she quietly but determinedly removed it with her own hand as if it were an unwelcome insect which had landed there. June looked at her father's face to confirm that the poise and authority she had always imagined he possessed was still in position. She couldn't be sure it was.

'I think . . .' he said, flushed, and looked very pointedly in the direction of two other dark-suited men, sitting in the side-aisle. These individuals rose together, and went to take up positions at either end of the pew in which the woman was standing, like two steers sent into a ring to round up a bull on the rampage.

For tense seconds June thought the woman would have to be forcibly removed, carried bodily perhaps, horizontal and kicking, from the scene. But the incident had rather a tame ending. 'It's all right, I won't be staying,' the woman said, 'not if I'm not going to get a civil answer to a civil question. Perhaps there isn't an answer, and that's it.' She left, with dignity, under her own steam. 'Thank you, dear,' she said audibly to the woman beside her who handed her her gloves, which she had been going to leave behind.

She pushed with difficulty sideways to the end of her pew, for she was stout, and left down the centre aisle, donning her gloves as she went, walking at a moderate speed. June saw her face as she passed, not flushed, not worried, not especially pleased with itself, certainly not triumphant, just a very ordinary face. The sidesmen marched superfluously behind her.

Recovering, father tried to make use of the incident. 'I'm sorry about our friend,' he said with a smile, when the west door was firmly closed again. 'She's obviously suffering from that temporary withdrawal of faith which comes to us all at some time in our lives. I hope I may have the privilege of talking to her in private one day soon. We must meanwhile all pray for her. The little incident illustrates what I was saying, does it not, that belief *cannot* only be based on fact, that it requires that leap of faith which Christ himself enjoined us to pray for . . .'

If that had been all, June might have taken it in her stride. Though she wasn't a great one for leaps of any kind at this time, including those of faith, the familiar formula of words would probably have been enough to lull her back into her former state of acceptance. But the repercussions of the incident prevented this. Father never seemed to stop talking about it. As far as June knew, he never made any effort to contact the woman, but that didn't prevent him from discussing her behaviour with everyone who came to the vicarage. It was clear to him the woman was deranged, he said. He found out she was an artist who lived alone (if six cats can be excepted) in a small studio flat. This was sufficient in itself apparently to explain a state of

82

derangement. How sad loneliness was, he kept saying

Bit by bit June realised three things. First that the woman wasn't mad but entirely sane, second that she wanted herself to ask the same question she had asked, and third that father himself wasn't so water-tight on the matter of faith as he made out. Wasn't it just that, like the rest of the clergy, his livelihood depended on believing the tenets of the Christian church? What *was* the authority for it all - for the creed, the dogma, the huge edifice of ritual - yes, even the story itself? She found she couldn't so confidently believe all these things had happened in the way it was reported they did. It seemed to her that Christianity was like everything else which claimed to be sure - like the headmistress at her school, like judges, like party politicians, like father. It seemed to her the priesthood had fixed the prices and closed the betting. She didn't say anything. She even continued to go to church. But from that day it was never the same. She had discovered that the phrase 'the truth' which she had heard so often had no meaning for her.

When she was at university reading languages, father died. Her mother, who was French and had never much cared for English life, went to live in a small house in a Paris suburb. During the summer vacation after her final exams, in which she obtained a medium grade degree, June went to stay with her mother. She did a lot of sightseeing by herself, and one morning, relaxing after a visit to the Louvre, she met Alfonso in a cafe on the left bank. She became aware, sitting there unaccompanied with her drink, that he was seated at a table a few yards away and that he was drawing her on a sketch pad.

When she looked at him, he didn't seem to react in the usual way and went on drawing as if she were an object like a house. Embarrassed, she had to turn away. But when he had finished the drawing he came across to show it to her. She didn't actually think it very good - it had a somewhat massive quality, which didn't suggest he was all that good a draughtsman and which certainly wasn't flattering. But he sat down and they began talking. She soon knew quite a bit about him. She learnt that he was Mexican, that his father had paid for him to do a course in psychology at the Sorbonne, but that in fact, unknown to his family, he had got himself in with a well known French sculptor and was working in his studio. Sculpture had become his passion and chief aim in life.

She fell in love with him almost at once. What she found irresistible was his amazing good-humour and balance, his total devotion to his new work, and his certainty that sculpture was what he was good at and what he wanted to do for the rest of his life.

In order to remain in Paris, she decided to get herself a job. She had no ambition to work for a petrol company, but when she saw the job advertised she thought she would apply. The employment was very well paid, and from an early moment she realised that if they stayed together she would have to keep Alfonso as well as herself for as long as proved necessary. She thought she was capable of sound business administration if she put her mind to it, and she was virtually bilingual. Perhaps because it was necessary for Alfonso's well being, at the interview she never really thought she wouldn't get the job, and this perhaps they mistook for confidence. At all events she was offered the post.

She knew from early on there would be difficulties living with Alfonso. She was sure there would be other women from time to time. But she was sure of another thing, that whatever he did Alfonso was as inexorably tied to her as she was to him. He knew how deeply she valued the fact he was an artist and how highly she estimated his work. In consequence he knew that, centrally, within the extremes between which his estimate of himself oscillated, he needed her. It was he who after a time began to suggest a civil marriage, and eventually she agreed.

She hadn't expected to fall in love for a second time. But they were on holiday together in the Midi one summer. On one of their rambles into the countryside, they came across the empty Château, which was for sale. She knew at once how much she wanted it, and why. Abandoning religion didn't mean she had lost the need for an idealistic basis to her life. Supporting Alfonso was her main concern, but why not also a colony for artists and intellectuals, living together in common endeavour?

They found the Nice agency which was handling the property. The place was owned by a small order of nuns in the north of France. As the place had been on the market for a long time and the agents had long ago given up any hope of finding a buyer, they were willing to try to persuade the owners to accept a lump sum of 'key money' and a limited tenancy lease. This to June's delight they succeeded in doing. The lump sum and the rent were to June enormous but, as the agent was quick to point out, in relation to the costs of similar properties it was in the peppercorn category. With a bank loan to take care of the key money, June found it was just possible. When her mother died, there were a few years of lease on her property to sell. With this sum she didn't have to borrow any more. Her salary took care of the rent and the other outgoings.

When she had finished washing, June took the towel and went back into the room. While she stood drying her face she looked out of the open window on to the beautiful scene below. The sun, about to lift above the Mont des Lézards, was chasing away little veils of mist. The pink light of early morning was maturing into something nearer yellow. Her eye caught a movement in the landscape.

There about half a mile away two figures were walking in single file with about twenty yards between them. The figure ahead was certainly Hortense, en route for her site. The other, male, carrying an easel and a haversack, she realised was Steve. She frowned for a moment in perplexity, but then smiled broadly. How very unexpected and nice that what she had suggested to Steve in her letter as a possibility had been achieved with no intervention from her. She had been wondering a bit about what to do with Steve today. Jubilee would be easier to entertain on her own, she thought.

But when she had put on her clothes and was on her way down to the kitchen to find something to eat and drink, she had a second surprise. She was crossing the hall landing. Through the long window she saw Jubilee and Frederick walking towards the Addicots' hired car, which was parked in front of the house. Jubilee was about to open the door of the passenger seat. She saw Frederick bound forward to perform the act for her. Having shut her in, he nipped nimbly round to the driver's seat. They drove off together.

Damon was in the kitchen, stripped to the waist, using the sink to wash himself. Perplexed by what she had seen, she completely forgot about his vow of silence. 'Oh dear, the pump hasn't broken down again, has it?' she said. 'Though actually I wish you both *would* use the kitchen. It must sometimes be very chilly in the early morning outside.' She said this automatically, then stood thinking. 'I've just seen two most unexpected sights,' she went on. 'Hortense seems to have got over her dislike of Steve and has taken him painting with her, and Frederick has just taken Jubilee off in the Addicots' car.' She then realised how she had transgressed. Damon, sluicing away, was of course not answering her. 'Oh, I'm so sorry,' she said quickly, and to hide her confusion turned to take the lid off the earthenware bread bin.

She expected that he would simply not recognise her presence and not acknowledge she had spoken. He would finish his toilet and go. But when she turned round, there he was, facing her, towelling vigorously, and grinning.

Some people, notably Hortense, found Damon arrogant and withdrawn (even without a vow of silence). She never had. She knew, unlike the others except Liz, how deeply grateful he was to her for the chance to be a resident at the Château and how much and how profoundly he believed in her idea, even though he was sometimes flippant about some of his fellow occupants. She knew, as presumably did Liz, that he really had a warm and cooperative nature. She also knew he was a very brilliant man, as great an intellect as Alfonso was a great artist. As such, he was different anyway - not to be judged by normal standards. And now, without his spectacles, he looked almost boyish and vulnerable. She had a strong impulse of warmth towards him.

Removing one of the metal covers of the range with the lever, she put the kettle on the direct heat. She unhooked a mug from the dresser and spooned Nescafé into it. A little tentatively she then unhooked a second mug and looked at Damon. Humour still showed in his eyes. He bowed slightly in acceptance of the offer.

He put on his shirt, and his spectacles. She poured the hot water into the cups and they sat with the steaming mugs on either side of the table. She cut him bread, which he also accepted. She was not embarrassed by the silence, which she found harmonious and restful. They ate and drank. She continued to think about what she had seen from the spare room window and from the hall.

In a minute or two Damon got up. He washed the mug in the sink, dried and re-hung it. She expected him to go, but surprising her again he stood there and, suddenly, spoke. 'Providence at work? If so through a flawed vessel,' he said in a small voice but perfectly audibly. With this he departed.

She was so surprised, then flattered that he had made an exception to his vow by speaking to her, that for a moment she didn't consider properly what he had said. When she did, she realised at once what he had meant. 'Providence?' What else could he mean but Steve and the possibility that he might be induced to help the Château in some way? The flawed vessel - what could that be but Frederick? A further thought struck her, which made her blush. As she had feared might happen, had Damon thought she had asked Steve here with this purpose?

She reprimanded herself. Of course she hadn't, not so blatantly. If anything it was the possibility of obtaining some advice - Steve's advice as an accountant - which had been in her mind, nothing more.

11

'Prier de ne pas toucher les objets,' said Liz clearly, quoting one of the notices she'd had Frederick write for her in a commanding, gothic-looking script.   Her remark was addressed to a peasant in bright blue overalls who was handling a large chafing dish painted with a green and blue fish.   Without looking at the stall-owner, and without any apparent guilt, the man put the dish back among the other earthenware.

Liz was dressed in a white overall and was in the process of painting another plate which she had mounted on an easel in front of her and which would be later fired in June's kiln.   An aspect of France she approved of was that once you had a notice printed you could take refuge behind its legality and not be involved in the expense of unnecessary emotion.   Given a certain situation, other things followed, as day follows night.   *'C'est normal, c'est logique,'* was a phrase frequently heard.   Damon said it was something to do with the Cartesian philosophy, which was embedded deep in the French consciousness.   Whether it was or wasn't she was in no position to verify, but the practice suited her temperament.

She adored market day.   The funny grey houses with their cluttered balconies ringed the little *Place* in the most friendly way.   The village bustled with sensible French housewives with square rimless spectacles, carrying long loaves and saying *'bonjour monsieur, bonjour madame'* a great deal.   Under the broad abundant leaves of the plane trees, it was deliciously cool. Her donkeys liked it here, too.   Tied to one of the rings provided with such municipal forethought round the central stone fountain and trough, they could drink when they wanted to.   At present they were having their lunch from two nosebags she had improvised out of sacks.   She used the donkeys for transporting her stuff to and from the Château.

She had done very well this morning.   A huge modern bus had clambered into the square and, after a lot of hydraulic hissing and puffing, parked by the church.   It proved to be full of American tourists.   One of the women found her stall and bought a cup and saucer. In a matter of minutes she had nearly all of them clustered round. 'And the merchandise is so *reasonable*,' they kept saying. Liz liked their word 'merchandise', which smacked to her of oriental *souks*. And her wares *were* very reasonable in price, she thought. Frederick said she should treble the amount to foreigners. She had always refused, it wouldn't be right.

Cartesian philosophy did not apply to Americans, and discipline broke down completely. At one point almost her entire stock was being handled. But her artefacts remained miraculously intact. When the visitors discovered she was English, they were doubly delighted. Liz's French accent was usually proof against non-French speakers, but she unwittingly murmured a four-letter word in her native language when she found she was short of change, and so revealed herself. Did she really live in this lovely place and did she make all the pottery herself? She had to give a considerable amount of her time to such chatter.

She saw Frederick some time after the Americans had gone, when the rather frenetic clock in the church tower had struck one. It was now very hot, it was doubtful if there would be more sales until it was cooler, and she was beginning to think her nut, cheese and tomato chutney sandwich might be nice, and possibly a *blanc* at the cafe afterwards. She could afford it today. Frederick was standing by the *Mairie* with its two standard bunches of tricolour flags attached to iron balconies, and pointing to the seated figure of Voltaire before it, whose raised finger seemed to admonish humanity for its foolish ways. She then saw that the person with him, to whom he was pointing out the statue, was Jubilee.

She watched for several moments expecting Jubilee's husband to appear. When he didn't, she began to conjecture. As she conjectured, the couple turned, and it was suddenly obvious to her that Frederick knew she was there and had every intention of making for her stall. She could see he was on some kind of a high.

'Lady Elisabeth,' he said expansively, 'Jubilee and I are on a cultural tour of the village. I've shown her the church, the museum, the basket-ware factory, and I've told her of your wonderful weekly activity here in the market, which she's dying to see.'

Jubilee was taking in Liz's stall.   'Frederick has only just told me this is all your own work, Lady Elisabeth,' she said, delighted. 'I'd no idea that you, too, are an artist.   I find new amazing things to marvel at every moment here.'

Liz wasn't greatly pleased.   Frederick had an able mind - Damon said so.   But owing to a spoilt childhood, he was vain, idle, at times dishonest, and he wasted his talents.   When he used her title it didn't usually bode well.   What was he up to?   Why had he been so obviously complimentary about her to Jubilee? She looked at Jubilee's nubile figure.   Surely he couldn't have ambitions of that sort?   If he had, she didn't want to be involved. She hoped he would soon continue his cultural itinerary and leave her in peace.

But the conversation continued, and a little later he said, 'What about some lunch together?'   Jubilee acclaimed this idea.   She insisted it should be on her as Frederick had been so generous in giving up his whole morning for her entertainment.

Liz didn't see a way out.   Asking a neighbour to keep an eye on her stall and the donkeys, she found herself sitting, not at one of the outside tables watching the world go by as she had planned, but on one of the red plastic-covered benches inside, having *châteaubriand* and chips ordered for her as the waiter spread a clean paper cloth on the table followed by three *couverts,* a basket of cut bread, and a large carafe of red wine.

There was no shortage of conversation, with Frederick beatified in this way, and Jubilee was determined to recall every detail of her morning.   Liz began to think she might have something of her quiet lunch break after all.   By 'mming' fairly frequently, her own thoughts and her consumption of the food could go along quite merrily on a parallel course.   This was until they had drunk the wine between them and until liberal helpings of the rather nice ice cream they did here arrived.   There was then a noticeable change in the climate.

'Liz, we need your complicity in a complot,' Frederick said, in such a way that Liz suspected he'd had the statement waiting in the wings all along.   Jubilee, she noticed, shifted awkwardly in her seat, and lowered her eyes, as if she knew what was coming. 'As you've gathered, Jubilee has fallen in love with this place. In the short time she's been among us, she says she's had her eyes opened. This, I am sure, exaggerates our humble achievements, but it's undoubtedly what she feels . . .' He looked briefly in Jubilee's direction for confirmation. She nodded uncertainly. 'Now, as you know, the Addicots only planned to be here two days and Jubilee thinks her husband is rather likely to want to adhere to this schedule and continue on an African safari he has booked. She has made it clear that she wouldn't want to play any part in persuading him to do otherwise. But what I've put to her is that if he can just be persuaded to stay a day or two more, he might agree of his own accord to stay even longer. Jubilee is sure Steve has a talent for painting, which is what he is doing at this moment. I'm quite sure he has, and that once he gets into the swing of things here, the problem may be to get him to leave us at all. What we've got to do is try to help him believe he has artistic talent.'

He paused, and Liz inserted her long spoon into the pink flank of the sweet. 'I see,' she said, not entirely seeing, but beginning to think Frederick might be about to make an embarrassing request of her. She looked at Jubilee, who definitely didn't seem too comfortable, she thought.

'I think you could be right about Steve's painting, Frederick,' she said, 'but of course we'll have to see. We've paid for our tickets now, and even if Steve were to change his mind about staying it would be rather expensive not to go.'

Frederick leapt in. 'But would it, Jubilee? You'll get some sort of refund, I'm sure, and it'll actually cost you much less to stay here than to continue with your African holiday in terms of meals and so on. You'll almost certainly finish up in pocket. Don't you agree, Liz?'

Liz now saw exactly what Frederick was up to. He wanted her to add her powers of persuasion to his own. This she certainly wasn't going to do. If he wanted to persuade Steve to stay longer he could do it himself, she wasn't going to be a party to his machinations.

She was going to say something non-committal, but just at this moment there was a diversion. They all became aware that a young man was signalling strongly to Frederick from the pavement outside.   Somewhat fussed, Frederick got up and went out.

She and Jubilee watched the short exchange which took place under the awning.   Frederick didn't appear very happy about the encounter and seemed to want to make it as brief as possible. They saw him accept a large brown envelope.   He held it uncertainly for a moment as if contemplating that he might be able to fold it and put it out of sight in a pocket somewhere.   But being in shirtsleeves, there was obviously nowhere to stow it.   He returned, rather sneakily put the envelope beside him on the bench, said nothing about it, and tried to behave as if its delivery had been an irritating triviality.   But the interruption had the good result that the previous subject was dropped.   Frederick began to talk about things Jubilee might want to see that afternoon and made clear his wish that the lunch party be ended as soon as possible.

The envelope was no doubt part of another of his shady deals, Liz supposed, but its delivery had thankfully ended the embarrassment.   Liz supposed something else.   It was now a great deal too obvious why Frederick wished to prolong the stay of the Addicots.

12

Steve was in two minds whether to accept Hortense's invitation, so joyfully delivered by Frederick as he and Jubilee were finishing their breakfast. Of Hortense's enthusiasm he remained doubtful - could he believe she welcomed his intrusion into her day's work? But though it was perfectly clear to him what Frederick was up to, he was glad to see Jubilee's joy at the prospect of being shown round. It would surely be churlish to upset Frederick's plans. A more diplomatic thought succeeded this. If by any chance Frederick was foolish enough to make a pass at Jubilee - which she would surely find ludicrous, and rebuff - it might serve to throttle back her euphoria for this absurd community. Maybe they could leave a bit earlier and spend a five-star night in Nice before their on-going journey.

For the moment he put himself to a greater concern. 'By the drawbridge at nine' - this was the instruction relayed by Frederick. He hadn't lifted a pencil or a brush for several years. The last time was on a holiday he had taken with a person-not-to-be-named in Amalfi. He had done a painting of this picturesque cliff-side village, he remembered, in delicious chalky shades of pinks and blues and buffs. Today, he might have a complete blank and not be able to do a thing. He could imagine Hortense's contempt, and was surprised to find he could do without this. A competitive spirit was aroused.

He was at the drawbridge punctually. Hortense was five minutes late. As she appeared, burdened with an easel, a large wooden box, a portfolio-case tied at the edges with black ribbon, and with a haversack on her shoulders, he jumped off the wall and ran to her. 'Here, Hortense, let me . . .'

'You will carry the easel and the 'aversack, I will carry *les autres choses,*' she said imperiously, brushing aside his gallantry. 'It is being a *promenade* of four kilometres. I am much later than *d'habitude, et je ne pense flâner.* That is the maximum you are being able to carry.'

He wished to question this judgment. He wasn't completely de-energised by wealth and good living. But there didn't seem to be a choice.   She gave him the easels and the "aversack', and struck off at once along a path through trees.

The path was narrow most of the time, which would have imposed single file upon them anyway, but it was clear from Hortense's manner that she wasn't contemplating a day of conversation.   He was content, especially when after ten minutes of trudging he found he was quite fully enough engaged in keeping up.   Frequently the path gave out and they had to scramble up or down rocky stretches in whose interstices grew a particularly malicious variety of thorn bush. Wearing safari shorts, his legs were punctured several times by these.

There was no stop.   It seemed to Steve the countryside closed in on them from all sides.   An occasional small bird flew off into the pines or into the rather scruffy lower vegetation.   For a period, a very large bird wheeled silently above them in systematic circles. Apart from the rhythm of his breath and the beat of his feet on the path, there was an increasing sense of the overwhelming solidarity of the earth beneath them and of the sun climbing steadily above.   Ahead jutted the massive up-tilted slab of the Mont des Lézards.

Steve overcame a crisis of fatigue and found a second wind, but he was glad when after crossing an unexpected stream by means of the flat white stones which lay in its path and climbing the incline beyond, he saw that Hortense had stopped.   She continued to stand for a moment until Steve drew level and gazed at the mountain ahead of her through narrowed eyes.

'*Le voilà*,' she said.   'I shall stop 'ere.   It is a new location, half a kilometre from where I have worked last.   If I have luck it will give the new dimension I seek.   *Lézards, c'est une grande mystère*, you know.   It is giving its secrets, one by one, and only to the most *persévérent*.'

She set up her easel, changed her mind and moved it several paces.   Finally, when she had placed and secured her canvas and taken out her palette and brushes, she handed him a sketchpad from the portfolio, a soft pencil, a rubber and a sharpener. 'Right, *allez-vous en*.   I am not wanting to 'ave you near, I must be alone.   Find a *sujet* to draw.   I will regard it later.'

It was a time before Steve could settle to anything.   He left the art materials by a bush and reconnoitred. He looked at the mountain, the obvious thing to draw, but couldn't bring himself to tackle its inanimate bulk. He examined the countryside sloping away to the south but it seemed similarly to lack interest. He settled finally for a single pine tree. He wished she had given him paints and a canvas. He could have made something of the sunshine on the bark, he thought. But he made himself comfortable in a shady spot with his back against a smooth rock and got started.

While he worked he had some more thoughts about Hortense. He didn't object to her behaviour to him. He had dealt too much with inadequate personalities in the bankruptcy business not to be able to appreciate the rare appearance of someone who knew their own mind. If he had to spend a couple of days here, what better employment than to sit at her feet? He had also sensed a different attitude in her this morning to the one she had displayed last night - underneath her bombast. Perhaps it was only her marriage to Paul, he thought, which had made her acerbic. One could not believe Paul was much of a match for her strength of will. And he was on holiday, wasn't he?

He was so engrossed in the drawing he didn't hear her approach. He heard a strident laugh beside him. 'You are fearing and avoiding the Lézards, I see. I am not blaming you. He is Olympus, my Lézards, full of angry divine *tromperie.'* He overcame a reflex motivation to get up, and went on drawing. 'Are you wanting to swim?' he heard.

'What?' He looked up, shielding his eyes with a hand against the sun.

'There is a pool further up that stream we 'ave crossed. Then we will take an early lunch, *n'est-ce-pas?'* She gave an odd laugh. 'Yes, *à nu.* At least I will be. *Vous êtes géné?'*

He had no idea what *géné* was, but if it meant embarrassed, he certainly was. She was daring him, he was quite sure. Though of course they went in for this kind of thing down here.

'All right.'

They left the art gear, Hortense carried the food, and they walked back the way they had come as far as the stream, then struck up its bank. Above was, as she said, a deep pool imprisoned by rocks.

She began at once to take her clothes off. Standing, she unbuttoned her white shirt and pulled it backwards over her shoulders, then slipped from the undergarment. Acutely uncomfortable, he sat on a rock, choosing a point as far from her as was feasible. He began to do the same, dawdling to postpone the moment of revelation.

'Look, Steve, look at me. See what a beautiful body I 'ave. Are you fearful of it?'

Fearful indeed, he nonetheless looked up and saw. She was standing on the brink of the rock, facing him, fully nude, smoothing herself just under the full breasts with both hands. In her crotch blazed a triangle of black. A shock not unlike one from electricity passed through his body. He blinked, but resisted the impulse to look away.

'You see? You look at me. It is not an impossible thing to do. And now you must be doing the same. Strip.' She turned to the pool, raised her arms briefly and took off gracefully. There was a neat plop as she entered the water.

He would keep on his underpants, he thought, he wouldn't allow her to undermine his dignity. But he immediately un-thought this. If he kept on any clothing it would make him more ridiculous, not less - anyway, how would he dry the things? Stripping off the garment, he took off his glasses and rose. He stood for a moment on the rock edge as she had done, aware that she was looking at him from below. He held his nose and jumped. As he surfaced she was swimming towards him.

'So you 'ave made it. Well done, Steve. *C'est beau comme ça, n'est ce pas?* Soon we will be lying on the rock to dry ourselves, then we eat.'

The simple food she had brought tasted delicious - the Château bread had a body and a flavour absent from the productions of mass bakeries. There was salami sausage, a huge tomato, and a fragrant pear. Hortense had filled a small flask with the cold water from the stream. He ate and drank heartily, and felt pleased with himself. It would be amusing to compare notes with Jubilee tonight, though he wasn't sure he would mention the nude swim.

They finished the meal, and returned to the place where Hortense was working. She began talking about her own work, which was obviously heavy abstract. He didn't understand what she was saying, nor the painting taking shape on the easel beside them. If the easel hadn't been set up in the direction of the mountain and he hadn't heard her remarks, he would have been hard put to say it was the subject of the work. The picture seemed to be a series of coloured layers, one on top of the other, with mysterious cavern-like areas between them in which unidentifiable creatures seemed to lurk. While she talked he lay on the ground with his hand behind his head. She was using terminology he didn't understand, most of it French. He heard phrases like '*pouvoir primordial*,' and '*l'ésotérisme obscur de l'époque Tertiaire.*' While she talked, he felt extremely drowsy and finally must have dropped off.

Waking, he realised from the changed position of the sun that he must have slept some time. Ubiquitously, seeming to occupy all the space with their noise, cicadas throbbed. The sky, the landscape, seemed even emptier, and now prostrate, like himself, in the heat of the day. Hortense was working, standing up with her back to him. She had said she didn't believe in sitting down to work, and indeed had no seat with her. She had put on a light floppy hat and seemed to tower over his recumbent figure with cool disconcerting force. To think, day after day, she stood here in this burning heat, wrestling with whatever it was which engaged her. No wonder she was contemptuous. Maybe, he conceded, she had a right to be. Not stirring, he watched her.

He remembered then his drawing of the pine tree, lying there on the portfolio case. She had said nothing about it. Why not, he thought? It surely wasn't bad - a first effort after all this time? At least you could see what it was. He yawned loudly, sat up and picked it up.

She took no notice. Down again went the head as she dipped the brush on to the palette, taking paint from here, there, making a little roue of it and returning to the canvas for the careful minuscule stroke. He had an access of confidence. 'You didn't criticize my effort,' he said. 'I thought I was going to get a

97

lesson'.

He thought she was going to ignore him. She continued to work. Then unexpectedly she put the palette and the brushes on the ground and moved into the shade of the rock where he was sitting. She took off her hat and sat beside him, her white-trousered legs wide, her elbows on her knees. 'One is not estimating the performance of a climber *au pied de la montagne,*' she said.

'That bad, am I?'

'You have some skill probably. But of course *finalement,* it is a matter of *manière de penser.'*

'Translated?'

'It is a matter of attitude.'

'I see. What's my attitude?'

'I have told you last night.' She let this sink in. 'You are also going away. You will go to this African holiday, then return to your . . . occupation.'

'Which you despise.'

She shrugged her shoulders in a way entirely peculiar to the French nationality. 'I thought you were asking me to estimate your drawing.'

Against his intention his annoyance was escalating. 'Well perhaps I was changing the subject,' he said testily.

She looked away. 'Very well,' she said. 'If you wish. You ask me if I am despising your profession. The answer is that I am not. I am not despising *it,* that is. I simply find it *inapplicable* - irrelevant, you say.'

'That's surely rather arrogant.'

'Truth cannot be arrogant.'

'People can have different versions of what truth is, don't you think?' Again, the shrug. He really felt unusually put out. He got up. 'Well,' he said, 'I can see I'm in your way here. I'll be getting back if you don't mind. Done enough drawing for one day. In fact I've probably done enough drawing for another ten years. I'll take some of the gear.'

She didn't stir for a moment or two, then she rose, too, but taking her time about it. She gave him the haversack into which she put the sketch-pad he had used and one or two other things.

Finally she faced him, and smiled. 'I'm sorry you 'ave 'ad enough,' she said. 'I thought you are beginning to absorb the *ambiance.* I thought you try to draw me while I work perhaps. I also was thinking a little later we could again swim. Your *petite* Jubilee, I am sure, will be very occupied today.'

Two buttons of her blouse were undone, revealing a quantity of those fine breasts to a point well below the line of sunburn. His eyes dropped to them involuntarily, and while they did so she reached her hand forward and laid it flat on the inside of his bare leg and drew it upwards. 'Given talent, art is a question of *perspective* of life, Steve. I think, here, in this place I touch, you have very good *perspective.'*

He realised that in fact he was having an involuntary reaction to her act. He fled. He fancied he heard a laugh behind him

By the time Steve got back to the Château he was physically exhausted and mentally in turmoil. He had hopelessly lost all sense of direction and the journey had taken over two hours.

On his way in he saw Alfonso's head protruding from the top of one of the towers. He shouted up to him to ask if he had seen Jubilee. He shook his absurd bearded head as if this question was amusing. Steve searched fruitlessly in the outhouses, and just as he was standing beside the moat he saw Damon at his table in the basement window below. Damon was observing him with an interrogative look. Caught in the act as their eyes met, he looked down at his desk in a leisurely way. This goddam place, Steve thought, it was a lunatic asylum.

He went into the living room. It was empty except for a squirrel eating crumbs left under the table from the meal last night. Obviously no one had swept. At a leisurely pace the creature loped out of an open widow. Then, through the other window he saw that the car was missing. It was clear Frederick the Hapsburg had taken Jubilee off somewhere.

Extremely displeased, he went up to the stuffy room they had been allotted to sleep in, which for some reason had been papered with a brown hessian material - what could be a more unsuitable choice for this climate? In the ornate bathroom, big enough for a hotel cloakroom, he swallowed two glasses-full of tepid water -

with it no doubt a variety of infection - then flung the windows wide open in the bedroom and lay on the bed. How was he going to endure another day of this?

Jubilee didn't come in until nearly seven. Hearing the car he rushed to the window in time to see it reach the top of the drive before it went out of sight round the building. He imagined Frederick get out of the driving seat and sprinting round to hand Jubilee out, kissing her hand perhaps. Steve jerked himself away from the window. The sooner they left here . . .

He decided nonetheless to behave in a normal way. The last thing he wanted was to let these people get under his skin. A dignified distance, he thought, with a touch of ironic humour - that's what fitted the bill.

Jubilee burst into the room. 'Steve, I've had the most wonderful day,' she said, kicking off her shoes and jumping on the bed beside him in a single movement. 'Frederick's shown me *everything* - Alfonso's incredible huge sculpture made out of poles - he's doing it inside one of the towers - June's craft studio - she does the most lovely jewellery and has promised to give me a lesson - and Lady Elisabeth's pottery stall in the village market. Do you know she makes all the things she sells herself? This afternoon Frederick took me on a drive round the countryside. He knows all about the origin of place-names. It was fascinating . . .' The avalanche of description went on for at least five minutes. It extinguished him. When breathlessly she paused and said, 'And how did you get on with Hortense?' he found himself hardly able to reply.

'Oh, I did a silly sketch.'

She jumped off the bed and made him show it to her. 'But it's good, Steve. I knew you'd draw again if you came here. I bet Hortense was impressed. Was she?'

There was worse. He mentioned the car and, though he hadn't meant to show he was peeved, pointed out that the insurance did not include a third driver. Jubilee swept this aside. 'Oh dear, yes, I did forget that. Well, I'll drive tomorrow. Frederick's promised to take me to Nice to show me a modern art museum.' She went on to announce her further news that she had decided to cook the dinner tonight, which Frederick had acclaimed as a good idea. She had made Frederick stop outside 'the better of the two butchers' in the village and bought filet steak. 'You don't mind, Steve darling, do you?' she added here. 'I thought it was the best possible way of repaying June, and all of them, for being so kind and hospitable to us. Now I think of it, June did make it clear in her letter that we're all expected to take our turns. With Frederick's expert help and suggestions I also bought wine and some other nice things. I must be off to start the cooking. Frederick's going to be my "kitchen boy", as he calls it.

The appointed hour for dinner was not until nine, as Jubilee would need time. Steve didn't bother to be punctual this time and things were in full swing when he went down.

News of the impending menu and its cook had got around. Everyone except Damon was mustered. Paul handed him a very full glass of *Tio Pepe* sherry, an amenity which was not present last night and which Steve had to assume was part of Jubilee's largesse. 'Well this is a good start,' he said nonetheless. He had by this time determined to do his best to enjoy the evening. He felt proud that Jubilee was going to have the chance to show what a fine cook she was. He might also, he thought, derive some marginal status for having been the financial provider of the treat. He approached the group amiably.

He tried first to nobble the giant Alfonso - to ask him, as an aperitif to conversation, about this great work of his in the tower. After a few monosyllables, finding his glass empty, Alfonso turned aside and went off in search of replenishment. Steve had a similar experience with Lady Elisabeth to whom he put questions about pottery. They had only been talking a minute or two when she, too, broke off. 'Look, please forgive me, but I have just remembered I absolutely *must* speak to Alfonso. I want to borrow one of his steel rods to solve a problem I have in my greenhouse. One never sees the man in daytime.' Just at this moment he saw Hortense eyeing him. Her expression reminded him brazenly of earlier events and for good measure connoted that she had noticed his temporary isolation from conversation and could supply an explanation for it. He turned away. She could stew, he thought. He decided he didn't have to make conversation with anyone.   He stood, amiably sipping the wine and observing the babble.

Frederick then appeared in a white chef's overall and said, '*Mesdames, messieurs, à table s'il vous plaît.   On attend le premier plat.*' There was an immediate movement to the table.

Frederick saw to it that Jubilee's entrance was given maximum effect.   He seized a huge hand-bell from the cupboard and rang it heartily.   At that moment Jubilee appeared, shy but triumphant in the doorway, carrying a tray. '*Caviar à la suprème de Jubilee,*' announced Frederick.   There was a burst of applause as he began to unload plates from Jubilee's tray and distribute them.

It was a dish Steve was familiar with, which Jubilee concocted sometimes when they had guests they especially wished to impress.   In England she did it with monkfish roes from tins, which resembled caviar, but he had to wonder if under Frederick's epicurean guidance a similar economy had been practised in this case.   The black roe at least looked genuine.

Next there were some exquisite pieces of steamed fish with a mustard sauce.   While these were being consumed Frederick took orders for the steaks.   A superior white wine had been served with the first course.   Paul was now putting out a second lot of glasses.   There were four bottles of red wine on the marble top of the baroque chest with their labels to the wall.   For the first time he could remember, Steve had an uncharitable thought about his beautiful young wife.   If she had asked him about the purchase of these luxuries he would have readily agreed.   But she hadn't consulted him, in the same way she hadn't consulted him about using the car.   He had the definite thought that the place was going to her head and asked himself where it might end.

Jubilee had been too busy with her duties downstairs to join the table.   After the delivery of the fish she came to sit down. Frederick had undertaken to do the steaks.   Immediately there was a commotion.   'The head of the table, she must have the seat of honour,' almost shouted Paul, into whose voice, Steve thought, had entered an element of hysteria.   What was getting to *him?* There were two empty seats on either side of Steve.   Steve was looking forward to Jubilee's return to his side.   But she was whisked from him. Alfonso, vacating his seat at the end of the table, occupied one of them. Jubilee was showered with compliments for her cooking.

When the steak arrived and Paul began to circulate the red wine, Steve made up his mind he was going to say something He had never been one to sulk, and knew surely, better than most probably, the value of initiative in human relations. He felt he was losing the initiative and that this was a downward slope.

Paul's hand was - Steve thought deliberately - obscuring the label of the bottle as it came over his right shoulder. 'Can I be allowed to see the name of the wine you've bought for us?' he said loudly.

Conversation ceased as if he had thrown a switch. He saw Paul glancing at Frederick, who was sitting on his left side. The label was held so that he could see it. *'Côte de Beaûne. Premier cru. 1976,'* he read aloud. 'I'm delighted. A very good year I seem to remember. I'm quite sure you have very good taste, Frederick.'

The silence deepened. Frederick's body straightened. 'Your wife asked me to select a pleasing wine for her,' he said. 'Naturally, in view of the fact that the *entrée . . .'*

'Oh quite, don't get me wrong. I'm very glad you did pick a vintage wine. I was just interested to see what you'd chosen for us, that's all.'

Was this the opportunity to say something? He certainly had an audience at hand, which for once was silent. It would be perfectly possible, and a lot easier, just to put his napkin to his lips and let the moment pass, but didn't he have a *duty* to speak? Didn't all his training and experience demand that he put another perspective before these no doubt talented but not worldly-wise people? It wasn't that he was bitter or wanted to get even with them in any way. He wasn't being small-minded, or defensive.

He leaned back in his chair and looped one arm round the back in a gesture he hoped would seem non-judgemental. 'You know, like Jubilee, I've had a most interesting day,' he began easily, 'a reflective day one way and another.' He paused, glancing round the assembly, as if to bring them all in. 'Reflective about the

Château Lamartine.　Now I haven't seen too much yet of your operation here and how it's financed, but from what I heard last night at this table, I rather think your excellent enterprise is very sadly on the brink of going under.　Isn't that so?　I see from the expression on your faces I've something like hit the nail on the head.　What I've gathered is that for some time you've been depending on the wonderful effort June has made to keep the place going out of the income from her job in Paris.　Through her, Damon has been able to get on with his history, Alfonso with his sculpture, Paul with his - er, music, Hortense with her abstract paintings, and so on.　But the fact is that June, through no fault of her own but through the harsh realities of the business world, is now no longer able to support you.

'I know I'm an outsider, but I hope you won't mind my suggesting a few things on this score.　As you know, I've had some experience in affairs.　Dealing with bankruptcy brings one in touch with human nature at quite an intimate level.　A receiver also has to have the ability to sum up a situation quickly, to reduce it to essentials.　So what I have to say is this.　I'd guess the place doesn't need to go under.　To put it baldly, what you artists and intellectuals have got to do for a change is think how to rub a few francs together.　It's perfectly possible.　I know this won't be something that comes naturally to you, for up to now it hasn't been necessary, but you already have some potentially lucrative assets.　There's Liz's horticulture - and her pottery - which surely could be developed, and there is, I understand, a large sum of money realisable from the sale of Alfonso's tower if things could be expedited more rapidly in that direction.　What I'm saying is that I'm sure that, with a little thought, each one of you probably has the means to convert your erudite studies and your excellent skills into hard cash.　It's just a question of finding the formula and the right frame of mind for doing it.

'If I can help in any way, just let me know.　I might concoct a few ideas if I were asked to put my mind to it.'　He paused, drawing in a long breath.　'Let me pounce on a single example. Our Hortense here - her excellent pictures shouldn't be standing against her studio wall.　Marketed in the proper way, I'm certain they could soon be adorning the walls of the rich and prosperous who can afford the high prices I'm sure they deserve. I tell you, with a little energy, a little *self-promotion,* the Château Lamartine could be coining it. You could be eating steak and drinking Côte de Beaûne every night.'

He thought afterwards that including Hortense in this bold way was a masterstroke. Wasn't he now evens with her? Her face, flushed and furiously turned away from him, seemed to indicate he was.

13

A heavy silence followed Steve's speech. Jaws circulated, hands reached for glasses, Frederick's immaculate table linen was raised to lips glistening with beef fat, glances were exchanged.

What would have been said had Jubilee not rescued them? 'Steve's very good at the money side of life,' she explained with a look on her face of the plainest goodwill.

She had allies. 'As good as your cooking, Jubilee,' volunteered Frederick jauntily, after only the slightest pause.

Paul eagerly took up this theme and began to question Jubilee about where she learnt her skill. In this way, like a dance at which only one couple had taken the floor, others then took the plunge. The subject continued to be food. The prowess of June and Liz was brought in. The conversation broadened. A stranger looking in about ten minutes after the bombshell would have noticed nothing unusual about the gathering except for the apparent isolation of one of the diners.

This would have been a misleading conclusion, however. The dinner proved to be the precursor of a night of unusual emotion at the Château Lamartine.

There was even friction between June and Alfonso, who usually conducted their relationship in a mutually considerate way.

Alfonso chose tonight to trim his beard. June was normally amused by this ritual but, the bathroom basin being occupied, she was compelled to wash from the bath tap. She was irritated by what seemed to her his finicky snippings in front of the mirror.

'When *are* you going to finish that sculpture?' she said with edge, her emphasis of the one word picking up Steve's mention of the matter.

'Eh?'

She repeated the question, but this time got no reply at all. 'We must have money from the World Council,' she continued, 'it's ridiculous they should expect you to labour away without even the certainty that they'll take the work when it's finished. You must get them down here again.' Alfonso had reached a crucial point in his beard clipping. Inclining his head and projecting his chin, he moved as near the glass as he could get, the large scissors poised. 'I said you must get them down here and negotiate an advance.'

Alfonso's accuracy was impaired. An irrecoverably large segment of hair fell to the basin. '*Coño,*' he said loudly.

Hispanic rage followed. Couldn't June see, he roared, that he was cutting his beard? Didn't she realise she had caused the most lop-sided effect which it would take a month to grow out?

For once June lost that ever-present tact which normally made her put Alfonso's art before any other consideration. Hadn't he realised, she said with raised voice, that only her golden handshake - and not so golden a shake at that - avoided their leaving the Château at once? Hadn't he realised she could no longer provide for the leisurely attitude he took to his work and its sale?

'Leisurely' was an escalatory word. Alfonso pounced on it. '*Perezoso,* am I?' he shouted. 'I e-sweat all day' - he pulled a tight-fitting, yellowing vest graphically from his armpits to illustrate his point - 'and you say I lazy. I work all night also - perhaps you then satisfied? I know *porque,* I know why you speak so. That rich *burro* Steve, you think he right tonight. That's why you invite him here. To tell us sermons. We artists here, big artists, big thinkers, not *mercantos.* We need not *consejos . . .*'

June fell silent, for she knew actually the last thing Alfonso was was lazy in the sense of physical labour. He worked from dawn till dusk most days of the year. He had been taking the sculpture part of his work with him to do in Paris. His lassitude, if such it was, was of another order, which in her distress and confusion she hadn't properly defined. She would not anyway be able to compete with such an output of words. Like all good orators, Alfonso would say nothing he hadn't said in his first sentence but would find new ever more intricately baroque and persuasive ways to repeat his theme. She was already supine on the mattress in the bedroom before, perhaps from lack of oxygen, the storm at last abated as suddenly as it had started.

'June,' he said in quite a different tone and descending himself onto the mattress, 'my little Junio, you not cross with your Alfo? I finish tower soon. Promise.'

Mollified, half-guilty, June turned her head. 'You'll get them down here next week?'

'I get them here *this* week. Make them pay beeg money.'

June had to keep her stern manner to avoid weeping.

Hortense Beerbohmer's sources of disquiet were more complex and very different from June's, but she was in a similarly nervous state when she and Paul reached the privacy of their suite and similarly in need of speech to relieve her tension. 'Wasn't that too *amusant*?' she said, whirling herself in front of one of the mirrors and observing the effect, 'the poor little man just doesn't know what 'as 'it 'im 'ere at Lamartine.'

Paul had gone immediately to his piano on entering the room, and was rummaging for something in the stool. 'In my opinion Steve, in some aspects, was rather making sense,' he said, with the air of someone adding a casual footnote, no more.

'Oh, you do?   Really, how intrigu-*ing.*'

'Some of us here do need to think a little more commercially maybe, and behave less like sponges.'

'Oh?   Sponges, you say?   And of whom are you thinking, I wonder?'   There was a silence at this. 'Me perhaps?   *C'est ça que tu veux dire?*'

Paul found what he had been looking for, a Bach sonata. He placed the score on the rest, looked at it a moment, arching his right wrist in mid air, but he didn't open the piano. Apparently he was making preparations for the following morning. 'You'd be a candidate,' he remarked then, getting up and making his way to the bathroom, 'when did you last *sell* a picture?'

Hortense took a nail file from the dressing table and stood using it, lolling in the doorway. 'But not yourself, *on suppose?* You are not being a sponge. You are not including yourself in this condemnation?'

'I've already contributed to the Château a lot more than my share, as you know,' said the musician, squeezing a striped caterpillar of toothpaste onto his brush.

'Oh, I see, we are excusing ourselves, are we? We are giving a proportion of money, and are not writing a note of music any person is wanting to hear, *et tu te crois autorisé* ...' A gust of rage overtook Hortense unexpectedly. 'I think that little man is *risible*,' she said, simultaneously breaking the file by making too sudden a movement. 'If you are thinking he isn't, you also are *risible.*'

Unlike the Aguas de Villanovas, the Beerbohmers went to bed with their dispute intact.

After dinner Frederick announced that he would be clearing away and washing up. As he had hoped, Jubilee volunteered to help him. But a chorus of opinion from the others forbade this. Jubilee had contributed more than enough to their evening, it was said. It was finally Damon, whom Frederick unwillingly summoned from his room, not Jubilee, who filled the breach.

Frederick, assuming the task of washing, donned a handsome full-length apron with navy-blue and white stripes, and Damon seized a tea towel. The greasy dishes were efficiently washed, dried and put away.

As Damon stowed the last item and was about to walk past him and leave, Frederick had an idea. He raised his hand in a gesture of urgent detention. He crossed the kitchen, opened one of the high wall-cupboards, which only he or Alfonso could have reached without a chair to stand on. He took out two bottles and held the labels towards his friend. '*Côte de Beaûne. Premier Cru. 1976,*' Damon read.

'I thought this an opportunity to repay you and Liz for your great hospitality to me on many occasions,' Frederick said, 'and there's another pressing reason to breach at least one of the bottles immediately.' He saw Damon's frown and that, because of it, he would have to explain the bottles. 'While advising Jubilee in the village on food and drink,' he continued in a tone which implied he was now dealing with a secondary matter, 'it occurred to me that by far the best way of compensating myself for my guiding services and a day's work lost, was this one. A great deal less embarrassing for Jubilee, and of course a very modest remuneration . . .' He paused again to indicate this lesser matter was now despatched. 'As I say, we have a pressing reason to talk.'

Damon's expression gave no further hint of what he was thinking. He seemed to reflect for a moment but then, seeming to make a concessionary movement of his shoulders, he proceeded towards his room down the corridor. Frederick followed.

Liz was not only into ceramics. She did a very acceptable home made wine, she spun yarn, and made clothes. She also made mats. The men discovered her embarking on her latest creation in this latter field. Sitting on one of the upright chairs, she had a largely completed work over her knees. Using a metal hook with a wooden handle, she was nimbly pulling the strands of home spun, home dyed wool through the canvas base on which she had painted her pattern. She was selecting strands of different colours from several cardboard boxes at her feet.

Frederick explained the two reasons for his visit, his offer of the bottles to repay some of Liz's past hospitality - when they had drunk her home-made wine - and, second, the fact that the remarks he had begun to make to Liz at their lunch with Jubilee in the village that day now needed something added.

'How can we talk with Damon silent?' Liz said.

'Ah, I think that can be arranged,' said Frederick. 'We know well how eloquent Damon's silences can be. I'm sure we'll be able to know his thoughts. 'I may?' he asked Damon, already opening the drawer where he knew the corkscrew to be. As Damon was already settling himself into one of the decrepit chairs and made no demur, it seemed he might. Frederick also found three glasses, and set about opening the first bottle.

When Frederick finished filling the glasses and was about to distribute them, he saw that Liz was frowning heavily. 'I'm sorry, Frederick,' she said, 'but as I indicated before I can't help you about the Addicots. Whether they stay on here or not is their business not mine. Since you've raised the matter, though, in view of what has just happened at dinner I must say it might

110

be a good idea if they left as arranged. In principle, as it happens I broadly agree with what Steve said, but I don't think we need an accountant to tell us what's obvious, well-intentioned as he may be.'

'But my dear Liz, with respect, Steve's speech has nothing to do with this. At lunch time today when I mentioned the matter to you, Steve hadn't made a speech. The matter concerns the feelings of our other guest, who has expressed a clear wish to stay on here. I'm merely acting on her behalf.'

'You're saying Jubilee asked you to act on her behalf?'

'It's reasonable to think she implied this, yes. You heard her say as much. She loves it here.'

'I heard her say nothing of the sort. No doubt she loves it here and would like to prolong her stay, but that doesn't mean she wants to inveigle her husband into doing something he doesn't want and which hasn't been planned. She did even say that, rather clearly.'

Frederick looked hurt. 'I'd hardly use the word inveigle, Liz.'

'Wouldn't you? I'd've thought it the right word. What is it you want me to do, anyway?'

Frederick eased himself on his seat. 'You heard Jubilee's remarks about the drawing Steve might be doing today. Well, I now have news. Jubilee told me in the kitchen this evening when she was preparing our delicious dinner that he has accomplished a work, a very promising work in her opinion. It appears however that he is less than excited about it himself.'

'So?'

'It's obvious - what's necessary is encouragement. What's necessary is that someone like you admires what's been done. You're an artist, he'll listen to what you say.'

'I'm not an artist, I'm a potter. Hortense is surely the person to make any art criticisms, not me. If Steve went out with her today to be given a lesson, I'm sure she's already made comments.'

'I imagine she has.'

'And they're complementary?'

'One might imagine so.'

'But you do not *know* so. Do you?'

Frederick could see an unusual amount of patience was called for. 'Liz, I think we aren't yet quite seeing eye to eye.'

'We certainly aren't.'

'All right, maybe you're right. Maybe Hortense wasn't especially gushing about Steve's work - for that matter when has she ever been enthusiastic about any work other than her own?'

'That's rather severe, isn't it?'

'If severe, true. I'm quite sure she *was* disparaging to Steve - whatever she thought. But it's *in consequence* of this, I think it's our duty to help Jubilee, and Steve, by giving Steve a more balanced judgement.'

Liz paused, drawing up a tuft with an exceptionally robust upward thrust. Her cheeks had coloured. 'If so, we all know why you think that. *You* know why.'

'I assure you, my dear Liz, I don't.'

'My opinion is that no more needs saying.'

Frederick gave a passable appearance of being dumbfounded, until he allowed some knowledge of Liz's implication to dawn. 'Liz,' he said then, 'I have to believe you're drawing a totally wrong conclusion. You're suggesting my motives in this are less than disinterested. I can see very clearly that a good deal more *does* need saying. You think I have some personal reason for detaining Jubilee here? Is that what you're implying?'

'What other reason?'

'I must say, my dear Liz, I'd've hoped to have earned from you a rather higher profile than that. Pleasure in Jubilee's company? Of course I have that. Who doesn't? She's a charming and intelligent girl. But you've entirely misconstrued my ends, which are of course from start to finish the community's interest. I really wouldn't have thought I'd need to spell this out. If Jubilee and Steve were to stay here a few more days and Steve had a further opportunity to see what we're achieving, wouldn't there be every chance he might wish to make an investment here if it were put to him? I'd've thought what he said at dinner tonight is a very good indication that he could be interested if approached in the right way, perhaps if approached through Jubilee . . .'

Frederick elaborated his case. He referred to the practice of patronage throughout history. Surely patronage of the arts was one of the oldest and noblest practices in civilised Europe. If Steve could by some lucky chance be brought to the idea of making a loan, or even a donation, which would save the Château, surely they owed it to all they were trying to achieve to accept it with grace? Did Leonardo da Vinci, he debated, spurn the commissions of the Duke of Sforza, other great artists the remuneration of Popes?

Liz seemed not to appreciate these historical parallels. The rate at which new knots were appearing on her canvas had noticeably increased. Her face began to flush. 'Frankly, Frederick,' she said at an apogee of annoyance, 'at best what you are suggesting is self-deception. The fact is plain, you're just keen on the girl, nothing more. And as far as your hoping Steve might give us money is concerned, I'd call that straight cadging. Why should he contribute to this place, it's nothing to do with him? Blast.'

An imperial purple knot had appeared in a square destined for one of carnation pink. It was a diversion fortunate for Frederick. He used it, both to control the effect on his nerves of this sally, and for a necessary switch of tactics.

'Well, it's time we heard from Damon,' he continued as evenly as he could while Liz was busy unpicking the errant strand of wool. 'If I'm not mistaken, Damon may have some thoughts not dissimilar from mine. Damon perhaps, being a realist, will be seeing things in a wider, less personal context . . .'

Darkness had begun to close, it would be a thick hot night. Damon put down his glass on the edge of the desk and rose suddenly. He took a box of matches, removed the glass cover from one of the paraffin lamps, raised the wick, and lit it. He replaced the cover, re-adjusted the wick again, and did the same with another lamp. While he attended to the second one, a moth came through one of the open windows and blundered frenetically round the green glass shade. A pair of owls were keeping in touch with each other as they hunted the pine woods

113

around the Château.   There was a growing tension between the trio.

'A wider context . . .' Frederick prompted.

But all Damon did was return to his seat and swallow the remainder of his wine.   He made no gesture and kept his eyes averted.

Frederick was chagrined.   Vows or not, surely this was scant reward for the wine.   Somehow he must bring them to understand the opportunity they were missing, he thought.   To gain time, he introduced the subject of earwigs and Liz's peaches.   But the creatures were no longer posing a threat, he was told with a minimum of words.   Suddenly Liz abandoned her rug making and embarked on a number of conversation-breaking tasks about the room.   'I'm going to bed,' she announced finally.   'This will be either here, or I shall sling my hammock in the stable.'

As she had correctly calculated, Frederick was forced to jump to his feet.   He knew he was for the moment defeated. He was obliged to leave.   Liz would sleep as usual beside Damon, normally and comfortably on their mattress.

14

Steve knew Jubilee was in a subdued frame of mind as they went up to their room after dinner, one that required some treatment.

'That was the most delicious dinner you put on, Jubilee,' he said at once as he closed the door behind them. 'I'm afraid it greatly outclassed the one we ate last night. I'm glad you thought of the idea.'

Jubilee was taking her rings off, standing by the dressing table. She presented to her husband her very shapely back. 'Only because we're able to spend more,' she said after a pause. 'Any cook who buys caviar and filet steak is going to get praise. I wouldn't have been so extravagant if Frederick hadn't rather pressed me into it. It was, I'm afraid, a bit ostentatious. I'd actually thought of doing just a nice fish dish.'

Steve approached and from behind her took Jubilee round the waist, placing his head over her right shoulder so that both their faces appeared in the mirror side by side. 'Whatever you bought would have been made delicious,' he said.

Jubilee didn't reject this embrace. But neither, Steve had to admit, did she entirely accept it in her usual warm and accommodating way. 'Why did you say all that at the end of the meal?' she asked.

Steve released her and began to undo his gold cuff links. He was glad for the chance to explain, and gave a chortle. 'Because I meant it, every word. To be quite frank, earlier on I felt a bit low. I mean, because you're so delightfully adaptable and because of your interest in art, you've been able to fit in here very quickly. It hasn't been quite the same for me. I'm a business man, not an artist or an intellectual, there's no good pretending anything else. I've been feeling quite a bit left out of things. Then suddenly, when there was that silence at table tonight, I thought I saw a chance to do a bit of *my* thing for a moment or two. No good skulking in corners, is it? I thought I'd give them a bit of clear thinking - it's what I'm good at. I'd say they've been needing someone to say what I said to them for some time.'

Jubilee swivelled on the dressing-table stool so that she sat with her back to the mirror, facing him. 'But it wasn't the right thing to say in the way you did, Steve. You could surely tell from the way they behaved afterwards that no one liked what you said at all.'

Steve removed his glasses and pulled his shirt over his head. 'No one would, would they - in the circumstances? No one exactly leaps at hard facts when they're unpleasant. I'll bet you June did, though. June's the one who's been keeping them all this time. I wonder where *she* thinks the next francs are coming from.'

'June above all didn't like what you said. I saw her face. Her eyes dropped to her plate when you were talking. She looked *furious*, more furious than anyone else as a matter of fact, and that isn't like her.'

'Oh well, even if you're right, which I do doubt - you must give it to me that I do know a little bit about the business side of life. I don't regret what I said. They may not accept the truth about themselves now, but when we've gone it's very likely they'll come to look on what I said in a different light.'

'But the truth about them . . .'

Steve thought he knew what Jubilee was going to say. She was going to say that the truth about the inmates of the Château Lamartine was that they were artists and thinkers, not business people, and couldn't be put in the same category as bankrupts in some manufacturing enterprise and lectured to.

He couldn't of course agree with this, but he thought it was better things were halted at this stage, for how could Jubilee know otherwise? Her experience of life had not, he was pleased to think, had to encompass the hard realities of economics. Might it continue that way, he reflected. He would certainly do all in his power to protect her. Beginning to whistle, he made his way to the bathroom for a cold shower. Having, as it were, tested out his opinion by stating it to Jubilee, he felt totally vindicated. Jubilee, too, he thought, recognising his certainty and lack of guilt, would surely on reflection come too appreciate he might be right.

The shower he did not enjoy, however. Enough water issued from the greened metal of the shower unit for Steve to get a good lather of soap over his entire muscular and hairy body, but it wasn't enough for its dispersal. Half way through the operation it gave out altogether, and Steve had to remove a good deal of soap on the towel. 'Goddam it, I've a good mind to take them in hand myself,' he said, rubbing vigorously as Jubilee came in. 'With Alfonso's skills, you'd think he'd at least have the plumbing functioning.'

Jubilee was not yet her usual self. For some reason there was still water in the basin taps. Rather reflectively she began to make use of it. While she was drying her face on the towel, she stopped the movement suddenly and turned to look at Steve. 'Steve, shall we not go to Africa and stay here? We could cancel the tickets, couldn't we?'

Steve couldn't have been more astounded. This was hardly the reaction from her he expected. 'Cancel? Of course not,' he said - much more sharply than he intended - 'we've paid for them.'

'They'd refund, wouldn't they? You'd get most of it back - and the amount we'd spend here would be much less than the refund. We'd probably be in pocket on it.'

'But Jubilee . . .'

'I know you aren't enjoying it as much as I am yet. But I think that's only because you've *decided* not to like it here. If you changed your mind, you could have as much fun as I'm having. You're always saying that you need to do more on the cultural side of life. That drawing you did today is super. I didn't tell you - I took it downstairs to the kitchen and showed it to Frederick. He thought it was tremendously good.'

'Big deal.'

'He said he thought Hortense probably thought it was good, too, but she never says what she means.'

'I'd've thought Hortense says exactly what she means.'

'Well maybe, but whatever they all think, does it matter? What matters is what *we* think. I'm sure it'd do you as well as me a lot more good staying here than putting up in luxury hotels in Africa and looking at wild animals who ought to be left alone and not pestered by humans.'

A very extreme thought came to Steve, which he wouldn't until this moment have thought himself capable of having. It dropped so precipitously into his mind, he had no time to censor it. 'You just want more time to go about with that absurd Frederick,' he was horrified to hear himself say, 'that's all this is about.'

He hoped he might find that he was saying this in a joking tone of voice, but he knew at once this was not the case and that his remark couldn't, wouldn't, be taken as humorous. Jubilee was blinking at him as if she had never seen him before and he had suddenly appeared out of the undergrowth. 'As a matter of fact,' she managed to say, 'tomorrow I'm going to spend with Lady Elisabeth. She's invited me to help with her gardening.'

After this, Steve didn't feel he was in charge of what he was saying at all. Confident in himself, had he thought? No, you're not,' he said, 'you're not spending the day with Lady Elisabeth or anyone else in this absurd dump. We're leaving a day early - tomorrow. We'll book into a decent hotel in Nice where the plumbing works and where we can expect to meet some interesting people - the Negresco if we can get in. We shall have dinner in Monte Carlo and play the tables. The following day we shall continue with our planned journey.'

15

Damon Raspin was the first to know of the precipitous departure of the Addicots. He had succeeded the previous afternoon in teasing free a few more strands from the thickly knotted ball of the Eastern Question. These concerned the motivation of those Bashi Bazooks, those Novi Bazaars, who had so freely massacred the Bulgarian Christians under their charge in the 1870's and whom William Gladstone had hoped to drive from the Balkan Peninsular together with their 'bag and baggage.' He had worked all night to the accompaniment of the even breathing of his peacefully sleeping consort.

Just as the first greyness was beginning to dilute the night, he heard footsteps in the drive above him. Steve Addicot appeared with *his* bag and baggage He was yoked between the two large items, and was walking purposefully despite the burden towards the hired car. Behind him, not quite so purposefully, trailed Jubilee. There was no speech between them. Steve stowed the two suitcases into the boot and they both got in. There was some minor trouble with the ignition, then the engine caught and they drove away.

Damon yawned, stretched, and smiled. So much for Hapsburg's heavy philandering, so much for the 'white knight solution' - the Hapsburg phrase which had slipped out at one stage, beyond Liz's hearing. So much also, he admitted, for his own flimsier more tentative thoughts in the direction of some financial rescue. It occurred to him he was tired, and that to climb into bed beside Liz and her warmth would be soothing.

Frederick's discovery of the flight was less gratifying. He had an intimation of disaster even as he stood knocking at the Addicots' door a couple of hours after Damon's observations, the set of Viennese china poised on the same tray above his right shoulder. There was no answer to his knock - and, mystified, he saw the door wasn't properly shut. He went in to find no trace of the Addicots except for an envelope on the dressing table addressed to June. An inspection of the drive showed the car was gone. Decimated, he returned to his room in the tower. The double breakfast was poor compensation for his devastating loss.

By evening, everyone knew except the Beerbohmers. Hortense, not anticipating company today, had left early for her day's work, and Paul, at work on his new technique as applied to the playing of the Bach Sonata, had no contact with other inmates all day. It was he who asked Frederick where their visitors were.

'How and why should I know?' snapped Frederick, turning away ill humouredly.

It was left to June to inform Paul that the Addicots had decided to leave a day early, 'as they wanted to see a bit of Nice before their flight tomorrow.' June clearly didn't enjoy being the spokesperson. Hortense, at Paul's side in these moments, gave a sniff - in the *haute Parisienne* category. 'To be expected, are you not thinking?' she said, carelessly throwing a tail of chiffon over her shoulder. 'Un *pédant lâche comme lui.* I hope, *au moins*, he has paid you some money, June.'

June looked pained, and blushed. 'He left signed travellers' cheques to the value of two hundred pounds,' she said, 'which was very generous of him, especially after the lovely dinner we ate last night. I feel very uncomfortable about it. I invited him as a guest.'

It was impossible to know if anyone shared her discomfort. It being her cooking evening, at this moment Liz entered with a massive tureen, which she thumped on to the table. It contained a miscellaneous vegetable soup. There was, however, something squarer and more resolute than usual about the set of her jaw as she began to ladle generously into the bowls. 'I'm afraid this is all there is - plus bread, fruit and cheese,' she said. 'And by the way, I claim Conclave.'

To which of Frederick's personal characteristics did the 'Charter of Rights and Duties' owe its existence? Damon, in a playful mood, said it was that lust for legalities so often to be found in people skilled in avoiding them. June might privately have wondered if such formality was necessary 'among friends and colleagues,' but concentrated on praising Frederick's 'beautiful calligraphy,' for the document was written on a scroll of vellum and illuminated like a medieval psaltery or Bible. She framed it, and hung it, on Frederick's request, on the wall of her bedroom.

The Charter had not proved a dead letter, however. One phrase particularly had been useful.

'If any person or persons may have at any time any wish to make a proposal which purports to be for the common good of the community, he, she, or they may - by "Claiming Conclave" - oblige the attendance of all permanent inmates at such a meeting. Proposals must then be debated, in the chapel, behind closed doors, until a unanimous decision is reached on the basis of common reason. During this period of discussion no food may be partaken of nor any beverage consumed.'

It might be thought that a group of people like this one, possessing an above-average quantity of individuality - and also one which liked its food and drink - wouldn't ever have wished to subject itself to such rigour. But the charter had been invoked several times. A Conclave was convened by Paul for example on the subject of non-domesticated animals inside the walls of the Château. No great research is necessary to discover who had been the cause of this. Paul's action had been precipitated by the fact that Liz had been keeping a sick stray sheep in her room (gained of necessity by a route through the main hall, which Paul designated 'indisputably a public thoroughfare'). Her chickens had also enjoyed free access to the building ever since Paul could remember, and had even been found on the first floor. Among more aesthetic arguments, Paul stated that he was allergic to feathers and wool. A fierce debate had raged, but Hortense had been Liz's only real advocate. After three hours of talk, and with hunger and thirst gnawing increasingly in seven empty bellies, Liz gave way.

Liz's soup was consumed at a speed which was, unconsciously, faster than normal. All other food on offer was also consumed. Who knew whether a hump would be necessary? Everyone knew the Conclave would take place that evening, and no one doubted that it concerned in some way the departed Addicots. Were they to be morally castigated in some way? Yet it was not Liz's style to castigate unless some practical point were involved. Mystery persisted.

The rare occasion of a Conclave was the only one on which the small private chapel was used. The building was in even greater decay than was the house. Blistered plaster fell at intervals from the ceiling and walls, together with the frescoes painted on it, and spattered onto the cracked, uneven tiles of the floor. Cobwebs sagged between the gilded pinnacles of the reredos. Several lights were missing from the stained-glass windows. In spite of the hot summer there was a damp mouldy smell. As the inmates filed into the once fine wooden stalls which faced each other in two rows across the short aisle, several creatures, probably rodents, scuttled audibly for refuge and a jackdaw hopped its way along an iron bar and escaped through one of the broken windows.

It was not yet dark but rapidly growing so. Liz had prudently brought with her two large candles and a box of matches. She removed the glass from two holders at the end of each of the lower rows of stalls and placed the candles into them. She lit the candles, replaced the glass covers, and immediately took position between them in the aisle with her back to the altar.

'June, I hope you'll forgive me for this,' she began when all were present, 'but you've told us that your wonderful hospitality, which has kept us all through these years - whatever small contributions some of us have made - must now soon end.

'Now it may be you don't wish the community to continue. If that is so, none of us is in any position to question your decision. But if, as I think and hope, you do want us all to stay and go on working, my proposal is that you should tell us the sum of money we need to raise, that we should then divide this sum by seven and that each one of us should be responsible for contributing that figure, whatever diverse arrangements we've worked with hitherto. I further propose that each of us here should, at a further Conclave - maybe in a week's time - state how he or she is going to raise the money. If at that meeting anyone is unable to convince the rest of us his or her proposal is sensible, regretfully they must resign their place to someone new who is able to make an acceptable undertaking.

'Can I first ask you, June, if I have correctly summed up the situation and your wish for the community to continue?'

Everyone looked in June's direction. June's head, semi-concealed in the most shadowy part of the stalls, was bowed. 'Of course I want us to go on,' she said in a small voice.

'Are you willing to say how much money is needed, say, per annum?'

'About three hundred thousand,' June finally revealed.

'Francs of course?' June nodded. 'And that, presumably, is for rent and running costs alone? It leaves out any kind of improvements, which of course the Château desperately needs?' Again there was assent. 'Right,' said Liz with an executive air. 'Add, say, another fifty thousand, then divide by seven?'

There was silence while, presumably, division sums took place in several heads. Certainly it began to take place in Liz's head. She gripped the spread wing of the bronze lectern eagle to assist her.

'Fifty thousand,' said a male voice.

'Is that it?' said Liz, relieved that someone had managed the calculation. 'Right, fifty thousand it is then. I beg to move.' After this impressive phrase, which completed the brief and impressive address, Liz took her seat in a vacant stall.

There was an even longer silence in which the mantle of twilight seemed visibly to tighten around them. A pew cracked like a pistol shot and one of the owls fluted outside. 'Why don't you float a mortgage on the lease, Liz?' said Paul then who, from his position of having contributed more cash than anyone in the past except June, felt himself justified in offering this less personally hurtful solution. 'It must be worth something.'

Alfonso, whom June had quietly dug in the ribs, answered this very practical point. 'Is not possible,' he said, wagging a large finger in front of his nose. 'Mort Gage not possible. Already have tried.'

There were some further suggestions of greater and lesser practicality for collective efforts which might raise money. Frederick, for instance, suggested they should 'throw the Château open to the public.' He foresaw a line of buses parked nose to tail down the drive and himself and Damon conducting large parties of Japanese and Americans round 'the public rooms.' He wasn't daunted when Hortense pointed out there was only one 'furnished public room' she knew of apart from this chapel and the kitchen. Nor was he dismayed by Paul's moral indignation at his idea of the 'use of imagination' in writing a colourful history of the place to subsidize the real one, which as far as they knew rather lacked colour. Suggestions continued as darkness began to fall. The candles were lit, and projected leaping grotesque versions of their silhouettes on to the walls and ceiling - as if they were devils engaged in a ritual dance. But in the end it was recognised that, interesting as many of these ideas were, and taken up as some of them might be, the succinctness of Liz's original proposal remained undiminished before them. At five to midnight, in an atmosphere of some emotion and dedication, it was adopted *nemeni con*, and Paul pronounced the meeting to be a historic one. The further meeting was fixed a week hence.

Before they left the chapel June, with tears on her cheeks, came out from the shadows and embraced Lady Elisabeth in full view.

16

Her three large leather suitcases ready in the hall behind her, Mrs Wilhelmina Hapsburg-Trench stood in the bay window of her modest bungalow pulling on the pale mauve gloves which echoed her lilac-coloured summer suit. She was a lady of statuesque proportions. With a wide-brimmed hat in position, the crown of which was encircled with a piece of material of the same colour as the gloves, she gave the impression of a fine flagship under full sail about to put to sea.

She was not unaccustomed to long journeys but, looking down on the view over a familiar Cornish estuary, she owned to being not entirely happy. After a life which had confirmed in her a complacent view of her achievements, Mrs Hapsburg-Trench didn't expect to feel disturbed. Yet she quite definitely *was* disturbed. Frowning a little, she put herself to discover the reason.

The taxi was late certainly, but that was to be expected and was allowed for. She was about to leave unattended all her possessions, including the Chippendale chairs, with the risk of a break-in and robbery. But all the pieces were heavily insured. Perhaps it was her darling Sophie who was troubling her?

Here she did ponder a little. It was the first time she had been parted from Sophie. Leaving the Home, and hearing the pitiful cries behind her, she had almost cancelled the trip. She imagined her now, miserable amid the alien scents, denied her favourite foods, too miserable to bark in that abominable cage. But, like Socrates, she knew what not to think about. Suffer as she had from this thought, she had decided finally that this was the way it had to be, and that was that. It wasn't the temporary abandonment of her darling which bothered her.

The taxi still didn't come. Sitting down, she took Frederick's letter from her bag, the second letter she had received in a remarkably short space of time. She was taking it with her for the address in case she forgot it.

'*Dearest Mums,*' she read, now for the third time. '*I sincerely hope that your health is good, and that of your devoted canine.*

'Though ever-cheerful in adversity - a fine virtue you taught me from infancy along with many others - I cannot entirely claim to be in perfect health myself at present. I mentioned to you in my last letter that poor June Aguas de Villanova has lost her job. This has of course placed on us all severe restraints of diet at the same time as increased responsibility for bread winning. I have of course refused to reduce by five minutes a day those humble efforts I make to keep flowing my small tributary to the great flow of European culture, but inevitably Nature claims its toll. I have to own to one or two curious fainting spells - I am sure not at all serious.

'What I am writing to say is that I would dearly love to see you. I would make the journey to you, but - well - as you may deduce, my circumstances make it impossible. Would you consider a second journey out here? As you know, standards of hygiene at the Château are not, cannot be, of the highest, but I think you found last time that those of our local hostelry were tolerable in the short term.

'Your ever-devoted son and admirer, Frederick.'

There was a P.S. *'Embrace for me the admirable Miss Sophie.'*

That was it - that last phrase, thought Mrs Hapsburg-Trench with an indrawn breath and with an emotion between relief - at having isolated the cause of her malaise - and alarm. The words had struck her before, but now she was thinking about them in isolation, she realised their full implication.

Never before had Frederick made any such literary reference to her beloved poodle. On a visit home once he'd had the effrontery to suggest that she be kennelled outside the house during his stay, on the grounds that he was allergic to dog hairs. She knew of course what it was - he was jealous of the place Sophie had in her affections. In the letter she hadn't taken greatly to the first reference. The word 'canine' even with the adjective 'devoted' could well have been one of his cynical games. But that P.S. was surely unequivocal. She considered what it must have cost him to write it, and drew the only

126

conclusion possible. The boy *was* ill. He needed her, and in his extremity had signalled the fact in this desperate way.

She had been imagining that a good part of her reasons for going was pleasure. She realised now that primarily it was duty. This confusion was what had been bothering her. What the unfortunate boy was saying was that if she didn't go now she might not see him again.

At this moment she saw the shiny black bonnet of Mr Tregarth's vehicle climbing the hill at a sedate pace towards her. She rose and again exercised her fingers inside the gloves.

The afternoon, Frederick thought, was refusing to acknowledge the importance of the occasion. Standing in his suit and tie in the open window of his room, the atmosphere inside and outside the Château was depressingly normal. The cicadas screeched, the place was deserted. Only faintly, from the direction of Alfonso's tower, he heard the muffled strains of the *paso doble* emanating from a small cassette machine he kept with him when working.

Frederick also felt agitated. Just when he needed all his composure, he felt deserted by his colleagues. At the second ('action') Conclave he had made his suggestion for raising a sum which would not only provide his share of the necessary funds but also those of several others. It had been met with a scepticism verging on the hostile. '*Donc, on attendra,*' Hortense had said in a most offensively ironic manner. Where now was that fine spirit of cooperation which had descended so pentecostically on the night of the first Conclave? Where was the support he needed for what was probably the supreme moment of his life so far, for the act which was going to save the Château and its precious cargo of human talent?

His alert ears caught the distant note of an engine. A few seconds confirmed that a car was approaching. He found himself rushing downstairs and had to check himself half way and remember that he was an invalid.

'Mums.'

'Dearest Frederick.'

Frederick had thought to lean against the cracked cornucopia at the foot of the entrance steps as the car pulled up, only the joy of seeing his mother enabling him to part company with its support. In the event he almost sprinted to open the door for her. It was not until he was in the middle of their embrace he remembered to falter a little.

'I'm decimated,' he said, 'I wanted so much to meet your train in Nice, but . . .'

'I did not expect you to, dear,' said the lady who, having emerged from the car and the embrace was already sizing up her surroundings. 'I say, things *have* gone down in the world since I was last here. Do you employ a gardener?'

'Er - no, mother. Not for some time as a matter of fact. We all do our best of course - now and then when our other labours permit . . .'

'I would also have recommended a tree surgeon. It's a great mistake to let nature take over, you know. You have far too many trees here, and they need severe lopping. Still, it is hardly my place . . . Now, I have hired this car for the three days of my stay, and the chauffeur. I presume you are going to offer me some refreshment here. Possibly also some arrangement can be made for Jules . . .'

'Dearest Mums, I thought first you would like to settle in to your hotel.'

Mrs Hapsburg-Trench hadn't had such a thought, but for once found herself guided by her son, who was simultaneously holding open the door of the car for her to re-enter while he instructed Jules about the route to the village. She had envisaged taking tea in 'the enchanted tower' which Frederick had described to her - he'd had lowlier accommodation on her last visit - and renewing her acquaintance with her set of Viennese china which she had sometimes regretted parting company with. Perhaps the fatigue of the journey was temporarily affecting her.

In the back seat of the Mercedes Benz, gripping a leather strap which helped her stability on the bends, she embarked on an extended account of her journey, which featured in particular the deterioration of service on French trains since she had last patronised them. During this, Frederick was also clinging to the strap on his side of the car, but for a different reason. He developed a prolonged fit of coughing. His mother appeared not to be affected. Her instruction to Jules to drive more slowly was probably on her own behalf, not Frederick's. 'These Latins all drive like the *Mistral*,' she remarked, not very *sotto voce.*

At the *auberge,* just off the main square of the village where Lady Elisabeth sold her ceramic-ware, Frederick gave another display of his deteriorated health. Attempting to lift one of the large suitcases - the driver was managing the other two - having staggered a few paces and begun to pant, he was obliged to abandon the effort and steady himself with the back of one of the seats, set to tables in front of the building.

'My dear, leave it,' said Mrs Hapsburg-Trench airily. 'Jules and the men here will deal with it, I'm sure.'

She concerned herself with the act of registration inside, together with various instructions to Madame, which concerned her comfort. 'There's no need at all for you to come up,' she said to Frederick, to whom the woman was about to hand the key. She took down, as from a shelf, a selection of her very serviceable French. '*Madame, je suis sûre, m'accompagnera à ma chambre, et le monsieur y portera mes baggages.*'

Madame was almost certainly not counting on performing this service with the key, but in the event, if with a lack of grace, did. 'You'd perhaps like to order us some tea, Frederick dear,' Mrs Hapsburg-Trench suggested. 'I for one am in need of some. I will rejoin you presently.'

Frederick had decided that his mother should meet only a selection of his colleagues, under strict control. Dinner at the Château was therefore out of the question. The meals would have to be at the *auberge.* He planned Damon and Liz for the first evening, June and Alfonso for the second - possibly June alone if Alfonso could be detached. For the third and last evening he foresaw himself dining *à deux.* His behaviour on this crucial occasion he had rehearsed meticulously.

But nothing would work to plan if his initial conversation with his mother was not successful. As she appeared and at once by her very presence made seem minusculely inadequate the small area of tables between the house and the low hedge which protected it from the pavement, Frederick rose and had no need to feign weakness.

'It is as usual,' his mother said, eyeing the seat untrustingly for cleanliness. 'They hide the single pillow in the wardrobe, hoping, I suppose, that you will not find it and endure that abominable bolster thing. The two lights in the room are wired, so that if one is on the other goes off, and in the bathroom one is forced to keep the basin taps running whilst washing, as their primitive metal contraptions have no hope of holding the water. You would think that an enterprising English plug merchant would make a fortune in this country. Do we not now have a common market?'

It wasn't an auspicious start. Frederick only hoped that the other two people present didn't have too firm a grasp of English.

Mrs Hapsburg-Trench didn't care at all for the minute toggle she saw protruding from the lid of the teapot, which betrayed the shameful bag to which it was attached. Neither did she welcome the choice which had to be made between common market milk and a moon-size slice of lemon floating in her milkless cup - the lesser of two evils. But she was not a negative person. Protests were made - identification of imperfection had to be registered - but this was peripheral. She was soon noticing more pleasing aspects of her surroundings - a donkey which trotted prettily past them, loaded with firewood, the single heavy boom of the church bell, which rather inexplicably expressed itself in this monosyllabic and unapropos way. Its reverberation lingered pleasantly on the rosy evening air. A party of swifts came out and began an energetic screaming race above their heads. With these events, the lady seemed to acclimatise herself to her arrival. Frederick adjudged the moment right.

'I thought we'd dine here tonight, Mums,' he said, nervously sipping the iced Cinzano. 'In fact I thought we'd do the same each night you're with us. We were naturally all looking forward to entertaining you *en fête* at the Château, but the fact is the Beerbohmers have proved an insurmountable problem. We all agreed, including them, that the best arrangement is the one I've suggested.'

'The Beerbohmers - a problem?'

'If you insist on the details, Mums dear, I'll have to give them to you. Paul Beerbohmer is suffering from a mysterious rash all over his body. Our doctor tells us it is a fungus. The spores are air-borne, and we're all of us to some extent therefore at risk. But we're assured that until any of the rest of us is infected, if we are to be, we aren't - in advance as it were - infectious. Therefore there is no risk to you in being in contact with me. But the Château isn't at present a totally healthy place to be. I fear the affliction is one of the results of our restricted diet.'

Frederick congratulated himself on this speech, made under duress, but there was a moment of doubt in which Mrs Hapsburg-Trench took an elegant sip of her tea, touched her mouth with the paper napkin, and stared upwards for a moment. 'Naturally,' Frederick had to add, on tenterhooks, 'the meals will be on me.'

Whether this was the crucial point will not be known. But Frederick's mother came down finally from her reflection. 'Then it seems there's no alternative,' she said distantly.

Driving back to the Château in the hired car, Frederick felt pleased. Liz and Damon (now happily released from his vow of silence) had provisionally agreed to the engagement this evening and had also agreed to make clear, at a suitable point, the new financial arrangements for which Liz had been responsible in her Conclaves. Neither, he knew, would skirmish with the truth, but it was no more than the truth he wanted from them. That his mother should hear from lips other than his own that he was responsible for the provision of fifty thousand francs a year if his accommodation at the Château was to be continued, was obviously sound. The avoidance by himself of any mention of the new burden would surely take on in her mind an aspect of concern for her pocket. (He remembered that his last quite recent appeal for funds had been met with silence and no funds at all). But he was arraigned suddenly by an atrocious thought.

As soon as the car drew up, he suggested that Jules might like to stroll in the grounds for half an hour or so. He went straight to the moat and signalled to the academic seated at the window below. Damon looked up, then glanced down at his watch. It was an hour earlier than their agreed *rendez-vous*, but Damon's movements made it clear that, though inconvenient, he was approachable. Frederick hurried back to the front door and down to the basement. Fortunately, Liz was not there.

'You've failed?' said Damon.

'On the contrary,' Frederick said. 'I've succeeded brilliantly. The invitation stands. But I've just realised there's a problem of nomenclature. I've referred of course in letters to my mother over a number of years to the Lady Elisabeth Elder-Fynes, though never to the fact that she enjoys the title in her own right, not by marriage. I've also from time to time referred to you by your Christian name. I've made it plain - I must have made it plain by inference - that you and Liz . . .'

'Cohabit?'

'Precisely. My mother is, as you know, a person who has skipped a generation in her mentality, perhaps two.'

'You mean you want to call the dinner off?'

'Of course not. As I've explained - apart from the pleasure of your company, which is of course paramount - your presence together tonight is of vital importance to my plans, all our plans . . .' Frederick gathered his mental resources. 'Damon, for this evening I have to bestow on you a hereditary knighthood. Not necessarily the surname, but the accolade. I thought I would say, "Mother, Lady Elisabeth Elder-Fynes, and Sir Damon." You can accept that, surely? If I slur the "Sir" you could quite easily have failed to hear it. Mother's sensitivity will remain un-bruised and your integrity intact.'

Damon sniffed, though not without humour. 'More of your crooked tricks, Hapsburg.'

'I mean I myself could have been under a false impression all these years about you and Liz. I could have reasonably assumed your knighthood. You'll do it?'

'It doesn't seem to be me who has to "do" anything.'

'Oh thank God. What a relief. I thought for one moment the

whole thing would be ruined. And Liz . . .'

'I will inform Liz what to expect, certainly.'

There was no hitch. Frederick introduced 'Sir Damon' and there was no tell-tale faltering in his mother's response. She had perhaps herself awarded Damon this status from the wording of Frederick's letters.

'What a pleasure, Sir Damon,' she said with an unaffected simplicity which would no doubt have conformed with those modes of court life to which historical accident had denied her access. Liz gave one of her most concentrated frowns, but a mild look from Damon seemed just to overcome her lust for clarity. Fortunately - having as it were crashed the sound barrier of the title - for the rest of the dinner they were through to first names.

It was a successful evening. Quite early in the conversation Frederick introduced the subject of Liz's animals. He pointed out how wonderful it was that with Liz's efforts they were able to eat a modicum at least of fresh wholesome food. Liz was encouraged to give an extensive description of her animals and what she called 'her tilth.' It was not long before, in reply, the habits and character of 'darling Miss Sophie' were being substantially delineated. Frederick and Damon were able to concentrate on eating.

There was an awkward moment when their silence made an impression at last on the social instincts of the visitor. Liz, who wore contact lenses, had lost one of them. Having recovered it with a moistened finger from the rich depths of her helping of *sauce Béarnais* she had temporarily to leave the table to clean and refit it. Damon was exposed. 'Now you are a quite brilliant historian - er, Damon,' said Mrs Hapsburg-Trench, resting her elbows on either side of her plate and clenching her hands. 'Frederick has told me about you. You're writing a very long book, I understand.' Damon gave a brisk nod and continued eating.

Mrs Hapsburg-Trench blushed faintly. Such brevity was surely hardly an adequate response to her civil question. Frederick had to rush in to the rescue. He explained energetically that the work concerned the Eastern Question, a matter of labyrinthine complexity which be-straddled a century of European history. He embarked on some outline of what the question was. But the damage was done. His mother wasn't used to be being dealt with by proxy. She returned to a rather prolonged and severe bout of eating, with lowered eyes.

The matter was not laid to rest until Liz returned. Slowly then, Mrs Hapsburg-Trench recovered her poise. Liz began to describe her plans for 'extending her tilth.' With pressure from Frederick's foot under the table, she was reminded of what was required of her. She led on in a natural sequence to give the reasons for this extra activity. She touched on June's recent misfortune, and described the Conclave she had called and the proposal she had made that each one of them should help to save the Château. During this description Frederick modestly lowered his eyes to his plate.

The next day further progress was made. Frederick suggested to his mother a drive in the car. Jules came up to the Château to collect him about eleven. He had indicated to his mother that he would be rising at four in order to 'clear his day for the pleasure of her company.'

In Nice, where the lady said there were certain 'old memories she'd like to renew,' the subject of lunch came up. Frederick said he didn't normally eat lunch, but he would willingly accompany her if she felt like a light snack. The upshot was that they both ate a succulent pork chop *à la broche,* supported by artichoke hearts and *petit pois and* followed by *mille-feuille* pastries burdened with fresh cream. Frederick had no difficulty in allowing her to pay the bill in view of his own generosity in having offered to pay for the evening meals at the hotel.

He didn't overdo his physical weakness, confining himself to a single performance some time after lunch when they were on their way back. He had to ask Jules if he would mind stopping for a while. He didn't disappear into the undergrowth as might have been expected, but sat on a stone only a few yards away in full view. He gripped his temples between the little finger and thumb of one hand.

He smiled wanly as he regained his seat. 'Please excuse me, mother,' he said. 'It was, I fear, the sudden unaccustomed ingestion of rich food at midday.'

'You feel sick?' enquired his mother.

'It has passed,' said Frederick steadily.

Dinner with June and Alfonso proceeded admirably. No one could take exception to June - and Alfonso, who in a vivacious and gallant mood described the duplicity and rapacity of a certain Quango which was failing to reward him for his herculean efforts on their behalf, could surely only be seen as further grist to Frederick's mill.

The following day Frederick suggested another outing to his mother, inland this time, to enjoy some mountain scenery. They ate another hearty lunch of beer and sausages at an alpine-type restaurant - followed this time by no gastronomic upheaval for Frederick. He must muster his resources for that evening, he told himself, on whose outcome his fate and that of the Château depended.

It didn't worry him that his mother had taken no initiative of her own to refer to his physical condition and its cause. He had experience of her mentality. He knew her maternal instincts had grown sluggish with her advancing years. They would have to be pressed to the limits before they could become fully operative. There were to be two preliminary tremors, spaced during the meal, the second more severe than the first, before a final eruption. With the *hors d'oeuvres* it was simply a matter of the fingers gripping the forehead again, closed eyes, and a little swaying of the head and upper torso, followed by some vigorous shaking of the head to throw off the attack, and a courageous return to normality. This was elaborated in the attack that accompanied the arrival of the cheese-board, but had the same *dénouement* of a return to stability.

'Feeling a little unwell, dear, are you?' his mother enquired again, though not, he noticed with some disappointment, interrupting her selection of cheeses.

He decided he would have to forego the very delectable dessert trolley. He lurched forward suddenly, half-rose and, like

135

a good lumberjack felling a tree, estimated his headlong fall so as to avoid tables and chairs. Supine, he drew his body into the simulation of a fit, drawing up his legs and bending forward his head so that his chin pressed into his chest and caused severe pressure on the back of his neck. It was this latter movement he had practised. He had found that what he had read was true. By a prolonged and determined holding of this posture he could induce a faint.

He had timed his exits from consciousness in these rehearsals, and the results had varied. They had lasted on either side of a minute. He couldn't be sure of the time span of this faint, but it must have been roughly similar. When he came to, he was being carried upstairs by the proprietor and another male guest. He gave no sign of his recovery and allowed himself to be laid on his mother's bed. He then listened with satisfaction to a Gallic quartet - his bearers had been joined by Madame and a grown-up daughter. Their theories about the cause of his collapse, none of which concerned the hotel food, were interrupted by his mother's voice. '*Voulez-vous vous en aller, s'il vous plaît?*' she instructed.

As the door closed he began to murmur feverishly. 'Fifty thousand francs,' he moaned. 'My work. Miss Sophie. Mummy,' he concluded.

He heard the curtains being drawn sharply, some other brisk movements, and finally speech. 'Now this charade has gone far enough,' he heard. 'Your attempt to deceive me, in two ways, is quite disgraceful. You would hardly expect me, Frederick, not to have consulted my up-to-date edition of De Bret before leaving home. The Lady Elisabeth Elder-Fynes is of course a real enough personage. She is unmarried and bears the courtesy title from her father's Marquisate. But if she had married, she would hardly have bestowed her name on her spouse. There is no Sir Damon Elder-Fynes. This was a puerile invention of yours to cover the plain fact that the pair are living in sin. At the time I went along with it, I had no wish for a scene. No wonder the man had nothing to say for himself. Secondly, and much more importantly, you are deceiving me about your physical condition.'

Frederick moaned pitifully. It was perhaps his most realistic simulation of the evening.

'You're not ill at all. If you are, it is self-induced. I'm perfectly well aware what you're up to. There was a moment in England, I confess, when I did wonder if your health was sound. Now I'm more than certain it's as robust as it ever was. You will listen to me. I know very well what this is about. Having failed to obtain money from me by letter, you're hoping by winning my sympathy for your physical condition to induce me to settle a sum of money on you to rescue you from this very minor problem you have. Let me make it plain - I have no such intention. There should be no difficulty at all for a man of your ability to earn the paltry sum of five thousand pounds a year. If you put one half of the energy you've expended in trying to deceive me into earning a living you'd earn several times that.'

Frederick opened his eyes and groped for clarity of mind. He was obliged to in face of this brutal realism. 'But mother I'm not well,' he wailed. 'You can surely see to what extremity I'm pushed.' He risked an even more lucid statement. 'And I'm only asking you after all for an advance on what will eventually be mine.'

At this she struck with the effect of the guillotine. 'You can count on nothing which will "eventually be yours." I've no doubt you've fixed your rapacious sight on Mr Chippendale's furniture. Well I have some information for you. I'm selling it all in the near future, together with the original bills in the master craftsman's hand. I'm certainly not leaving it to executors to sell it and take their percentage. As you well know, your father hardly left me a rich woman. I intend to enjoy some of the benefits from the one substantial asset I possess before I die. You should also know I've re-made my will recently. If in my remaining years you're able to go some way towards the elimination from my mind of the impression this abominable display has left on it, you may hope to inherit some percentage of what's left. But I warn you there'll be other beneficiaries, including our local animal-care centre, who will have instructions for Miss Sophie's welfare if she outlives me.' She wasn't yet done. 'What I have done for you is to bring that suitcase.' She pointed to this item, resting on top of the wardrobe. 'You'll find it full of natural remedies for any real illness you're likely to contract. Now I think it's time you were going. Jules will run you back. Tomorrow I depart.'

17

From earliest childhood Alfonso had been scared of heights. Near the Mexican village where he was born was a quarry. Apparently, in infancy he had screamed his head off if he were taken anywhere near the place. Wells, high-rise buildings, even pictures of these, would set him off. He had a recurrent nightmare in which he was always sitting on a cloud with the fear that its substance wouldn't be enough to keep him airborne. The fearful climax of the dream was that, after a desperate period of clutching, he began to slip through the vaporous support and was finally precipitated into a dizzy headlong plunge earthwards.

In adolescence he strove to overcome the phobia and largely succeeded. He made himself walk near precipitous cliffs. He joined a team of American speleologists working in his neighbourhood and underwent several hideous expeditions underground, which involved the exploration of gigantic hellish caverns. Finally, when he reached the age for military service, he deliberately joined a special operations unit, which he knew would require him to learn how to scale cliffs.

It was during this training that he had an experience which made a deep impression on him. They were in the middle of the course, and had had their confidence built to a point where, both in terms of skill and mental courage, they could tackle solo climbs of cliffs some hundred feet high. They were still on safety ropes, however. A colleague, out of sight at the top of the cliff, would be belayed to a boulder or if necessary a stake driven firmly into the ground. As the climber rose beneath him, with the rope fed over one shoulder he would take in the slack with both hands so that if there were a fall he could contain it by bracing his leg and back muscles against the strain.

Alfonso was doing his first major climb on a sea-cliff. Below him were cruel rocks and a sea which swelled over them, breaking in places into an angry foam - like a pit of snakes, he imagined, hungry at the thought of their next victim. On the way up, he overcame several crises of confidence and at last was near the top. As he breasted it, a terrible situation met his eyes. His colleague was not belayed at all, neither was the rope round his shoulders. He was talking to another soldier and idly taking in the slack of rope with one hand. Alfonso very nearly fell back with the shock. Only by a supreme effort did he overcome his vertigo and scramble to safety. It put back his training, and he had to join the next course to recover the lost ground.

He was aware that the giant structure he was constructing for the W.C.H.I.S.A.R. had links with his old weakness and his determination to overcome it. He wasn't fully conscious of this until very late in the construction when, one hot afternoon when the temperature was in the middle thirties centigrade, he was in his forge. This was some time after his difference of opinion with June about his failure to contribute enough to the Château and, following this, Liz's Conclave.

He had been striving to finish the work, knowing that June had written to the people in Paris and that a final inspection visit was imminent. The telescope itself, inside the tower, was virtually in place as were those representations of celestial bodies such as the Sun and the Moon, which were to be attached inside the telescope as if they were in the moment of being observed by the astronomer peering through the aperture far below. As yet unfinished were one or two of the symbolic creations which were to be sited in a ring on the ground below and linked by thin metal rods to the stars or planets with which they were associated. The Sun for instance was yet to have the model pylon to which it would be joined - this link suggesting the greatly enhanced use of that star's energy, which the Quango was researching.

Alfonso had been only dimly aware that within the telescope at its highest point there would be one last symbolic creation to unify the whole concept. He was not in any overt way religious, but at the back of his mind he had thought rather vaguely that the figure or object occupying this crucial position would need in some way to represent ultimate power. Perhaps - in some purely symbolic form - it could be a deity. He had pushed away this final task, only conscious that there was something there at the back of his mind which would eventually become manifest if he didn't challenge its exact nature too frontally.

Stripped to the waist in the inferno in which he was working on this sweltering afternoon, he knew what it was going to be. This crowning sculpture would be roped in ownership to each of the celestial objects further down the telescope, he thought. Were not the Sun, the Moon, all the other countless bodies in our galaxy as much the property of the Almighty as any living creature? And of course they would be *roped* - a vital word - of course they would be roped. He began to laugh. He was a large man, and his laughter was also loud. Someone outside the forge would have thought there was a madman within. Seizing a section of rod, he buried it in the smouldering coals and worked the bellows energetically. The flames speared upwards to a white heat, illuminating his bearded face and sweating body looming over it like a figure in a Pre-Raphaelite painting. Still laughing, Alfonso bore the red-hot tip to the anvil and seizing the hammer began to fashion it into a large hook. The complete sculpture had dropped into his mind like a vision. He wouldn't need a drawing.

Being about to turn off the *autoroute*, both Miss Greta Svensson and her young assistant Jan Topolski were leaning forwards looking for the signboard. Jan was the first to spot it. 'Ah, there it is,' he said.

'I think you are right, Jan, thank you,' said Miss Svensson, crossing into the nearside lane. 'We'll be there in good time for our appointment.' Mr Topolski nodded and both administrators relaxed again. Miss Svensson made an adjustment to the large sunglasses she was wearing.

The different tempo of their progress on the secondary road also altered the mood of their relationship. The night before, they had put up in a motel together (naturally in single rooms) and jointly eaten dinner in the motel restaurant. But the fact that they had driven over eight hundred kilometres of motorway since leaving Versailles the morning before had induced a kind of torpor into what was, anyway, a business-like office relationship which was formalised further by the difference in their ages and nationality. Miss Svensson was in her later fifties and Norwegian, Jan Topolski twenty-two and originally Polish. But - perhaps it was the fact of what they had as it were endured together - there was induced involuntarily a certain camaraderie which hadn't been present before. 'It will be an interesting mission,' Miss Svensson said.

'Interesting indeed.'

'We bear a heavy responsibility.'

'We do.'

'We must leave no aspect unexamined. There must be no possibility of offence to any reasonable sensibility.'

The pair hadn't been involved in either of the two previous visits, the first of which had been to establish with the artist the 'parameters' of the work and to approve the drawing-board stage, the second to inspect the work when half-done. They had difficulty finding the way. But by trial and error and some rather erratic local advice, suddenly the Château appeared and they turned into a wide forecourt. A male figure who had been sitting on the steps leading to the front door rose hastily, leaving a book on top of the balustrade.

'Miss Svensson? Welcome to Château Lamartine.'

Miss Svensson found her door being opened for her and a crooked forearm presented as if she were about to be escorted into dinner on some grand occasion. Embarrassed, she ignored the arm. 'This is Jan Topolski, who's assisting me on my mission,' she said instead, trying when she had got out of the car to stretch her limbs not too obviously. 'And your name is . . .'

This was not to be vouchsafed. Having shaken hands with Jan, the man turned on his heel. 'You'd perhaps care to follow me,' he said. Was she mistaken - could he be some kind of a butler?

They were ushered into a rather sparsely furnished room whose main feature was a large refectory table on which stood an enormous bowl of tastefully arranged wild flowers. The not unhandsome but curiously visaged figure withdrew with a bow. 'I'll inform the interested parties that you've arrived, Miss Svensson,' he said. 'Please take seats.'

She had been warned in her colleague's report that it was an eccentric community. This seemed borne out. The visitors did as they had been bid.

As they sat, above them there was sudden outbreak of someone playing repeated arpeggios of chords on a piano. A grey squirrel appeared in the open french-windows, was about to come inside, but thought better of it. Miss Svensson raised her eyes and saw stains on the ceiling, presumably from some plumbing disaster. A piece of the very faded wallpaper hung back from the wall. 'A somewhat decayed establishment,' she remarked. 'Let's hope "The Telescope" is not infected.' Her colleague was strongly in favour of this statement.

At last from the afternoon drowse and silence - the arpeggios seemed quickly to have exhausted themselves - there were light footsteps. The door opened and a rather distraught female appeared. Her hair seemed to be damp. The couple rose.

'I'm so sorry to have kept you waiting. I really expected you this evening. I was having a shower.'

'I think we *did* say three.'

'I'm sure we did. It's entirely my fault. Anyway - I'm June Aguas de Villanova.' Handshakes were exchanged. 'Now I expect you'd like . . .'

Miss Svensson moved into territory which she connoted by her bearing and manner was more familiar to her than people having showers and mistaking times of appointments. 'As I explained in my letter,' she began, 'what we have in mind for this initial visit this afternoon is to interface with your husband and establish the guide-lines of our visit. With a firm agenda agreed, I think Mr Topolski and I could then withdraw to our hotel in the village, which I'm sure you *have* arranged? We shall then be in a position to begin our work at eight a.m. in the morning in an orderly fashion. I foresee a further period of withdrawal, perhaps over the luncheon period - naturally, Mr Topolski and I will need to confer upon what we have seen. A final on-site session is then envisaged to clear up any secondary matters which may have arisen.'

'Then you'll be able to tell us the verdict?'

Miss Svensson paused. She was beginning to think a number of pauses were going to be needed during these proceedings to overcome such naiveties. 'Not, naturally, tomorrow evening, Madame Aguas de Villanova. I'm quite sure, on maturer thought, you wouldn't expect a large organisation like ours, contemplating the expenditure of a considerable sum of public money, to make its decision in so precipitate a way. I shall make my report. The public relations committee will deliberate, then the finance committee, and in due course, certainly within three months, you'll be informed of our decision.'

'*Three months*? But I thought this visit was just a matter of form? Alfonso has laboured for over a year on this work, you know. He hasn't been able to do anything else . . .'

'I'm of course aware of the time span of the construction. But I'm sure I don't have to remind you of the terms of the agreement. All expenses are paid in advance. In the event of a cancellation of the project by ourselves a courtesy fee is payable, but we do have the right to cancel - as we had at the half way, and have now in this the final stage. I'm in no way saying we're going to recommend a cancellation, but I must stress that my investigation is far from being "a matter of form." Now perhaps you'd be kind enough to lead me to your husband, or lead him here.'

June tightened her resolve. She knew very well from her twenty years in business how these committee-bound bureaucrats worked. She herself had been a committee-bound bureaucrat. It was only at the Château, in which she donned her *alter ego,* that she became as informal as she obviously had been about the time. Formality was *de rigeur*, she saw. She altered her tone. 'Alfonso is working in his forge on the last touches to one of the sculptures, which will be finished in the morning. He has asked me to discuss the matter of the agenda with you. I can also take you on a preliminary inspection of the telescope.'

The change, the almost miraculous descent of authority into a being she had already begun to think possessed little, momentarily threw Miss Svensson. She agreed rather tamely.

Unknown to Alfonso, the Château was in a state of highly-strung tension. Liz had decided to raise the price of her pottery and to increase her output. She would take a stall in the market on both days it operated, instead of just the one. She had also undertaken, with the proffered assistance of Paul and Frederick (on different days - they refused to work together) to increase her output of food. June was also now turning out jewellery and batik-wear and selling it on Liz's stall. Hortense was organising an exhibition of her work in a Nice Gallery. Damon was hinting, if darkly, at a 'plumpish bird which could come home to roost,' and it had to be assumed that The Eastern Question was becoming less of an enigma to him and that publication was imminent.

On the other hand the outcome of Frederick's bid to claim an advance on his inheritance, so confidently forecast as the single-handed means of the community's rescue, was clearly a failure even though he had declared that his mother was giving his request 'deep consideration.' Unspoken was the notion that even if all their other expectations were fulfilled, it wouldn't be enough to stave off the inevitable. It was as if they lived over a geological fault. At any moment the tremor would come, and who knew then what and who would be left standing?

Alfonso's telescope, however, was seen in a different light from the other enterprises. It was there, tangibly. Some money had been paid down for it. Money, big money, was promised - in writing. Displays of anticipation were absent of course - such ostentation would have been vulgar. But anticipation there was. Subtly, in ways it was doubtful if Alfonso noticed, everyone was politer to him, even deferential. Several visited the telescope and made complimentary remarks on recent progress. Paul Beerbohmer's enthusiastic daily commentary, normally dismissed as sycophantic trivia, was listened to and nodded upon.

Alfonso might be oblivious to all this but he was being driven by unusually strong impulses from within himself. Never one to shirk, he had recently almost doubled his hours of work. It was symptomatic of this immense effort that, while June was talking to the visitors, he was in the forge wrestling with the final touches to his 'deity' with a fervour unmatched by any displayed previously. He finished it soon after midnight and, too tired to go up to the room, slept on the floor there in the forge.

In the hotel that evening, with an enthusiasm relatively equal to Alfonso's, Greta Svensson ordered a bottle of vintage wine to go with her dinner and that of her young assistant. The previous night they had made do with a carafe of house wine. And the meal would be concluded with glasses of cognac, she decided - an unprecedented occurrence in the travels of the Norwegian public relations expert.

In her earlier visit to the 'artefact' with the artist's wife, she had with difficulty hung on to any vestiges of those caveats and reservations upon which wise administration must be based. From the moment she entered the romantic tower and the floodlighting had been switched on, she had been bowled over by the magnitude and daring of the thing. She couldn't believe that one man had created it single-handed. Surely there would be machine-hire involved in the expense account she must later examine. That the marvel would be drawn finally from its stone sheath by a helicopter was an even greater wonder. It reminded her of those words written by an English poet - 'Excalibur - mystic, wonderful.' She would make use of this striking phrase, she thought, in the report she would be writing.

She imagined the telescope at Headquarters being lowered gently into its waiting cradle, watched by a multitude, and she imagined the glittering reception which must surely be planned. The artist would be rightfully in the main limelight, but would not she too receive her small acclaim? She would certainly be expected to make one of the speeches.

When she mounted the quaint and perilous circular staircase to examine the various sculptures attached to the telescope, she was engaged in a different way. As with a caricaturist's pen, Aguas de Villanova had sketched by means of a few brilliantly-wrought metal plates the objects he was representing, the sun and the moon and so on. Wonderful, wonderful. June explained there would be other figures which would be sited on the ground at the foot of the telescope and which would correspond with those heavenly objects she had seen in the mounted positions. These were all in the forge and she would be seeing them tomorrow. Finally she was told with some added excitement that there was one crowning piece of sculpture missing. This was the one which would be fixed right at the top of the telescope. It was to be a surprise. Even June didn't know yet what it was, except she understood it would represent some kind of deity. Alfonso had been locking himself in the forge for the last few days. Miss Svensson said she had no doubt it was going to be a fitting *piéce de résistance.*

She was at the Château with Topolski precisely at the agreed hour the next morning. There was no one about. She tried the bell-pull but it didn't seem to be connected. Thinking that the *rendez-vous* was perhaps at the tower itself, she suggested to her companion that they walked round.

They were passing some outhouses when a huge bearded figure emerged from one of them, naked to the waist and carrying a not very clean-looking towel. He took no notice of them and made his way to a pump in the yard. Inducing a heavy sluice of water by manipulating the handle, he began to wash himself vigorously. Was this yet another servant? There seemed to be more servants than artists in this place.

'Excuse me, but we have arrived for an appointment with a Mr Alfonso Aguas de Villanova . . .' The strenuous ablutions continued. The very hairy torso was now receiving attention. 'The meeting was scheduled for O eight hundred hours,' Miss Svensson added more crisply.

There was a change in the demeanour of the individual, though not, Miss Svensson adjudged, because of what she had said. It was probably that he had finished washing and was switching to the drying phase. But he turned towards her and grinned hugely. 'Have arrived right spot,' he said. 'Me sleep forge all night. This my bath room.' He interrupted his towelling to wave an arm in a circle, indicating the perimeter of the yard. Information was arriving in Miss Svensson's brain from her colleague's report. 'A large man, only semi-skilled in the English language, of unpredictable habits.'

'I believe . . .' she began. She was overwhelmed by sudden recognition.

'Jew Norvega lady come look at my telescope - right? OK, I show jew. Very beautiful. Feeneeshed. I feeneesh for jew. I work half night. Mucha work. First we see telescope, jes? *Espere un momento* - I put on shirt.'

During her second and much more detailed examination of the telescope, her feelings enhanced by the presence of the artist himself, Miss Svensson was even more transported than she had been the previous evening. Literary phrases began to suggest

147

themselves for use in her report. 'The forceful and *joyful* personality of the artist, so majestically transmogrified into the soaring lines of the telescope . . .' 'A sensitive mind which has seized and glorified, through art, the major aims of our organisation . . .' She was aware that this enthusiasm was disallowing her from asking him all the questions she had prepared, but she permitted it, permitted it not only out of necessity but increasingly she noted from a *wish* to submit herself to it. They were engaged on the inspection for more than two hours.

As they emerged from the tower, Greta Svensson felt *herself* transmogrified. At a vertiginous height she had been asked to reveal her first name. It was the essence of her professional instincts to keep a friendly distance during missions of this sort, but she had revealed her name, and Jan had been asked to reveal his. 'And now, Greta,' Alfonso said, 'I show jew masterpiece.'

They walked to the forge. There were only two small windows high up in the walls - which were grimy and strung with soot-encrusted cobwebs. For a moment in the darkness she could hardly make out more than the central fireplace raised some three feet above the floor and mounted between four brick pillars, and a metal canopy above it to collect and funnel the smoke into the chimney. Embers still glowed faintly among the ash.

Then Alfonso lit two paraffin lamps, and from the shadows leapt the shapes she had been brought to see. She saw the plough which would turn the soils of the planets for food production, a pylon which represented the energy that the harnessing of natural resources like the sun's heat could release for the benefit of mankind - and the other symbols which would lie at the foot of the column and be umbilically joined to the corresponding symbols of pure scientific research mounted above. But in the corner, shrouded in a smutty sheet, was a hidden object. She knew at once this would be the 'deity', which the artist's wife had spoken of the previous evening.

She was aware that Alfonso was keeping this until the last and, not to spoil the *dénouement,* she dutifully restrained her excitement and made herself concentrate on the other objects as he explained them one by one. At last he was ready to remove the sheet.   Holding one corner of it, he grinned broadly.   '*Y ahora,*' he said, 'I show my God.'

There was a flopping noise as he wrenched off the sheet.   A cloud of dust exploded and rose slowly in the lamplight. Revealed was a large steel hammock slung between two poles. In the hammock was the outline of a huge, naked, fully equipped male figure with a beard, reclining with one knee raised, reading a book held above him with one hand.   The other hand was idly engaged apparently in hauling the rope upwards.   The slack that had been already taken up was coiled untidily under the hammock.

Miss Svensson had a curious sensation.   For the first time since her contact with this work of art she was not clear. Everything to this point had been so very lucid.   The figure was plain enough - it had a majestic Michelangelo quality about it. But the rest of the imagery . . .

'That is - God?' she said, intending this to be a statement, but finding her words came out interrogatively.

'That is some God, jes,' said Alfonso.

'And he's reading - a tome of science perhaps?'

'I think lighter work,' Alfonso said.   'A *romanza* perhaps.'

At this point Miss Svensson noticed another object on the far side of the body.   It greatly resembled a box of chocolates, and now that she was alerted to this concept she saw that the outline of the deity's cheek was markedly convex.   'Your God seems very relaxed,' she remarked.   'But the rope . . .'

'Ah, the rope.'

'One rope?'

'It will be - how jew say? - split.   More split down telescope. Split in six.   One rope each object.'

Miss Svensson's slight dismay began to disperse.   'Ah, I see. You wish to link all the planets, and the great endeavours on earth below to which they are linked, to the Godhead.   What a fine sentiment.   And it is a great Godhead - so recognisably a Godhead.   It is not of course the Christian God, nor the Moslem, nor the Hindu, not the God of any one religion - an international Almighty.   Only atheists will be disappointed.   I'm beginning to think it succeeds admirably.'

Alfonso had begun to chuckle.   'And he not care,' he muttered.   He was no longer addressing her, Miss Svensson thought, he was gazing at the sculpture.   'He not care two buggers.   He not care if they all fall below and smash into theirselves - big black hole.   He have good book, nice chocolates. My God, he sit right at top of telescope in very cum-fort-uble position.'

18.

'Dear Señor Aguas de Villanova,

'I must first thank you and your wife for not only providing me and my colleague with hospitality at the Château Lamartine, but also for giving us a unique cultural experience.

'Naturally, you would not expect me at this stage in any way to preempt the decision of the Board to which I am responsible, but I do not think I depart from any protocol in saying to you that, whatever the decision about the erection of your work in front of the headquarters of the W.C.H.I.S.A.R., from a purely personal point of view I found "The Telescope" intellectually challenging and aesthetically most elevating.

'There is, as you know, a small problem - the crowning figure, your "deity." I realise that, in the first flush of creation, you could not consider very deeply the very mild (and, let me stress, footnotal) criticism I had to make of certain aspects of this figure which, as I endeavour to explain to you, arise from purely practical criteria. I am certain, however, that now you have had time for more mature reflection, you will have realised we could not allow such - yes, I use the word - such a note of flippancy to mar what is otherwise so suitably grave a tone, and an addition that nowhere appears in the agreed blueprint. Will you allow me - though clearly a lay person in the realms of art - to make a simple suggestion which would involve the minimum of effort on your part? Remove the box of chocolates, modify the curve of the deity's cheek, and have him grasp the incoming rope with <u>both</u> hands. A further thought occurs to me, now I grapple with the subject. Perhaps the hammock could be removed, and the figure poised upon some other less recreational support, a throne perhaps?

'I shall delay the submission of my report until I have read from you further, an event which I hope to enjoy in the soonest future.

Meanwhile, I remain your admirer and, I trust, good friend, Greta Svensson.'

'Dear Señor Aguas de Villanova,

'Your short, succinct letter has both surprised and pained me. Surely this is not your well considered position? I delay yet in the presentation of my report in the hope that even at this eleventh hour you will reconsider - not only the interests of this organisation - but also your own. Where else will you be able to place this work, so specifically planned for our needs? Do you realise - apart from all other considerations, that you will be forfeiting all but a very small portion of a large fee? I can give you until the end of this week to change your mind.

Yours sincerely,

Greta Svensson.'

A third letter exists, which arrived at the Château some three weeks after the second.

'Dear Señor Aguas de Villanova,

'With great regret I am to inform you that the Public Relations Committee of this Organisation has declined to accept your submitted work for the adornment of the space before this Headquarters building. I think you will be aware of the main burden of the reasons for this decision.

'Please find enclosed a cheque in full and final payment of our obligation to you. The sum includes settlement of the five per cent cancellation charge, as per contract, and up to date expenses. You will note that a deduction has been made from the latter under the heading of "fuel consumption." While examining the electricity meter in your tower just before we left in order to take a final reading, my colleague discovered that an unauthorised cable had been led off this meter which, as far as he could tell, had been used to illuminate a room in another of your towers, the one that is roofed and inhabited. The deduction is estimated but, I think you may agree, conservatively.

'Yours faithfully,

'Greta Svensson (Public Relations Executive.)'

It was June who had collected this correspondence. She was in fact the only person in the community who had read all three letters - Alfonso had only read the first. June discovered it when she suspected from Alfonso's demeanour that something might have come, and, on searching, found it discarded on the floor of the forge. The other two letters he had left unopened in the living room, where the postman left the rare mail addressed to the Château, and where June had seized them. When she had tried to give them to Alfonso he had refused even to open the envelopes. She had pleaded with him, most unusually lost her temper, but he was unmoved. 'Take my telescope, take my God, part and parcel,' he chuckled.

June was in despair. She thought of enlisting the others who, she knew, had expectations of Alfonso's success almost as great as her own. But she knew she couldn't do this. In a curious way, childish and obstinate as Alfonso's stand was, she couldn't in her deepest feelings condemn him. The mistake had been to take on this contract in the first place, which she was guilty of having encouraged him to do. His contempt for this self-important Quango had always been there. She herself had it. How could art and business, art and politics, ever successfully marry? The remainder of the Château lease would have to be sold - if it was saleable. The community would break up.

Early one beautiful September afternoon when, at the nadir of her spirits, June was standing in the window of her bedroom unable to work or do anything constructive, she heard a car approaching the Château. She looked at her watch. It couldn't be the post, it was too late. She dreamed it was the Svensson woman returning to say that all was forgiven and that the telescope would be bought after all, deity included.

It wasn't Miss Svensson. Quite an expensive-looking car appeared with shiny black paint. It disappeared from her view on the way to the front door. In a few seconds a man in a cap, who looked like a chauffeur, appeared round the corner, obviously bewildered to find no one about. Suddenly galvanised, June rushed down.

When the man saw her approaching, he marched towards her with some relief. '*Château Lamartine? Je cherche . . . Madame*

Aguas de Villanova.' As he said this, he was looking down at an envelope he carried in his hand for guidance in the pronunciation of the name.

When she said she was this person, he behaved in an odd way. First he asked her if she was sure she was. Apparently satisfied, he then looked about him furtively as if any witness to their conversation might be detrimental. *'Je dois vous donner cette lettre,'* he said quickly and in a lowered voice.

The handwriting was familiar. She tore open the envelope. The letter was written on the notepaper of the Negresco Hotel in Nice with today's date. Her eye went automatically to the bottom of the page. It was from Steve Addicot.

'Dear June,' she read, *'I know you'll be surprised to get this - in this rather cloak and dagger way. But the fact is something's happened which is - which I think is <u>bound</u> to be - important to you. I'm back here in Nice and would like to meet you - this evening if possible. The chauffeur will bring you here and, naturally, take you back afterwards. If this is too short notice for you, will you come tomorrow? The man can find himself a room in the village, at my expense. At all events I'll wait here until you come.*

'There's one thing I'd ask you to comply with. I'd prefer at this stage that no one, not even your husband, knows I've written to you in this way and that you've come to see me. If someone finds out that this letter has come, would you temporarily think of some explanation other than the real one?

'I hope you'll come here. I'll then of course explain all.

'Yours ever, Steve.'

19

Steve had apologised to Jubilee in Nice for the silly outburst which abruptly terminated their stay at the Château Lamartine. He said it was because he had been jealous, loving her as much as he did, jealous that she had fitted in so well with everything going on there when he had felt estranged by it. She had accepted his apology, if gravely, and the safari holiday had been quite a success. Jubilee had been thrilled by the animals. He was sure a spell at home would disperse the unpleasant memory.

On the business side, everything was going right for him. A number of collapsed medium-size firms fell into his hands to sort out. His reputation, paralleling his income, was multiplying at a compound rate of interest, and he could choose the cases he took on. Surely he was in the harvest-time of his life, he thought, when the ripe produce of his hard labour was streaming in. And he had Dolly Sevenoke to remind him that it wasn't just business which drove him.

One morning some two weeks after the holiday, he had a particular feeling of pleasant anticipation as he drove his Rover through the huge wrought-iron gates of Dolly's estate, which wasn't many miles from home. Ahead of him stretched the long white drive, neatly fenced on either side, dividing fields where a healthy herd of Frisians grazed. At the summit of a slight incline, frankly exposed against the sky, rose the great house with its impressive Palladian portico.

Coming here as he did about once a fortnight was something quite different from the rest of his work, for Dolly had long since ceased to be just a client. He thought of her now, that small vivid presence sitting in the vast space in there, waiting for him with her simple clear language, her sharp mind, and the power she wielded so light-heartedly over her well-run domain. It was flattering to him to think she looked forward to his visits.

As well as doing the farm and the estate accounts, Steve advised Mrs Sevenoke on the management of her personal fortune. But she hardly looked at the papers he brought. 'All right, you decide that for me,' she'd say. 'As you say, sell the inflation-hedged stuff and buy the bonds, sounds sense. Now I want your opinion on something much more important. What are we going to have in the front flower-beds this year?' Sometimes she asked his advice about her family. 'What am I going to give my great-nephew, Andrew, for his birthday?'

In front of the house were some well-sited trees and lawns in perfect trim, which ran between colourful flowerbeds. As Steve entered this area and slowed the Rover, the upper half of Jim Moody, the head gardener, appeared from a thicket of shrubs. Moody waved, Steve waved back. Owens, the butler, continued the welcome at the front door. 'Mrs Sevenoke is waiting for you in the morning room,' he said leading the way. Steve entered the sunlit room and marched to the diminutive figure seated at the desk in the bay window and heard Owens discreetly close the door behind him.

Dolly finished screwing on the cap of a fountain pen, dexterously swung her invalid chair away from the desk and confronted him, smiling. 'My dear Steve, how nice, you are ten minutes early.' She extended her frail white hand, which he sandwiched gently in both of his.

Sitting in the armchair, he began to rummage in his large black bag. 'I've got some good news, Dolly. You've probably seen. These new pharmaceutical shares you bought . . .' He found the file in the bag. She was putting away her spectacles in the case.

'No business today, Steve - not now anyway. First I have something to say to you. But I want you to promise me something before I tell you what it is. I want you to promise that, when I've finished, you won't speak about it - not now, or ever. Will you promise that?' Mystified, he agreed. 'Right. Well it's quite simple really. I'm still going strong, I suppose, but I've had the feeling lately I'm not going to last much longer. About a month ago, I remade my will. The house and the property is taken care of - as you know, I've left it to the National Trust. Having no children, in an earlier will I'd chopped up the money among the various members of what is called, I believe, my "extended" family, who consider they have a right to it. They'll all get something, but I've come to the conclusion they don't deserve the considerable sum which will be left when probate has fed off the corpse of my estate. I've never liked people who assume things, and I've always considered that money is to be used productively and not squandered, which is undoubtedly what will happen if that lot get their hands on it . . .

'So I set myself to think who or what might best make use of it. There are charities of course, but I've never had much use for corporate bodies, even philanthropic ones. It's individuals who do and create things, not organisations. And what individual whom I know and care anything for would make best use of the tidy little sum there'll be? Why, Steve Addicot, I thought. He understands money. He'll make good use of it. And of all the people I've known in my life - of those who are left - you're the person I'm fondest of. You come here as often as you can and cheer me up - just by being yourself. It's a great gift you have, Steve, the greater because you probably don't even realise you've got it. To someone like me, someone of my age, being cheered up is the most important thing in the world.

'There now, I've got it off my chest. And that's all there is to say. You are to inherit my dough when I kick it. That makes me very happy. Now, I suppose we have some business to despatch - then I suggest a game of draughts. Best of three and it's your turn to start first. You may recall I thrashed you the last twice.'

Steve realised at once he didn't want the money. How could he possibly accept it? He knew how large the sum was likely to be. Why should she do such a thing, which was bound to alter the basis of their friendship? Almost the next day, a fellow accountant in the partnership made a remark to him. 'Getting along all right with the Sevenoke portfolio, Steve? Play your cards right in that direction and you could soon be in for a little windfall, right?' The remark was casual, humorously meant, but it shattered him. This, plainly, was how other people saw his relationship with Dolly. Was it true then? Had he had a mercenary motive all along? Had he helped Dolly with all

157

these family matters, listened to her, told her about his own life, visited her regularly even when business didn't demand it and he couldn't spare the time, brought her flowers, out of an ulterior motive so deep he hadn't been aware of it? He couldn't believe it, but had to consider it was a possibility.

His partner's remark decided him.   True or not - and he didn't think, after wrestling with himself, he could ever know the truth - he couldn't live with it.   He went to see Dolly at once.

'Dolly, I'm sorry, but I've got to break the promise I made to you.   I've got to make just one remark about what you said to me. I, too, want to make it and don't want you to comment afterwards, in order that things can go on as they were before. Will you please accept this?'   He hurried on in case she should demur.   'I'm deeply touched that you should want to leave me your money.   The *thought* of it flatters me and I am very grateful.   It has deepened our friendship - on my side at least. But I don't want it.   I want you to take me out of your will.   I think you should leave the money to charities if there's really no one else you want to have it.   I can help you decide which ones, if you like.'

She was looking at him steadily.   'People are talking, are they?'

'No, not specially, it isn't that.   It's me, my own feeling, nothing to do with anyone else.'

'You don't want my money.'

'No. I feel it'd spoil - what we have.'

She surprised him greatly.   An enigmatic smile showed for a moment.   'All right, I understand,' she said at once.   'If you prefer.   Perhaps you'd like an object or two then to remember me by? You shall choose. Is that better?'

'Enormously better.   *One* object would be lovely.'

He could feel relief swelling through him.   He couldn't believe the rectification had been achieved so effortlessly, almost casually.   What an understanding woman she was. With a little switch of her mind she had restored their relationship to its former light-heartedness. She said she would think about some suitable charities and consult her lawyer again.

He chose for his gift a suit of armour that stood in the hall, which had always intrigued him, and they didn't refer to the matter again except for a little remark she made as he was going that day. 'After all, what's money worth?' she said with a grin as he took her hand, 'certainly only what you want to buy with it, we both know that. And if one has everything one wants . . .'

A month later Mrs Sevenoke died. Various members of her family received modest legacies. The house, the farm, and a considerable sum of money was given as she had promised to the National Trust. She left ten million pounds to Steve Addicot, also the suit of armour he had selected.

When he opened the lawyer's letter, Steve couldn't avoid an initial leap of excitement. Ten million - he was no longer rich, he was filthy rich. A manor house, lands surrounding it, drifted into his vision - tenant farmers, a bailiff, even a yacht perhaps with someone to run it . . .

But this feeling was almost at once superseded by an unspecified fear. He found himself rounding on Dolly. Why had she so deliberately flouted his wishes in this way? It quite clearly *was* deliberate. Because the suit of armour was included in the legacy, there was no question of her having forgotten to change her will after their conversation. He recalled her words: 'Money is only worth what you want to buy with it.' Was it some sort of a rich woman's joke she had indulged in to amuse her in her last days?

He couldn't believe this, and very soon discerned what was bothering him. What he feared was how Jubilee would take the news. Jubilee knew the legacy had been offered before and that he had turned it down. Would she now think he had lied to her, that he had not turned the legacy down, that he had *worked* for it?

Since their return from holiday, Jubilee's interest in reading and pictures had increased. She seemed to be for ever in that summer-house of hers. There was more than one occasion when there was no dinner when he got in because she had been immersed in some tome and had forgotten the time. She had started taking herself off to London for the day to visit the art galleries, and sometimes exhibitions. She also had regularly to visit her Open University tutor. He didn't object to this. He was glad she had such a fulfilling hobby to occupy her when he was away. What worried him was what had worried him for some time - the fact that here he was earning all this money and it seemed there was no way he could find of spending it on her. There was an occasion recently when after buying her a very expensive, jewelled ring-box for her dressing-table, he found it a week later in a drawer in the kitchen, still in its box and wrapping-paper just as she had opened it. What was the point of spending all this energy, and now inheriting this fortune, if Jubilee wouldn't enjoy the fruits it yielded? If only they had been able to have children, he thought, it might be different. They would be thinking of them and their future, not just themselves.

He said nothing to Jubilee about the legacy, knowing this was foolish. Though probate could take months, it could only be a matter of days before she would find out. A big legacy like this, involving the National Trust, would be in the national newspapers, let alone the local rag in which it would probably be on the front page. The phone would never stop ringing. He, and inevitably Jubilee when he was away, might be besieged by journalists and people wanting donations. He knew, if by some fluke this didn't happen - and it was true Jubilee never looked at a newspaper - his mother would know, and would phone. But he didn't tell either of them. He lived under an anaesthetic.

As he had guessed would be the case, mother got to the news first. She even beat the journalists arriving at his door. She didn't phone, she arrived in a taxi soon after Steve had got in from a day's work. Slumped with his whisky and the mail, he heard the front door bell ring and the confused conversation with Jubilee in the hall. Mother came rocking in like one of those Russian dolls with no feet. 'Steve, you should have told me. I've just been told by a neighbour who saw it in the London evening newspaper. Looked a right Charlie I did, knowing nothing about it . . .' She was observing him. 'Oh, so we're that complacent about it, are we?   It's just another million or two to you, is it?   And here am I wondering how to scrape together enough cash to buy a new cooker.'

Steve was aware of Jubilee lurking behind her.   He couldn't look at either of them and could barely stir himself.   He hadn't got up when mother came in.   He went on reading the letter he had spread on his upper leg and took a sip of his drink.   'I told her I didn't want it some weeks ago,' he muttered.

'Did you now?   Well you seem to have got the right formula then.   You've certainly *got* it all right.   Good tactics it seems it was.'

To his alarm Jubilee was sidling out, back into the kitchen.   'I'll probably be giving it to charity.   We don't need it,' he found himself saying, dully.

Mother stayed to supper.   She did practically all the talking and provided some imaginative thoughts on how the fortune might be spent or invested.   In these proposals, charities did not figure, for 'where does charity start but in the home,' she explained.   Steve went in for some grave nodding.   The only practical result of the evening was that he promised his mother a very substantial cash sum, which would look after a number of necessities in addition to the cooker.   During this time, Jubilee showed some interest and listened to the conversation, but made no comments.

When mother had gone, he knew there would have to be a proper conversation with Jubilee about it.   Jubilee said she was glad for him, and that if he was really going to give the money away - and did he really want to do that? - it would be nice for the people he chose to give it to.   She also said how much Dolly Sevenoke must have appreciated him to have taken such a major step, when he had made it plain he didn't want anything.   He asked her if she had any ideas of how they might spend some of it.

She thought for a moment.   'I suppose there could be some things.   I'll have to think,' she said.   She was embarrassed, he could see.

After this, by a tacit understanding, the matter was dropped for the evening. They then did a number of routine things and eventually went to bed. What gave Stephen the greatest cause for concern was that he didn't feel Jubilee was holding out on him in any way. There was no tension emanating from her, apart from the fact that she couldn't immediately think of anything she wanted which she hadn't got. What was patent from her manner was, not that the legacy was undesirable in any way, but that she had simply nothing to say about it, that she saw it probably as an irrelevance. In bed, as usual, she read. It was an exceptionally heavy looking book she must have got from the public library. He noticed it was called 'Middlemarch'. A dreadful thought engulfed him. Was Jubilee growing away from him? Was his concern for material welfare slowly strangling her love for him? Would it end like . . . This he could not contemplate.

He had turned out the light on his side. It was usual for him to do this. After his day's work he was usually asleep in a few minutes. Tonight he knew there was no chance of sleep. He listened to the rustle of the pages of Jubilee's book as she turned them over. For a quite unfathomable reason he found himself counting them, and felt very low.

The idea came to him, as ideas of such simplicity and magnitude often do, at the very nadir of his chagrin. He sat up with a jerk. 'Of course, Jubilee. How slow can one get? I've got the perfect solution to the problem. Dolly would rejoice. Do you know I'm not sure she didn't know all along that this was what I'd come to think?'

20

June's first reaction when she was handed Steve's letter by the car-driver was to feel further depressed. Did she ever want to see Steve again after his recent visit - his bumptious and tactless words at the dinner table, and his precipitate departure? But there was a tone in the letter which intrigued her. She re-read the brief paragraphs. The tone was kind, concessive - but determined, she thought, just as she had always known him to be. The chauffeur had half-turned away from her and was apparently examining the south-west tower. She made up her mind. '*Voulez-vous m'attendre quelques minutes, Monsieur,*' she said. She went back to her room to change.

Feeling self-conscious in one of her Paris outfits, a navy and white ensemble, she went downstairs almost furtively, and was thankful not to encounter anyone. She got hurriedly into the back seat of the limousine.

It was nearly four o'clock when they reached Nice and joined the jostle of cars which still thronged the *Boulevard des Anglais* though it was nearly the end of summer. She had turned her back on the sophisticated life of big cities since leaving Paris. She didn't belong to it any more, she told herself, any more than she belonged to the money-orientated thoughts of people like Steve Addicot. Yet when she saw the palms, and ahead of them the reptilian grey dome of the luxurious Hotel Negresco, she couldn't control a quickening of her pulse, and breathlessness. What was it he had to say to her?

She had hoped to be able to slip into the cloakroom to tidy up, but he was sitting in the hall and, seeing her, at once jumped up like a schoolboy and came rapidly towards her. 'June, you've come. How wonderful of you - and you look, if I may say so, quite ravishing.'

She was sure she must appear stern. She always felt this on the rare occasions when people paid her compliments. She also on reflex asked if Jubilee was with him. She wasn't.

He insisted on tea, though she told him she never had 'tea' and had almost forgotten what it was. He flicked his fingers in mid-air to attract a waiter. She eventually submitted to a cream cake because it was easier than trying to refuse. While she severed cream-stuffed pieces of éclair with a two-pronged fork, he chattered about Jubilee, about how sad he was that it hadn't been practical for her to come, about his journey, and about the reasons why he found this hotel so agreeable. During one absurdly long passage he cross-examined her about her opinions - of which she had none - about Nice hotels and whether the Negresco surpassed the others. The one notable thing was that the Château wasn't once mentioned. But at a certain point she noticed that he was no longer giving his energy to this meaningless conversation. He finished his cake, dabbed his mouth with the paper napkin and seemed to take some sort of bull by the horns.

'June, I'm going to make a suggestion. The public rooms down here are, well, a little public. With my purpose in mind I did take a room *en suite* with a sitting room. I suggest we go up there where total privacy is guaranteed. If you'd rather not, naturally . . .'

She found the circumlocution amusing. What a quaint mixture he was of the brash and the over-sensitive. But as they mounted together in the lift, bereft now of even banalities of speech, her apprehension reached a climax. What on earth was he up to?

They sat in the luxurious room, narcissistically duplicated in a huge gilt mirror - the light-coloured Empire-style furniture, the gilded chairs upholstered in emerald green velvet. He came to the point with brutal suddenness. 'The fact is, June, I've bought the freehold of the Château Lamartine.' He left a pause, as if she would need it to absorb the shock of this. 'As you know, the previous owners are a rather scatty order of nuns, who scarcely realised they owned the place and left the collection of your rent to the agent. They fortunately weren't scatty, however, when it came to talking about price. They eventually agreed, with the agent's encouragement, that the repair and modernisation of their convent with the capital sum which would be forthcoming from the sale - with a large sum of money left over to invest as well - was better than owning two derelict buildings.'

June was beginning to get her thoughts back. 'But *why*, Steve? Why on earth would you want to do this?'

Steve looked sheepish. 'You may well ask,' he said with a titter, 'you may well ask indeed. I've asked myself over and over.'

'And . . .'

'And what?'

'Well, what answer have you given yourself?'

Steve abandoned the chair and marched to the window, which overlooked the beach and promenade and beyond it the placid blue of the Mediterranean. He put one hand behind his back in a Napoleonic gesture and addressed her, his face unseen. 'I'll be brief about my motives. As you know, Jubilee fell in love with the Château even before she saw it. For a long time now she's been trying to catch up on the things she was unable to learn at school, and working for an Open University degree. She was enraptured by your idea of artists and intellectuals living together in the way you do. On our return to England I increasingly thought that her rapture had become an obsession. She never said anything about the Château, but I knew it was constantly on her mind. The knowledge of it was there between us every day. As you may have surmised, Jubilee and I are very close. I slowly came to realise that our life together would deteriorate, without either of us wishing it, if in some way our connection with the Château was not renewed.'

'I see.'

'There's another aspect of the matter. As you know, I've been pretty successful as an accountant. Since our holiday here, during the summer I've been even busier, and among other things I came into a very large legacy. This, you'd have thought, would have been rather nice - a reward for long years of hard work. But probably because I knew Jubilee probably wouldn't care about the money, I began to wonder if I did see it that way. What would we spend it on?' Steve turned slowly and faced her. 'On the evening in which news of my windfall became public knowledge, things reached a sort of climax. I discussed things with Jubilee of course, but it was almost an embarrassment. It was clear she really didn't care one way or the other. I'd almost come to the conclusion I'd give the money away to charities, when later in the evening, Jubilee I had a miraculous idea which would allow

Jubilee, myself, you, all of us, to be gratified.'

He returned to a chair nearer hers and actually took possession of her wrist as if she needed leading somewhere. 'My dear June, I am now your freehold landlord. What I want you to do is sell me the remaining years of your lease - naturally at a price generously advantageous to yourself. In return I am - I was going to say, "I am willing, willing to allow you" - but that's quite the wrong phraseology. In return I positively *want* you and your friends to go on living at the Château, rent free, and with only the most minimal compliance with the ideas I have for developing the place . . .

'I've made my plans. First I shall completely restore the house and the grounds to their original glory. Then I'll set about running the Château on the commercial basis I've devised for it. Of course I shall provide all the safeguards against damage to the feelings of you and your colleagues, and absolute guarantees, legally established guarantees, of their tenancies, including of course, it goes without mention, your own.'

June was still bemused. 'A "commercial basis?"' was all she could utter faintly.

'I've told you that the last thing I am these days is mercenary, but in terms of natural economy, if the venture is to succeed, there must be some return on the very substantial capital I'm expending. Ends must at least meet. I've thought this side of things through very carefully. My idea is for an exclusive luxury hotel, one that will be discreetly famous, world wide - yes, to the rich. It will offer superb accommodation, a cuisine to please the most refined palettes - even French ones - *and a range of activities which have never to my knowledge been offered by any such establishment before.* I have to confess the project has taken over my life. Your happy compliance with my plans is the one remaining item to put in place. If you give it, I, Jubilee, I trust you - all of us - will soar.'

'"Compliance?"'

'Ah, my dear June, another speech deficiency of mine and you rightly seize on it. Compliance is quite the wrong word, implying, as it does, the overcoming of resistance. I can quite imagine that some of your colleagues may have some initial

166

resistance, but not, I hope, yourself, who has been in the business world and understands the workings of ordinary mankind. "Cooperation," "coincidence of vision," maybe are the sort of words I should use . . .

'Now I come to the crunch. You heard me mention "activities." What kind of amenities does a normal luxury hotel usually offer? Swimming pools, tennis courts, a golf course, fishing rights, skin-diving, in remoter continents safari treks and the viewing of exotic animals at their water-holes whilst sipping iced alcohol in an observation lounge. As you know, Jubilee and I experienced the latter after we left you earlier in the summer. Very enjoyable it was, too. But you see I've come to believe we've arrived at a moment in history when our leisured plutocrats are hunting for something new. Who knows but that at this very moment other entrepreneurs are not scenting on the wind this very same idea?'

June was essentially a pacific person inclined to a leisurely pace of life, but years in the administration of oil had conditioned her, when necessary, to the speedy despatch of affairs. Over her initial shock at having changed landlords, Steve was beginning to make her feel she was being entangled in verbiage, as she had felt when dealing with Miss Svensson's locutions on her arrival. 'What do you want us to do?' she almost rapped.

The change of tone had its effect. Steve abandoned his euphoric tone. 'What our clients want these days is academic and aesthetic interest,' he replied in an equally brisk tone of voice. 'I look at myself and see the prototype. I myself, fully engaged as I've been, have felt in idle moments a certain area of emptiness. If I have done, others much grander and richer, will have felt the same. And within the present boundaries of Lamartine, don't you see, we have it all . . .

'You have your own expertise, so does Lady Elisabeth, in the field of crafts. In the arts we have Alfonso and the Beerbohmers - Paul in music, Hortense in painting. To uphold the world of the intellect there is a fine historian and our place-name expert. All in their several ways can contribute unforgettable experiences to our clients. If I'm not very mistaken, given the international bush telegraph which exists among the select group of people we shall hope to interest, we'll only initially need to advertise in a few exclusive outlets. We'll soon be inundated with bookings.'

'You mean we'd all teach in some way?'

'Yes, you could call it that - and in exchange, it goes without saying, for no rent now being due. But leave the detail aside for one moment. Be assured, I've thought everything through. Let's just deal with the principle. What do you say, June? What *can* you say but yes?' Steve made an abrupt switch. 'Do you remember that bird?'

'Bird?'

'At our school. The one I was alleged to have let out of the headmistress's greenhouse. It threw us together, did it not, that childhood incident? I've thought that that liberated rook could be the centrepiece of our emblem. Its origin can be a secret between us.'

On her way back to the Château in the hired limousine, June's mind was drawn inexorably back to a morning at the charity school in Kentish Town thirty years ago, which she hadn't remembered for a long time. They would both have been about nine or ten.

She had known as soon as she arrived at the school and clumped down the wooden corridor to her locker that something was up. Wherever you went in that building, except in the headmistress's study, there was an odour she could still conjure, compounded of mud, sweat, ink, greens, and a clammy sweet smell of stew. But this morning there had been something else. Was it fear?

The chapel bell was tolling for prayers as usual - a single monotonous inescapably protestant summons, but she had caught sight of the teacher pulling on the rope behind the thin scarlet curtain. She was putting more into it than usual. Most of all, it was Miss Cleaver's face which told her some new oppression was imminent. She stood as always at the chapel entrance viewing them as they filed in as if to cleanse them of the contagion they had collected by being at home all night. A tint of excitement seemed to enliven her sallow cheeks.

They prayed, sang a hymn, then there she was, Miss Arabella

Cleaver, MA (Cantab), mounted behind the brassy eagle's beak. The pews creaked loudly in the silence her presence there caused. 'I have a disappointing event to announce . . .'

June had had no contact with Steve Addicot. It was a girls' school which took some dozen or so small boys aged under ten. The boys were an unruly ghetto, to be watched in the way wasps may be watched when having tea in the garden - with some vigilance but no fuss. She noticed him first because of the bird.

It was a young rook, still with grey fluff. It crouched motionless on the wooden slats in Miss Cleaver's locked greenhouse, eyeing them uncomfortably with black eyes as they stared at it from various angles outside the glass. Miss Cleaver had said its wing was damaged. She had left food - some chopped meat on a saucer - and a bowl of water. Neither food nor water had been touched by the bird.

During break when they were watching, unexpectedly the creature stretched upwards and flapped its wings vigorously. It was then June noticed Steve. 'That bird isn't hurt at all,' he said, 'it's just a fledgling that hasn't learnt to fly yet. Trust *her* to want to go and lock it up.'

June thought this might be true. She observed Steve and thought what a nice boy he looked - eager, humorous, direct, and in an engaging way innocent.

Later they learnt that someone had broken a pane in the greenhouse and the bird had gone. In their class, Miss Cleaver took some time - quite a long time, which drove an agreeably large salient into first period - to point out how evil this was. It was not just, she said, that a bird she was caring for had been sent to its certain death, which was cruel and thoughtless, but that an act of vandalism and burglary had taken place. She went to lengths to reiterate the amenities supplied by the Christian church, which allowed for the rehabilitation of sinners provided they truly confessed and repented. She set a kind of alarm clock for this process to work through. If by lunchtime, she announced, the sinner had summoned the courage to come forward, nothing further would be said about the incident. If not, she would be forced 'to take further steps.'

In that day's break rumours whispered in the classrooms

became public. A boy of course was the culprit. How could so barbaric an act be female? A girl in June's class and age group, who had witnessed Steve's statement about the bird, spoke of what he had said. Her revelation was swept up by some older girls and borne to Miss Cleaver. Steve was arraigned.

He denied the charge. But he had been given lines after school the previous day. What more obvious confirmation of his guilt was there than that he had wreaked his revenge in this way before going home? Once, twice that day he was plucked from class. The first time he came back dry-eyed, defiant. From the second interrogation he didn't return. He was seen being collected at the front door by grave relations. This door was never used by students except when they came for the first time with their parents.

He appeared the next day mid-morning, not a lot different. All the girls and most of the boys shunned him, a leper. Miss Cleaver had announced in prayers that after 'some persuasion' the culprit had confessed, so the incident could be put behind them. But her words and manner didn't connote that the full processes of Christian forgiveness had been deployed. Steve continued to deny having released the bird. 'I only told her I had to keep her quiet,' he announced. 'Now I wish I *had* let the bird out - she's a cow.'

June believed Steve. The weekend after, by which time Steve had been sent to coventry by the entire school, she saw him in the town looking with concentration into the window of a toy shop. She underwent a crisis of emotion and went up to him. 'You really didn't do it, Steve, did you?' she said.

His frank, open face swung to her. 'Of course not.'

'I believe you.'

He turned back to the window with a shrug of his shoulders. She remained standing beside him. 'Thanks,' he said after a moment.

'Would you like to come to tea?' she asked. Steve came to tea, she went to tea in return with Steve, whose mother June thought was a character. June found she didn't have a great deal in common with Steve. He was after all a boy and she was a girl.

Steve left the school at half term and went to the state primary.

But they kept up their acquaintance through their adolescence and even afterwards. They had always exchanged Christmas cards on which a few words were scribbled, and there had been the one occasion when Steve had visited the Château.

Now this. June was confused. Her logic told her that what Steve had done was totally unacceptable. Even if she were to agree, how would the others respond to being bought in this barefaced way? But she discovered a curious thing. This childhood incident had always been with her - in a way it was a bond still. At a moment during the journey she caught herself smiling. There was something so delightfully impish about Steve and, yes, courageous. She had always rated courage highly.

21

For months a band of workers overran the Château Lamartine, craftsmen of all the skills - carpenters, stonemasons, glaziers, blacksmiths, tilers, plumbers, sign-writers, heating and air-conditioning experts, fresco-restorers, roof experts, dry-rot specialists, master plasterers capable of repairing and restoring the most delicate historic mouldings, suppliers and fitters of kitchen equipment, landscape gardeners, horticulturalists. Even a specialist firm had been called in to restore the drawbridge to working order. Finally a white-overalled, slow-moving army of decorators took possession, both inside and out. In their improvised hats made out of newspaper, they lent over the balustrades, whistled on the scaffoldings, and stood in their perilous cages winched from their moorings above. A powerful smell of paint engulfed the Château as it emerged, spankingly, dazzlingly, from the cast-off dirt and decay of its crumbled past.

Throughout this period of renewal, Steve was energy personified. He and Jubilee originally stayed in the village *auberge*, but a quite separate and priority operation was to convert one of the outhouses, which had been some kind of a barn, into a comfortable modern dwelling for themselves. Only the outer stone wall of the original building was to remain. This was now finished, so Steve could be on the *chantier* day and night - *chantier* being a French word he had very happily added to his growing vocabulary.

By day he was seldom not occupied with supervising some aspect of the work or choosing new materials, and when the workers had gone back to their homes in Nice and the surrounding countryside, he was frequently to be found by himself planning a new feature, or discussing it with June and Alfonso. Though legally he was now master, he made a point of trying to take this couple with him at every stage. It seemed to him essential to avoid implying by the smallest inflection of speech, by manner or deed, that the change in economic arrangements in any way infringed their sovereignty on the cultural side. Alfonso, he found, was not much interested, but it was particularly important that he should take June with him. Steve had never been under any kind of illusion, whatever June said, that he would easily command the respect and cooperation of the other inmates. When he happened to bump into one or other of them about the place, they responded to his persistently cheerful greetings with bare civility. He didn't persevere with his greetings in Hortense's case indeed, for she gave no answer at all but tossed her comely blonde head aside in a gesture of haughty severance. Hortense, he suspected would prove a more residual element against his erosive bonhomie than the others. But Steve didn't despair, or for the moment care - there was far too much to do. When the work was finished, that would be soon enough to turn his mind to the problem.

Jubilee was in her seventh heaven, as well as probably all the other six, at being back at the Château. She continued to pursue her own studies with the books and instructions which were being despatched to her regularly from England, but immediately found a number of ways in which to include herself in the life of the place. She helped Lady Elisabeth sell her pottery in the village on market days. She assisted June with her enamelling and was learning the skill herself. Most remarkably, she had even penetrated the fastnesses of Damon's work. It seemed she was involved somehow in card indexing for him. In the extravagant descriptions she gave him of these activities of hers, Steve half-consciously diagnosed an avenue for his own eventual acceptance. Intellectuals and artists are quite possibly the most conservative people in society, he thought. They needed time - and maybe, yes, the offices of a very charming and beautiful girl - to adapt to change.

He was reminded, however, that an irksome problem lay in wait for him on the very day the external scaffolding came down, the interior of the house being already finished. He happened to encounter June outside the front door, which had been handsomely sanded and varnished in French style. She was just setting off to the village on her bicycle. He invited her to gaze with him for a moment at the front facade, and in what he felt was the intimacy of this moment he had an idea. 'I think, this being a red-letter day,' he said, 'I think we ought to celebrate somehow.

173

Shall we have a banquet tonight - on me of course?'

June held the handlebars of her machine and put her leg through on to the further pedal, shaping to depart. 'Well, you could ask people certainly, Steve,' she said.

Though as part of the agreement they had all retained their original rooms, the eating arrangements of the community had retreated from their old venue on the ground floor down to the kitchen, the one common room in the house which had, by consent, not been touched by the renovators. A second, modern de-luxe kitchen had been created on the ground floor for the new activities of the Château.

'We could perhaps christen the new hotel dining room,' Steve added.

To his disappointment, June didn't linger. 'Perhaps we could,' she said over her shoulder.

He decided to ignore the reservation lurking in her manner. He thought perhaps tomorrow might be a better idea for a banquet than today. This would allow him to think about food and drink with the newly arrived chef - and the delay would give him time to distribute formal invitation cards, which he would buy in the village.

This latter task he undertook later in the morning. He found some cards in the newspaper-cum-everything shop. They were of reasonable elegance, though written in French of course. He took care in the filling in of the bits which required handwriting, and himself went down to the old kitchen where he knew mail was now left. He left them in a fan on the kitchen table. The cards had R.S.V.P. clearly printed on them.

He had done all this without consulting Jubilee, for he was quite certain she would be as delighted at the idea as she had been on that other occasion, on their previous visit, when she had cooked the dinner. They had all their meals now in 'The Barn,' as they had named their new house. Eating a salad Jubilee had hastily concocted on her return from a morning with Liz on her now much extended 'Patch,' he told her.

They had created a charming patio on the shady side of the house, making use of an olive tree. They had also built a fountain, which was functioning well even in the dry season as a result of the massive repairs which had been made to the Château's water supply. Jubilee's reaction wasn't at all as he had expected.

Steve had noticed already that Jubilee's manner had undergone some small changes since their return to the Château. She was as excitable and enthusiastic as ever, as loving to him - her natural love, he guessed, reinforced by a degree of gratitude for the huge change he had made in his life - very largely on her behalf. But underneath these customary characteristics there was a certain gravity, a certain dawning certainty maybe, a confidence that left her not quite so sweetly open to novelty. Several times recently she had responded to things he said with a look, if not quite of reservation, of withheld knowledge. He had always seen their relationship in terms of a dance, an old-fashioned ballroom dance, in which he, the male, naturally chose the direction of their movements, and she with instinctive skill followed and subtly embellished them. Just occasionally recently he had felt it was she, not himself, who was leading the steps. It was so on this occasion.

'You can ask them but I doubt if they'll come,' she said with a small laugh.

'But of course they'll come. I've never known them pass up a good meal, have you?' He had an alarming thought. Did she think he was asking her to do the work, and she was less than willing this time? 'Our new chef's going to do the cooking,' he added.

'Oh it isn't that, Steve. If Chef wasn't doing the work, I'd do it willingly. What I mean is what I say. I just don't think they'll accept in their present mood.'

'You mean they're sulking?'

Jubilee fixed her eyes on a lizard which had performed a short run on the stones round the fountain and was now standing as stationary as a piece of costume jewellery in the sunshine. 'You think they're sulking, do you?' she said musingly.

'I'm sure of it. I've saved the Château, I've restored it to its original glory, I've created a safe environment in which their endeavours can quietly proceed and flourish, and they're sulking like spoilt children because "business" has performed it. Don't they understand that the luxuries of the priesthood, of the art world, of the activities of philosophers and historians and intellectuals, down the rungs of time, have ever been the result of business?'

Jubilee smiled. 'Why, Steve, you're getting quite lyrical.'

'Maybe,' said Steve, who had indeed become a little breathless and had a slight flush on his cheeks.

But these innovatory and interesting thoughts were punctured by a sound which both Addicots instantly realised as that of their well sprung, brand new, brass letter-box snapping shut after consuming a delivery. The couple looked at each other. It was Steve who rose.

It was, as he had thought, not the day's mail at this hour. He recognised at once the stylish calligraphy on the single expensive-looking envelope which lay on the tiled floor. With difficulty he slit the heavy envelope with his little finger. A sheet of notepaper akin to vellum was revealed.

'Mr Frederick Hapsburg-Trench thanks Mr and Mrs Stephen Addicot for their kind invitation to dinner tomorrow, but regrets that he is unable to attend owing to another engagement.' The letter was signed with a baroque flourish.

By the evening Steve had received no other R.S.V.P.s. He was sure they just hadn't bothered and would come, but because Jubilee remained doubtful he went up to June's room.

The Villanova's room, like those of all the inmates (including Alfonso's tower which alone of the four remained unrestored) was unchanged. It sported still the dismal hessian on the walls. June was sitting at the small table in the window painting a china pig. He said he was sorry to trouble her and he was probably being overanxious - she and her colleagues weren't perhaps used to formal invitations such as those he had distributed. But could she assure him everyone was coming? Clearly the Chef needed to know numbers.

June was obviously much embarrassed. He suspected it was this which made her abrupt. 'Oh I don't think any of them will be coming, I'm afraid,' she said. He asked the reason. 'The reason is they haven't taken at all kindly to the changes.'

He spared her the question as to whether, despite the ink she had implanted to their agreement, she was to any degree a party to this view. 'Oh dear, that's disappointing,' he said instead. June made no comment and went on painting. He left at once.

22

Hortense sat dispiritedly in the large armchair she kept in her studio, her brushes untouched, her easel empty of a canvas. She couldn't understand herself. This, to a person of her temperament, was the most worrying thing of all. It had in some way to be her work. To a true artist like herself, any strong emotion must relate to the state of her creative being. What else was of importance to her? Certainly not her redundant marriage. There was no doubt her creative being was in crisis.

She had worked on Lézards and its mysteries for over a year now, mysteries which she had so confidently felt she was penetrating and on the point of understanding. They seemed now further from her than they had ever been. Like a mirage to the desert traveller, the image seemed mockingly to advance ahead of her. For two days she had been mooning about like this. She hadn't been outside the Château grounds.

She stood by the large open window, gazing down savagely on the turning sprinklers which were watering the newly turfed lawns, and upon the gardener tending the new beds below, which had been planted out with thriving floribunda roses. A pair of workmen in white coats, the last of the painters, were painstakingly at work on the newly rendered balustrade which ran the length of the terrace. Was it the changes wrought by the unspeakable Addicot which troubled her? Surely they were responsible? Was not environment all-important to an artist?

At a deeper level, she knew, Steve was not the root of her malaise, merely its form of expression. Given an outlet in a different direction through which, released, her spirit would soar, of what significance to her was a man of Steve's calibre? It was love her psyche craved, not hate, a love which was burning there, pressed down by the workaday concerns of convention. What was she doing to release this healing gift?

The thought galvanised her into a sudden spasm of energy. As on another occasion not long ago when similar thoughts had inspired her, she moved briskly down from her attic workplace to her bedroom two floors below and sat at her dressing table. In a state of intense excitement she combed out her naturally styled hair so that it sprung outwards and the curves were emphasised. She mascara-ed her eyelids, rouged her lips. She was a highly attractive woman, she thought, thrown away. What was she doing wasting herself like this? Standing before her long mirror, she stretched back her shoulders, re-tucked her shirt and smoothed her waist and hips. She turned sideways and admired what she saw, first one way then the other. Art, to burgeon, must be fed. Feed it she would.

Liz, she knew, would be in the new carnation beds. She had said at breakfast that was what she would do today. Satisfied at last that she looked her best, she poured concentrated lemonade into a thermos flask and went down to the empty modern kitchen where she topped it up with water and dropped into it several ice-cubes from the fridge. In the deserted hall she took a last look in the new gilt mirror and for a moment imagined herself reproduced on the cover of Vogue Magazine, two Afghan hounds in attendance, leaning elegantly against one of the pillars in an ultimate *haute-couture* pose.

Liz, red-faced from her exertions and with two rivers of sweat pouring down her cheeks, was standing in the centre of the wide area of grey-green plants whose plump buds were just beginning to show gussets of scarlet. She had just finished adjusting the nozzle of a new high jet sprinkler Steve Addicot had provided. Hortense stood for a moment framed in the arched gateway through the wall hoping Liz would see and greet her.

But Liz was too absorbed. Hortense watched her friend turn away and march towards the tap on the further side. She saw her twist it on, then stand back, shielding her eyes against the sun, to observe the effect. There was a pause, a loud gurgle, and a powerful jet rose and began to turn a fine horsetail of spray over the almost blooming crop. Still, Liz didn't see her. Hortense had to make her approach, unacknowledged. She was only a yard or two away when Liz saw her.

'Oh, hallo Hortense, out for a stroll?' Liz turned back to her sprayer. It was clear she was in a good mood. 'God, if I'd only had one of these things before . . .' Her eyes were alight, Hortense noted, with this alien and irrelevant enthusiasm. Liz began to talk about the angle of the jet. Had she got it precisely right? Perhaps the outer perimeter of plants were not getting enough.

Hortense feigned an interest, and meanwhile observed the grubby plump hands hanging at Liz's side, the bedraggled hair, the proud wide shoulders which rivalled any man's, the fine bust which could so masterfully press into hers. She had to draw breath to counteract a sensation of faintness.

'Another five degrees upwards, don't you think?'

Hortense moved in quickly. 'I've brought you some lemonade, Liz,' she said.

Lemonade was not what was on Liz's mind. She frowned. 'Lemonade?'

'Yes. I thought you'd be thirsty.'

'Oh.' Mystified, Liz came to terms with the unexpected. 'Well, thanks, that's nice of you. I am thirsty actually. It's getting hot.'

There was an old wooden seat with a missing slat, which had escaped Steve's rehabilitating eye. To Hortense's delight, Liz accepted a break in her activities. Together they dragged the seat a small way into the shade of a young walnut tree. Hortense poured into the plastic top of the thermos. Watching the stout neck swallowing the liquid at a go with strong greedy gulps, she had a moment or two of intense happiness. 'You *are* thirsty,' she laughed, taking back the cup, 'another?'

Liz shook her head, wiped her mouth with the back of her hand and left a mark of soil on her cheek. She went back to the subject uppermost in her mind. 'It's going to be a super crop - not bad for my first attempt. I'm rather pleased. One sees the effect of proper nutrients. It should really make something for us if I can do the packaging right. I've got a buyer in London through a friend.'

'But that's marvellous, Liz. You are so - *habile.*'

'I don't know about *habile.* It's a question of equipment really, resources. I must say I'm grateful to Steve.'

This wasn't a subject, either, which Hortense welcomed. She scotched it quickly. 'I wish I could feel as successful as you are with my work,' she said with a languid sigh.

Liz was again looking at the jet. 'You are being successful, aren't you?'

'Since three days I am not touching my canvas.'

'That's bound to happen sometimes. Do something else.'

Hortense gave a little laugh she hoped indicated that foothills wouldn't do when mountains were under discussion. 'I'm afraid it's a little more complex than that, *ma chérie*. My difficulty is *spirituel*. You see, Liz - I feel you are so *sympa* and I can speak to you. You see . . . you must know . . . that my marriage with Paul . . .'

'Damn,' Liz said, 'now how the hell did I do that?'

To Hortense's disappointment, she saw that Liz was studying her thumb. There was congealed blood on it. Liz took a grimy handkerchief from her pocket, licked a corner, and began to rub the wound with it. Desperately, Hortense watched. Was it possible Liz could be so concerned with a minor injury at such a moment? She had a wild impulse to say it all, as she had so often imagined herself doing - to say she was lonely, that she loved Liz, that she wanted her love in return, that they could both love each other in a finer deeper way than either had experienced before, and that, if they did, all her own creative problems would be solved in a trice. But she was tongue-tied.

'Your problem, you know, Hortense,' she heard Liz continue, 'is that you don't do anything practical apart from your painting. You should take up embroidery or something like that. That would take you through periods of difficulty, I'm sure. You'll be all right in a day or two. It's probably just a *crise de foie*. It usually is with me. I take cenapods. Remind me to give you some later. Clear you out in a day. Now I must get on. Thanks for the lemonade.'

Out of sight of Liz, Hortense kicked a stone with her sandal and hurt her toe. She felt for a moment or two near tears. Her whole past, with its massive injustice, welled up. She recalled the lowly Auvergne village and its impossible provincialdom, the dowdy visionless school, father beatified in his ex-wartime, ex-Resistance-hero's role, which he re-lived in the fourth-rate bar he frequented. She remembered mother, her spirit eroded by toil and hardship, reduced to mere existence and the manipulation of the handful of clichés she used for speech. The day returned to her when father won a large sum on the national lottery, and she had the supreme joy of knowing that this meant her release from a life sentence. The time at the Paris art school was the best in her life, the only time she had really lived, when she had met Paul and was too young - and yes, then, too provincial - to realise that he, like so many other Americans with money, was imagining himself, with the help of Europe, to be other than his origins determined him to be for life. Since then, faithful to her talent, she had toiled on, meeting June one day, coming to the Château, and then, as she saw it now, running downhill. She had been dragged down, she reflected bitterly, by an early innocence and a harsh fate.

As she approached the stables she caught sight of Frederick ahead of her, bending in some long grass. She saw him put something into his trouser pocket. Seeing her, he moved guiltily and began beating the grass two or three paces away with a stick he had.

'Lost a franc piece somewhere here,' he began.

She didn't believe him, made no effort to help, and stood watching his phoney efforts. As he gave up with a charade of resignation, she noticed under the rotten bottom timber of the un-restored stable a chicken's egg. She smothered a desire to confront him with his petty theft. They faced each other in an unusual embarrassment. They only, ever, communicated over necessities, and there was no necessity at the moment.

She expected him to slope off with some shifty excuse. But to her surprise he stood his ground. Something, she saw, was going on behind those busy grey eyes which never quite met yours but which seemed ever-alert. 'You're not working today, Hortense?' he said amiably.

'You see I'm not.'

'Could I then take advantage of this rare event and offer you a cup of tea *chez-moi?*'

Out of chagrin, perhaps from curiosity, she found herself accepting. She had never set foot in Frederick's tower, let alone inside his rooms. She wasn't pleased to see that, despite the common resolve of the community to refuse to allow any alterations to their private quarters, this hadn't prevented the considerable refurbishment of Frederick's tower. The spiral stone staircase had been repaired. A handsome scarlet rope handrail had been installed, held by gold-coloured rings, and down the centre of the steps flowed a brand new carpet of the same colour as the rope. At intervals, expensive bronze sconces had been mounted on the wall. But she restrained herself from making comment.

By all appearances, the room itself hadn't been touched, however. It was a jungle of his junky things, and overall hung a disagreeable smell of less than hygienic maleness. 'You must pardon the mess I live in,' he said.

She didn't know what made her respond in the way she did, only that it was the result of an intuitive impulse. '*Peût-être tu a besoin d'une femme,*' she realised she had said.

He looked at her in amazement. 'You think so?'

'I am thinking so. You will become a *célibataire inguérissable.*'

While she sank into one of the armchairs whose inadequacies were uncomfortably concealed by the faded and stained tartan rug spread over it, he began to busy himself with the kettle. Having filled it, he placed it on an electric ring in an alcove, curtained with a brown blanket. He then regarded her with unwonted intensity. 'You have just made the most penetrating observation,' he said, eyes lowered.

'Oh, have I?'

'I have, as it happens, been thinking very deeply about my bachelorhood in recent days.'

'Frederick, you cannot be telling me you are in love?'

'I cannot allow myself to think so.'

'But - *quelle mystère* - why not, if you are?'

'Because there's an obstacle.'

'It is a girl in the village? There are *raisons de famille*

183

perhaps?'

'Worse. The obstacle is built-in, permanent, unscaleable, and a great deal nearer at hand than in the village.'

She was amused. 'An obstacle - to a man of your energy and ability?'

He sat on the arm of the other chair and seemed to take a decision. 'You know, Hortense, I have reason to think this could be a historic meeting between us.'

'*Tu le dites?*'

'Permit me to be personal. All of us at Lamartine - even, tacitly, I hazard a guess, June, who's been in a particular position of difficulty - have been united in regretting recent events. Even if, in our extremity, we might have been able to accept that some change and sacrifice were necessary, the *manner* in which the changes have been carried out has been unspeakably vulgar. You, I believe, have probably felt more keenly than anyone the debasement of our life which is taking place. Would I be right in saying that you might have an especially *personal* disgust in addition to the more generalised one we all feel?' Hortense was beginning to be perplexed. She blinked rapidly to cover the sensation. 'I see you don't quite follow me. I think I must be wholly frank with you. Hortense, it is a married woman I love. It is . . . Jubilee Addicot. I must at all costs detach her from that ageing philistine - who is crushing, with his monstrous materialism, that tender desire for culture which Jubilee has daily displayed to us since her first day here.'

'Jubilee?'

'She's a darling, an angel, the most adorable female I've ever set eyes on. I'm bewitched and possessed by her.'

Hortense remembered now that she had heard some gossip about this, which she had at once dismissed as an absurd irrelevance. How could Frederick, of all men, hope to catch such a fortified prize? Faced with the reality, she found other nebulous considerations taking shape.

Frederick also appeared to have considerations, rather less nebulous than hers. 'Hortense, what exactly is your attitude to Steve Addicot?'

'Mine? As you have suggested, *on suppose.*'

'Exactly. And, also as I suggested, felt more keenly than anyone else - with the exception of myself.'

'I don't know about that. I find the man *odieux* - that is all.'

'More than that, I have cause to believe. A great deal more than that.'

Again there was an interruption. During their conversation the grousing of the ancient kettle had turned into noisy turbulence, now to a smooth purr of billowing steam. Frederick rose and took down two cups and an ornate teapot from a set of china occupying one of the bookshelves. Turning his back on her, from the kettle he poured some of the water into the teapot then swilled it inside, holding the object in both hands. Finally, having tipped out the water into the basin, substituted tea, and filled the pot, he returned to her and in a moment or two began to pour into the cups.

'I think you may be forgiven for being perplexed,' he went on. 'As perplexed as I now feel embarrassed.'

'Why are you feeling embarrassed?'

'Why indeed?   Never did I think for a moment I'd ever arrive at this juncture. A corrupt act is a corrupt act, one to be buried at once by anyone with the power to do so - as I have the power to do.'

'*Merde,* Frederick, *de quoi parles-tu?* '

'That day, a year ago - we must cast our minds back - the first day of the Addicots' presence among us - do you recall it? Inadvertently I brought you and Steve together, and on the same day, acting out of simple hospitality I showed Jubilee the Château, the village and the environs.   For me it was the beginning of everything. For you . . .'

'Well, what about ""for me?""'

'For you it was also a traumatic day, wasn't it?   One reads between lines.'

She felt a tremor of uneasiness. 'It was a wasted day, certainly. The man has *aucun dons artistique,* let alone in other directions.'

'Quite so.'

'*A quoi tu veux en venir?* '

Frederick had remained standing since pouring the tea. He moved now to a shabby trunk against the wall which had on the top in faded black lettering 'F.HAPSBURG-TRENCH. 660' - a relic no doubt of his English schooldays. He opened it, rummaged, and came up with a large brown envelope. This he held across his chest with folded hands as he returned to her, as if it were some religious relic. It occurred to her he looked disagreeably triumphant.

'The village of Vigny-les-Pins would seem to a visitor, sleepy and backward. I've no doubt it's both those things. But I'm afraid it also contains its contingent of provincial venality. Anonymously, soon after that significant day - when you were out at Lézards with Steve Addicot, and I in the company of Jubilee - I received this package from a stranger, without comment. It happened most embarrassingly when Jubilee and I and Liz were having lunch in the village restaurant. Fortunately, an intimation that it might contain something regrettable came to me, and I didn't open this envelope in front of them. Why I should have been selected as the beneficiary of such a disgraceful intrusion upon decency I've never been able to imagine. I can only think the sender was some demented, anonymous moralist and thought I, as another inhabitant of Lamartine, was the person to contact. Naturally until this moment now - this moment of our common cause - I'd completely forgotten about the incident. I tossed the envelope into that trunk and wiped its memory from my mind. It's the most embarrassing moment of my life, one I have to force on myself, but I think now you must look upon the contents of this envelope. When you have done so, shocking as the experience may be for you, you'll come, I'm sure, to have the same thoughts about the paradoxical potentiality of the situation which I've just had.'

She took the envelope and drew out colour photographs - apparently amateur, probably Polaroid, but clear enough. The first was of a lake set in a pine forest upon whose glassy surface appeared two heads, the rest of their bodies concealed in the water, one male, one female. One head, she realised, was hers, the other that of Steve Addicot. The second photograph showed them both basking in the nude on a rock beside the lake, he face down, herself face up. The third was of herself waist-deep in the water and Addicot in full frontal nudity posed on the rock ready to make his jump.

Her breath had seized up. Destroy them, she thought. They must at once been torn up and burnt. It was blackmail. In some despicable way, Frederick was threatening her. She must destroy them now while they were in her hands. But perhaps because of her lack of oxygen she couldn't move.

It seemed Frederick was reading her thoughts. 'The photographs can of course immediately be destroyed,' he said, 'though I'm sure there's a perfectly natural explanation for what they depict, which makes that quite unnecessary. If you wish, they'll be destroyed at once. On the other hand, as I say . . .'

'This is *épouvantable,*' she burst out. 'Peasants hiding in the bushes, you accepting the disgusting fruits of such *désir lascif.* There was absolutely nothing that day . . .'

'Quite so. And that is the way any sane person seeing the photos would take it. I see it that way - the heat of the day, a natural response to it, your naturally liberated attitudes . . . On the other hand it occurs to me that, seeing the matter from a different perspective, by correct use of the disgracefully acquired and maliciously delivered photographs both our purposes could admirably be achieved and the purposes of our community served. No other motive than this could have spurred me to take this initiative. The photographs would have remained forgotten in that trunk . . .

'Hortense, it must now be dawning upon you that - if we were to adopt, let's say, a certain attitude - we have the means both to rid ourselves of our persecutor *and keep Jubilee.*'

23

It's so much nicer eating down here,' said the Lady Elisabeth, her cheeks bulging with a mixture of potato and savoury red pepper, 'it's much more convenient for the cooks.   I don't know why we didn't before.'

Hortense agreed heartily as, standing as close to the Marquis's daughter as she could get, she lit the second paraffin lamp and turned up the wick.   New electricity wiring and fitments had been installed everywhere, but the community adhered rigidly to the untouchability of what they regarded as their territory.   For safety reasons the electricians had refused to join the new system to the ancient arteries which used to bring light to this part of the house, so they remained unnourished by power.

'It is much more *intime*,' Hortense said.

'Intimate for as long as he doesn't get the idea of restoring an eighteenth century kitchen for the amusement of the guests,' remarked Frederick, who had finished his first helping and was returning to the large pan on the range to search for any food remaining.

'And requiring us to wear cut-away coats, knee-breeches, hooped skirts and wigs,' said Damon.

Damon's contributions to general conversation were rare. When they occurred, they were liable to be of significance.   All heads immediately turned to him.   'What's that you say, Damon?' enquired Frederick.

Damon didn't interrupt his eating.   He seemed more amused than concerned.   'From your daily scavengings for information, Hapsburg, haven't you observed the brochures which have been arriving in the post recently, addressed to Steve Addicot, from Woburn, Longleat, and several other such places?   He's clearly been seeking to plagiarize them, I'd say.   Now, this week, we have a series of parcels from a theatrical outfitters' in Nice.   I find it difficult not to connect the two events.   *Someone*, for sure, is to wear the garments.'

'Not us, surely?' said Hortense, breaking a fairly solid rule not to speak to Damon, nor indeed to add any comment to a context in which he had a part. 'Naturally, the clothes will be for the hotel servants.'

Damon's raised shoulders to express the comic possibility that this could be so, but that on the other hand it might be otherwise. 'You would surely feel at home in the costume of an Auvergne peasant, Hortense,' he remarked.

Hortense turned vermilion, and chose to avoid the sally. '*C'est incroyable.* If he thinks of practising such *infamie*, I shall be plainly refusing. We never agreed to such humiliation.'

There was another general movement of heads, this time in Frederick's direction as a legality seemed to be involved. 'I suppose it's just within the terms,' Frederick muttered gravely. '"Such cooperation as can be reasonably required in pursuance of the non-capital viability of the premises." I think that's something like how the relevant phrase would read in English.'

June seemed to shrink lower in her chair. She had only been picking at her food. 'I know I'm responsible. I should never have signed that document,' she said, shaking her head. 'It's no rescue, this, there'll be no end to it - it'll get worse. We'll all be driven out by such antics. I've let you all down. Perhaps we should go now when we still have our dignity. We could rent somewhere else with the money I got for relinquishing the lease.'

A heavy silence followed this statement. No doubt Hortense thought of the still unravelled mysteries of the Mont des Lézards, Paul Beerbohmer of the yet-to-be-made discoveries of his research into wrist-angles - which the upheaval of a change of venue must surely withdraw even further from his grasp. Maybe Damon thought of his books and the difficulty of their transportation, Liz of the many ramifications of the now teeming results of her husbandry, not to mention the welfare of her livestock. In the one tower, which had not yet been restored or roofed, lay Alfonso's rejected creation, like a rocket in its silo, so difficult to extract without the use of a helicopter. If such were the thoughts, it was Frederick who collected them and gave them articulation in a single phrase.

'We don't move from here - he does,' he said. 'The facts

are simple. The place is saved financially, it is true, but without the male Addicot on the premises, and with the addition of a little paint, the place is the same as it ever was. We have the same security of tenure - which your lawyer so ably arranged for us, June. All we've done is exchange a bankruptcy accountant for a nunnery as freeholder, and no longer pay rent. We now have the surely relatively simple task of removing the freeholder from the premises, and with him his absurd plans.'

The change in the atmosphere was palpable. Alfonso spoke in a jovial baritone. 'What we do? Suspend him by neck in my tower?'

'Nothing so extreme, Alfonso.' Frederick addressed all present. 'You'll recall that my efforts to deliver my share of the agreement reached at our last Conclave, dependent as they were on the cooperation of another person were not wholly fruitful. I'm confident now that, with June's permission, I'm in a position to honour my pledge.'

June was looking wan again. 'There can't be any physical violence, Frederick.'

'Nobody's talking about physical violence.'

'Nor the threat of it.'

'No such threat. I may take it I have your blessing then?'

June looked about her distractedly, her gaze fastening finally for guidance on Damon. But Damon's head was non-committally lowered. 'It can't be right for him to be here, if this sort of thing is to happen,' June said. 'It's not within the *spirit* of our agreement. And he'll never enjoy it. It isn't his scene. He has only come because of Jubilee, and . . .'

It was never clear just what June was going to add to this - possibly something about Jubilee. But whatever it was, it was manifest to all present that, Damon having given her no indication of his judgment either way, she had *de facto* at least given her consent to whatever Frederick planned.

Had Damon a reason for his silence?

Damon had never imagined he could work in the presence of a virtual stranger. A dozing or a sleeping Liz was the nearest he had ever been to accompaniment. He had never intended that Jubilee should invade his privacy in this way. It was to have been a morning or two in response to her urgent request that she might help with some cross referencing which he had got rather behind with. He had happened to talk to Frederick about this need of his, and Frederick had told her. She had approached him and it had seemed churlish to refuse.

Not only, Damon found, did Jubilee not disturb him, he found her presence at the other table in his room strangely soothing. She worked quietly - and as he now knew efficiently - and with an intelligence he couldn't have guessed at. She never spoke until he got up at the end of the morning, and only then to put to him any questions she had.

After several consecutive mornings he realised he must put a stop to it. Apart from other considerations, there was the question of payment. He couldn't continue to accept her services without some recompense. Money, even if he'd had it to offer, would have been inappropriate. But on the morning he had decided to speak to her she surprisingly pre-empted him.

'Damon,' she said, 'I really do enjoy doing this work for you, you know. I think we've both realised there are many ways in which I could be useful to you - not only with cataloguing information but also with typing, which wastes your time. Now, I can see - if this is so - that you might not want to employ me because of the question of payment. I don't want payment, but I can see it would be embarrassing for you if you can't reimburse me somehow. Last night I thought of a way. You could, if you were willing, teach me some history. Nothing could be more wonderful for me than this. I'd ask you for, say a quarter of an hour of your time each day I work for you. You will perhaps set me things to read. I'll read them and then have questions to ask you. I'd like to know for a start about the Crimean War, which comes into my syllabus.'

In her interest as much as his own, Damon guardedly suggested a trial period of a month. After that, either side could withdraw without giving a reason, and there would be no hard feelings. She thought this most fair, and they began. She worked every morning.

In a very few days, Damon came to the conclusion that

191

Jubilee was a fine example of a potential mind which the British education system had not only failed to cultivate but wantonly overlooked. In no way did he resent the time he gave to talking to her, whose length she was always protesting was far beyond their agreement. Very soon there was a new development.

Whatever Frederick was plotting for the discomfiture of Steve, he was equally active in his thoughts about Jubilee. Every day when they walked together, Damon was burdened with his tergiversations on the subject. Frederick's difficulty was of course to know if Jubilee in any way - the very smallest way - reciprocated his own feelings. How could he make an overt approach, he repeatedly said, without the encouragement of knowing he had a bridgehead? It wasn't long before Frederick saw an opportunity for himself - 'in the context,' as he put it, of 'their auld alliance.' Couldn't he, Damon, under cover of his professional relationship with Jubilee, somehow sound her out?

Damon had no wish to, but didn't refuse. Frederick frequently badgered him for news of what he called 'progress.' 'Anything this morning?' he would say, 'did my name crop up at all?' When nothing happened, Damon had finally to agree he would try to make a more frontal approach.

Jubilee's questions on her reading the following morning were especially abundant and complex to answer. He made a quick decision. If she would like to walk with him that afternoon, he said, he would give her the best of his mind on the matters she had raised. At lunch he told Frederick he had done this. Perhaps, he said, the more intimate circumstances of a walk would yield an opportunity. Frederick was delighted.

Damon had thought his conversation with Jubilee would start by being historical and that it would have to be himself who switched it to personal topics. To his surprise the reverse happened. The trees had scarcely closed the gleaming Château from their sight before she began. 'You know, Damon, I do so love it here,' she said. 'For me it's like starting a new life. I'm so grateful to Steve for making it possible. I think I'm really a scholar *manqué*.' She gave a small laugh. 'That is to say of course I haven't the brain to be clever - I'll never be a scholar as you are - but I didn't get what I wanted from my teachers at school. There weren't enough of them, too many of us, and most of the students didn't want to learn.'

She was so light and attractive in her pink cotton dress and wide straw hat, she made him feel awkward in his hot English clothes. He didn't know where to put his hands. To have them dangling at his side seemed wrong. He tried putting the fingers of his right hand between the buttons of his shirt. This seemed too studied. He finished putting both hands behind his back. This was also wrong - it made him seem more avuncular than he wished to appear.

'I think you could very well be a scholar if you wish,' he said.

She turned to him. 'You're just saying it to be nice. I'm a 'B' Stream Comprehensive girl.'

'What does your school matter?' He hesitated. He must not, tempting as it was, depart from his strict rules of accuracy. 'I think you can be a good historian,' he said carefully.

They relapsed into a long period of silence after this. This surprised him. He expected her to take up his mild and qualified compliment. But after looking grave for a moment and making as if to say something further, she seemed to dismiss the subject.

The rough tracks through the pine woods were usually narrow, as this one proved. Single file became necessary. He went ahead of her, only stopping now and then to hold back too rampant a thorn which had encroached, once to extend a hand she asked for as she scrambled down a protruding boulder. The perfume of rosemary and the even beating of the cicadas suggested their increasing isolation in a vast landscape not greatly concerned with humans.

Damon knew as they walked that he couldn't speak of Frederick today. What would they talk about then? Presumably the Crimean War. He had a thought which left him breathless for several paces. Supposing, after an hour or two together, they didn't talk at all about the war? Would he dare to think that she, like himself, had preferred to enjoy the occasion for some other reason?

He planned to descend to the bottom of the valley, to the riverside. This, after half an hour, they achieved. He chose a shady spot under some birches beside a pool of some breadth. Downstream they could hear the gentle rush of the water escaping over a mini-rapid of rounded white stones. The pool was calm, the water moving out contentedly into the wider space in slow thoughtful eddies. They sat on some grass, still green from the spring, and Jubilee took off her hat and began to finger the pink ribbon which ran round the crown.

'Damon, do you mind if I ask you something?' she said. 'In confidence.'

'No?'

'You're sure you don't mind? It's rather personal.'

'I'm pretty sure I won't mind.'

She looked into the water at their feet. 'It's about Frederick. I know you two are close friends and I thought perhaps for that reason you'd be able to . . . well, advise me. I really don't know how to put it, but you know how kind and attentive he was to me when we came out here before? On that first memorable day he gave up all his time to take me round and show me everything. And since we've been here permanently, it's been the same. At least once a week he's spent an entire day to show me things. The other day he wanted me to go up to his room to have tea. I'd never been in that tower, which has always especially intrigued me, and I accepted.

'Well, we had tea off that Viennese china he seems so proud of - apparently it's an heirloom. He was talking, as he often does, about his work. He'd just got up to get me a second cup of tea and had actually put it down on the little table he'd pulled to my seat. He was standing very close, unnecessarily close I thought, when he said something.

'He spoke very quickly and for a moment I wasn't clear what he'd said. Immediately afterwards he poured himself another cup and went to sit in the chair opposite, where he'd been before. We continued our previous conversation as if nothing had happened. Then - you know how it is, you get a sort of play back of something you've heard and not fully registered in the moment. I realised what he'd said. What he'd said was -

the exact words - "you must leave that dolt of a husband of yours and marry me."

'You can imagine how embarrassed I was. I began to question whether he'd really spoken those words. If he had, I argued, why had he done so in such a peculiar way? I mean, if he were in love with me or something, he'd surely have said so in the way men usually do. But the more I thought about it, the more sure I was I'd imagined nothing. What am I to do?'

Damon's mouth had gone dry. As a person who had always felt himself to be about twenty years older than he was, he was experiencing the most odd sensation that he was actually younger than Jubilee. He saw himself for a moment as she must see him - a not at all attractive man with a rather red face and spectacles and gingery hair - dressed in twill trousers and a lumberjack shirt which a schoolboy might have worn. He heard his voice, pretending to be the speech of a life-experienced sage, coming out like the utterance of some fourth-former acting too dramatically a role in the school play.

'I take it that you in no way reciprocate his feelings?'

'Of course not.'

'Then if I were you I'd simply pretend the words were never spoken, that you didn't hear them.'

'But if he were to repeat them?'

'If he were to repeat them, you'd know how to dispose of them perhaps?'

What amazed Damon was that she seemed to take his feeble advice as a voice from the clouds. 'Thanks, Damon,' she said, 'you've set my mind at rest. That is of course exactly what I must do, or not do. If I do nothing, I'm sure that after a time Frederick will come to forget that he said anything so foolish and we can get back to our normal relationship. I think, though, don't you, I should somehow contrive not to see quite so much of him - without hurting his feelings of course? I am after all quite busy now, helping you and June and Liz, and doing my own academic work. Damon, you are wise. I suppose I've been a bit innocent.'

Was Jubilee innocent? This was a question, among others, which Damon inwardly debated as they began the return journey. Was this episode, for example, to be taken at face value? That she had no feelings for Frederick was plain, but why had she chosen to say so to himself? Was it because, as she had said, he was a friend of Frederick? Did she hope he might somehow warn Frederick off an act of even greater embarrassment to her? This was not the most convincing explanation, but it served. He clung to it. An alternative would be either gross immodesty on his part, or, as was more likely, wishful thinking. It would also be an assault on Jubilee's no doubt loving relations with her husband.

On the way back, they stopped again to rest. It was even hotter and they had been going uphill. They sat together on a fallen log. 'You agree with what Steve's doing here, don't you, Damon?' she said with a directness he was beginning to expect from her, but which he nonetheless found devastating each time it happened.

'Er - doing?'

'Yes. The purchase, the renovation work, the way in which the Château will be made to earn its keep?'

He stalled for time. He stared at the ground between his knees. 'You mention three quite separate things there all in one sentence,' he said, grinning in case she happened to be looking at him.

'Well, take them in turn.'

'I'm sure June is grateful about the purchase - despite some difficulties.'

'But you - are *you* grateful?'

'We seem to be still here at least, still doing our work.'

'But I'm asking you if you're grateful. That isn't quite the same thing as you're saying, is it? Would you want to have to move all your books somewhere else, to disrupt your studies? Isn't it, for yourself personally - selfishly if you like - a positively good thing?'

'In most aspects perhaps.'

'Right. *That*'s settled. Now, number two. What about the renovation? The house was crumbling, there were rats. All those beautiful ceilings and mouldings were falling to bits. The nuns would never have done anything about the decay, and June wasn't in a position to. The work has caused you all inconvenience, I know, but it has been tastefully carried out, wouldn't you agree? There must be few country houses in France in such apple-pie order?'

Damon didn't know which way to look. The ground between his legs no longer seemed a haven. He turned his head away from her sharply, and fixed his eyes on the trunk of a tree. 'The work has been well done,' he said doggedly.

'And you welcome it, and what'll follow?'

He couldn't say more. There was what seemed to him a very long silence. During it his mind raced this way and that. What *did* he think? He had in an easy-going way added his support to the common feeling. He had scorned above all what had seemed the brash and arrogant assumption of 'business' that it, and the pragmatic values it embraced, could regulate and promote any aspect of life to which it chose to turn its attention. It was surely the *tone* as much as the reality of Addicot's revolution which was offensive?

It was as if Jubilee were reading his mind. 'I see you *don't* welcome it,' she said at last. 'And I'm quite sure you welcome even less what's likely to be proposed for the future.'

Damon risked a quick look in her direction. She was blushing lightly and, like himself, was staring at the ground in front of her, as if gathering courage.

'My husband means the best for all of you, you know,' she said. 'It isn't just for me he's bought the Château and given up his practice in England. He does really believe that thought, the arts, and beauty, need encouragement, and space and time to work in.'

'You mean you do.'

'Steve does as well.'

'It's patronage.' His tone had turned acerbic involuntarily.

'Is that a bad word?'

'Yes - if it's patron*ising* at the same time, as in this case.' He stood up. 'Perhaps we'd better get back,' he said.

She also stood up, alarmed. 'Oh Damon, I've upset you. I really am sorry. I had no wish to do that, I've no right to do that. I do understand what I thought would be your feelings.

It's just that I also thought . . .'

'You've every right to say what you have, but I must get back. I'll think more about what you've said.'

She tripped anxiously beside him as he began to stride in the direction of the Château. 'Oh dear, I *have* upset you, I know I have.'

'Not a bit.'

'But Steve does mean well,' she repeated, almost as a cry of despair. 'Deep down. He needs understanding, and if you all go on treating him badly I fear you'll drive him to do things he doesn't mean to. He's very obstinate, you know - and actually very *passionate.*'

Her distress confused Damon as greatly as had her plea for support. He couldn't deal with it. He left her by the pump (now pristinely restored, painted black, and ringed with flowers) with a gruffness which fringed on the impolite. Of one thing he was now sure. Jubilee Addicot was no innocent.

24

Steve wasn't greatly upset by the refusal of the Château inmates to attend his dinner party. Such a sulk was to be expected from people who had not yet understood they could enjoy the comforts of life at the same time as being producers of culture. He had only to persist, they would come round in the end. Now the restoration was almost finished, he would have time and energy to devote to the tantrums of his distinguished residents.

A couple of mornings later Jubilee left the villa early. It was market day and she was accompanying Liz and the donkeys down to the village. He had tried to get Liz to substitute the Peugeot estate car he had bought for such a primitive method of transport, but had met with predictable failure - with Jubilee as much as with Liz. Almost for the first time since they had been here, Steve endured moments of isolation. There were plenty of things waiting for him to do. Three girls were coming for interviews for the secretarial post he had advertised, in the afternoon he had to see short-listed applicants for the crucial post of hotel manager. But would it all work, he thought? Could his aspirations and those of the Damons and the Fredericks and the Hortenses of this world really be brought into happy communion? Had he the ability and the courage to pull it off? The silence dwelt heavily about him and suggested he might not.

Steve adopted his usual tactic for combating doubt. He would go to his office in the main house earlier than he had planned and get cracking, he thought. As he was about to open the front door, he noticed a large white envelope sticking through the letterbox. He released it from the brass jaws. His name, printed in small letters, appeared in the middle of the envelope. He recognised the type and realised it had been cut out of the new brochure he had just had printed, and stuck on the paper. In the top left hand corner in individual letters, also printed, were the words 'Private and Confidential.' He slit the top of the envelope and drew out a brief note, which was similarly written to protect the identity of the sender.

'You are not welcome here.'

There was a piece of stiff card inside the envelope. The letter had been nestled in the cavity between the card and the outside of the envelope. He drew out the card and a photograph fell to the floor. He picked it up and stared in astonishment. It took him a moment to realise what it was and who were the two nude bodies, one a female standing waist high in a lake looking upwards with amused expectation towards the other, a male, who was standing on a rock about to make the plunge.

Steve's office faced into the small area which was recessed into the rear side of the Château. Laid with attractive terracotta tiles and set with white iron chairs and tables, this was where the guests would sit under apricot-coloured canopies taking an aperitif in the warm evening air before moving into the ornate dining room beside it. The men were here today positioning the dwarf tamarisk trees, ready planted in white tubs, which he had ordered as additional decoration between the tables.

Sitting at his desk, he attempted to control the violent feelings which assaulted him. He would get rid of the lot, he thought, in a surge of rage. He would send them legal notices to quit. If they refused to go they would be trespassing on his property. He would call up the gendarmerie and have them put outside the main gates with their baggage. He knew, however, even as he thought this, that it was a daydream. The contract prevented it.

He went to the safe, and in frenzy seized the file which held the document. He took it back to the desk and, with an eye skilled in the rapid extraction of relevance from official and legal jargon, began to search for some loophole. At the time of signing he had been overjoyed that June was so willing to be cooperative. It had seemed the arrangement was so beneficial to all that it would be accepted in a spirit of goodwill. He hadn't given too much attention to the detail, leaving this to the English lawyer he had found in Nice.

He realised now, after reading two pages that, if he hadn't given attention, June, or her French lawyer, or more likely her colleagues, had. The agreement was stuffed with provisos protecting their narrow, ridiculous lives. He jumped impatiently to the last page where, he knew, his lawyer had set out his own wishes. Triumphantly then he isolated the phrase he was looking for - the one concession he had thought it right to call upon the inmates to supply.

'The Residents agree, in return for free accommodation (in such quarters as they at present occupy, defined in the schedule below) to render to the Landlord on two days a week and for a maximum of eight hours on each of these days, such reasonable services as, in the Landlord's estimation may best contribute to the well-being of his enterprise.'

'In the Landlord's estimation.' He remembered there had been some discussion about that phrase. June's lawyer had wanted another wording which indicated prior agreement on the form of the services to be rendered. He had held out. He had to have flexibility on this point, he had argued. Thank God he had.

He had them screwed. His fever receded a bit. If they wanted to play tricks, there were a great number more in the bag he could play. He imagined Frederick doing a day's work for once in his life, carrying luggage to the visitors' rooms, or Hortense pressed into acting as a waitress in the dining room. It had not of course been these roles he'd had in mind for them, but why not if they wouldn't cooperate and if it would help to bring them to their senses?

His discovery meant he spent a much more amiable day than he had anticipated. The girls who came for interview were not all he had hoped for, but one of them had presentable skills.

The afternoon interviews of candidates for the post of hotel manager went triumphantly well. The qualifications of Albert Tricot, which he had read in the application papers, had already struck him. In person the man was even more impressive. Quietly spoken (and with English grammatically perfect - and embellished, not diminished, Steve thought, by an appealing French accent) knowledgeable in depth on all aspects of hotel work, it was plain within five minutes he was the man for the job.

What especially pleased Steve was that Tricot seemed drawn to the place. Steve had warned himself to be on the look-out for a Gallic resentment against what might be construed as an Anglo-Saxon invasion of French territory, particularly as he planned to remain on the premises himself and look after finance and all external communications, promotion and so forth. His caution, he decided, in Tricot's case, was superfluous.

By late afternoon Steve felt almost normal again. The photograph was a prank, he was sure - another example of the puerility of these highly-strung people. He was convinced that June, a sensible woman, knew nothing about it and would be shocked and disgusted if she did. What he had to do was soldier on as ever. To show he cared about such trivia would only make them try on more tricks.

Albert Tricot had gone. He thought he would walk down the drive and intercept Jubilee, Liz, and the donkeys on their way back. About half way down the drive, he heard a sound in the woods sloping away to his left. It sounded like someone's laugh. Probably some villagers trespassing, he thought. Were they poaching? Poaching was the most likely explanation, though he couldn't think what anyone could hope to snare in this parched land. He stepped off the newly tarmacked road onto the bed of pine needles, which conveniently muffled his footsteps.

He heard voices. He thought there were two. Suddenly, he saw them, a male and a female figure sitting on a fallen log some hundred yards ahead with their backs to him. He realised with alarm that it was Damon - and Jubilee.

He dodged behind an outcrop of rocks. He noticed that his pulses were racing as if he were in face of some danger. He raised his head slowly. They were talking - that was to say Damon was talking - in a low voice. Jubilee's head was turned to him with an attention which suggested she needed to catch every syllable. He couldn't hear what Damon was saying.

Steve ducked behind the rock again. Why was he behaving in this cloak and dagger fashion? Why didn't he approach them naturally, say he had heard voices and had come to investigate? But he knew he wouldn't do this. All he could think of was that Jubilee had said she was spending the day with Liz in the village market and here she was elsewhere. It occurred to him for the first time in his life that Jubilee, as 'another person' had once done, could have been deceiving him ever since they had been here. Frederick had been one thing - but this Damon? A dark horse if ever there was one.

He remembered the photograph and his pulses broke out again. If Jubilee were ever to see that, what would she think? And if she were being tempted at the same time by a young suitor? To cut this disagreeable line of thought, he turned back from the rocks and began to retrace his footsteps.

Steve had been going to make some of the preparation for their supper that evening. One effect of the Château had been to make him wish to be involved in domesticalities. He thought he could put on the trolley all the things necessary for the laying of the table. He wouldn't actually lay it, knowing he would never get it to look as Jubilee did - pretty and appetising. He thought he might also peel potatoes, which he remembered Jubilee saying at breakfast would be featuring on the menu. But on his way to the kitchen he encountered an unexpected resistance to the idea. He'd had a hard enough day, Jubilee's activities were voluntary. Why should he assist in a duty which was hers?

This rude lack of charity shocked him. He didn't *have* thoughts of this kind about Jubilee. But his decision was not altered. It was as if it had been taken over, over his head, by a higher authority. He poured himself a double whisky, took the two-day old copy of the Financial Times which he had delivered especially from Nice twice a week, and went into the patio to read it.

Jubilee didn't come in for another hour. He heard her call as she opened the front door. He didn't answer or move the paper, which he held up in front of him until she actually entered the patio. 'I've had the most scrumptious day,' she said. She looked radiant, he thought, as she flopped herself into the other cushioned basket chair. 'We were swamped with buyers. Liz said she's never had such a good day. Sold everything - the donkeys had a burden-free walk up the hill. June did well, too. There were three bus loads of tourists. They descended on us like locusts.'

Steve felt he was looking at his wife through a slit in a castle wall. Clandestinely he waited, waited for her to explain why she had not accompanied the donkeys on the way home. She didn't mention this.

'I can't think why you don't phone me from the village to pick you up,' was all he could contribute when she finished her account of her day.

She laughed at this. 'But what you never realise, Steve darling, is that I love walking up with the donkeys.'

It was on the tip of his tongue to ask how she had managed to enjoy the company of the donkeys this evening when she had been with Damon, but he dithered and the opportunity was lost.

'I do like Liz,' he heard her continuing, 'I feel I'm really getting to know her. She's beginning to tell me things, intimate things - about her childhood and so on. I mean she doesn't set about it - I don't get it all in one heavy heap. She ekes out the information in interesting snippets, as she thinks of them - apropos of whatever it is we are talking about.' Steve noticed the word 'apropos,' definitely a new arrival in Jubilee's vocabulary. Such additions were an increasing phenomenon since she had been helping Damon. 'Obviously she was a neglected child. Her elder sister seems to have brought her up. Her father - the Marquis - seemed always to be away from home, and her mother led a wild social life. She said today she and her sister Gertrude used to sleep in the same bed - "like lovers", that was her phrase. They used to cuddle each other in winter because, though they lived in a huge house and were presumably rich, there was never much heating. Now you might think with someone else that this was a bit unhealthy. With Liz you don't. It all seems so natural. I think she's the most natural person I've ever met.'

'And do you think the other people here are "natural,"' he was surprised to hear himself say, in a tone which had the ring of cross-examination about it.

Jubilee didn't take it in this sense. She put her head on one side. 'No, I don't think they are. Not all of them. June is. June is sweet. I don't think June ever has bad thoughts about anyone. She doesn't seem to be programmed for bad thoughts. And she is so beautifully passionate about art and culture. Alfonso, too, is natural. He's a real artist. Nothing matters to him except his work - at least, other things are secondary. And he's so funny, he tells wonderful stories about Mexico. I go into his forge sometimes. If he's working, I might just as well not be there. He doesn't even notice me. But if he's feeling lazy, which I always hope he will be, he talks. Hortense isn't natural. I don't really understand her. She seems shut away. Paul is shut away, too - I think really his spirit still lives in America. Frederick . . .'

'Frederick?'

Jubilee smiled. 'I think Frederick is rather a rogue,' she said, 'perhaps a "natural" rogue, but I like him, don't you? He does have a kind of fervour, too, though I suspect not much of it is applied to his work. You might think Frederick is rather devious and dangerous, but I've come to the conclusion he isn't dangerous at all. What he really needs is someone to look after him, to take the place of his mother, who seems by all accounts to be rather a powerful sort of person and who probably pounded away his confidence when he was young.'

She stopped. The fountain tinkled in a teasingly monotonous tone. Did not its invariability mock the undulations of human emotions, Steve thought. A couple of magpies, pleased that the day's heat had surrendered a little, were chuckling in the vicinity. Steve had one of the most unpleasant sensations of his life. He had the idea that things were going on, like the magpies and the fountain, things which he had always regarded as inconsequential but which were actually what life was about. For a fleeting moment he thought that all the little things which Jubilee had always been concerned with was what life *was* about, and that he, travelling inexorably the road he had always travelled and thought so important, was moving away from it, that somewhere, way back probably, he had confidently taken a wrong turning, and in consequence finished up in a desert, featureless and empty, by himself.

He called upon rage to assist him. Frederick, no, he had always known Frederick was no contest, but he with the red hair and spectacles, he of monastic vows and silences, he of the book that was never finished and of the so-called intellect, he who had been so conspicuously not mentioned by Jubilee in her inventory of Lamartine characters. Here, surely, was something tangible to clutch, to hate?

'And Damon?'

'Ah, Damon . . .' Ah, Damon indeed. Jubilee looked quickly at her watch. 'Heavens, look at the time, I must see to the supper, you must be famished.' She danced up, seized the laden baskets, and disappeared. In a while he heard her humming. He suspected the tune was from an opera. Damon listened to opera. Steve had heard it coming from that pigsty of a room in the basement. The fact hit him like a stone.

He had drunk too much - the whisky, and now the bottle of light Provençal rosé Jubilee had selected to accompany her deliciously flavoured veal escalopes. Jubilee was becoming very knowledgeable about wines. She was talking at length on a subject which was driving him to the borders of irritability - needless to say 'The Eastern Question.'

'I shall begin recruitment tomorrow,' he said, interrupting a passage about some Turk having an affair with an 'odalisque' - whatever that was. She didn't absorb what he had said, still with her Turkish amours and taking a reflective sip of the rosé. He had to repeat the phrase.

She looked up. 'But I thought you began today, Steve?' she said, making the effort to come over to his thoughts, and resuming her eating.

'I don't mean domestic staff, I mean the inmates.' He gave the latter word more than usual emphasis. 'I intend to put them to work in the very near future. They agreed, after all. Our first guests arrive in two weeks. There'll need to be rehearsals. I've been thinking what I'll require them to do. There'll be excursions. Frederick, it seems, will be the perfect man for those. He looked after you very well, I remember, on our first visit here. Paul will be in charge of all evening activities, which must include music of course - *light* music. Hortense, Alfonso, June and Liz will give day courses in their respective arts and crafts. Which leaves Damon. History is not a subject which quite lends itself to a course, is it?'

Jubilee's eyes remained concentrated on her plate. 'He could perhaps take people on rambles,' she murmured.

'In this heat? I don't think there'd be any takers, Jubilee. No, not rambling, I think. Something a little more stationary and mute, is my plan. He isn't a very communicative person, is he? I was thinking about it today, what is the most stationary, mute profession there is - that, surely, of the commissionaire? One recalls them in the old days outside cinemas, dressed in red tunics and gold braid. You see them in our own age gladdening the pavements in front of large London hotels in long brown coats and smart beaver hats, whistling for taxis for film-star clients. I don't think the Château Lamartine can be complete without a similar figure. As a matter of fact, until costumes can be made for the hotel staff, I've hired some from a theatrical outfitter in Nice. One of these will do very nicely. Damon will have to smarten himself a little. He'll in fact have to be prepared to speak to a few ordinary mortals here and there on extremely normal topics. I'll require him on duty on the first and last days of our weekly courses. He will stand by the front door and answer any queries our guests may have.'

Steve had been carried away by this speech. He hadn't noticed during it how abnormally Jubilee had been behaving. 'You can't do that, Steve,' she said now, with a broad flush on her cheeks.

'I can't?'

'It's quite unsuitable for someone like Damon, it'd be most undignified.'

'If he feels it beneath his dignity, perhaps he should be considering his position here then.'

'Steve, you *can't* do this.'

'I intend to.'

'I think you must be doing it on purpose.'

'Really? And what purpose do you think I might have, if that were so?'

'I don't know. I think you may be jealous in some way jealous of Damon's intellect - perhaps you're jealous of them all here.'

'I have a funny way of showing it then, don't I? Buying up their decaying dwelling at hyper cost and putting them all on their feet. It might be a little more relevant to talk, not of my jealousy, but of their gratitude.   Gratitude is not something I've seen a great deal of recently.'

Jubilee softened a little. 'But that's just it, Steve. It's difficult for them to show gratitude at present, but I think they feel it underneath. I think they secretly envy you for your energy and enterprise. What they need is time. I think they all understand they must contribute.   The things you've thought of for all the others to do are excellent, and they won't in the long run disagree about them.   But if you do this to Damon, you'll upset the whole plan.   They'll all take sides against you, and all the goodwill will be undone.'

'They've taken sides already.'

'Only on the surface - and they're divided.   Given time I'm absolutely sure goodwill will prevail.'

'They're united in their condemnation of everything that makes their cosy little activities possible.   That much is stark clear. They're united, but I'll break them.   I'll teach them the lesson of their lives.   I'm the most cooperative soul alive, but in business I've never been taken for a ride in my life.   I won't be taken for a ride by this lot.   Damon for footman, full stop.   I've no more to say on the subject.   Will you pass the salt?'

25

Twenty-eight Americans descended the mobile staircase which had been married with the door at the first class end of the Pan American jet. Nearly all were over sixty and the great majority were women.

There was a noticeable variation in the agility of the tourists as they began to emerge from the plane. A lady of stout proportions in a pink silk dress and carrying a large handbag, paused lengthily at the top of the steps, giving herself time to bring down the spectacles which had been poised on the front part of her head. Only then, making firm contact with the handrail, did she, head down, commit herself to the perilous descent. On the other hand the sprinkling of males were conspicuous by their wish to appear spryer than they were. One, loaded with two sizeable pieces of hand luggage, took it too fast. Towards the bottom, he tripped, stumbled, half-recovered, and arrived on French soil on one knee. He danced up, chuckling, dusting his trouser leg energetically before recovering his fallen luggage.

'Hey, watch it there, Logan,' said a comrade behind him, 'you're not making it to the bar any faster that way.'

The party filed good-humouredly into the open doors of a transit bus and stood quipping until eventually it sneezed shut its doors and jolted into movement towards the airport building.

They submitted good-humouredly to the scrutiny of passports, to the wait they had to endure with the other passengers while luggage of a very varied standard rode up the conveyor belt and spilled clumsily on to the carousel. But at last, walking through customs un-accosted, they were returned to first-class status.

Waiting to welcome them in the crowded concourse was an interesting-looking male figure with a severe plateau of wiry greying hair and demonic features, this macho image being confused, however, by a wisp of lilac-coloured chiffon round his neck trailed stylishly over one shoulder.

'Ladies and gentlemen destined for the Château Lamartine, will you foregather here, if you please?' the man said repeatedly, holding a kind of standard on a pole announcing the luxury hotel in large Gothic lettering. As they arrived with their trolleys, the Americans were pleased to be relieved of their luggage by two porters who loaded it on to a large carrier.

'Are you our guide?' asked a lady with a Chicagan accent. She received a slight inclination of the head, not in her direction. One of the men was still less fortunate. 'What's the name, mine's Lew Kordelman,' he said, holding his hand forward. He received no acknowledgement at all. Glances were exchanged, a couple of heads were wagged sideways, but final judgement was suspended. This was Europe, where you couldn't expect things to be the same. They were here for the differences, weren't they?

Seated in the luxury bus, things became clearer. Cokes and other familiar thirst-quenchers were offered by the driver - a Frenchman in a blue overall. With ice tinkling in their glasses, their mentor then vouchsafed to speak. Turned away from them in his single seat beside the driver's, he plucked a microphone out of its socket and after a couple of soft blowings to test its cooperation looked straight ahead of him and began.

'Ladies and gentlemen, welcome to France. My name is Frederick Von Hapsburg-Trench. It's my pleasure and duty to convey you to the Château Lamartine where a very warm - I might say a hot - welcome awaits you. Let me say on behalf of my colleagues that it will be the object of all of us to make your brief stay with us an unforgettable event in your lives.'

These words were the prelude to a considerable speech. It was clear to the Americans after a very few sentence that this was no ordinary tourist employee. The cultured *British* voice, the appearance, the nature of the spiel, indicated this. It began with a complex but highly informative examination of the name of the town they had landed in - not Nice at all apparently in origin but 'Nikka', a Greek word meaning 'victory.' This suggesting they had already embarked on that 'cultural journey' the brochure had forecast for them, they settled more comfortably.

'Hey this is a *deal*,' whispered a lady. The judgement seemed to run round the bus. The pretty terrain, the glimpses of the Mediterranean behind them, the cicada chorus - which tripped a further Hapsburg-Trench treatise on how exactly this noise was produced biologically - prepared them for a collective response which, when the Château wound into view, outdid anything hitherto. 'Now ain't that sumthin'?' said one of the men. 'Done up like noo. Sam, just take a look at those towers.' By the front door was a magnificent fella got up in red - golden epaulettes sprouting from his shoulders, standing there like he was growing out of a garden pot.

The collective eulogy sub-divided into no less individual performances of appreciation as the guests were shown into their sumptuous apartments - that of the Shrebanskis for example. 'Now this place sure has class,' said Eunice Shrebanski as the door closed on a French boy dressed in brown corduroy breeches and a frilly white shirt, who had accompanied them. She ran a jewelled finger along the end of the four-poster bed which had curtains and all and the letters C and L entwined with suggestive amorousness at the centre of the intricately-moulded, pastel-coloured footboard. She opened the door to the adjoining bathroom. 'Take a look at this, Marty, it's solid marble.'

While his wife inventoried the luxury of their quarters, Marty stood at the window, whose slatted outer shutters, tethered at forty-five degrees against the afternoon sun, he opened fully. Could there be game in these wooded hills? It hadn't said a thing about game in the publicity and there was no sign of water anywhere which could possibly harbour fish, but he would bet a thousand to nothing there was something to shoot out there, maybe wild boar. He imagined coming at him an evil tusked snout released like a missile from the undergrowth, his cool and level aim . . .

'There's money here all right,' Eunice announced. She had re-entered the bedroom and was looking up at the chandelier which hung centrally. 'You don't get this sort of shine on cents.' Marty allowed his dream to be superseded. 'Sure thing you don't,' he said.

Eunice ran her arm round her husband's broad shoulders. 'Pleased you came then, honey?'

'Sure as hell I am. Like Von Freddie said, this ain't something we're gonna forget in a hurry.'

Steve sped about the place almost holding his breath. He couldn't believe it. A week ago, without consulting Jubilee further, by individually written invitations he had called all the permanent residents together in the salon. At the appointed hour there they'd all been, deployed about the room among the expensive new chintzes, waiting for him in silence. Hortense had extended herself on the *chaise-longue*.

After the briefest mention of the contract and the legitimacy it gave him, he had launched straight in. He didn't precisely give them the option to depart from his 'guideline suggestions', but did say that he would be very willing to listen to any comments they might want to make after he had read them out. Any sign of bolshieness - over Damon's role for instance - would have provoked him to pull no punches. But there was no dissent of any kind, they listened in silence. Aware of their apparent cooperation, he made a last minute amendment when referring to Damon's duties. He had been going to describe Damon as the 'commissionaire'; he modified this to 'welcome officer.'

There were no questions or comments after his address. When he had asked them to submit to him written plans showing the detail of how they would carry out their duties and indicated that was all, they simply rose in a leisurely fashion and filed out.

Returning to Jubilee later, he told her the meeting had gone off perfectly civilly. 'I guess they know which side their bread's buttered,' he added. Jubilee didn't comment and went on reading.

In the days which followed, Steve's spirits went up and down like a twin escalator. On reflection he did wonder if the silence at the meeting was worrying. Had it been sullen? Had it concealed a decision to boycott his arrangements after the guests had arrived? The worst of his fears centred on Jubilee. Neither she nor he had referred again to Damon's new role, but a coolness between them did not dissipate. Her daily sessions in Damon's room also continued. Had they discussed the matter, he wondered? On the other hand the 'plans of intention' came in very properly from June, Liz and Paul (who had agreed to a selection of Chopin Preludes for the first after-dinner evening recital he was to give), and June reported that Alfonso, not it seemed at his best on paper in English, had a 'sensible' programme of sculpture demonstration which she had been over with him. As his contribution, Frederick had mapped a comprehensive tour of the neighbourhood, which included lunch at the Hotel Negresco. All programmes had been, as far as Steve could tell, exhaustively - though not, he realised, over-modestly - costed. Liz put a P.S. on the bottom of the handwritten outline of her own elementary pottery class to the effect that Damon's suit 'seemed to fit him.'

These were omens it was difficult to take ill, but on the day Steve was on tenterhooks. He rose an hour earlier than usual and went on a tour of the guest rooms, which he had already done the day before. The housekeeper whom Tricot had hired had taken care of every detail. He also made another reconnaissance of the new kitchens where copper pans gleamed on the walls, and the brand new steel stoves, shelving, *bain-maries* and chopping boards, stood pristine and ready for use. He even visited the chapel, completely restored to its former glory, where an ecumenical service jointly conducted by the local curé and a protestant reverend from Nice would take place on Sunday morning. Would his luck hold?

Not wishing to intrude when the guests were arriving, Steve stationed himself in a concealed position on the roof from which he could observe the scene. He spotted the approach of his magnificent brand new bus when it was a mile off, a wink of sharp light, like a signal, from the blue haze that hung in the valley below. Soon it was beginning its ascent of their newly tarmacked drive. Just before it swung into view and turned on to the freshly-gravelled area in front of the Château, Damon came round the outside of the building resplendent in his uniform, pulling on white gloves. He saw a groomed and besuited Hapsburg-Trench descend from the door of the parked vehicle and lift out the hinged block which halved the drop the elderly Americans must negotiate. He stood handing them down, making each time a slight bow as if he had been born to the job.

It was only later Steve really believed it was all happening. As the dinner hour approached, from his office window he saw the guests arriving in the patio and sitting themselves at the white iron tables, amid the potted tamarisk, orange and lemon trees.

Waiters hired from the village and rapidly instructed, took orders for daquiris, manhattans, white ladies and dry martinis. When all had moved into the dining room he plucked up courage. Putting on the coat of the glossy blue summer suit he had bought to celebrate the opening, he walked across the patio and entered the elegant dining-room.

For a moment he felt a stranger among the pink-laced tablecloths, the gleaming silver, the monogrammed table-ware (the same C and L entwined), the carnations on each table and the two majestic arrangements of red gladioli on sideboards, not to mention the slick operations of the waiters, transformed by their white shirts and evening-dress trousers, who were handling the leather-bound menu and wine-list holders like professionals. Tricot certainly knew his business. Tricot himself, watching discreetly in the shadows of the screened exit to the kitchens with the eye of a croupier for the smallest departure from excellence, then winked at him across the enthralled diners.

Steve felt turned on by this simple act, like a light. It was all his, it came upon him - his vision, his executed dream. Where he had been invisible, he was thrown suddenly into relief. As if to confirm this, a lady, delivered of her order and having put away her spectacles into a 'purse' of Gladstonian proportions, was eyeing him with dawning knowledge. 'Something's telling me, sir, that you're Mr Stephen Addicot, to whom we owe all this splendour,' she said.

In this moment Steve knew what he had become, the resident owner of an exclusive international hotel of unique type. He only wished Jubilee were here to share the moment. But it was her evening for enamel-work with June, she had said, and she would rather not miss that if he didn't mind.

26

When Steve had asked Jubilee to put on an elegant dress and accompany him to the dining room, she knew how much he wanted her to say she would. She knew he wanted her to share the excitement of their first evening, after all his planning and hard work. It was mean of her not to go, but it was an important evening for her, too. She had been looking at her watch when Steve spoke to her. There was only another hour to go.

She was in the pottery early. In the corner stood the kiln, humming to itself. Thank goodness it hadn't fused this time, thanks to the new wiring which June had sensibly allowed the hotel men to install. If her creation were imperfect it wouldn't be the kiln's fault. She sat down, watching the kiln. Every few seconds it clicked, as if notching up its approach to success.

June came in. 'Keeping vigil, Jubilee?' she said merrily. 'This lot's going to be all right, I'm sure. But say a prayer.'

As Jubilee said one, June went to the switch, paused a moment, smoothed her hand down her hips, and plunged. The red light went out and the humming ceased. Jubilee jumped up. 'I can't wait,' she said, 'it's like opening a tomb which may be full of jewels.'

'Oh, we can't open yet. We'll have to let it cool down a bit first. The sudden change of temperature would crack the glazes.'

Jubilee subsided in disappointment. She knew this, but had forgotten in her excitement. They got on with other work. June was making the plasticine model for a dainty chain necklace, and Jubilee began to play on the drawing board with the idea of a medallion for Damon with the motif of a Sultan in the centre of a harem. She was sure he wouldn't wear it, but she wanted to do something to show how grateful she was for the interest he was taking in her education.

She had a good light-hearted relationship with June, she thought, one she greatly valued. But - it was funny - it only seemed to function when they were alone together like this. When other people were present, it seemed to go into eclipse and became quite insubstantial. It was, she supposed, because in at least one respect they were very alike. The sort of things they wanted to talk about were very similar. Conversely, the sort of things other people discussed were not ones on which either of them had much to contribute. In the presence of others therefore, their own sources seemed to dry up.

Tonight there were an unusual number of important, even menacing items concerning the community which seemed to be at hand, confidently expecting comment. But in a kind of conspiracy neither, skittishly, referred to them. They sent them to coventry. 'There's a regatta of water-boatmen going on in the new swimming-pool,' announced June out of the blue. 'They haven't lost much time moving in there.'

Jubilee laughed like a schoolgirl. 'I know, I saw them, too. How on earth do you think they got in? I love your idea of a regatta. They're just like that, or like pleasure-seekers in rowing boats on a lake. A pity, I suppose one of the gardeners will have to remove them.'

There were other similarly light-hearted topics. Carried away, they allowed the kiln longer than it needed.

Jubilee's pair of cuff links, her first finished enamel-work, were perfect. Meant to represent two scarabs, they were of a bright emerald colour, tiny veins on the shells picked out in a rich gold. June was as delighted as she was herself. 'Steve will love them,' she said generously. Jubilee thought he would, too. Privately, she hoped they might make up for her absence at his side this evening.

They were both examining the other items in the kiln, June's things, when they heard a noise outside. The door opened to reveal Damon, apparently bent on making an unusual visit to this room. Jubilee thought he looked sheepish. 'Thought I'd come and have a look at them,' he said gruffly.

She exchanged a puzzled look with June over his lowered eyes. Them? What did he mean? Then she remembered she had said something to him about her cuff links yesterday. 'But how nice of you, Damon,' she said. She held out the cuff links in the palm of her hand for him to see. He took them and examined them closely like a jeweller with a glass screwed into one eye.

'Both unflawed, well done.'

Jubilee found herself blushing. She had quite decided, after a previous incident in which he had paid her a compliment, and her nervous system had reacted in this same way, that it had absolutely no cause to. She would always have guessed that Damon was a level headed person who would pay compliments when they were due, and that no conclusion need be drawn from them beyond the matter in hand. But here she was again, apparently doing just that. 'June taught me,' she said.

'Hardly,' June said. 'You learnt by watching, and in half the time it usually takes.'

There was a long silence, the rigid sort, which closes the buds of the human spirit. Jubilee relied on June to provide some general topic which would rescue them. It was surely her duty, as a kind of third party? But to her great agitation she saw June was turning down the role. 'Well, I must be getting upstairs,' she said, removing the last object from the kiln. 'I really only came down to turn this off. And I've just remembered Alfonso's gone and ripped his trousers again. If I don't have them decent by the morning I'll be for it. Night, both of you.'

There was worse. Accepting this contrived departure with a content too apparent for Jubilee's ease of mind, Damon sat down back to front on one of the hard chairs, laid his arms along the back, and rested his chin on them. He faced her.

'You're very gifted, Jubilee,' he said as soon as the door had closed.

When he had sauntered up to Jubilee's pottery stall in the village those few days ago, she had accepted his offer to walk her home as quite natural. His afternoon walk had just happened to bring him through the village and the thought had occurred to him. Why not? There was an item of historical business to conduct, which was in fact what they talked about. Liz encouraged her to go. 'I can handle the mokes,' she had said cheerfully. Tonight there was no historical matter outstanding.

'I don't think I'm gifted,' Jubilee said. 'Eager, and rather starved in the past of things I want to do, that's all.'

'Gifted - hands and head in unison in the spirit of the Greeks. I envy you. If I have gifts they're in the upper region only.

It's a lopsided arrangement, and a handicap.'

She felt a trifle easier and found she could afford to give him a small laugh. 'Ah, but you're a specialist. If I'm anything at all, I'm probably an all-rounder.'

'All-roundering is the right thing to have. Specialists dig down and eventually disappear from sight.'

'But look at the treasures you find down there. Treasures are seldom mined open-cast.'

'Treasures the majority of people don't much care about having.'

In spite of her instinct that she should weigh her words, she felt a devil-may-care feeling descending on her. 'But you enjoy doing it - isn't that the point?' she said lightly. 'If everyone did what they enjoyed, there'd be no serious problems in the world. You're lucky to know what you enjoy.'

'I enjoy your company.'

'I enjoy yours, too.'

'Your company is different from any other here.'

'Thank you.'

She knew he was limbering up for something else. But she was entirely confident all of a sudden that she could keep it at bay. It was a dangerous pastime. What if she should stumble, she thought - not without a frisson. But she had a sudden confidence that this was an area in which her footwork was quicker than his.

'Come and have a drink with us,' she said. 'Steve should be back now from talking to his Yankees.'

She saw the shadow fall across his face, and she knew she had won this round anyway. 'No,' he said at last, back to his grumpy-sounding monosyllables. 'No, I shan't do that, thank you.' He rose.

She found herself taking guilty pleasure in this baleful reply.

27

Steve was to address his guests the next morning in the main lounge. Before the agreed hour of nine, all were present. An air of positive optimism prevailed. 'Here we are, rearin' to go, Mr Steve, sir,' said Alice Alighetti, an unmarried plastic-wear salesperson of more than pensionable age who was in her own words 'still going strong.' Miss Alighetti had already established herself as one who didn't mind giving her mind in public.

'That's darned right, rearin' for the old culture, said Logan Ford with singsong intonation. He was the energetic tourist who had arrived on French soil on one knee.

Steve's spirits kindled as he threaded his way through the brand new furniture towards the remodelled mantelpiece, on which a genuine Louis Quinze clock was just chiming nine. He had wondered if anyone would show, and here they all were, eager to start. Perhaps he should have been an American, he thought. He would have been better understood.

'Good breakfast? All settled comfortably, folks?' he began, standing with his back to the fireplace, where brass glinted and a large red azalea bloomed. 'Well now, you're going to have to put in a spot of work on this little obstacle course we've designed for you.' He harvested the smiles and titters from their eager faces. Wasn't this the difference between the Americans and the English? With Americans you are right until you prove yourself wrong. He switched to the serious.

'I'm going to tell you something. I was never a hotelier. I'm an accountant by profession. I suppose you might say I didn't exactly fail at being an accountant. I did bankruptcy work, and the British weren't so bad at going bankrupt until latterly. But you know, helped by my wife, Jubilee - whom I hope you'll very soon be meeting by the way, she was busy behind the scenes last night - helped by Jubilee, I got to feel I was missing something in life. I won't go into the whole story. Sufficient to say I happened to run into this bunch of people here, every one of them a proven master or a mistress in a chosen field, and got this idea. The community wasn't in such fine shape in the economic sphere - the building was falling apart for a start. Why couldn't I rescue the place, I thought, and at the same time do the world a favour. I banked on the fact there'd be a lot of folk like me - dare I say it, like you? - who have the same kind of feelings about art and books I had, who don't just want to hear music, read, look at pictures and the work of fine craftsmen, but also meet the men and women who produce these things, talk to them, get an idea what it takes to do what they do, and where possible to have a go at it themselves.'

When he finished his speech, he felt he had emerged into a new existence. Several heads were nodding. He started into the action straight away. He first listed the opportunities available to them, then said something about each of the people who would be handling the subjects, something of their achievements in the world of art and thought.

He got off to a good start, he thought, with the Lady Elisabeth Elder-Fynes - he gave her her full style, why not? Liz, he explained - in the relaxed atmosphere of the Château she would prefer them to call her that - Liz would introduce them to various techniques of ceramic work, give a demonstration of her own method and the materials she used, and get them moving on creations of their own. Liz, of all the residents, had offered her services all the week. She was also prepared to do a horticulture course, demonstrating her use of 'modest' resources in 'limiting climatic conditions.'

June Aguas de Villanova would take *aficionados* of enamel and batique work in much the same way, though she would only be available on two days. Paul Beerbohmer's contribution, apart from evening recitals on the piano, would be only for those who were already musicians and had attained some degree of proficiency. He would introduce his principles of 'manual posture' in musical production which, he claimed, might be applicable, with adaptation, to any instrument. June's husband, Alfonso, was also available, though probably to a minority of guests - those who might have interest in metals. Artists, or those interested in beginning to draw or paint, would join

Hortense Beerbohmer. Hortense would outline what she was trying to achieve in her own work and give two or three demonstration classes - on perspective, the use of colour, and so on - then set her students going on creations of their own which she would later comment on.

'And now,' said Steve. He smiled, and left a pause. 'Now I come to the intellectual of our community. You may be surprised to hear you've already met him. He is Mr Frederick Hapsburg-Trench, who accompanied you on the bus from Nice airport. Frederick is an expert on local place-names. We considered hard and long whether we could include this enthralling subject in our schedule of delights, but decided finally that it wouldn't be quite as suitable as some of the others. We were certain of this when Frederick came up with an alternative. Frederick is not only an expert in the derivation of place-names, he has a secondary interest in the medicinal properties of wild herbs - which are to be found in abundance in our surrounding countryside. After an introductory talk, he plans two 'rambles', which he assures me will prove of interest to all nature-lovers as they will include observation of fauna as well as flora. He will also - I quote him verbatim - "stray here and there into aspects of alternative medicine."'

Steve ended with an outline of the excursion which was to take place on one day each week, to be led, again, by Frederick, the highlights of this enthralling day being a visit to a perfume factory at Grasse and to the Matisse Chapel at Vence, lunch at well known restaurant in Nice, followed by a restful Corniche drive, ending with a 'patisserie tea' and a visit to the gaming-rooms at Monte Carlo's famous Casino. After this Steve sat down, and was strongly applauded.

The rest of the week needed detailed organisation. Yvette, Steve's secretary was called in, and a complex session of signing up took place. Fortunately the residents were flexible about times. By eleven the timetable was set, by midday the first introductory sessions were operative.

There was only one thing which marred Steve's content at the way things were going. Being a man with a capacity for self-criticism to whom forgiveness came easily, he was already wondering if his act of making Damon play the degrading role of commissionaire was vindictive.

The previous morning, before the arrival of the guests and when on his way into the Château, he had bumped into Liz outside the refurbished stables. 'Oh, by the way, Damon says his contribution will be to organise and accompany an outing to those caves somewhere to the north of us which have prehistoric drawings. He's got some plan to set them problems which they'll have to solve.'

Damon had left it until practically the last moment to send in his activity-plan, and through an intermediary, but he was cooperating. When later in the day, from his roof-top vintage point Steve saw Damon in his regalia emerging from the house below, his contrition was immediate and total. The man was doing what he had been asked to do, and more. He decided at once he had been jumping to too many conclusions about him and Jubilee. He would rescind the commissionaire business at once, he thought. Next week Damon would be included in the activities as he had requested and his own vendetta would be forgotten.

Had Steve been able to tune in to the various conversations which took place in the guests' dining room at lunch time he would have felt doubly pleased. An unmarried, not entirely unattractive blond woman in her thirties called Anita Ström who was travelling with her mother - certainly the only guest not in the older category - had spent the most 'electrifying' hour, she said, closeted in a sound-proof studio (a gift of Steve's to 'his maestro'). Mr Paul Beerbohmer, she described graphically, was a man with 'the most active and sensitive mind.' He had introduced her to a 'whole new tactile structure,' which she was quite sure was going to revolutionise her approach to piano playing 'at a stroke.' And apart from the 'intellectual content' of her lesson she had had such 'a deeply inward-going interface' with this plainly gifted *American* pianist.

Another table was ecstatic about Lady Elisabeth - despite Lamartine's relaxed atmosphere they couldn't yet manage the disennobled version of her name. What confidence, what style - and how beautifully she spoke English. (A four letter word uttered when a lump of clay she was pounding fell on her shoe had been expunged from memory, it could after all have been misheard).

Steve was not a witness to these eulogies, but the following day curiosity prompted him to follow three men he saw on their way to Alfonso's tower where they were due for a session on metalwork. By the time he entered the tower behind them, they had climbed to the first stage above him where Alfonso was working. One of the men, a parts manufacturer for one of the U.S. space projects, was clearly fascinated by Alfonso's welding expertise and by his deep understanding of metal tension properties, even though Alfonso's discourse was delivered in nouns and verbs unaccompanied by the usual leaven of other parts of speech and frequently with Spanish words whose meaning they had to guess at.

While Steve stood there they moved up to the higher stage. He replaced them on the middle one. As they clambered into what June had recently dubbed 'the crow's nest' - the highest part of the structure - he heard a more aesthetic conversation.

'You're telling me that's Gaa-d, Alfonso?' one man said.

'The great mighty, *el mismo.*'

'But the guy's in a hammock for Chris'sake.'

"Ammick, jes. He tek it easy.'

'And the ropes . . .'

'Ropes loose. God not care two buggers for cosmic accident, you think?'

There was a pause. Steve held his breath and counted to five. There was a burst of laughter. 'Why you cynical son-of-a-bitch. And he's got the old boy eating something. What the heck's that he's got there beside him?'

Steve feared the women might take a less catholic viewpoint when they heard about it, but he didn't have to worry. The story was round in no time. Alfonso, an artist, a Mexican to boot, his telescope a visible and indisputable evidence of his genius, was granted wide dispensations.

Hortense was also at work this morning. She had a dozen

women deployed about the grounds dressed in bermudas, sitting at easels and attempting to capture the perspective of the drawbridge or of one of the three (restored) towers. With the help of a pair of binoculars kept at her side, one lady was drawing a gargoyle crouching under the parapet at the top of one of the downpipes.

'Everything going well?' Steve dared to ask as he met Hortense walking briskly between two of her charges. Hortense's manner was no more complimentary to him than it ever was, but her very air of business-like involvement implied cooperation - on her own terms, she alone had demanded payment for her services, some part of which he had agreed to.

'Madame Beerbohmer sure doesn't give us any quarter,' remarked the lady she was on her way to assist. Hortense took no notice, but seized the pencil and began to make some brisk modifications.

It was a matter of time, Steve thought - time and tactful silence. The expertise of the residents was actively involved. Who could resist the flattery of being needed, especially when this was accompanied by economic security?

Frederick's room had two windows. On this glorious morning he was split between them. From one, with the aid of his heavy ship's binoculars, he had in view a tantalising lower section of Jubilee's bare right leg as she sat reading in the patio of her house. The view had alternated with one of her left leg. For a brief period he had seen both limbs together - one crossed leg had begun to swing backwards and forwards. His mind was concentrated on the fact that as the sun rose, the shadow thrown by the house was also moving. With it Jubilee might also move to another position which would be more advantageous from both their points of view. He was, he admitted, now quite obsessed. He would never again be at peace until . . .until what? The answer to this question was in a way the centre of his dilemma. Originally he had thought that a simple token of his esteem such as the one he had delivered would be enough to keep his wheel of dreams and fantasies turning for life. But recent events, and Hortense - wicked Hortense - had raised his expectations.

It had been touch and go - that encounter with Hortense in his rooms, as he had known it would be. But she was cooperating. And with Steve off the scene who could say what result *could* ensue from a suit firmly pressed? Hortense had been a great deal more encouraging than Damon in the matter. In fact he was beginning to doubt the extent of Damon's usefulness.

Addicot, the Arch-Fiend, was abroad. He had seen him enter Liz's pottery shed. A crunch of footsteps on the gravel below had him darting to the other window. The Fiend had emerged and was approaching Hortense's painters, dotted here and there on the lawns.

As Frederick gyrated the serrated wheel on the bridge of the binoculars and brought the self-satisfied face into sharp vision, he focused all his violent dislike. Cheap plebeian, cradle-robber, rich vulture who fed from the carcasses of nobler souls. He must be crushed, banished, and Jubilee rescued.

Could he kidnap her, he thought wildly - temporarily, during the heat of the crisis - to prevent a precipitate flight, to allow her time to realise it was freedom she enjoyed, not duress? But first things first, there must *be* first that crisis. He couldn't wait until the evening. He would have an audience of five, Yvette the secretary had said - just the right number. Not too many that a tone of intimacy couldn't be set, enough for the rapid dissemination of what he would convey.

Frederick realised he must radically amend the tone he had affected on the bus from the airport. 'Good evening, ladies,' he said benignly, as he approached them standing together clearly nervously in the porch.

'Good evening, Frederick,' said one of the ladies, 'we're looking forward to our ramble.'

'I'm much looking forward to it also. I'm flattered you should wish to hear what I have to say. Shall we?' He led them to one of the round wooden tables set about the front lawn, each with a gaily-coloured sunshade, which would accommodate six. 'I thought we might begin with a short informal discussion.'

They arranged themselves at the table. 'Ladies,' he began,

hands clasped in his lap and head bowed in a position he had practised in front of the long mirror in his room and was confident suggested humility. 'I'm going to start with a statement which may at once isolate me from your affections, thought I dearly hope it won't. I have the greatest regard for the medical profession. A grandfather of mine on my father's side was a doctor. But I have also the profoundest belief that God, in permitting, for his inscrutable purposes, the free operation of physical pain and suffering among us, has also provided the means, the *natural* means, of offsetting this evil. We have to my mind only to look around us, to experiment, and also to accept in this too severely scientific age that people who lived before us were not devoid of wisdom and have in fact found many remedies at which - yes, I'll state it - at which our noble medical profession sometimes looks askance. As I see it, God has laid for us a kind of treasure hunt. He has given us clues, and we must search. We must search the meadows, the woodlands and the mountains to find what he has put there for us. Our walk this afternoon *will*, I hope, be something of a treasure hunt.'

Frederick paused, and was certain he had his audience in the palm of his hand. A French Impressionist artist, he thought, might well have depicted the scene - himself the Messianic centre of a group of people receiving some Biblical vision, their faces turned up, lit with the evening light which had already that mysterious pink tinge to it.

The walk was a total success. Having imparted such knowledge as he could remember from his mother's many ministrations, they were soon listing to him the fruits of their own experience and the miraculous cures they had achieved. He had only to point out here and there a particular fern, the resin to be obtained from a rarer species of pine - once a colony of fungus at the foot of a rotting ilex, a distillation from which, on inspiration, he decided was a five hundred year old cure for leprosy - to maintain the illusion he was taking them for the walk and not the reverse, which was nearer the truth. In his second session with them, he thought, he would reveal the as yet unopened caseful of herbal remedies Mums had left.

By the time they got back, goodwill and confidence was running in full spate. There was no question now of their being intimidated by his intellect. It was their idea, not his, to offer him a drink at the same table on the lawn before they went in to dress for dinner. When Providence Casburger, a schoolmistress from Cincinnati who had come into a large inheritance, introduced the subject of the Château and what a wonderful concept it was, Frederick knew his cue was at hand.

He allowed a number of compliments, giving especially welcoming nods to those which referred to 'the community'. As he had been sure would be the case, at last there was reference to Addicot. 'What a fine man he must be,' declared Beezy Wallace, an Indianapolis housewife who owned a chain of teetotal restaurants. 'I know a bit about the hotel and catering industry and I can tell you the place you've got here is tops. Steve also knows us Americans. He knows our weak spots . . .'

'He should do,' said Frederick quickly. Simultaneously he found something very interesting in the middle of his glass. Squinting at it through one eye he raised it to the sunlight.

For a moment he was afraid his comment had been too quick, too softly uttered. But Eugenie Sperling, a research laboratory assistant, and not the leading conversationalist, took it up. She prided herself on listening for things other people missed. '*Should* do? What do you mean, Frederick?' she said, blinking,

Frederick did his best to look embarrassed. 'Eh?' he said distractedly.

'You said Steve Addicot *should* know us Americans and understand our soft spots.'

'Did I?'

'You certainly did, Freddie boy,' said Beezy who was rapidly settling back into being American again after a brief excursion into withdrawnness in Frederick's presence. 'Come on, out with it.'

Frederick lowered his eyes and affected extreme unhappiness. 'Oh, I mean that I understand Mr Addicot was once married to an American lady.'

'You mean to say . . .'

'That his present wife is his second, yes.'

'His first died?'

'Divorced.   I fear she ran away from him - or so one gathers.'

'Ran?'

'I believe she didn't feel - er - compatible.'

'And this explains why Steve understands us, you're saying?'

Frederick paused, he hoped with effect.   'You *might* put it that way.'   He gave the remark a particular edge, as if their question, like a prospector's spade, had struck on a very solid metal object but one which he preferred not to disinter.   'I must no longer keep you from your dinner,' he said instead, rising. 'It has been for me at least a most rewarding session.   I much look forward to our second.'

A satisfactory planting of the bomb, he thought returning to his room.   Could he say the fuse was now ticking?

The crisis in Frederick's life was duplicated by the one Hortense was undergoing.   There was first the weight upon her of her impending exhibition in Nice, now only three weeks ahead. Had her relations with the Mont des Lézards been in a satisfactory phase, she might have been better able to withstand the thought of this vulgar exposure to public gaze.   But they weren't.   In some moods indeed she felt the Mont de Lézards was drifting away from her.   If she were away for a fortnight, which she would have to be for the exhibition, when she returned to set up her easel before its massive fastness what further sense of alienation would she experience?

Her doubts about whether Liz would ever acknowledge, let alone respond to, the passionate love which lay waiting for her, were an even greater burden each day they were not dispelled. She took even more care over her appearance at times when Liz might have the opportunity to gaze on it.   She invested in a new heavy perfume which would penetrate, surely, the stoutest resistance.   Drenched in it, she sat next to Liz at mealtimes. There was no evidence Liz even noticed the lure.

Hortense took refuge from these adversities in a virulent hatred of Steve Addicot.   It was his invasion of their privacy, she inveighed to herself, his vulgarisation of their surroundings, and his assault on their creative psyche which was responsible for her malaise. Overcoming an instinctive dislike at any scheme initiated by Frederick, particularly one which exposed her, literally, in so stark a way, she had gone along with his idea of getting rid of Steve, only stipulating that the photograph could not be used except in an extremity and after further consultation with her.

An event then occurred which shifted her perspective. She was in her studio one evening - as so often lately not working but staring listlessly through the window. Her window commanded a fine view northwards over the escarpment on which the Château was built. About a quarter of a mile away she saw two figures walking together. She saw they were Damon and Jubilee.

While she watched they stopped walking and faced each other. Damon was gesticulating, no doubt engaged in making a point. His arms then seemed to freeze in the air. He lowered them and took a step towards the girl. Unbelievably, as they resumed their walk, he encircled her waist with his arm and for a moment allowed his hand to rest on her body.

Hortense knew that Frederick had enlisted Damon in the furtherance of his surely ludicrous ambition in Jubilee's direction. It was possible what she had seen was Damon carrying out his comradely task. But she didn't believe it, she didn't believe the gesture she had seen was in any way comradely. It had all the hallmarks of a caress, the act of a man who already had cause to think his advances found favour. Liz, as far as she knew, had been faithful to Damon in the time they had shared the room, but had Damon reciprocated? It was known he hadn't. Liz was ten years older than Damon, and there had been at least one girl in the village who had, some time ago, temporarily diverted Damon's affections. Was it not just possible, was it entirely wishful thinking on her part? Damon in love with Jubilee, Liz unmoored from Damon's arms, and adrift? Her pulses raced recklessly.

She made a swift decision. The photograph, she thought, with no provisos, should now be used as Frederick saw fit. No means were now to be neglected for Steve's summary removal from the Château, especially if this could be achieved while leaving Jubilee here. Very soon after this she had a further opportunity to contribute to this goal.

It happened that among her American art students was the almost silent Eugenie Sperling, who had twinned painting with her interest in 'herbology' under Frederick's tutelage. Eugenie had decided in the short time available to sketch as many of Liz's vegetables as she could. On her round the next morning, Hortense visited her as she sat in a secluded corner of 'The Patch', endeavouring to pay homage to a fennel plant.

Hortense found it more effective not to speak to her charges but to seize their brush or crayon and express with a few defining strokes some elementary point they were missing. She was doing this with Eugenie. Eugenie, she had noticed in their first session, had slightly more ability than the others and was less given to substituting babble for her lack of expertise. She was struggling with the shrinking perspective of the rounded bulb of the vegetable.

In a small access of generosity Hortense gave some extra moments of her time. She shoo-ed Eugenie off her canvas seat, addressed the easel, and scribbled in a few of those little tricks of shading that achieved the *trompe l'oeil.* While she did this, Eugenie sat cross-legged on the patch of grass beside her. She watched dutifully for a moment or two, then her attention seemed to slide. Her back as upright as a Hindu's, she put her hands together under her chin, indeed like a fakir saying his prayers. 'You don't like Steve Addicot, do you, Hortense?' she said.

Hortense was not often taken by surprise. *'Vous le dites?'*

'I've noticed when he passes you withdraw your spirit - like a mother calling in her children in face of some menace.'

This unexpectedly romantic image further perplexed the artist. 'I am doing that?'

'I don't like him, either.' Eugenie paused, and dropped her hands. 'Frederick told us yesterday he was once married to an American woman.'

'C'est vrai?'

'Say very vray, and - pardon me if I say it - but I have a feeling, Hortense, you know that perfectly well.   Could I be right?'

'*J'ai certainement entendu parler de cela, oui.*'

'Frederick also said the American woman ran away from him.'

One of Liz's goats began loud bleating on the other side of the wall.   Hortense was grateful for the interruption.   It gave her a moment to think.   Frederick had told her of this incident. He had said he had been careful not to over-dispense the poison. Wasn't this the chance to increase the dose?

'It's true perhaps that Steve has never been quite recovering from the experience,' she said carefully.

'She ran away from him, Frederick said.   Then he jumps into marriage with this coloured girl, who could almost be his daughter - if she were a different colour, I mean.   She's very innocent, isn't she?'

Maybe not so innocent, Hortense thought, but she didn't elaborate this.   'You are very *sensible* - very, how are you saying it in English - very penetrating, Eugenie,' she said instead.

'Oh, do you think so?'   Eugenie gave a little sniff of laughter. 'Well in that case I'll let you into a secret.   You see, I don't usually have very much to say, but I do notice things other people miss.   I think what Frederick was meaning was that Steve doesn't like us Americans - that he pretends to like us, but that really he's despising us all the time.   Is it possible, do you think, that Steve is punishing us for his bad experience - which he probably thoroughly deserved?   It's the way he laughs, so rapidly, almost hysterically.'

Hortense carefully put down the charcoal stick, and rose. '*Comme je vous ai dit, vous êtes bien sensible.   Je crois que vous avez tout compript.*'   Hortense put her head to one side. 'You are having quite a nice feel for the fennel, Eugenie,' she added.   'You must persevere with it.'

28

Two male members of the American group had made especial friends. Logan Ford and Marty Shrebanski and their wives sat together at mealtimes and the men met regularly in the bar beforehand. They were now joined by a third couple. Art Lipstein was a stout and amiable person of recent German origin. A retired funeral home director, he had become rich from the dressing up of corpses in a favourable light for their relatives' last view of them, and from other delicate massagings of grief.

None of the three men had taken the positive initiative for the holiday and their attitude to it was mixed. They had been most impressed by their joint session with the Mexican sculptor and entertained by his less than sedate attitude to art. The insouciant and chocolate-eating deity had figured more than once in their jovial bar discussions. Their day with Damon on the other hand, in which they had visited a prehistoric cave, had been less rewarding to them. Damon had talked to a large degree over their heads. The museum near the caves, with its casefuls of flints and bones, lacked drama in their eyes, and the 'problems' they had been set, which asked for possible explanations of things they had seen, left them scratching their heads. They took refuge in flippancy. Logan had suggested a smoothed cavity in the cave floor, which turned out to be a place for pounding grain, was a stone-age armchair.

On the evening of the second 'working' day, in which they had taken a bus tour under the guidance of Frederick Hapsburg-Trench, whom the three unanimously decided was a 'right ponce', they had had enough and were in a mood for diversion. Marty Shrebanski was the first down to the bar. Seating himself on one of the bar stools, he reached into his pocket for his cigarettes and drew out instead a small envelope which was edged with black.

He held out the envelope at arm's length, squinting at his name printed on it in gold lettering. He took out his spectacles.

It looked as if the letters had been cut out of something.   He opened the envelope.   There was a dwarf-size piece of writing-paper, also edged with black, with more gold lettering and, underneath, a group of rather active-looking black demons.

'If you would care for a little excitement, be at the drawbridge at midnight.   You have been personally selected for this experience.   If you value the offer, tell no one of your rendezvous.   Come alone.'

There was no signature.

Had someone been reading his thoughts about wanting a diversion?   Someone had obviously been into his room and slipped the note into his suit pocket.   He was about to show it to the barman, but at that moment Logan jumped through the door like a jack-in-the-box.   Marty held his fire and asked the barman for a double slug of Logan's poison.   'Take a look a this, Logie boy,' he said when they had both made an impression on their drinks.   Logan then discovered he had a similar invitation in his coat pocket.

They were ready for Art Lipstein when he came in, but Art beat them to it.   He had already discovered his envelope on his way down in the elevator.   Had all the fellas got similar invites then, they asked themselves, the women, too?   Scrutiny of other people in the bar revealed no extra excitement.   Exclusive offer to them then, was it, because they were friends?   They decided it must be and that they would keep it dark for the moment, especially from their wives.   It could be a lark.

After dinner, when they had completed a couple of rubbers and the women had decided on an early retirement, tired after the day's strenuous activities, they went back to the bar.

As midnight approached there was only a small party playing dice noisily at a table.   They slipped out.   There was no one in the hall.   What was it - some kind of black magic session?   A night hunting session, Marty had thought hopefully - a covert badger-cull perhaps.   An orgy more like, Logan had suggested.   Perhaps they had up some women up from the village.   More likely it was nothing so exciting - probably a practical joke.

Nevertheless, as the three slid as unobtrusively as they could through the front door, they were not without apprehension. Supposing it were an orgy they were being invited to participate in? Each one considered the practicalities of such an indulgence. Would they, could they, actually participate? How would their absence be explained upstairs afterwards?

Dwelling on these uncertainties in the windless darkness surrounding the Château was different from doing so in the brightly lit interior. As they left the welcoming arc of the front door lights, the woods surrounding seemed to heave towards them. The night was clear but close, and there was no moon. An owl hooted and was answered by its mate, as if signals were being passed ahead of them. The drawn curtains in the Château windows seemed to deny them access to all that was familiar. 'Ain't this just something?' said Logan, to test he still had a voice which could say things he recognised. They reached the drawbridge and stood there in a knot, facing all ways, as if at bay. There was nothing, except from somewhere inside the house the faint pulse of music from one of the bedrooms.

'It's a spoof, like I said,' said Art. Familiarity with death had perhaps conditioned him not to expect the unexpected. His companions were inclined to agree, until Marty saw the very small light - on the ground was it, on the far side of the drawbridge?

'Watch your step, Logie boy,' said Marty, not entirely in jest, as Logie bounded in its direction, 'you'll find yourself in the moat or down one of those watchercallits into the dungeons.'

The light was a small candle, little bigger than the kind you stick on a cake, wedged between two boards of the drawbridge. Behind it, propped against the closed heavy door, was another of the envelopes, addressed this time to 'The Three Musketeers.'

As Logie lifted the candle it occurred to Marty that someone just ahead of them had just lit it. It had hardly started to reduce the wax. Art opened the envelope.

'The chapel awaits you,' it said. There were more demons emphasising this point.

The men exchanged looks in the candlelight.   'I tell you guys, it's an orgy,' said Logie. 'French Moonies?'

Art knew where the chapel was. His old profession of undertaker had drawn him to look at it. He had stood there on the first evening imagining a catafalque, candles, a vigil perhaps - four men hired to stand, heads down, at the corners - discreetly piped organ music, anything which could be paid for.

As they approached the chapel a surprising thing happened. The place was in total darkness, but a small light seemed to grow inside, dimly visible through the windows. Then they saw, because of the light inside, that a small side-door was ajar. Again, Marty sensed the figure moving ahead of them. His hunter's instinct was aroused.

The light was another candle, a huge one this time at the end of the choir stalls. The newly lit flame was just taking hold and was steadying to a vertical plume as straight as a cat's tail. Its light threw huge shadows on to the walls. 'Someone's right ahead of us,' said Marty.

'John the Baptist,' said Art.

'It'd better be good,' said Logan, 'the build up's getting hot, though I ain't seen no dancing girls yet.'

On the altar hung a sizeable black arrow with a couple of demons hanging on to the shaft with both hands stretched above them. It pointed to the left. They went to the left, into shadow.

Suddenly, only a metre or two ahead of them, a bright light seemed to leap out of the floor. For a second or two it disturbed their vision, now accustomed to darkness. Then they saw that a large hinged flagstone was uplifted and propped by a bar, that there was a flight of stone steps going down and that the electric light which had been switched on came from some kind of a room below - a crypt?

The same thought seemed to occur to all three simultaneously. They looked at each other in the up-flung light. 'Two of us at a time?' suggested Marty. 'If someone removes that bar, no one's ever going to know we're down there, right?' Art volunteered to be watchman.

The other two went down. It was a small chamber, clean, un-dank. The stone had been recently refaced by the looks. It *was* presumably the crypt. At the altar end, between two of the six stout pillars, three on each side, had been rigged what at first sight seemed to be a series of montages. In the first, propped against a pillar, was a bronze eagle such as might be part of a church lectern. Through its breast and protruding the other side was an arrow, cunningly made from welded lengths of steel bar. A black cap covered its head. In the second a large placard was propped, covered with photographs apparently cut from newspapers and magazines. It didn't take more than a few moments to realize that all depicted war and suffering. There was one shot of planes apparently dropping napalm, others of mangled scorched corpses, ailing hungry children with pot-bellies, grief-stricken mothers, desperate lines of refugees. It was quite decisively a depiction of war. 'VIETNAM,' shrieked a black headline stuck sideways. There were others - 'KOREA', 'LEBANON', 'NICARAGUA', 'LIBYA', 'IRAN', 'PANAMA', 'MOGADISHU', 'IRAQ', 'KOSOVO'. Prominent was a large shot of a wall somewhere on which was chalked, 'AMERICANS GO HOME.'

A third montage was devoted to drugs, a fourth apparently to sexual depravity - the cuttings referred to notorious sex scandals, two presidential (one notoriously recent), to rape and violence, all American. But it was the centre-piece which drew the amazed attention of Marty and Logan most forcibly. This was sited between the two rows of pillars and intended to be a kind of altar. Again the artistry of a certain sculptor, whose identity they now recognised, had been in operation. What was plainly an old-fashioned Parisian *pissoir* had been raised above a very dirty and tattered example of the Stars and Stripes lying rumpled on the ground. By some contrivance water was falling from the contraption above on to the sacred cloth.

'Holy cow,' said Marty Shrebanski through clenched teeth.

Art was calling down from above, eager for news of what was going on. He was just about to be informed when there was a loud click and something went live. The words were strange, recorded certainly, but spaced and clipped.

'Americans . . . have . . . pissed . . . on . . . the . . . world.'

There was then a long peel of rapid laughter which went on for some ten seconds. Unmistakeably they were listening to the voice of Steve Addicot.

'Say, what the hell's going on down there?' called Art.

'Art,' said Marty, 'we're getting the feeling someone round here doesn't like us too much.'

Before they went back into the hotel the three Americans sat on the balustrade outside the front door. They lit cigarettes and held a conference. They decided it was the work of the nutty Mexican. Mexico was full of anti-American slobs. No question the arrow and the *pissoir* were his handiwork, and anyone who could rig up a thing like that telescope in the tower was crazy enough to do this.

'But the voice,' reminded Logan, 'that was Steve Addicot all right, how d'you explain that?'

'Could've been fixed,' said Marty, a bit snappish. He was beginning to think they had been made monkeys of in a way a veteran shouldn't be, and he wanted to be in his bed. 'It was certainly recorded, an audio-montage. You record a long tract of someone speaking then snip out the bits you want, easy.'

'It's true the guy'd hardly want to mess on his own act,' agreed Art.

They called it a night on this. Probably the best thing was to say nothing, except to wives, no point in making a fuss. Marty volunteered to have a quiet word about it with Addicot tomorrow. He should know what was going on behind his back.

But Logan had hardly finished telling his wife upstairs when the phone rang. It was Marty. 'Say look, there's a bit of a shenanigin developed. Eunice has thrown a couple of sticks on the fire. You and the better half feel like coming on over? We'll get up some room service.'

The night porter brought them beer. Eunice had something to say. She had struck up something of an acquaintance with Eugenie Sperling. On her way up to their room earlier they had met in the corridor and got talking. Eunice invited her in, suspecting Marty wouldn't be up awhiles. Eugenie had let fall what she had heard from Frederick and from the French artist a day or two before, and added her own diagnosis. When Marty came up with the news of what they had been up to this evening, Eugenie had gone but Eunice was ready to put two and two together.

Eunice was a homely woman, but it was not for nothing she was a leading light in the All Arkansas Patriotic League of Women. To the astonishment of the three men, their decision taken outside the front door was lightly swept aside as 'wishy-washy.' 'It's quite clear to me what this is,' said Eunice, 'it's a deliberate insult to our nation, carried out by the English proprietor of the place, if not by him directly on his orders. It's obvious since his first, American, wife took to her heels, he has nursed a deep-seated grudge. He's responsible, and in my opinion you men've got to do something about it tomorrow. One of you's gotta stand up during breakfast and make a statement to the rest of the party. I suggest you announce a meeting.' Her words were reinforced by Betty's fervent nodding.

The two men sat staring at the ground between their legs. Logan was the first to look up. 'What Eunice says does put another angle on things, Marty,' he said, 'wouldn't you say?'

Marty still thought it strange for a man to spend all this money and then put it at risk in this way, but psychology had never been a strong subject with him. It was a field in which he tended to yield almost a hundred per cent to women in general and to Eunice in particular. 'It's an angle certainly,' he said.

'And you'll act?'

Logan was caught in a cross fire of two female gazes. 'I'll certainly sleep on it,' he said.

Steve sensed something was afoot on his way to the office the next morning. He passed two ladies coming out of the breakfast room. He said good morning to them in his brightest early-morning way. 'Good morning, Mr Addicot,' they said in unison as if they had been rehearsing the phrase. Neither smiled, and the animated conversation they had been having before the exchange was discontinued.

Albert Tricot came into the office for their morning conference. 'They want the salon for a meeting,' he said in his attractive Gallic English.

'All of them?' asked Steve.

'Apparently.'

'What for?'

'I don't know. A waiter said one of them got up during breakfast and made a speech about something. I'm having the room set up right away.'

Steve didn't give it much more thought. They were probably considering some form of extra remuneration for the academic and artistic staff. He had a great deal to dictate to Yvette, whose shorthand speed was tested to the limit. He had just about finished the work when there was a strong burst of clapping from the direction of the salon, followed by some chords apparently being struck on the piano. Singing began and after a few moments it became clear it was the national anthem which was being lustily rendered. Steve looked in his diary which had a list of international festivals. There was nothing to explain this unusual display of patriotism.

Five minutes later there was a knock on the door. Two male guests wished to see him. He recognised them and, as it happened, knew their names. 'Mr Shrebanski, Mr Ford, a pleasure,' he said, leaping up and lifting another chair to place beside the one on which Yvette had been perched. 'What can I do for you? You all seem in a very patriotic frame of mind this morning.'

It was obvious that whatever he could do for them was going to take a few moments to unravel. They first wanted Yvette to go, and when this had been achieved took their time about sitting down. Then Shrebanksi gathered himself. 'We want an explanation, and it'd better be a good one,' he said.

'An explanation? Of what?'

'You know very well what we're referring to.'

'I don't, I'm afraid. Is everything all right? You've all had a meeting, I gather.'

'I'll say we've had a meeting, and it's been decided. If we

239

don't get a satisfactory explanation immediately, we want five star accommodation with meals at your expense in Nice for the remaining nights of our stay, a bus to transfer us there, and a transfer to the airport in two days' time. We're not staying here a minute longer to get this sort of treatment.'

'There's a misunderstanding somewhere, Mr Shrebanksi - a failure of communication. What exactly's worrying you?'

'Playing dumb, are you? Well I'll give it to you straight then. You've been married twice, right?'

Steve flushed. 'Yes, as it happens, I have. Jubilee is my second wife. I fail to see however . . .'

'Your first wife was American?'

'As a matter of fact she was, but . . .'

'And she ran out on you?'

'Really Shrebanski, I can't think you mean to be so personal . . .'

'That's right, she ran out on you. So now you want to take it out on the rest of us - that's just what they're saying. Well I can tell you right here, Mister, we don't take to it. Whether or not it was you leading us to that pigsty you've got down there last night is to my way of thinking immaterial. It's there, you know it's there, and you're responsible for it being there. I tell you, if this wasn't France I'd kick your arse and have you in court. You know it's an offence in the U.S. to desecrate the flag? You can go to gaol for it.'

29

Jubilee was pleased at the way in which the community had cooperated with Steve's plans and delighted that Steve had relieved Damon of the duty of doorman. Steve's natural goodwill had supplanted a temporary mood of fractiousness. But she felt an unease she couldn't explain. She had just finished helping June with her enamel class. 'Well, that seemed to go all right,' she remarked.

'Oh yes, all the *classes* are going all right,' June said. The stressed word indicated something, what could it be? She had an exchange with Damon about his visit to the prehistoric cave. He just chuckled and changed the subject when she asked him how it had gone. It seemed as if something were awaited.

On the day on which the Americans had sung their national anthem, it was one of Jubilee's mornings off from working for Damon. She was with Liz in the greenhouses helping her to water a bench full of orchid plants, which were to embellish the dining-room tables of the hotel. In the presence of Liz's common sense, she was convinced she was imagining things. Then, as she crossed the drive on her way back, feeling very hot and sweaty after her efforts, she witnessed what seemed like the entire hotel clientele clambering on to a bus whose engine was running. She thought it must be another excursion, but then she saw it was not the Château bus but the rather shabby one from the village, also that the people were lugging their own heavy suitcases. The driver was stacking them in the open racks in the under-belly of the vehicle. She was at once alarmed.

She stood watching. Everyone seemed to be in a hurry to go. There came a moment when all seemed to be aboard, and the driver, a Frenchman she knew, also from Vigny-les-Pins, was stowing the last piece of luggage. She approached. '*Mais qu'est ce qu'arrive?*' she asked in her now passable French.

'*Ils partent.*'

'*En definitive?*'

'*En définitive. A Nice.*'

'Mais pourquoi? Ils doivent rester encore deux jours.

There was an emphasised heaving of the shoulders as the locker doors were slammed and the key turned. *'Vous me permettez, madame?'* She stood aside while the man went aboard. As the bus pulled away, one or two female heads were turned to her with a definite content of pity. Most were held steadfastly in a forward direction without expression.

Her first instinct was to go to Steve, whose absence from this precipitate departure was the strangest and most alarming thing of all. Did he know about it? But remembering her earlier intimations she overrode her instinct. She thought instead of Damon. Damon would be working, but she decided to make an exception to the rule of not disturbing him.

She went at once into the hall, down the back stairs, knocked and entered his room in one movement. 'Damon - sorry - but what's happening? You *know* what's happening, don't you?'

He turned his head back sharply to his work, but she refused to feel guilty. She advanced and stood between him and the window so he had to look at her. He took off his glasses and began to polish them with his handkerchief.

'You've known something's been going on all the week, haven't you?'

He seemed to accept the disturbance and grinned faintly. 'I gather a slight case of national chauvinism has set in.'

'A case of *what*?'

'The guests have seen fit to feel their nationality insulted.'

'Damon, explain. What's this about?'

'You've spoken to your husband?'

'No, I haven't.' She found herself blushing. 'Not yet.'

'When you do, he'll no doubt give you a full account.'

'But I want it from you, now. What happened?'

He refitted the spectacles and made a fussy little movement with his chair. Despite her embarrassment she watched him like a stalking cat. She was going to get it out of him even if it was the end of their relationship. Sparely, he told her - largely by suggestion and hints rather than by straight narrative.

'I'm going to look,' she said as soon as she had got the gist of the 'exhibition' in the crypt of the chapel.

'You'll waste your time,' she heard behind her before she reached the door. She stopped and turned. 'It's was all dismantled during the night. Anyway, I doubt if you'll get into the crypt. The hinged flagstone leading down to it is locked.'

She returned slowly to his side. 'You knew about this before it happened, didn't you?' He was silent - guiltily silent, she was sure. 'You knew and did nothing.'

He hung his head and kept his lips fastened. Then he took up his pen. She was furious. No doubt he had taken part, too. God, what a lot they were, Damon included, a lot of schoolchildren. 'You make me feel sick,' she said before she left. 'All right, Steve isn't always as tactful as he could be, but he's done all this for you, and this is how you repay him. I'd've thought you at least would've had more sense.'

Poor Steve. She now felt only for him. As she rushed up the stairs she was faint with apprehension as to what he must be feeling - after all his effort and enthusiasm. If what Damon had told her was true, she would never speak to any of them again until they had grovelled and apologised. She burst headlong into the hall and turned sightlessly towards the door on the further side, which led to the office. As she did so she collided with two waiters standing in the centre under the great chandelier. She became aware they were greatly embarrassed - surely not just because she had bumped into them.

'*Pardon, madame,*' muttered one.

On the landing half way up the stairs was a boy wearing a long white apron. He must be one of the kitchen staff. She realised they had all been giggling about something. While she stood taking in the scene, the two waiters beside her vanished into the dining room, the boy on the stairs via the upper landing and the door on the first floor. It was one of the pictures which had absorbed their attention, the one where the boy was standing.

Steve had had a number of coloured Provençal prints enlarged and framed to adorn the staircase. Her heart pounding, she mounted the stairs. One of the prints had been removed, and a blown-up photograph substituted in the same frame. She saw with horror what it was.

Not knowing what she was doing, she went back to their house. She went up to the bedroom, opened the windows wide and drew up a chair so she could see the view over the pinewoods to the valley below. From here the roofs at one end of Vigny were just visible, and the belfry of the church. She concentrated her mind on the village and how she loved to go shopping in it or sell pottery and enamel work with Liz and June. She thought of the housewives with long *baguettes* sticking upright in their bicycle baskets, the *curé* in his round black hat, not too clean cassock and worn shoes, buying a cake for himself in the fragrant *patisserie* where there was always brisk business at any time of the day. She thought of the knife-sharpener, his feet peddling his painted machine at the corner of the square on market days, of the amiable clerks in the bank who always gave you the impression they were more interested in chatting to you than in money. She thought of the animals - the dogs, usually in twos and threes, who seemed to have a village community of their own and were usually busily up to some pranks together, the cats which basked on sunny window-sills, the mules, Liz's donkeys tied up at the fountain. All these good things had not changed, she thought. Such sense and beauty must surely prevail?

She heard a noise below. Steve must have come in. She waited for him to call or come upstairs. She heard him in the kitchen. She thought he was running the tap, having a drink. Then there was silence, a new kind of silence. Not the pleasant perennial one which surrounded them every day and which was broken only when the mistral blew and soughed in the pine needles. It was a human silence, which wasn't silence at all but increasingly a cry, a cry of distress and disequilibrium.

After a few minutes, she couldn't bear it. She went down. He was sitting slumped in one of the basket chairs in the patio, an empty glass on the table beside him. For a moment, out of the dictates of their normal relationship, his unusual dejection moved her. Until she remembered the picture. She stood there where she was and didn't speak.

'We're finished. We'll have to go. It won't work. They're too diabolical. I can't get rid of them, and if I stay they'll do it again. They're determined to get me out. Tricot can run it until

I decide what to do with it. We'll go home - which we should never have left.'

In spite of everything she suspended her own feelings. 'They're children,' she said. 'One or two of them are children.'

He sniffed with disgust. 'Infant prodigies in that case - prodigies of evil.'

'You're exaggerating, allowing an inferiority complex about "intellectuals" to warp your judgement.'

He looked at her in amazement - an amazement, she thought, which could be justified. It was true she had changed a great deal in the last weeks. 'You're telling me I've got an inferiority complex?' he said. 'What do you know about it? Do you imagine, just because you've been sidling up to that self-satisfied lunatic who thinks he's someone because he keeps his head buried in books all day, that you, too, have taken on his phoney wisdom? I'm the one in this place who knows about the world. They know nothing of it, they've lived off others all their lives. I've spent my life in the market place. I've dealt with the men and women whose energies have paid for all this games playing. I'm one of them. So don't talk to me about inferiority complexes, Jubilee.'

'You can't see that all you have to do is give way to them in certain directions - and begin to learn, as I have, something about what they're up to.'

She thought he was going to lose control. He stood up and faced her. The bare patch on top of his head had turned bright pink. His voice rose to something nearer a scream. 'You're one of them. You've become one of them. You're up that bloody Damon, who in my opinion is the ringleader. Like my first wife, you've let me down, betrayed me, ratted on me.'

She turned cold with disgust. '"Ratted?"' "Up?" Are those your horrible words? And you, I suppose, can lie naked on a rock with Hortense Beerbohmer and escape any kind of censure under those headings?'

He froze as if bewitched into stone, his eyes staring at her as if he were dead on his feet. 'What are you talking about?' he said.

'What I imagine every employee in the hotel is now talking about. I'm talking about the photograph of you and Hortense, which is framed half way up the main staircase. You're telling me you haven't seen it?'

He gave a kind of a whimper, then ran out of the house. She heard his footsteps beat away into silence. Through the window she saw him making for the Château.

Steve, beside himself, and in control of nothing beyond his determination to remove the abomination, rushed into the hall. Watched by one of the female cleaners, and another whom she quickly summoned from the salon, he raced up the stairs. He clawed at the frame, but it was screwed to the wall by invisible means. He gave a stifled shout, rushed down to the hall again, seized the bronze shovel from the gloved hand of the astonished salon cleaner, and remounted to the half way landing. He swung the shovel three times at the glass, shattered it, removed the photograph and tore it into small shreds.

By this time his audience had swollen to five, and a sixth figure was just adding itself. This latter was Mr Tricot, who was just in time to see the shredding operation completed.

'Take over, Tricot. You must take over,' he was surprised to hear. 'My job as well as yours - bookings, publicity, finance everything. I'll write to you. I'm leaving this madhouse now.'

At least the latter part of this statement proved to be true. Tricot made a determined effort to restrain his employer, or at least to delay his departure until he'd had more time to reflect, but Steve was adamant.

'I'll write to you,' he repeated, only a trifle more in control of himself.

Steve didn't even take a suitcase with him. He didn't speak again to Jubilee. He called for the village taxi to take him to Nice.

30

A heavy pair of naval binoculars in use at the Battle of Jutland on the German side were again in constant use on this fatal morning, observing broadsides, direct hits, sinkings, and finally an enemy retreat. When the engagement was over, Frederick Hapsburg-Trench, mounted in his tower, unlike his naval ancestor had no doubt a great victory had taken place.

He knew last night that his bait had been taken. Concealed in the chapel in the antique confession box, he had listened to the promising comments of the insulted Americans. Inspired by these, in the early hours, he had placed the photograph in the hall. Now, this morning, there had been this miraculous climax of events. First, walking under the open salon windows just after nine, he had heard Shrebanski's speech. From a further distance he heard the American national anthem being sung. He was aware from what he had overheard that some kind of a confrontation with Addicot was imminent. He couldn't be sure how this would go, but before midday from his window he had witnessed the total departure of the American party. Finally, beyond his most fervent dreams, he had witnessed the return to his house of the dejected Addicot. He'd had him in view, sitting alone in his patio, for a full ten minutes, then talking to Jubilee, clearly with emotion involved. Addicot's precipitate and apparently frenzied departure from the house, his destructive behaviour in the hall - so satisfactorily well-witnessed - and his blessed departure in a taxi, was surely a triumph not one of his colleagues could question. A later conversation with the urbane Tricot, which Frederick naturally conducted with an air of anxiety and concern for the well-being of the Château, completed his information. All the signs were that Steve Addicot had attempted to explain to Jubilee his innocence of intercourse with Hortense Beerbohmer and had not been believed. His business wrecked in a single morning, his second marriage surely in danger of shipwreck like the first, he had fled, leaving behind him unattended the beautiful prize.

Frederick thought of going immediately to Hortense. She hadn't gone out today and was almost certainly in her quarters. The Beerbohmer rooms, he also knew, contained a number of liquid items which would have been worthy of the occasion. But a single thought deflected him from the pleasure of celebration, for he knew human nature. Before the event, in the thick of the unpleasantness of Addicot's presence among them, all but one of their number had been effectively for Addicot's removal. Now that Addicot was gone, could that mealy-mouthed hyena known as the liberal conscience be relied on to stay away? He couldn't yet be sure there wouldn't be a counter-reaction.

He decided there must be no overt crowing. The business in the chapel could be said to be a collective act, which several people had known about in advance and which was therefore a common responsibility. But the photograph was another matter. This was better left as an anonymous act. He and Hortense must not be seen together in any circumstances which might implicate them. Tricot had told him that he had been charged with the running of the hotel. Surely things could go smoothly ahead now with a minimum of words and no fuss.

Resolving this, Frederick felt he could give himself to the matter which had greater priority in his mind. He knew, with a hunter's instinct, that in this matter as with the other there must be a period of lying low. Shock is an unpredictable state, and from some kind of shock Jubilee must surely be suffering, however great might be her underlying relief at being free from her unfortunate and unsuitable entanglement.

Later in the morning he saw her emerge from her house and make for the Château. He quickly went into the Château and emerged from a door which would ensure their paths crossed. As they did so, he kept his eyes lowered, only as they passed sending her a quick look of anxiety and concern. She wasn't looking in his direction and might not even, from the set look of her features, have been aware he was there, but Frederick wasn't disappointed. He had always believed in the power of telepathic communication. His glance of condolence, he thought, if not overtly acknowledged, would have been subconsciously registered. He was able during that day and the next to engineer three more occasions when his path crossed Jubilee's, so that similar subliminal messages could be passed.

Then he received some definite encouragement. As days passed and Steve didn't return, it became clear that Jubilee, far from being in a shocked daze as he had imagined, was playing an active part in the running of the hotel. Early every morning she was closeted with Tricot in the office. Jubilee, it seemed, had assumed Addicot's mantle. What could be better? If she did this, and a profit was made, Addicot would be less likely to sell the place, a possibility which had not occurred to him but which Damon had sardonically mentioned as a probable result of his departure. On the fourth day after *les événements,* he decided a move could be made.

About six in the evening he saw that Jubilee was in her home. He washed, changed his shirt and neckerchief, dabbed a little of an unguent he had invested in on his wrists and temples, and set off. There was a knocker on Jubilee's door, no bell. He didn't like having to use this - a loud clatter would seem to suggest forcible entry and violence - but there was no alternative. He raised it and gave two intimate raps. After a long pause, Jubilee came to the door.

He couldn't overcome the need to swallow at the sight of her beauty. In doing so he must have paused too long. 'Well?' she said, still holding the door-handle.

'Jubilee, I think I can guess something of what you may be feeling . . .'

'What is it you want?'

'I . . . I'd appreciate it if I could talk to you for a few minutes, inside perhaps?'

She looked at him as if he were a stranger. By all the saints, she had changed, he thought. Not in beauty - if it were possible she was even more radiant - but in mien. Where now was that lovely innocence? 'It'd better be brief then,' she said.

She turned on her heel and marched ahead of him. As he followed her in, in his confusion he left the door open. She led the way, not to the patio in whose cool fragrance he had imagined their conversation would take place, but to the rather stuffy sitting room which with its white leather chairs and pristine newness looked as if it were never used. She stood at the mantelpiece with her back to him, fiddling with an ornament.

'Could we - er - sit down?' As she didn't answer, he did so in one of the white armchairs, she remaining standing. This, he felt, put him even more at a disadvantage. 'Jubilee, I - we - do, all of us, I think, know what has befallen. What I have to say is . . . that we feel most deeply for you.'

'Do you? That's why you played this absurd prank in the chapel, I suppose?'

'Jubilee, I do believe there is genuine regret about that. It was, as you say, a prank. I don't think it was ever intended . . .'

'Lie number one. You had every intention that the outcome would be exactly what it was. Protected by that nasty bit of legality you made sure of in the contract, which prevents you from being booted out, you wanted to show that the Château couldn't be run as a hotel. Right?'

She turned and faced him, and he began to see what he was up against. But he had a dialogue going with her, he thought, at least he had a dialogue. He must hang on and widen the bridgehead. He summoned all his powers. 'Yes, Jubilee, I suppose that the organiser of the little episode did *herself* feel in some directions a little more strongly than some of us. But the general intention, I ask you to believe, was not so overt, nor so malicious. We've been a close community for some time. Some of us do, I concede, at times behave in a way that more sophisticated people like yourself must find a little - well yes - childish.'

He saw that what he said had some effect. She turned away again and he had a renewed view of her delicious neck, her slender waist, her perfect brown legs, which finished in a dainty pair of golden sandals. '*She,* you say?' she said.

'I beg your pardon?'

'You say it was a woman who organised that anti-American charade?'

'Did I?'

'You know you did. Are you saying it was Hortense? It wasn't Liz, and it certainly wasn't June. Are you saying Hortense did that *as well*?'

Frederick knew this was the most crucial moment - perhaps of his life - far more so than that fatal night in the village hotel when he had thrown a fit for Mums. He had a surge of confidence. He rose. 'I can't say for sure,' he said, and heard his voice - firm but understanding, as he wished it to be. 'One can only guess in such circumstances. All one can say is that Hortense does have a vindictive streak. She is after all very French.'

'What do you mean?'

'Forgive me, but you do ask. There was, there must have been, some sort of a quarrel between them? Steve, well . . . perhaps he'd thought better of whatever had taken place between them. Given this, it isn't difficult to predict how the lady in question would behave.'

Jubilee didn't reply, and with an excess of emotion of his own, which he knew he must control, he saw she was weeping. Her head bowed, her shoulders shaking, she was clutching the mantel as if it were all that prevented her from falling into an abyss. His passion overtook him. It was the moment, it must be the moment. He advanced, actually put his hand upon her waist and felt the flesh firm and warm under the thin garment. 'Oh Jubilee, my love, do not be sad. He isn't worthy of you. I love you, don't you know that?'

He enjoyed a moment of ecstasy, a moment he would surely treasure all his life. Then an extraordinary thing happened. He was aware that he had been sent reeling backwards. It was a moment or two before he realised why. She had turned violently, thrown back his arm from her waist and delivered a brutal punch into the middle of his face. His nose, he suspected, was bleeding - quite possibly it was broken.

'Get out of here, you slimy hypocrite,' he heard. 'Get out of the Château. I never want to see you again. You're malevolent and repulsive.'

31

Hortense was again in a state of high tension. She couldn't sleep. It wasn't Paul's presence which troubled her, she had moved him out of her bed permanently now. He slept either in the sitting room or on a camp bed he had erected in his ridiculous soundproof studio.

Was it then the *vernissage* of her exhibition in Nice tomorrow evening which kept her awake? What if none of the critics came, or if they tore her work ragged - or worse, if they didn't mention it in the papers at all? What if none of her work was sold and she was unable to recoup the outlay of her total savings, which Paul's meanness had forced her to put at risk?

She did have these fears, but knew they weren't central. She undulated fitfully between waking and sleeping and had strange visions of the Mont des Lézards, which took on gross humanistic forms. Once it developed a mouth between two of its giant strata. She realised it was Liz's mouth, laughing at her disquietude.

She slept finally and woke late. The brightness of the sun visible in the chink between the heavy curtains told her she had overslept. It was nearly nine, she saw from her clock. She leapt from the bed, bounded to the window and snatched back the curtains. Here she was checked. Blinking in the light, she had to shade her eyes to see what was happening in the drive below.

Damon, clutching a large package, was climbing into the passenger seat of the Addicot estate wagon. At the wheel, leaning to open the door for him, was Jubilee. Hortense jumped back to hide herself from view. She saw them drive off.

Hortense sat down on the bed, her pulses thumping like a pop concert. What did it portend, what *could* it portend except the most glorious possibility for herself? She dressed hurriedly and went down, almost hysterical with anticipation. Tricot was in the office. She put her head round the door and asked for Madame Addicot.

Tricot's handsome frame had been seated at the big desk. As Hortense entered, he rose with that automatic flunkey's deference of his.   He spoke to her in English indicating his total subjection to his Anglo-Saxon paymaster. 'She is not here, Madame Beerbohmer.'

'*Comme je peux voir,*' she snapped.

No sign of irritation appeared on the wax-doll features.   'What I intended to say is that Madame Addicot is not in the Château.'

'*Vous savez où elle est?*'

'I believe she has gone to Lyon, madame.'

'*Pourquoi?*'

Tricot sat down again at the desk.   At last, in the act of picking up his golden fountain pen, he revealed the tail end of an emotion. 'I am afraid I am unable to help you, madame.'

Idiot.   She slammed the door behind her.   He knew all right. But so did she, she realised suddenly.   The parcel?   Lyon?   She remembered Damon had once said something about an English publishing house which had an office in Lyon.   The incredible had happened - he had finished his book - and, more relevantly, surely he must also be making progress with Jubilee.

A thrill of anticipation passed through her.   Was it possible it could happen so soon, with such gloriously indecent haste? Why not?   Jubilee was young, Damon was young, Steve had been prised.   From Jubilee's point of view her marriage had probably failed a long while ago.   Steve's departure, and the reason for it, merely made the fact apparent to her.   The child should be grateful to her benefactors.

It was precipitate, but it was surely now or never.   She went first to the fields.   In one, four separately tethered goats grazed fanatically as if they had no time to lose, untended.   In another, dense maize foliage stood, silently glossy, no figure seeing to their irrigation.   The stable and greenhouses were similarly deserted.   She searched the public rooms, descended to the kitchen.   It was while she was in the kitchen she thought of a last resort.   Damon was away.   It was just possible for once Liz was enjoying the privacy of her own room during the morning hours. She went down the dark corridor at once and knocked on the door.   Liz's voice told her to enter.

Liz was sitting on a chair mending a torn skirt.   'Liz, I am looking for you *partout,*' Hortense said.   'I am *désespéré.*' Liz continued to sew.   She had about half a metre of thread on the needle and, at the apogee of her stitch, her right hand was level with the top of her head.   'You know it is the *vernissage* this evening?'   Liz didn't raise her eyes.   'You would not, I suppose, be accompanying me?   I have a car hired.   I am needing someone to help me to speak to the English-speaking critics, to the foreign press.'   A nice touch occurred to her.   'Maybe Damon will also be coming?   His silence can be so *distingué* . . .'

'Damon's not here,' Liz said quickly.

'Not in the Château, you mean?'

'He's gone with Jubilee to deliver his manuscript.'

She allowed significant pause.   'But he will be returning before . . .'

'They've gone to Lyon.'   It was a difficult moment, one that stretched Hortense's abilities to the limit.   Should she show sympathy, bewilderment?   But she was relieved of her dilemma. 'All right, I'll come,' Liz said.

She had to rein back her delight.   'You will?   Oh, *splendide*. If you come, it will be a success.   *J'en suis sûre.'*

In the car descending the road to Nice, Hortense exercised a draconian discipline on herself.   The unbelievably unbelievable had happened.   During a snack lunch, which they had prepared together in the kitchen and taken outside to eat, she had a further idea.   The reception wouldn't be over until after eight.   She had intended to return to the Château afterwards, but why didn't they have a posh dinner at her expense, she suggested, stay the night at a small hotel, and return at leisure in the morning?   Liz - in a mood of distracted resignation, Hortense thought - accepted.

They found a hotel without difficulty.   Liz had to change into the dress she had brought and Hortense put finishing touches to her appearance - thinking before that she would be returning that evening, she had already changed.   As they entered the small but elite gallery, Hortense experienced, in Liz's presence, what she was sure would turn out to be one of the most exalted moments of her life.

In the white, brilliantly lit modern room they were surrounded by her work.   On one side, engagingly hung, were the products of her earlier period, which Brabazon, the gallery-owner - a small man with something of Tricot's faceless courtesy - had suggested would probably be the pictures which would sell to what he called 'the general public.' On the other were the creations of her 'middle epoch,' which showed her transition to pure abstract. Upstairs was her mature work, which 'grappled', as the brochure put it under her instruction, with 'the cosmic mysteries of Jurassic land-forms.'

Brabazon approached, eyes closed, head bowed, hand stretched, in a gesture which suggested informed submission to artistic excellence. Hortense introduced 'a colleague and a dear friend of hers' - the Lady Elisabeth Elder-Fynes - who had kindly consented to help her with their guests. Brabazon at once asked Liz if she was also an artist, and showed no facial sign of being disconcerted when he was told, 'No, I grow things.' Only Hortense noticed his eyes flick to her fingernails for confirmation of this information. Brabazon, with an explosive click of his own finely manicured fingers then had one of the waiters open the first bottle of champagne. He lifted his glass. 'To the success you so richly deserve, Hortense.'

Hortense knew she looked her best this evening. Dress shops in Nice, in the season, were to all intents and purposes a microcosm of Paris. She had bought the dress for the occasion, silk, huge golden blobs on a greyish background, décolleté to show her ivory shoulders. She was drenched in newly applied Marcel Rochas. It was all far too much for a reception like this, but she intended it. No dowdy art-in-jeans image for her, slinking into a corner. The journalists were going to be pushing to speak to her. And Liz, darling Liz, how perfect she looked, too, for the role she was to play. Her old brown dress - did she really have nothing else? - but with just that wisp of discreet make-up which, with her cheek bones and flawless English complexion, hinted at lineage before she opened her mouth.

As they had entered the *Boulevard des Anglais* the sun had withdrawn behind a massive cloud. Like a power failure, its thousand reflections - on the sea, on the metal of the endlessly moving cars - had fused. A storm threatened. In the excitement, and under the bright lights of the gallery, Hortense hadn't registered until now how dark it had grown. The air was yellowish and crisp with electricity. 'Oh my God,' she said, looking towards the door, 'there'll be a storm. No one will come.'

Brabazon laughed. 'To the Gallerie Emile? *Ma chérie, n'inquiet-toi.* Jove himself will not stop them.'

She had to endure some twenty minutes while Liz and Brabazon discussed roses, which Brabazon grew in his Cap Ferrat villa. The first lightning fingered, thunder retched and boomed. The reception was doomed, she thought. Everyone would stay at home. The rain and wind came suddenly with brutal force. Palms and exotic trees in a park on the other side of the road, which had been static and perfectly visible, were suddenly leaning at forty-five degrees and were almost obliterated from view. The rain drenched down. Two rivers, one on either side of the road, swelled and ran every moment more swiftly. A cataract from the roof torrented on to the pavement outside. Then the first taxi drew up. Brabazon had his assistant take out a large striped umbrella.

Hortense's anxiety redoubled. One or two damp people, short on conversation, would be worse than none. Then, in a matter of a minute or two it seemed to her, the gallery was filling. And the rain, far from being a stay, turned out to be a stimulus. Laughter and raincoats shed, people turned a brighter animation to each other and the pictures. Soon the white-coated waiters were holding their trays aloft as they circulated, the noise became deafening.

Hortense was in the thick of it. She went upstairs. Many perhaps would never get up there, but she must be, she thought, at the side of her latest achievements. She needn't have worried. Critics, editors, cognoscenti of the art world - they all sought her out, cornered her. She was brilliant, she felt, sipping from her champagne glass, discussing, bantering, wheeling on her heel. 'Such texture', 'such penetration', 'such insight', she heard. 'Your landscapes reveal the mysteries of geological time,' said one well-known columnist already trying out his text. Once, as he passed , Brabazon hissed at her out of the corner of his mouth. 'Six sold already downstairs. I should have doubled the prices.'

Hortense was not tired. She felt her energies stirred to a pitch. She could have out-talked them all. But at length she became aware that the throng was less. More of the more sincere people, who had waited to see her in a less thronged moment, were coming upstairs to give their congratulations. Then they, too were gone, and she and Liz were downstairs. with Brabazon closing the door on the last departing guest. The waiters had begun to clear up.

'Well, my dear, you believe me now?' Brabazon said. 'It's the greatest success we've had for some time. They all came, you know - Des Marnes, Laporte, Michèle Garnier, the lot, twittering like budgerigars. They'll do you fine, they won't *dare* not to. Even Schultz. I saw his face looking at one of the recent Lézards, *trying* not to like it. I'm certain he didn't succeed - the sheer *weight* of your work. Now look, you're dining *expensively* with me, both of you. No arguments. I've booked the table.'

Maurice - he became Maurice during the meal - said he wanted to drive them back to the hotel afterwards in his Porsche. From Hortense's point of view, it was the one difficulty of the evening.

While coffee was being poured she slipped out to order the taxi - they were miles outside Nice somewhere along the Middle Corniche. When the page came to announce its arrival, Maurice got awkward. She had booked a taxi? Well then, send it away - someone else would take it. She had to whisk Liz to the ladies'.

'We 'ave to take the taxi,' she said, out of earshot of the attendant. 'He cannot be seeing the hotel.'

Liz didn't understand. How could something like this be understood by an English Marquis's daughter, whose thoughts attained the imprimatur of legitimacy by virtue merely of being thought? It doubled Hortense's discomforture to have to insist against her as well as against Maurice.

'No, Maurice, you are being much too kind already - and we are fatigued,' she had to blurt as they reappeared in the dining room. They left him perplexed, if not annoyed, standing by the door. Liz, equally bemused, had to follow.

Hortense was quickly able to throw off the indelicacy. The storm had retreated, though it continued to boom inland, as if from some neighbouring battlefield. Rain fell quietly but insistently. The wipers of the vehicle, wheeling rhythmically, soothed her. She was alone in the back seat with Liz, the night lay ahead of them in an anonymous hotel. What did she care about an upstart gallery owner? It was the night of her life, she thought, for which she had lived thirty-five years.

'Thank you, my dear Liz,' she said gratefully.

'Oh, that's all right, I enjoyed it.'

It was well after twelve. There was only one light in the hall of the hotel and an elderly male came out of an inner room to give them their keys. Hortense had imagined a bar where an exchange, oblique but nonetheless unequivocal, could have prepared the way. As it was, here they were mounting the stairs together, unprepared, facing the imminent banality of separated sleep in two single rooms, which weren't even adjoining. At Liz's door, Liz gave a leonine yawn. 'Well goodnight,' she said.

'Liz?'

'What?'

'Nothing.'

The door shut, the corridor stretched, the timed light went out, and she had to fumble for the dimly lit switch.

She lay awake for two hours, a distant clock tracking her wakefulness. The room grew unbearably stuffy. She got up, threw back the curtains and opened the window. Rain was still falling dismally into the deserted street below. A neon light switched on, off, maniacally, as if a child were playing a game. She knew what she was going to do. She had known for some time, only lacking the courage. Surely Liz would accept the lifelong devotion she had to give her? It was the moment now, she thought, when in a semi-conscious drowse such a secretly welcome visitor would be admitted. Liz had forgotten to lock her door. She was sure of this.

She put on her dressing gown, but not her slippers. She opened her door and listened. A muffled snore came from one of the rooms. She crept along the corridor in the dark. She knew Liz's door from its relation to the illuminated switch. Outside, she listened again. No sound from below.

Gently she twisted the handle and applied the smallest

pressure. It was as she had thought, the door gave, Liz had not bothered to lock it. She smiled in the darkness. Liz would not conceive of the dangers of an open door. Or, she allowed herself to consider for a wild moment of ecstasy, could it have been deliberate? She felt her pulses, battering her throat and wrists, must be audible. She heard Liz's breath, deep and even, on the other side of the room. With both hands she closed the door behind her.

She approached the bed. How to wake and yet not alarm her? How to control her own now trembling body? She knelt by the bed, slipped the dressing gown from her shoulders and pulled the nightdress over her head. Static electricity flickered dryly. Slowly she infiltrated her hand into the warmth. She was so close she could feel Liz's breath on her hand. She encountered the naked broad shoulder and travelled onward, under the nightdress, to that swelling breast.

'Liz, *ma chérie*, it is me, your Hortense.'

Liz started up. 'Who's there?' Roughly, she pulled away to the other side of the bed. A light went on and, bent towards her loomed the huge adorable torso. 'What on earth are you doing, Hortense?'

'I cannot sleep. I am not sleeping again unless . . .'

'Look, what the hell is this? You've got nothing on.'

'Liz, *tu sais bien*, I love you. And I think, just a little you are loving me. Let me enter - beside you.'

There was an appalled silence. The eyeballs bulged as they ranged over her nakedness. 'Have you taken leave of your senses?'

'You are loving me, Liz. We are *in* love. We are always being in love. Damon is not loving you. You are not loving him. And now there is this girl. There is nothing now which is impeding . . .'

Liz was getting up and putting on her dressing gown. Flushed and huge, to Hortense she was like some great classical goddess. 'Look, I think you'd better get back to your room at once,' she said.

'No,' Hortense pleaded.

Liz opened the door. 'Do you want me to call the man?'

32

Damon and Jubilee didn't take the *autoroute*. Poring over a map, Damon worked out a devious way that branched off the *route nationale* and took them through huge landscapes with long blue ranges of stony mountains clothed with pines, and plains stretched with spaced olive trees and golden harvested grain-fields. They passed through picturesque old villages of yellowish stone, in which little squares were shaded from the day's heat by spreading plane trees. High on a hilltop was a castle ruin. A magnificently towered château was inhabited, at its masthead flew a bright flag.

They didn't speak much. Jubilee drove alertly, both hands on the wheel. Her expression, Damon could see, bore still the wounds of her recent experience but - was it his imagination - did the tensions relax as they progressed? If so, was it the beauty of the landscape which effected the cure, or the habit of harmonious silence they had formed from their long mornings of work together? He liked to think the latter was part of it. They passed a huge field, violet with lavender. Jubilee gasped. 'How lavishly beautiful,' she said. He nodded.

A little later they entered one of the villages. It was mid-morning and a market was in progress, two lines of makeshift stalls under the plane trees. Their progress was slow through the throng of people. On one side Damon saw a cafe with tables set outside. 'A drink?' he said. He hadn't allowed himself to think what might be between them, and still didn't. They stopped and had *citron pressé.*

They reached the Rhône valley and ran north along the crest of its eastern flank. In the village, Jubilee had insisted on buying a picnic. They found a leafy spot overlooking the grand view. The river which divided it was so massive it didn't seem to move and was more like a lake in the middle distance. Half a dozen heavy barges spaced themselves along it, imperceptibly voyaging. A train, whose noise didn't reach them, moved southwards, and a stretch of motorway was visible like a double track of busy ants. On both banks towns smouldered in the haze. While they watched, three French Air Force fighter planes appeared from nowhere and scorched across the sky.

Kneeling on the dry grass, she began to unwrap the food - a baguette, *camambert* cheese, fruit, chocolate, and a can of lemonade they were to share. They ate, amused at their savage hunger. Afterwards, wriggling herself into a comfortable position, Jubilee lay back and closed her eyes. 'We don't have to go on just yet, do we?'

Damon slept with girls from time to time. Though never discussed, it was understood between him and Liz. Liz had once had an affair, too, similarly open yet tacit. It had never seemed necessary to debate something which was irrelevant to their more timeless arrangements. Not too long ago Damon had had an affair with a village girl, even staying away overnight sometimes. He hadn't seduced the girl. That is to say, she knew as much as he did about what was happening and about what would be the outcome. It went on amicably until she went away to Nice.

Why couldn't it be the same with Jubilee, he thought, observing her stretched beside him? He could lean over her now and kiss her. He thought there was a good chance she wouldn't object if he did. Kindling, his ambition leapt ahead to tonight - a hotel somewhere, a double room? They hadn't discussed where they would spend the night, but both knew they wouldn't get back to the Château.

As soon as he had thought it, he rejected the idea. With Jubilee, he knew, it would never be a casual affair, neither from his point of view nor hers. He and Jubilee would not just 'make' love. It would have to be all or it would be nothing. If the former, it would be the end of him and Liz.

As if sensing what he was thinking, she opened her eyes and didn't need to move her head to encounter his gaze - she was looking straight at him. Seeing what was in his eyes she smiled, neither advancing nor rejecting him. Just as he had been, she was waiting, he thought, waiting for a decision from an umpire who sat above them both but who hadn't yet pronounced.

He found himself immediately looking away. He picked a

dried stem of grass, and gripped it between his teeth. After a few moments he recognised there was one thing to be said. He had been trying to pretend it wasn't there. He removed the grass from his mouth. 'Steve didn't have an affair with Hortense,' he said. 'Knowing Hortense, I'd guess she dared him to strip that day. I suppose you could say that people in this part of the world do go in for this sort of thing, and Hortense was more than probably taking advantage of this fact. In face of the challenge, Steve maybe was under some kind of pressure. It's very probable it was in no way amorous. As for the photography, you may have guessed who was behind that. The party might well have guessed something like the swim was on the cards.' Jubilee turned her head away. 'What I'm saying is it's very probable Steve has been misjudged.'

His statement was made, submitted as it were. She made no comment. Freed of it, he could relax again. Jubilee drove on at a moderate pace, now in total silence, but he was aware that she had her eyes exclusively on the road. She was no longer noticing things as she had on the morning drive. He made a few comments at things they passed. She nodded, not looking. As time was getting on, they went down on to the motorway. He regretted this. The competitive rush destroyed the idyll of their morning drive. They stopped for petrol at one of the roadside establishments and, still dazed with speed like all the other people there, went into the self-service restaurant for cups of coffee. It was as they left this place that she took his arm suddenly, hugged it to her, and gave a skip. 'You're one of the nicest, warmest, funniest men I've ever known,' she said. 'And we have a lovely deep friendship, don't we?'

33

Arriving in Nice after his flight from the Château Lamartine, Steve had had the driver drop him in a street full of small hotels. It was doubtful if he would get a flight tonight, and anyway he felt tired and confused.   In the morning, things would be clearer. Maybe he wouldn't go. He was lucky in the first hotel he tried. He lay down on the bed in his clothes and fell asleep.

When he woke it was light. He looked at his watch and saw it was six. He had slept nearly twelve hours. He had dreamed he was in a small chamber whose ceiling was being lowered by some hydraulic mechanism. He would be crushed and pressed into a rectangular package of flesh. He still had the sensation of appalling constriction. There was only one consolation. His American wife left him. This time he had pre-empted the disaster.

He decided to have a bath, but there was no hot water at this hour. He surveyed the functional room, which smelt of toothpaste. He rejected the idea of going back to bed, he wouldn't sleep again. A return to the Château? Impossible, so soon - what would be changed? He saw there was a phone.

He called the airport. There was no answer. The world slept on, indifferent. For a human voice to speak to, he dialled his mother's number, which he knew by heart.   With the hour change it would be five in England, but mother had been up at this hour every day of her life. The ringing tone pleaded fruitlessly twelve times. He rang again.

When three attempts produced the same result, he grew alarmed. Mother was never away. After much palaver with a night operator on enquiries, he got the number of a friend of mother's who lived up the road.   There was a pause as the woman took in who was phoning at this hour, then the voice came at him unsurprised, accusatory. Didn't he *know* about his mother's fall in the street two days ago, the stroke, the hospital? Yes, the Royal County hospital. Yes, she *was* critically ill. Everyone had done their best of course, visiting her, making sure she was as comfortable as she could be . . . as there was no one else, no *family* at hand.

He brought the conversation to an abrupt close. Harpy. The woman was enjoying every moment of it. He rang the hospital. Mother was unconscious, and, yes, very ill.

What did he feel? Nothing especially new, he found, beyond the thought he had often had before - that one of these days she would be pushing off like this. She'd had a hard but essentially good life. His main, peripheral feeling, he realised guiltily, was one of relief that at least his immediate actions had been determined for him. There was no question now of his not going to England at once. It was a certainty to cling to.

Later, the airlines resumed communication with the outside world. There was a seat on a flight at ten.

England was defiantly, doggedly the same. Cool and windy though August, litter flew about wantonly outside the terminal, where he joined a silent queue waiting for taxis. Each time a taxi came the people inched forward their suitcases. A double-decker bus wheeled in too fast and pulled up further on.

As if he had woken from an anaesthetic, he yearned suddenly for Jubilee. She should be with him now at this moment - which was meant to be a crisis in one's life, wasn't it? He imagined her brown softness in his arms again, her giving mouth - then thought of her, relieved of his banal presence, sleeping with that sinister egg-head. Too painful to contemplate, he snatched his mind away and made himself think of mother again. Unconscious, they had said - so he wouldn't be able to speak to her? Would she die, or would she be an invalid and he would have to look after her?

In the taxi to Liverpool Street, he asked the man - what banality - about the economic situation in Britain. The stoical 'can't grumble' phraseology was part of the sameness at the airport. Was stoicism, or the idea of it, even in the midst of relative plenty, all Britain had these days? Was it all *he* had?

He went straight to the hospital. They had put her in a public ward, but she had curtains drawn round her bed. The eyes of the other patients watched him as he entered, like a herd of cattle, he thought, eyeing an intruder in their field.

The familiar, imperious old head was centred on the raised pillows, the expression complacent, loftily critical. She was dead, he thought. To all intents and purposes, she was dead, and this was the pose she had chosen to die in. Her breath, moving in and out of her open mouth as if separate from her volition, was like small waves on a beach worrying something lying at the water's edge. It didn't belong to her. Soon, at will, the tide would withdraw and leave her bleached carcase stranded. For a moment he had a small rush of emotion. Despite the look, perhaps because of it, she was so tiny, so helpless. She was his mother, he needed to protect her.

Soon he briefly touched one of her responseless hands lying outside the bedclothes, and rose. As if to repair his nullity, his omission of any tenderness or grief, the nurse put her white hand on the old brow and unnecessarily re-tucked the sheet. In an office he spoke to the brisk sister in her Oxford blue uniform.

'We cannot be confident, I'm afraid, that she'll last the day, Mr Addicot. She's very weak.'

He asked if she could be moved to a private ward. There would be no point, he was told, and it might precipitate death to move her. The rest of the conversation, too prolonged, was their agreement that it would be pointless for him to stay. They would call him, yes, if there was any change.

His own house was let. He remembered Jubilee had stored a lot of clothes, including his, at mother's place. He had nothing with him except a razor and a canister of shaving cream he had bought at Nice airport. He supposed he would have to see to the house anyway, if mother died, and he may as well camp there.

He had to break in. He spent a miserable evening resisting the compulsive wish to lift the telephone perched on a small table in the hall and talk to Jubilee. That he didn't was largely because he had a greater fear that it would be Damon, not Jubilee, who would answer. Would he have moved in by now? Wasn't it justice that he would have done - Damon, who was Jubilee's age, who was the dispenser of her beloved culture? No, he had taken the right decision. The photograph had a simple and innocent explanation, that he hadn't given because he knew Jubilee wouldn't believe it, wouldn't believe it because she didn't want to. He had stolen something he had no right to by marrying her.

The phone rang at six in the morning. He'd had a beautiful dream in which he and Jubilee were reunited. He was so sure it was her ringing, he knocked the phone over getting to it. It was the hospital. His mother had just 'passed away.'

How admonitory society becomes when someone dies. It took him half a morning to register the death - finding the right office, waiting his turn with other recalcitrant people who had been indiscreet enough to lose their relatives. The clerk was irritable as he wrote down the irrelevant details. Worse was the undertaker. Steve ordered a funeral of medium proportions - not from meanness, but because the black-suited man began by saying he would arrange things with a sensitive appreciation of his mother's 'very respectable station in life.' How did the absurdly pompous figure assess what was respectable, and for that matter what were 'stations' in life? He heard his mother's abrasive tone in his own as he ordered the second cheapest coffin. He felt she at least approved of this.

Worst of all were the 'friends' who came to 'pay their respects' to him - the news seemed to get round that he was living in the bungalow. Respects took the form of lengthy selections from mother's virtues, and a montage of uplifting incidents in her life in which they had been involved. He felt much of it was forced, even lies. When he showed impatience, again he was reprimanded. There were scathing references to his wealth compared with Ethel's 'valiant struggle in life'.

Finally there was the cremation. The young minister of the chapel she attended made an effort to register the 'especial' importance of the life of 'our dear departed sister', and spoke with a synthetic smile of her 'ebullient energy and uplifting interest in others.' There was a fierce approving nod in his direction from one of the entirely female congregation. The minister insisted on the scattering of ashes in the Garden of Remembrance, which he said he was quite sure mother would have wished.   There was an extra fee for this.   It was while standing here in the dismal knot witnessing the ghoulish deed that Steve reached a kind of nadir.   As he got into the car he had hired he saw the disapproving faces.   They had clearly expected to be asked back to some kind of wake.   Freed of them as he now was, he felt a lifting of the spirit.   Nothing could be worse now.

Before he reached the bungalow the lifting of spirit became translated into a concrete thought.   They had lectured him for being rich, for being an absentee son, but it wasn't him they upbraided.   It was the dullness and sterility of their own lives. By allowing them to affect him, wasn't he attaching himself to the same subservience to fate?

What had fate got to do with it?   Hadn't he always believed in the possibility of achieving what he wanted?   He had thought his despair was born of his estrangement from Jubilee, but was it, entirely?   Wasn't it as much the Château?   He had taken on the Château for Jubilee of course - without her he wouldn't have been near the place after his first visit.   But hadn't there been another reason?   Hadn't he felt estranged from his life in England long before the question of the Château arose?   By buying the Château, making it his principle activity, hadn't he set out to prove something, and *wasn't he now taking defeat lying down*?   He made up his mind.   He wouldn't give in so easily.   He would go back and fight them - with humour and persistence.   It was his Château.   He could do what he liked with it.

And Jubilee?   What if Jubilee had left him and gone to live with Damon?   How would he be able to bear living in the same premises and seeing them together daily?   He pushed this unbearable prospect aside.   Let her first see him fighting for what he believed in.

34

Mr Jan Topolski sat at the large desk whose position he had modified. Greta Svensson, his late boss, a sterner character, had had it inclined away from the window, thus denying herself what she considered the frivolity of the fourteenth floor view. It was inspiring, he thought, when considering some weighty matter to see the semi-circle of international bunting stretched in a stiff breeze, and more distantly the massive outlines of the great Bourbon palace. The change was symbolic of the novelty he hoped to bring - a more outward-looking, less bureaucratic flavour in closer accord with the Organisation's global ideals.

He looked at his memo pad and saw there were a dozen letters to write. He savoured the thought. In a moment he would hold down the switch of his intercom and speak to Ann (no longer 'Miss Flowers') who was certainly as pleased at the use of her first name as he was. But she beat him to it. The machine went live as his hand moved towards it.

'Jan, are you frantically busy?' The soft English voice was still deliciously unused to the familiarity he had introduced.

'Not frantic. Actually, Ann, I have some mail, if you're free.'

'Of course,' she said. She kept the line open. 'Reception says there's someone to see you,' she continued in a lowered tone as if someone might be listening. 'I told him, via the desk, it's usual to make appointments, but the man apparently insists. I've had to have him come up. He's on his way. What do I do? Can you squeeze him in if . . .'

'Who is he?'

'Name of Addicot. From a Château somewhere. Lamartine is it?'

Addicot was not familiar, but Lamartine was. Suddenly he had it. Of course - the Midi, a crumbling ruin, the incredible metal sculpture in the tower, and the mad Mexican artist. Interest kindled as he remembered the storm the matter had raised. 'Ah yes, I *do* recall. All right, I'll see him.'

Not immediately, however. He wasn't rushing it. That much of Svensson style he was prepared to preserve. He had Ann Flowers in to do the letters and kept the visitor waiting outside for twenty minutes. Casual callers could never be given instant access, or where would they be? Between letters, he picked up an inkling or two about the caller.

'Short, energetic, rushed about my office like a terrier,' Ann said. 'He claims to be the owner of the Château.'

Funny, his impression was that the Mexican sculptor's wife had owned the place. But then - she must have sold out, he thought. Not so very surprising.

Ann's dog-simile was immediately borne out as Addicot was admitted. He literally bounded through the door as if just unleashed. 'Good of you to see me. I was just passing through Paris, and . . .' Topolski thought the handshake was the preliminary to some feat of ju-jitsu in which he would find himself twisted, lifted, and thrown on his back on the floor.

They settled, coffee was brought, and - another Svensson ploy - the pending subject was kept at bay. This technique, he conceded, produced in most people a nervous tension, which could often be advantageous at the business stage.

Addicot could be kept at bay for less time than most. The sugar and milk routine was complete, Topolski had at hand remarks about the view from the window, but the topic was abruptly aborted. 'Now look,' said Addicot, drawing his chair closer and ignoring the coffee steaming at his side, 'I understand a couple of years ago your organisation was involved with the Château in a matter of a large piece of sculpture you'd ordered.'

'It has an echo.'

'Good. Now you'll understand that at that time I had nothing to do with the place. I purchased it afterwards.'

'I see.'

Addicot gave a short laugh. 'I can well imagine how things didn't work out. The artist in question isn't entirely of this world. But then how few of them are - how few artists and intellectuals are?'

'You know of this man?'

'Of course. He's still one of my inmates. All the people

you met are still there.'

Steve explained the situation. He explained the changes he had made to the fabric and décor of the Château and how he had turned it into a very novel kind of luxury hotel by keeping on the previous occupants and, through their good offices, dispensing culture as well as comforts. He didn't of course refer to a working model of a latrine poised over the sacred emblem of a Superpower, nor to the consequences of its being viewed by some of his guests.

During this considerable outlay of words Topolski's mind was not inactive. He recalled in greater detail the loss of prestige his ex-boss had suffered as a result of the affair. He remembered that as a result of the fiasco the whole project of a sculpture had been put in abeyance. Greta had wanted to forget her (too precipitous) involvement with deology, which had earned her such unfavourable comments from their financial masters. Topolski's mind made several alterations of direction as Steve spoke, but it steadied finally into an attitude of wary interest, even excitement. Could this prove to be the first major matter in which he achieved a breakthrough from the past?

Addicot had finished his exposition. He was approaching the point. 'So,' he was saying, 'here we are. I see you haven't yet bought another sculpture to put in front of your building. To be frank I did make some enquiries before coming here and gathered your plans have been temporarily shelved rather than abandoned. Now the custom-built creation still stands in the north-west tower of my Château. What I've come to ask is this. Would your department, now that management our end is on a more business-like footing, consider re-opening negotiations? Naturally I have an entirely new contract in mind.' Addicot sat back in his chair and stretched his arm for his coffee.

Topolksi could imagine what Greta would be doing in this circumstance. 'Steady, make smoke, be affably inscrutable.' He could hear the Ibsenian gloom in her words. He grew excited. It was Polish not Norwegian blood which flowed in his veins. He also liked Addicot, who had a humour and a directness which appealed to him.

'I went to Larmartine myself, you know,' Jan said.

'You did?'

'I was at that time number two in this department. I saw the sculpture, and the artist.'

'All the better, you know what I'm talking about.'

'The abandonment of the project was indeed a great waste - from the point of view of the input of both parties.'

'It was.'

'But of course there was the - er - stumbling block. And surely the stumbling block remains?'

Addicot wiped his mouth on the paper napkin supplied, screwed it up and stuffed it into his empty cup. He crossed one leg over the other. 'Ah, the nitty, yes. If I'm right we're talking about a chocolate-eating god and a stubborn artistic mind. But do we need to stumble? Had your predecessor - has any of us - really thought how we can avoid doing so?'

Jan drew back a trifle. 'You must realise that a flippancy of that order could not be allowed, Mr Addicot. An organisation such as ours . . .'

'Of course, of course, it's unthinkable. But it surely wouldn't be difficult to find someone - any nimble plumber or blacksmith with a head for heights would do - who, after the work is installed here, could climb up, perhaps under cover of darkness, and make just those two or three small adjustments which are necessary.'

Topolski swallowed. 'Two or three . . .'

'The chocolates and the book could surely stay. No one's going to notice them at that height. The curve of the God's right cheek might need the smallest modification, and the hand which holds the book must join the other in order to give the impression that the rising cable is being grasped with more commitment. But that's all, in my submission.'

'But the hammock, Mr Addicot? The hammock remains. It was the reclining figure on the hammock which caused us the major concern. It's the hammock which is out of the question.'

Steve grinned. 'Hammock, what hammock? You must refer to the *cloud* upon which the Godhead is seated. The removal of the hammock's tethering ropes would immediately suggest this more celestial support, and of course it would be made clear in your explanatory literature that this is the case. I'm quite convinced that with these very trivial changes the effect of the God figure - to anyone who bothers to observe it with binoculars, which would be needed - will be one of fatherly concern, concern for the smooth functioning of the universe and for the brave endeavours of mankind labouring on earth below.'

'But even if we were to do this, it would surely interfere . . .'

'With the copyright? Correct. But at that stage the copyright would be yours, wouldn't it? There may be certain small adjustments that your lawyers will need to make in the small print of the new contract but, given that that work is done unobtrusively, you'll be in the clear in the unlikely circumstances of a rearguard action by the artist. Your bosses will gaze down upon an offence-free sculpture. Now what do you say, Mr Topolski, and how do you react to the idea of our having lunch?'

Jan Topolski had no objection to a shared lunch, especially as his own offer of the canteen paid for out of his own expense allowance was exchanged for a brighter prospect in the town at his visitor's expense. Already massing in his mind were those bureaucratic complexities which would be involved in any reopening of this file - but one step at a time, his whole training and experience was reminding him.

35

The Hotel Château Lamartine prospered under the professional expertise of Albert Tricot. Two more group bookings - which fortunately had not requested the cultural extra services available - arrived and enjoyed themselves without incident. But the permanent residents weren't happy. For reasons unconnected with the hotel, they felt rudderless and dispirited. At the evening meal when normally cheerful discourse flowed, there was virtual silence. Beyond an occasional appeal for salt or the water jug, it was a question of dogged eating. Plates clattered, cutlery chinked, and people drifted off as soon as they had finished.

Not the least melancholic was Frederick. He kept his eyes on his plate when he ate and had become a victim of chronic sighing. He sighed when he was passed something, he sighed when he had finished eating, sometimes he sighed with no apparent prompt. Liz spoke more than most, but because, being one of the cooks and very largely the caterer, at mealtimes there were more practicalities for her to attend to. But she, too, seemed heavy and distracted. Liz's apparent susceptibility to the contagion was especially unsettling to the others, accustomed as they were to her well-anchored attitudes. It was noticeable that the tacit bond between her and Damon, never overt but always present, was in some way missing. It was generally known that Damon and Jubilee had driven to Lyons and stayed the night there.

Hortense's absence also led to speculation. Paul made no comment and appeared to have no interest. Liz being the last person to have seen her was asked where she was. Liz shrugged her shoulders and said she had no idea, but her manner suggested she did have a very considerable idea. It added a further dimension to the unease. Was it just exigencies arising from her exhibition in Nice which detained Hortense?

Paul Beerbohmer was the exception to the general malaise. The soundproof room Steve had built for him had transformed his life. For some weeks now he had not, except for his lessons to an ardent young female American, given any of his time to the techniques of note playing. Aurally and physically inviolate in his new, lockable workplace, he indulged glorious hours among the syncopated rhythms of jazz music, secure in the knowledge that no one would know of his banal but joyful descent into folklore. Secretly he had sent one of two of the compositions he completed to an agent he used to know in Paris. They had been placed almost at once with a group which performed lucratively in left bank bars. More were being demanded. Hortense's absence was a bonus to Paul's well-being. He took long luxurious baths in the marble bathroom, slept again in the double bed and lingered in it as long as he pleased in the mornings.

The Aguas de Villanovas were no exception to the rule. In an idiomatic phrase Alfonso used - one of the few he had managed to pluck from the bewilderingly plentiful tree of the English language - June had 'gone into pieces.' She would not work, lay about reading, and replied listlessly when he spoke to her. 'Gwass wrong Juni? Everything all OK here now,' he said to her once.

'It's not all right, we'll have to go, my dream's shattered.'

'Is not shattered. We not go. We stay here. No Steve - ver' good. We all sit pretty.'

'It's not very good at all, and we aren't sitting pretty. The fact is we've taken advantage of Steve and we're paying for it. Quite apart from financial matters, the community will never be the same again. It's my fault. I knew when I invited Steve that something like this could happen. I sold us to Mammon, and Mammon's had his money's worth. Incidentally, Mammon has turned out to be rather nicer than any of us.'

Alfonso couldn't understand such convoluted reasoning. He shook his head. On another occasion he bellowed, but it made no difference to June. She just went back to her book. Soon, her attitude began to affect him. He depended on June - on her sense and reasonableness. This detachment was not reasonable. He, too, found he couldn't work. One night he took money from June's handbag and went drinking in the village. When, having slept in the square, he returned ill and repentant the next day, she showed no emotion either way.

The state of Jubilee's spirits was more complex. She had so enjoyed her trip to Lyons with Damon. Their relationship, she knew, had reached a new point. She had no doubt now that Damon was not just flirting, as she'd gathered he'd been known to do with other girls in the past, but was very fond of her. And this of course was not in the silly peacock way in which Frederick had temporarily convinced himself he was in love with her, but with a frightening depth and concentration - an intensity she might have expected from Damon, she told herself, had she thought about its possibility beforehand. She knew she had only to show the smallest sign and he might leave poor Liz and ask her for a permanent arrangement. What was her attitude to this?

She had been deeply moved by his forbearance when they were having the picnic overlooking the Rhône valley - his thought for her in not pressing anything too strongly, above all in his honesty about Steve and Hortense. That evening in the Lyons boarding house, when they were upstairs together after dinner and said goodnight in the corridor, she'd been profoundly tempted. She had felt his physical strength, like Steve's, and in addition his beautiful mind, pressing her with all its will. One movement of her eyes or lips, she knew, and he'd have come into her room. But in this moment of truth she found she couldn't make this movement, not yet, not at least until she knew for sure that Steve had left her, not until she'd had more time to think of Liz and what would happen to her. She'd put her hand on his. He'd gripped it fiercely, and they'd stood there for some moments like a frozen tableau.

Had Steve left her? She accepted Damon's version of the photograph. She could see that that explanation of Steve's behaviour was a possible, even a probable one. She'd even thought it herself. But in a way it made things worse. If he hadn't made love with Hortense, why had he been so secretive, and why when it came out he'd had a nude swim with her had he behaved in such a guilty adolescent fashion?

Above all she castigated him for something which had

nothing to do with Hortense - for his behaviour towards the community. Why had he been so sycophantic and provocative by turns? Why, for a period, had he been so vindictive towards Damon and then, when confronted by Damon's dignity, so abjectly repentant? Why had he allowed the prank in the crypt, which she was quite sure was only Frederick's silly doing, to get under his skin? His attitude, his inferiority complex about 'intellectuals,' his assertion of 'business' - not just as another, equal, but as a superior, human activity - diminished him. She tried to reinstate him in her mind, tried to feel sorry for him languishing somewhere - with his mother, was he? But she found she couldn't. She lived on, like a widow, happy in a way that Damon loved her, but bereft of initiative. Whatever her own feelings, how could she hurt Liz, she thought, whom she had come to love and respect?

An evening about a week after their journey to Lyons, Damon phoned her from the main house. This had never happened before. They didn't see each other in the evenings. 'It's me,' he just said when she lifted the phone, and left a long silence. What he wanted was to come round. He'd never been to her house. They'd always met in his room in the mornings - he was already beginning a new work - or for walks in the afternoons. She hesitated. She knew he meant the novelty to be significant. She said yes.

It amused her as she opened the door to notice he'd made no attempt to improve his appearance, as Frederick once had on an occasion whose superficial similarity she was forced to remember. Frederick, she recalled, had soaked himself in some disgusting scent. Damon was as ever wearing his very English whipcord trousers and a white shirt, which had once been slightly torn at the sleeve. She suspected he'd made the neat repair himself. His thick hair was naturally tidy, but it certainly hadn't been combed. He was carrying something in a small paper bag and held it out to her as he entered.

'What is it?' she said.

'Open it and see.' He came through the door and closed it behind him. He marched in the direction of the patio.

Following him, she pulled from the paper a beautiful royal

blue square with yellow medallions, in each of which was a veiled oriental lady in diaphanous clothing. In the centre medallion was a Sultan-like figure. 'Lyons silk,' he said gruffly, his head turned from her. She felt a gust of happiness. It was so unlike him - yet, given that he'd had the thought, paradoxically so totally in character. 'The Eastern Question?' she laughed.

He grinned. 'Something along those lines.'

She didn't care. She ran to him and kissed him on the cheek. 'Oh thank you, Damon. It's beautiful. I'll treasure it.'

It then became embarrassing. They stood together not knowing what to say, until she thought of making coffee. He followed her into the kitchen. He sat at the table while she handled the kettle and spun the shiny beans in the grinder. For some reason, she found she could talk freely again. 'Hortense still isn't back.'

'No.'

'Is she staying in Nice?'

'Possibly.'

'Albert told me the exhibition was a success. Apparently there was quite a piece about it in the "Nice Soir".' Damon was silent. 'Damon, what's up about Hortense? You know something?' He shrugged. 'You do know. What is it?'

Damon bent his head and touched his nose with his knuckles as if it were itching. 'I doubt if she'll be back here.'

'Why, because of the photograph business?'

'No. Because I suspect she made a pass at Liz.'

Jubilee took her hand off the kettle handle and stared. 'You mean . . .'

'I mean Hortense is that way inclined, yes.'

'And . . .'

'And Liz was hardly interested of course.'

'Liz told you about it?'

'Not in so many words.'

Jubilee sat down heavily. 'How very unpleasant,' she said. 'For Liz, I mean.'

'Oh I don't know. Liz is robust. I don't think she'll give it much thought now it's over and done with.'

Jubilee realised with discomfort why she'd instinctively raised the subject of Hortense. Suddenly, unannounced, their own matter and Liz's involvement in it was before them. If Hortense's pass wasn't the cause of Liz's being upset, it was perfectly clear what was. Jubilee had been observing her face in the last days. It wasn't hostile towards her, she thought, but blank. Since Lyons they hadn't exchanged a word. Jubilee hadn't been near the greenhouse or the pottery shed. She hadn't liked to. 'Poor Liz,' she said after a moment. 'She's so kind and generous, and courageous.'

Damon's chin was tucked into his neck. 'She's all of those things, certainly,' he said, almost inaudibly.

They were both conscious of the evening stillness through the open windows. The light was just beginning to fade and the bats were out. Their squeaking flickering presence expressed the electric atmosphere between them.

'I love you, Jubilee,' Damon said. 'I want to marry you. You are the only girl I've known I've felt about in this way.'

Jubilee realised a plume of steam had been blowing for some seconds from the English electric kettle. The lid had begun to rattle. As it switched itself off she jumped up. Standing with her back to him, she began to pour into the open funnel into which she'd shaken the coffee. The water didn't percolate at once and she was forced to wait, topping it up as it disappeared into the jug. Damon's words scalded her with pleasure and anticipation, but she fought to control these feelings, which could so easily lead to that embrace from which there would be no going back. The coffee was made. She removed the filter and, turning back to the table, began to pour into the cups.

'We must think of Liz,' she said.

'Liz will be hurt, but she understands. She's always understood that our relationship . . . has limits, for both of us. There's never been any hiding of that on either side.'

'No.'

'Then?'

'Then *that* perhaps, if you say so, could be all right, though I can't believe it's so simple. But there's something else. I have to see Steve again.' She'd said it. She'd known all along it would have to be said. Steve's departure had been unnatural, inconclusive.

'You'll go to England?'

'Possibly.'

'Why don't you phone him now?'

'Phone?'

'Ask him what his intentions are.'

'I don't know where he is.'

'You could at least discover *that*.'

'I might.'

'Will you - tonight?'

He made her promise, though she couldn't see what a phone call would achieve. Soon she asked him if he'd go. If she was going to speak to Steve she couldn't think what she'd say to him with Damon there. When he'd gone she regretted her promise. If she phoned, whatever she said, Steve would be bound to see it as an overture. She didn't feel like making an overture. Finally she thought of asking him about the hotel. What did he intend for it? Though she and Albert Tricot were keeping things going, he hadn't written to Albert as he'd apparently said he would. This was neutral enough territory, wasn't it? She could make herself sound purely practical. Steve might refuse to speak to her. Did she hope he would?

She rang his mother first. There was no reply. She tried their own house and got their tenant - the wife. 'Er - yes, Mrs Addicot, your husband did phone us - oh, some days ago - to see that all was well - which it is, we're very happy here. But I'm afraid I don't know where he is now unless he's still in his mother's house, where I believe he was when he phoned. We're so very sorry to hear about your loss. Your husband didn't mention it, but we saw the funeral announced in the local paper. I suppose that's why your husband is over here?'

Jubilee returned to the kitchen when she put the phone down. She sat at the table, put her head in her hand, and wept. She imagined a cremation chapel, the wreaths, the piped music, and Steve sitting alone in a dark suit on the front pew. Whatever else turned out to be the truth, she should have been there, at his side. She'd never known parents, but she could imagine what it

279

was like to lose them. She clung to this regret of hers. It was something at least which she felt clearly, like one limb which has recovered from paralysis.

The next morning Jubilee was having her daily interview with Albert. What a nice man he was, she thought, as he ran her through the week's menus for the group of international parliamentarians who were staying at the hotel - fortunately, again, not requiring the cultural activities. He didn't have to do this, even though she was beginning to be able to make good suggestions. He was just naturally courteous and sensible. He'd accepted without fuss that she'd wish to keep an eye 'while Steve was away' - the phrase he used.

It was eight o'clock, one of the times of day Jubilee most loved. On the way over to the main house the air had been fresh with the smell of dew, suggesting the promise of the day and, beyond it, the splendours of the autumn. Now the sun was flooding its light into the room, warming it steadily. Across the patio, from the direction of the kitchen, came the fragrance of the morning bread-bake, of bacon cooking and fresh French coffee. She'd had a strong feeling when she woke that her life would soon be resolved. Steve would phone. If he didn't, she'd go to England and find him.

They were in the middle of a debate Albert had instigated as to whether *Sole Bonne Femme* or *Langoustines Lamartine* went best with filet steak - the menus were all *table d'hôte* this week - when there was a rumpus in the hall, a slammed door and voices. The door burst open and Steve appeared. 'Jubilee, hard at it, I see. Albert. What a glorious morning.' Before she could compose herself he kissed her on the cheek, hugged her briefly, and flung himself into one of the chairs. 'Finished a certain little business concern yesterday, got a charter flight which left at an ungodly hour so as to get here sooner, and here I am. Yes, I'm back - for good. Call of the south and all that, beakerfuls of it. How did we ever live in England, Jubilee, it's horrible. I say, what about a spot of breakfast, Albert? I'm famished. Whistle up a waiter and have him bring it here, will you? I'll have the lot.'

Albert withdrew.   Steve picked up the handwritten menu she'd been pretending to read. 'Parliamentary fare, I see. *Compôte républicaine* - a nice touch. They're here, I see. Should be good, having them. Democracy has its uses. They'll have our name broadcast round the world.   Liking it, are they? No more *cryptic* pranks, I hope?'

Jubilee controlled her thoughts, which were jumping about like the frog Olympics. 'No pranks, no.'

'I didn't expect any.   You know I've been thinking about Frederick's little masterpiece - Frederick was behind it, I'm sure.   *Having* thought about it, I've come to the conclusion it was really very funny.   Those two Americans who came into my office the morning afterwards - I wish you could've seen their faces.   They looked like the riders arriving in Aix from Ghent, weighed down with the importance of their message.   It was the women of course who'd put them up to it.   If it'd been left to the four of us we could have sorted it out.   You know, we haven't been very sensible - correction, *I* haven't been very sensible.   If you're dealing with a bunch of highly talented folk like this lot, of course you're going to get some unusual occurrences from time to time. I didn't make enough allowances for them, that was my mistake.   Well, it's going to be different now.   I'll let them know I bear no grudges and we can all start from scratch . . .   Incidentally, talking about scratching, something's been eating me all the way from Nice.   A mosquito, I think.'   He pulled up the short sleeve of his red sports shirt and revealed a livid area on the plump part of his upper arm.

Jubilee had somehow to stop his flippancy. 'I'm sorry about mother,' she said, looking at her hands in her lap.

'You know about her?'

'I spoke to the tenants on the phone yesterday.   They'd seen the announcement.'

'You phoned the tenants?'   She didn't answer, but by leaving the silence indicated no concession. They did phone the tenants from time to time. She saw his hope die and his eyes fall away. 'Yes, it was sad,' he was forced to continue.   'I heard she'd had a stroke when I was in Nice. I happened to call her.   As there was no reply I spoke to one of her friends. This friend told me what had happened and which hospital mother was in. Mother was unconscious, and never recovered. She died the night after I arrived.'

'I'm so sorry.'

He looked stricken for a moment, then smiled. 'You know how she looked, lying there on that bed? *Slightly annoyed* - even when unconscious. I don't suppose she thought the hospital was up to standard.'

Jubilee accepted the humour, and mother's death, as a postponement. During the conversation her spirits had sunk about as low as they'd go. Did he really think he could breeze in like this and pick up their life as if nothing had happened? It was quite conceivable, if she allowed things to go on as before, he wouldn't even refer to what had happened between them.

For a moment she wished he hadn't returned. She should have gone to England to settle things. The others would massacre him, and one humiliation was enough to witness. It would be like one of those terrible Spanish bullfights, she thought - first those dreadful cruel arrows, then the sword thrust and the inevitable preordained death of the thoughtless courageous innocence of the bull.

36

17 Rue Fontaine
Marly-le-Roi
Seine et Oise.

Dear Señor Aguas de Villanova,

You may remember that I had the pleasure of making your acquaintance when two years ago I accompanied Miss Greta Svensson (at that time Director of the Public Relations Department of this Organisation) to make a final on-site inspection of your work of sculpture, which we had conditionally commissioned.

Recently Miss Svensson has been appointed to another post and I have succeeded to the Public Relations Directorship.

One of my strong objectives is to provide continuity in the work of this Department. The great majority of Miss Svensson's decisions are ones which have my unqualified accord - indeed, in most of them I played a supportive role in my capacity as her junior. But inevitably when a newcomer takes over a directorial position in this way, there will be one or two matters in which a different viewpoint is taken. One of these is your sculpture.

It was my view at the time (as indeed it was of Miss Svensson) that it was little short of a calamity, from your point of view as well as that of the W.C.H.I.S.A.R., that our negotiations should have fallen through as they did when the cause of disagreement was relatively minor. Miss Svensson, however, took the position that the extremely relaxed posture of one of your figures in the upper part of your 'telescope' and the apparent attitude it connoted was, if unmodified, so inimical to our aims as to render unacceptable the rest of the work. This is where I part company with my colleague.

Having had some contact with the art world, I think I do understand the fiercely uncompromising attitude taken by good artists to their work, and I would consider it a deterioration of our civilisation if they were less so. What I wish to put to you is that if you were to find yourself in a position to restore our severed relations, you will find me willing to reciprocate to the utmost of my powers. As I view it, your work should be re-offered to us - in the version I saw, and at the price agreed.

I must stress to you, however, my dear Señor Aguas de Villanova, that though I have taken a few discreet soundings of what <u>might</u> be the attitude of my superiors - among whom there have also been changes - nothing can be certain. What I would like you to do therefore, in the event of your sculpture still being available, is to you write to me at W.C.H.I.S.A.R. – not at this , my private address - with the exact form of words I suggest. Such an approach, I assure you, will help me to lubricate the giant wheels of bureaucracy. With it, I hope to facilitate a happy outcome of the affair from both our points of view.

I remain, most sincerely, your admirer,

Jan Topolski.

On the morning of Steve's return to the Château, Alfonso was roaming about the building, half-heartedly looking for one of the hotel employees who was Mexican, with whom he'd already had a couple of nostalgic conversations. In his listless and disillusioned frame of mind, he found the letter on the hall table, where mail was put these days.

Alfonso had never been greatly interested in mail, even when it was addressed to him. But on this occasion he took up the bulky envelope with both hands and regarded the handwriting and postmark with mild interest. He sat on the stairs to read it.

He was not expecting gold nuggets, but in the manner of a prospector his eye rapidly sifted through the complex phraseology and quickly alighted on the one bright fragment towards the end. He read the phrase three times. Undoubtedly, the point of principle was being yielded, an offer was being made. With only a modicum of effort compared with what he'd already expended, it seemed a large cheque was within his grasp. By its agency a change in June's mood could be effected.

Without telling anyone, he went immediately into the writing room. On a sheet of hotel notepaper he copied out the prepared letter which Topolski had enclosed, placed it in a crested hotel envelope and addressed it. He went to Yvette in the office for a stamp, and put it in the post-box in the hall.

ChâteauLamartine
Vigny-les-Pins
Alpes Maritimes.

Dear Mr Topolski,

Since our unfortunately ruptured negotiations of two years ago I have constantly regretted that we did not bring things to a satisfactory conclusion, especially when the difference between us was so relatively minor.

I regret that I am not able to yield on the one small point which divided us - I still maintain that my work fulfils the terms of my commission and that an artist cannot allow himself to be compromised even on small details. But I have heard that you have not yet commissioned another artist to produce another work. I have also gathered there has been a change of management in your Department, and that you have now assumed the responsibility. I do wonder if as a result I can hope for that slight re-orientation of policy which is all that is necessary for a positive conclusion to emerge.

May I hear from you?

Yours sincerely,

Alfonso Aguas de Villanova.

37

On her second night in Nice, Hortense Beerbohmer didn't remain in the small hotel in which Liz had so abruptly and inexplicably rejected the offer of her love. She probably wouldn't have done anyway. To have stayed near the scene of such a painful incident wouldn't have been pleasant. But in fact she had several offers of alternative accommodation.

On the first open day of the exhibition she was besieged with people wanting to make her acquaintance. Other journalists from the national press were down. One of these wanted her to accompany him to his hotel - not only, she sensed, for the further 'in depth' interview he was suggesting. Maurice Brabazon asked her to stay with him for the duration of the exhibition in his luxury villa, which he shared with a young male artist. There were at least two other men who, with a little encouragement, might have come up with offers similar to the journalist's.

In the end she made a decision quite independent of them all. She booked into the Elysée Palace Hotel. Her pictures were selling. Maurice doubled the prices after the *vernissage*. Why should she consider money now? She'd been elevated at last to that select group of the elite painters of France. She bought another smart outfit for the autumn, a range of underclothing, three new pairs of shoes, and an expensive suitcase. She imagined in not too distinct detail that she'd be removing to Paris in a few days, and rather waited for someone to make the arrangements - a furnished atelier temporarily vacant perhaps, which would allow her to find her feet.

When towards the end of the week no such offer was made, she was forced to concede that she'd have to return to Lamartine, albeit very temporarily. There was of course another point. As she had modestly pointed out to *cognoscenti*, she had but pierced the perimeters of the mystic secrets of the Mont des Lézards. Her work at the foot of that impressive feature was far from complete. The view was reinforced when she saw her hotel bill, which would necessitate a loan from Maurice. She decided the difficulty involved in seeing Liz again must be secondary to professional imperatives. It was thus that the Château was to witness a second prodigal return within the space of hours.

She didn't take a limousine for the journey. The public bus which took its place was unpleasing to her. At this time of day it carried exclusively women, it seemed, dowdily dressed with basketfuls of shopping, who got on and off at various points and chattered incessantly about the small matters of their lives. She kept her head steadfastly averted, and stared out of the window. The behaviour of the insolent driver was worse. At Vigny-les-Pins he opened the large locker under the bus where her suitcases were stored, then stood back and insisted she herself remove them without his assistance. She was relieved to sit back in the taxi for the last leg of the inconvenient journey up to the Château. Leaving the cases in the drive, she went inside and ordered a hotel employee loafing in the hall to carry them up to her rooms.

In her sitting room a further disagreeableness awaited her in the form of Paul lounging in one of the armchairs with his feet over the arm, sucking some sort of disgusting sweet on the end of a stick and reading a score. He didn't get up, and regarded her over the sheet with a distinct lack of welcome. 'Are you back for good?' was all he could find to say.

'The duration of my return, *c'est mon affaire.*' She went into the bedroom and witnessed an appalling mess. He'd clearly been using her bed, which was unmade. She returned to the sitting room. 'You will move your things out of here again.'

There was no reaction. He got up, but only to move to the Louis Quinze table in order to pick up a silver wind instrument lying on it. This looked new - a saxophone, was it? He produced two bars of syncopated noise from it, which sounded like a snatch of sound from a fourth-rate nightclub.

'Paul, have you gone out of your mind?'

'No, into it.'

She went back into the bedroom, tore the sheets off the bed, flung them into the sitting room and, taking the suitcases which had now arrived, retreated into the bedroom again, slamming the door behind her and locking it. In an hour or so she had calmed herself. It was of course the sort of behaviour to be expected from such a low mentality as Paul's.   She'd introduce divorce proceedings at the earliest opportunity.   Meanwhile he was to be ignored.

What was important was to renew her acquaintance with the rest of the community and, for as long as she chose to stay here, to make sure things continued as before.   Indeed, she told herself with an access of pleasure, she might expect to garner a little of that esteem which her success must have earned her.   Was it even possible that Liz might have had second thoughts, now there'd been time for the reality of their relationship to take root in her conservative nature?   She thought a tour of individual visits would be preferable to appearing unannounced at supper.   June should be her first port of call.

June was not in her workshop, and there was no smoke from Alfonso's forge, she noticed.   She put her head round the door and saw the place was empty.   She mounted in the new lift to June's room on the top floor.   At the door she paused.   There was some kind of a rumpus going on inside.   At first she thought it was a row, then she realised they were both laughing very loudly.   'Alfonso, you marvellous darling man,' she heard June say in a most uncharacteristically theatrical way.   She knocked.

They took their time.   There was more laughter and speech before in a moment or two June opened the door.   'Oh it's you, Hortense.   You're back.   We've all been wondering where you were.   Come in.   We've just had the most wonderful news.   It looks as if Alfonso has sold his telescope to the Quango after all. They seem to have given in over the changes they wanted, and are willing to offer a new contract with an even higher price.   Isn't it wonderful?'

Hortense had never seen June look so radiant.   She entered the untidy, gloomy, hessian-walled room, and found herself snatched round the waist by Alfonso who waltzed her in several dizzy circles.   'I sell big telescope,' he shouted in her ear, 'including lazy God.'

Hortense extricated herself, and a little order was restored. Stretching her arm fully forward she offered congratulations to each of them in turn.

June managed to quieten herself, though there were two silly tears half way down her cheeks. 'Oh, it's such a wonderful day, Hortense,' she said. 'Damon, too, has had a letter from his editor - which though not a definite acceptance of his book yet is very complimentary and encouraging. Alfonso has had this success, and then there is your marvellous exhibition. Liz has told us about the first evening, and we've read about it in the papers. Congratulations to *you*. We're all so pleased for you. At last, it seems, my idea has really worked - several things at once, as if it were planned and ordained from the start. It's all been so worth it. We'll have to have a celebration. I shall give a celebration . . .'

At this point Hortense was standing by the window and saw to her complete astonishment and chagrin that Steve Addicot was briskly passing below. She had quite a lot of difficulty breaking in to June's euphoria. '*Steve,* June,' she had to repeat. 'That is Stephen Addicot who is just passing below.'

June calmed herself. 'Yes, it seems Steve is back, too, she said. 'He returned this morning.'

'Permanently?'

'There's no reason to think not.'

'But - the others? You mean people are accepting it?'

'I'm really not too sure,' she muttered, looking at Alfonso, who was still grinning in his deranged way. 'Perhaps . . .'

'Perhaps *what*, June? There is surely not being perhaps about it. We have decided to banish him. We are not wanting him here. *De plus*, I am not imagining his wife . . .'

June found some resolution. 'I don't know what Jubilee thinks, Hortense,' she said. 'Maybe she's forgiven him. Perhaps it wasn't such a serious dispute after all? Anyway it's surely now no business of ours. Honestly, Hortense, with all this good news, I wonder if anyone is going to feel like doing anything drastic again.'

'What's good news got to do with it?'

'I should have thought it would make a difference. I'd've thought that you, too, with your success might . . .'

'Might what?'

June coloured. 'Well you, I imagine, were partly at least the cause of Steve's estrangement from Jubilee. I should have

289

thought you'd be pleased the damage may turn out to be limited, if it is. You told us once you had no feelings for Steve either way. I've always wondered actually why, given this, you did what you did. I'm sure it was your initiative, not Steve's, what happened that day - whatever *did* happen.'

Hortense was livid. Clearly Alfonso's little success had gone to the woman's essentially bourgeois head. They had for much too long, in her estimation, shown deference to June because she'd once owned the lease of the Château. Well now she didn't own it. What status had she - an enamel worker, a mere craftswoman? There were stronger spirits in the place to rally than her. It wasn't even worth showing annoyance.

'I think *autrement*. Addicot's presence is *inacceptable*. He is having no place here. I shall try for his second departure. This one will be final, *je t'assure.*'

The place was swarming with foreigners. In the hall Hortense saw three Japanese golfers with their gear, apparently waiting for a taxi. She was asked the time by some freakish woman in a hat - Scandinavian to judge by the accent. Outside she was stared at by a single man walking about alone under the trees with a shiny black skin. If she was expected to give this lot painting lessons, she'd refuse, she decided.

She strode purposefully in the direction of the north-west tower. This time it would need to be something a lot more direct than montages in the crypt and a photograph. A notion came to her. She mounted the spiral staircase and knocked on the door.

There was no reply. She knocked more loudly with the same result. She tried the handle. The door was locked. She was about to turn away when she heard a noise within.

'Frederick?'

There was a long wait, more sounds. Finally, three bolts were pulled back and the door opened. 'I am no company for anyone,' Frederick said. 'I am broken.'

She marched in past him. Clearly he'd been asleep in one of the chairs. The room was in worse chaos than June's, and smelt disgusting. She only just managed to stop herself going to both windows and flinging them wide open. Instead she sat in an upright and impermanent position in the other armchair. 'Steve Addicot is back.'

'It is immaterial.'

'It is not immaterial. Drastic steps are called for. I have to resume my work at once, and that is *impossible* as long as that man is *chez-nous.*'

Frederick sat and immediately sunk his head into both hands. 'I cannot go on. You know what has happened since you've been away? Damon has stolen Jubilee from me. He has deceived me. All the time he was pretending to help me win her affection, he was secretly courting her himself. They went to Lyon together and stayed the night. Every morning she is with him in his room, their walks together last two hours. One evening he went to her house . . .'

'Well if it's happened, it's happened. You'll just have to forget her. You probably never had much chance anyway.'

Frederick groaned. 'You are merciless. That isn't what you said before. You said I had every chance. You encouraged me.'

He was looking at her now in an accusatory way. *Merde*, the man was flabby. No wonder the Hapsburgs were a flop in history if this was the strain they bred. 'There is a simple solution. *Un incendie* - in his house. It ought to be very easy - in the day, when they're out. You will be able to do it.'

Frederick's look turned to one of horror, and total cowardice. 'Fire?'

'Un *truc electrique de quelque sorte* - no insurance company is being able to complain about that. "Faulty Midi workmanship" - *on peut imaginer la phrase.* But he will know of course, Addicot will know what we intend if he stays.'

Something was happening to Frederick. In a moment he got up. On the top of the worm-eaten chest-of-drawers stood a photograph of a majestic woman with an ample bosom wearing a large hat. This seemed to be the object of his pilgrimage. He stood facing it, with his back to her. 'I wish to have no further part in that sort of thing. I have nothing really against Steve Addicot. He's a decent enough fellow. Actually, in my personal grief, I've come to realise that apart from my feelings about Jubilee I've always been pleased he took over the Château. It would have crumbled otherwise and we couldn't have afforded to stay here. And I enjoy having the guests here. I enjoy taking them out on the bus. I believe I'm not alone in feeling under some sort of obligation to Steve. We've been unjust to him.'

Hortense also rose. 'You are not a man, you are *plasm.* I have been knowing always of course. So, *si les principes te manquent totalement,* I know where I shall go - to the man who "took" Jubilee from you. Actually of course he didn't take her. You were never having her. Damon at least *ne manquera pas à sa parole.'*

Returning to her rooms Hortense found her hands were shaking. For the first time in her life she realised she was afraid. She had always been acutely aware of Damon. She knew he was powerful, that he exercised a tacit influence over all of them. But because he so seldom took the initiative and, like a medieval prince, observed their goings-on through a secret aperture, she'd managed to isolate, even to disregard him. She had now, surely, to face him, perhaps even coerce him.

She sought to escape the ordeal. Why did she have to bother? She had public recognition of her talent now. She imagined herself leaving tomorrow morning for Lézards, setting up her easel. Wouldn't it be different, with most of her early work on the mountain already adorning the walls of the *cognoscenti?* Wouldn't she be powered by a new strength to step further into the mystery and put aside irrelevancies?

This was the horror. She would *not* find that strength, she realised - not automatically. Still haunting her would be those same Furies chanting the same questions. *Could* she do it again? What *new* ground would she break? How easily that sycophantic flock of crows who had crowded around her in Nice would abandon her if she didn't continue to deliver. In her uncertainty, her protective venom against Steve rose again to engulf her.

She remembered that scene in the kitchen when Frederick had demanded and received the vote of confidence for his plans to remove Steve. With the exception of Liz, there was no doubt, the vote had been *nemeni con,* including Damon. Damon hadn't spoken, but he must have known precisely what was intended and made no comment. To a man of his intellect and integrity that was collusion.

On the strength of this notion she took her courage in her hands and went down. She entered his room without knocking. On the far side by the table, Damon stood with Jubilee. They were not touching each other, but very close. They were in the middle of what seemed an intense discussion. Both looked at her in surprise. 'I must ask you to excuse me, Jubilee. I am wanting to speak to Damon alone.' The two exchanged a look. Damon raised his eyebrows in a way Hortense didn't find flattering. But Jubilee left without a word.

She kept it brisk. 'I'm sorry to come in like this but what I have to say is being urgent.' Damon was continuing to stand. 'Can we sit down please?'

Reluctantly he sat at the table. He indicated what apparently had been Jubilee's chair and table beside it. He turned his chair a fraction to face her. She felt extremely nervous. He wasn't giving her the slightest encouragement. She'd had a wild idea of beginning the discussion by referring to his interest - he, surely, as had been the case with Frederick before, could hardly regret the renewed absence of Addicot if it could be brought about? In the event, under his sardonic eye, she at once jettisoned this. Damon wasn't Frederick.

'You can guess why I've come?'

'I can guess.'

'We all took a decision of principle.'

'Did we?'

'You know we did. You included.' She had the satisfaction of seeing his eyes drop. 'Everyone had the chance to speak that evening when we discussed Addicot's purchase of the Château. Only Liz did. *June était d'accord. Tu étais d'accord.*'

'I don't recall expressing an opinion.'

'Neither did you make any opposition.'

His eyes fell again. 'That is correct,' he said quietly.

'I have always imagined you are not a man who is changing his mind for reasons of personal convenience.'

'I hope not. But where justice is involved it can be another matter, can't it?'

'You speak of justice?'

'Precisely that. The man has never been venal.'

'The man is *anathème* to the Château Lamartine.'

'It could be said he is its saviour.'

She stared in disbelief. '*Vous même?*'

'*Moi même.* And incidentally, if we're making accusations, I don't think your behaviour has been exactly honest, has it?'

'You are calling me a liar?'

'You permitted that photograph to be displayed. You permitted it to be thought that you had an affair with Steve Addicot. You allowed Jubilee to think it.'

'What people think, *ce n'est pas mon affaire.*'

'You permitted it - I submit, you wilfully permitted it. A prank is a prank. Your act, and Frederick's, was more than that. It was personally venomous. Liz apart, we've all been guilty in some way, you in a particular way.'

'*Tu veux trouver grâce auprès de Jubilee, c'est tout.*'

'You can think what you like.'

'*Merde,* what a lot of twisting English you all are. *Bien, tu m'as décidé. Je suis finis. Je pars toute de suite, aujourd'hui.*'

This proved to be a fine example of Hortense Beerbohmer's executive statements. She was as good as its intention. She was not seen again by her companions.

38

News was not usually disseminated at great speed at the Château Lamartine. There was a notable exception in this case. June Aguas de Villanova 'Claimed Conclave', the meeting to take place in the chapel at six pm that day. Not wishing to go round herself to issue invitations, she asked Albert Tricot if he could get one of his junior employees to carry out the task. On his agreement, she wrote out the appropriate number of cards.

Accordingly, just before the appointed hour, five people converged on the Château's beautifully refurbished chapel and with a mixture of puzzlement and anticipation on their faces silently filed into the two front rows of the stalls. *Vide*, five, not seven people. Hortense Beerbohmer was not among the number, and June had already taken up position at the bronze lectern as the others arrived. At last all noise ceased.

'Hortense should be here,' said June. 'She has returned.'

'And gone,' said Damon.

'She won't be here,' Paul confirmed. 'She's left for good - in both senses.'

This latter remark was made without bitterness, it was noted, even with an element of humour. It was perhaps because of this rare element of levity from Paul that June seemed to accept the news as being the truth.

'My dear friends,' she said, 'in the past when we've had conclaves it's always been to resolve some difficulty over which we haven't agreed. I believe this one will be different.

'My first object is to make an announcement. We are artists and thinkers. We believe we should do our work like monks and nuns, apart from the world. We have to be deeply critical of the work of course, but I think we all agree we shouldn't be too much concerned with external expectations of what we do. But I've always believed personally that, however much we resist allowing public demand to influence what we produce, we're nonetheless always hopeful that what we create will find a public reaction of some sort - yes, I'll use the word - find a market. We do after all belong to society as much as anyone does.

'Well, this is all very rigmarole-ish. I really don't want to make a speech. What I want to say, first, is that Damon has finished his book and delivered it to his publisher, and the first reactions seem favourable. Hortense, whatever we may sometimes feel about her, is a talented, perhaps an exceptional artist. She's had a deservedly great success with her exhibition in Nice. Lastly I'm happy to announce that Alfonso has heard today that W.C.H.I.S.AR. seems to have changed its mind about his sculpture. It's not yet absolutely certain, but they've invited him to re-submit his work and talk of a new contract with no mention of modifications . . .'

She left a moment or two for this unknown event to be received, but she was interrupted. As if controlled by some hidden mechanism, all those present quite spontaneously rose in their seats, turning some towards June some to Alfonso, and began to applaud. A large audience in a concert hall couldn't have produced a more rousing effect. As the clamour continued with no sign of abating, the speaker clutched the outspread wings of the bronze eagle as if for support and shook her head quite vigorously - more, it was plain, from emotion and confusion than from any wish to deny the acclaim.

Finally, after a final loud 'bravo Juny' from Frederick, the clapping ceased and the five re-took their seats. June regained herself. 'Thank you for that,' she said, and paused. 'Now I must put to you my second point - the reason why I have called this session. It concerns Steve.'

Steve had spent the day of his return in furious activity. Albert, with Jubilee's loyal support, he learnt, had been running the place with impeccable efficiency during his absence, but it was important to him to reconnect himself with everything going on. He read the files, looked at figures, visited the housekeeper, the chef and the head waiter, and chatted to a number of the lesser employees, asking them not only about their work but also about their families and their lives, of which he had already a considerable knowledge.

Necessary as this was, he was conscious of his inner need for this expenditure of extroverted energy. When at odd moments his activity slackened as inevitably it must, he was aware of 'questions' that lay in wait for him like wolves outside a door. He quelled them by thinking of some new direction in which to fling himself. Once for example when on a spirited circuit of the building to see that some new guttering had stood up to a recent outbreak of the mistral, he caught sight of Jubilee in Damon's room. Jubilee was seated and Damon was closely at her side. He was again, more starkly, brought face to face with the waiting predators. But he quickly averted his eyes and continued on his practical mission, which he later extended by a visit to the greenhouses where he found the Lady Elisabeth at work. He had thankfully no difficulty in engaging Liz in an animated conversation about the decorative cactus market into which she was thinking of plunging. She at least, his subconscious mind registered, didn't seem to have any objection to his return, which she took as a matter of course.

At the end of the morning he went into the bar to meet some of the guests. He became involved with the African section of the parliamentarians, a group of eight who kept together and sat at the same table for their meals. When they asked him to join them for lunch, he accepted gratefully.

Amid the first class decor, eating the gourmet food served so expertly by the waiters, they discussed the famous Gorges de Verdon, which the group had arranged to visit during the afternoon in the hotel bus. They invited him to come with them. The afternoon, and what he would do in it, had already been posing a problem to Steve. He accepted this further invitation with relief.

On the return journey he again became conscious of the unavoidable crisis which was closing in on him. He'd managed the initial scene in the office this morning rather well, he thought - but a whole evening alone with Jubilee in their house? Would it really be possible to pick things up where they'd been dropped and carry on as before? An appalling thought occurred to him. Was Jubilee living any longer in their house? He'd had half an ear cocked during his conversation with Liz to learn of any modification in her sleeping arrangements which might have taken place, but with no result. Leaving the Africans, he returned to the house. Jubilee wasn't in. Would she simply not return? He waited in agony.

She came in just before six when he'd drunk two whiskies in the patio and with a pocket dictionary at hand was battling with the journalistic French of *Le Figaro,* which Jubilee had insisted on having delivered. He heard her close the front door quietly and slip into the kitchen. She seemed to be washing her hands. 'Come and have a drink,' he called.

She took her time coming, but appeared at last, carrying a glass of orange juice. She sat beside him. Her face was a mask. He launched into an account of his day, which contained a long, he hoped amusing, passage about his conversations with the Africans. Twice she smiled in quite a natural way. 'Keep your nerve, soldier on,' he kept telling himself. Half the problems of the world would be solved if people avoided analysis and remained positive.

'Well, what sort of day have *you* had?' he asked finally, really out of guilt for having held the floor for so long.

She drank, then ran her finger round the rim of the glass. 'During the morning I mostly typed. Damon has a new article he's just written for an American historical journal. All the afternoon I've been in the pottery.'

Damon - she'd pronounced the word with no emphasis. Was it possible nothing had happened, that it was all platonic, that he'd allowed an inferiority complex to invent what had never taken place? He had to believe so. 'Sorry about lunch,' he went on. 'Hope you weren't expecting me. I actually ate with these good people in the dining room. I should've let you know.'

'It doesn't matter.'

'You mean you prepared lunch?'

'No. It was ready in the fridge if you came.'

He was lured on to more dangerous ground. 'I had an interesting talk with Liz this morning,' he said when they'd both carried out an extensive inspection of the reddening sky.

'You did? What about?'

'Cactus.' He waited. Should he allow that further pace forward? 'She seems in a very normal state of mind.'

'Normal?'

'I rather expected one or two of them might be somewhat hostile, after the little performance in the chapel when the Americans were here. She was entirely amiable.'

'Liz has never objected to the hotel.'

'No, you're right. It's Frederick and Hortense, I suppose, who were the trouble-makers.'

He was on the very point of adding Damon to the list when they both became aware of a disturbance on the other side of the house. It sounded like a group of people approaching. Steve's first thought was that it was some of the guests going for a pre-dinner walk in the grounds. Then there was a pregnant pause and the door bell rang.

Jubilee looked anxious and remained seated. 'My Africans again?' he said. She was silent.

He got up and went to the door. In the hall he could hear their movements outside, though none of them was speaking. He opened the door. It was the inmates, all six of them. June spoke from the centre of the group. 'We'd like to speak to you, Steve, if you have a few minutes.'

Steve found he was very short of breath. 'Speak?' he repeated helplessly. 'Yes, I suppose so. What about?'

June looked embarrassed. 'Could we perhaps come inside?'

He led them into the sitting room. On the way he saw Jubilee disappearing upstairs. 'Let them try any funny tricks,' he told himself. But he was far from feeling defiant. All he felt was a weakness at the knees. He'd been wrong. He'd always been wrong. He'd been trying to buy culture, and in this vain attempt he'd also been trying to buy Jubilee. Whatever he had coming to him he deserved. They sat down in the various chairs about the room. He sat in one of the window seats, facing them. Most bent their heads. Paul looked at the ceiling. Only June looked at him.

'When the community started its life together here,' she began, 'we agreed certain things. One thing was that if we ever had a dispute or if there was ever a need to make a common decision, any one of us could summon what we decided to call a "Conclave", which it'd be obligatory for everyone to attend. A Conclave has to continue until a unanimous decision is reached on the basis of reason. Incidentally, during these times we don't eat or drink.

'We've just held such a meeting. It was called to discuss our attitude to you and to the hotel. What we've come here to say is that we've decided unanimously, in a very short space of time, that we want to make a very sincere apology to you.

'I regard myself as the principle offender. I confess that when I first invited you here I had an ulterior motive at the back of my mind. It was nice to see you again after all the years, but I'd just lost my job at the time, financially we were in desperate straits, and of course I knew you were pretty wealthy. Although I never formulated then just how it might happen, in a vague way I think I did hope that somehow or other you might help, perhaps even rescue, us.

'Well, that's of course just what you did do, though hardly in the way I'd imagined. You met me that day in Nice . . . and everything that's happened followed from then. But having a vague idea of extracting money from you wasn't the really shameful thing I did. I suppose that wasn't very noble, but it wasn't in any way malicious. The shameful thing I did happened afterwards. As I'm sure you were only too well aware when you bought the Château, there was a general feeling of hostility towards you, as there so often is towards a benefactor. We resented that you repaired and made more beautiful "our" Château, and romantically thought it had been much nicer in its previous crumbling state. Although we honoured our contract to render our dues to you, we bitterly opposed the idea of the hotel and, above all, the energy you used to run it and make it a success. We wanted to force you to go. All of us knew that an attempt would be made to do so. In that sense we were all a party to what happened. We persuaded ourselves that wealth and business enterprise is the enemy of art and thought. We now realise we were wrong. Where, for example, on a much grander scale, would the Renaissance have been without the great patrons? This is what we want to say to you. I hope I've said it right. We want you to know that in the future you can count on our complete cooperation and support.'

All but one of the heads had risen. Paul's, Liz's, Alfonso's, even Frederick's. Alfonso, without doubt the architect of the levitated *pissoir*, was grinning hugely. But Steve realised one head was missing. 'Hortense isn't here,' he said.

'Hortense has left Lamartine.' June said.

'She isn't returning?'

'We don't think so.'

Paul was nodding at this, and seemed pleased to be making the confirmation. Steve was suddenly swept up into a lightness of spirit. He'd won, he'd won after all. He wanted to embrace them all, including Damon - who continued to sit with eyes lowered, he noticed. Jubilee should know at once. She couldn't have realised this was going to happen. 'This calls for a celebration,' he said, jumping up excitedly. 'I must call Jubilee. Champagne. It won't be on ice, but who cares?'

He began to bound towards the door, but was forced to check half way across the room. 'We think so, too, Steve,' June was saying as they all rose with her. 'We think a celebration's in order. We're planning a dinner tomorrow night, if you and Jubilee will come as guests of honour. If you don't mind we'd rather not celebrate tonight.' There were nods. 'There's one more thing we want to say. We want to offer you and Jubilee full membership of the community, which bestows of course the right to call and be summoned to Conclaves.'

He couldn't detain them. They began to file out. Damon, he thought, seemed to be hanging behind the others. Had he another, more personal, apology to make? He was ready to preempt the gesture by making one of his own. He was about to extend his hand. But at last Damon didn't falter. Seeming to decide something, he went out with the others, still averting his eyes.

As soon as the door closed he flew upstairs to the bedroom. Jubilee had started a new hobby of making artificial flowers in silk. She was kneeling on the floor, busily engaged in cutting out the pieces. Brown paper patterns were pinned to the material.

'Jubilee, they came to apologise. They want us to belong to their - thing.'

She didn't stop snipping. 'I'm so glad,' she said.

'You mean you know?'

'I thought it might be something like that when I saw them coming. When I heard the kind of noise there was coming from below, I was sure. It was June speaking, wasn't it?'

'Yes. She spoke for them all. But - you don't seem pleased?'

She put down the scissors, rose, and came to him. She put her arms round his neck and her cheek against his. 'Of course I'm pleased. It's what you deserve.' She gave him a short squeeze.

He was fevered with love for her. Had they found each other again? He withdrew his head to kiss her. She pulled away. He had to drop his arms and release her.

'Jubilee, I never, you know . . . that day with Hortense. She *dared* me to swim with her like that.'

'I know.'

'How do you know?'

'Damon told me. He talked to Frederick. Frederick set some minion of his from the village to follow you with a camera. He suspected that Hortense would get up to something of the sort. Apparently, it's a habit of hers to swim in the nude, regardless of the company. She's done it with other people, hoping to make them feel prudish if they don't do the same.'

'That's exactly what she did. So you don't . . .'

'I don't blame you for that day, no. I don't think I ever did. What I blame you for is concealing it, for making it so important when it was nothing. I blame you for your whole misunderstanding of the community, the worthwhileness of what they are doing - and also of course their silly childishness, which you shouldn't have taken so seriously.'

'But it's different now. I've learnt my lesson.'

'*Have* you?'

Her alienation hit him like a sandbag. He had to know all of a sudden. He couldn't keep up this fencing any longer, it wasn't

302

his nature. He had to know, even if it was news which would devastate his life. 'You're in love with Damon,' he said. She turned her head away. 'You've been having an affair.'

'No, that's not true.'

'You admire him because he has an academic mind and I have a prosaic business one.'

'I admire Damon's mind certainly.'

'And his youth. I'm too old for you.'

'No, I've never considered that.'

'Well, what are you going to do then - leave me?'

'I think you ought to remember that it was you who left me, Steve.'

'But now I'm back. So what are you going to do?' She kneeled and took up the scissors again. 'Damon wants you to leave me and marry him, is that it?'

She refused to answer. To hide a torment of misery which fell on him he went out. He went out and walked for a long time in the woods. When he returned she'd gone to bed. The light was out and she seemed to be asleep.

Jubilee's morning awakenings were nearly always joyful. Waking, to her, was like the opening of a door on to a new garden of wonders. She always lay for a minute or two thinking of what she would do that day and savouring the prospect.

The following morning this didn't happen. She'd had dreams which she couldn't remember but which she knew had been confused and difficult. She felt heavy. What pained her most was that she knew she'd have to go on being neutral, both to Steve and Damon. The truth was she didn't know what she felt.

She thought the best thing might be to do some enamelling, and as soon as she could escape the horribly non-committal breakfast she had with Steve, she slipped out. He, too, was heavy and sad. She couldn't bear to witness his distress, of which she was now undoubtedly the cause.

June came down when she'd been working for some time, full of Alfonso's success, of the reconciliation with Steve, of her natural joy that her idea of a cultural community had been so well vindicated. For a while Jubilee was able to elevate her spirits enough to join with her, but they soon fell back again. Did June know about her problem? Surely she must guess, after Lyon? She'd sensed that people were guessing a great deal more than was justified, and June must have noticed Liz's low spirits. But if she did, she gave no sign of it.

At lunchtime Jubilee went back to the house. She thought Steve would come in, and set about some lunch for him. It would be churlish, she thought, to be as casual as she had been yesterday. Before she went into the kitchen she went upstairs. The bedroom was a mess. In her haste earlier she hadn't made the bed and there were clothes everywhere.

Steve had hung the jacket of the light suit he was wearing yesterday on the back of a chair, the trousers flung carelessly over the top. She took the coat and as usual began to go through the pockets for bulky objects that would pull them out of shape. She made the usual harvest. Among the objects was a folder with his used air-ticket inside it. Opening it to make sure it was no longer valid, she noticed on the bottom copy, which remained, that his flight from London had been via Paris, where he appeared to have spent three days. Had he been sightseeing? Mildly interested, she threw the paper away.

That she mentioned it when they were eating a salad in the kitchen was from lack of things to say. 'Oh yes,' he said dully. 'I did drop in there for a couple of nights.'

'To sightsee?'

'I went to Versailles.' He had yesterday's Financial Times on his side-plate, folded at an article. His tone was flat, and he pretended to go on reading.

She debated whether to drop it. What was the point of trying to make conversation? But she was intrigued. Versailles, she asked herself. He couldn't have been to see the Palace for three days, and Steve had never voluntarily been sightseeing in his life.

'You saw the Palace?'

'No. The Quango.'

She began to guess. 'You mean the place which has bought Alfonso's telescope?'

Steve nodded. 'Yes, I gave them a ring from England and

304

found they hadn't yet commissioned another work of art to replace Alfonso's. Also there'd been a change of personnel director. I thought it was an opportunity. Anyway, to cut a fairly long story short, it turned out that, by a lucky chance, the new bloke was anxious to upstage his predecessor. I got him finally to send an unofficial letter to Alfonso asking him to re-apply. Apparently there've been some changes in the top brass as well, and he thought there were good odds they'd agree this time if it was handled right.'

'But what about the God business? How did you get over that? They're not insisting on changes any more, are they?'

He looked sheepish, and made as if he was returning to the paper. 'Oh, probably the less said about that the better.'

'Steve, tell me. How did you persuade them?'

'I think it's better it remains confidential. I probably did the wrong thing as usual.'

'I'm sure you didn't. What did you say?'

'I told Topolski to buy the thing, then make some minor adjustments. They'll own the copyright then, and there are to be some little jiggles in the small print. Hope no one here finds out I've been involved or I'll be for the high jump.'

'What "minor jiggles"?'

'Well, I thought leave the chocolates - no one will see them at that height. Make the hammock into a cloud, and let the old boy grab those ropes with both hands as if he meant to haul them up. Who the hell's going to care, or even notice, except Alfonso? I'm not even sure he would now.'

'You mean you're responsible for Alfonso selling his telescope, and you did all this for the Château - after what they did to you?'

'Yes.'

'But - why, Steve? Why have you done this?'

He looked sheepish again. 'I didn't tell you much about the funeral. The people who came were pretty slaggish. Blamed me for Mum's death almost. I neglected her, I was stingy to her - that's what they were all thinking. They hardly bothered to conceal it. But going back to Mum's house afterwards I found I couldn't blame them. Their lives aren't so interesting probably. They *need* something to blame, I thought. I found, when I thought about it, that that was OK by me. Perhaps I was sort of doing them a service by being a receptacle for their feelings. Then I thought of myself and the Château, and how I'd behaved to the inmates. Wasn't it the same thing really, in another disguise? They hadn't being doing so well either, then I came along and did what I did - in the way I did. It was natural, looking back, the way they reacted. I'd asked for it. Anyway, I made up my mind I was coming back. And this was quite apart from you. I've come back, and I'm staying, Jubilee, whatever you decide. I'm staying to do the job I decided to do. I might even stay here for good. I think I'm going to like the job.'

Jubilee couldn't understand what was happening to her. She was meant to be being serious, wasn't she, deeply upset because of the rift that had opened between them? She *had* been upset. But now she found she had only an overwhelming desire to giggle. It started somewhere down in her chest and crept upwards and downwards and outwards. It became a laugh. She was soon helpless.

Steve gaped at her. 'What's so funny?' he said.

'*You're* so funny. You're so hopelessly, darling-ly funny. You went to all that trouble for Alfonso - after what he and the others did to you. And you pulled it off - I can just imagine the serious civil servant in a plush office, and you running circles round him. Then you've turned them all round here and got them eating out of your hand. You run circles round everybody. You're so direct, and you understand so well what life's about. I love you. I've never stopped loving you. Don't you realise that, you silly man.'

It was a moment or two before Steve caught the wavelength. Then he, too, began to see his achievement from Jubilee's angle and found it funny as well. He wasn't quite sure which was his predominant emotion in these moments - amusement, surprise, relief, or being in love with Jubilee. Probably they were intermingled.

39

Summer was gone. When Frederick Hapsburg-Trench threw open his window the morning air had a nip which reminded him pleasingly of a fine autumn day in England. A light frost had whitened the dapper lawns below, and rosy sunshine was filtering through the pines. Turning away to the wash-basin in which he had decided to shave and wash, he began to whistle 'Men of Harlech.' Later, after towelling vigorously, he donned clean underclothing (for some months now he'd clandestinely used the hotel laundry services) and as a last thought opened the diminished bottle of after-shave, which he hadn't touched since a certain occasion.

They were expecting the second group of American tourists who, booked through another agency, were happily ignorant of the traumas experienced by their compatriots. They'd asked for the cultural activities - what Damon had recently named 'the ampler amenity.' Frederick was now involved with all the groups visiting the hotel, even those like the parliamentarians who had not elected for culture. By his own styling, he was 'Transport and Communications Officer,' a full-time post which commanded a salary. It was the latter which accounted for the well tailored dark-grey suit he now wore, and the flamboyant tie.

In good time he was off with the driver in the Château bus in the direction of Nice airport and another group of Americans who, emerging from customs and meeting a spruce figure awaiting them, would be puzzled anew by that unusual mixture of apparent subservience allied to an undoubtedly elevated level of culture.

The rising of Liz and Damon Raspin, if not having the overtones of pleasure as that of Frederick, had also some positive elements. Liz woke first. Looking at her consort's still sleeping face beside her, she was moved strongly.

She knew all that had happened. When there is less speech between two human beings other methods of communication develop. She knew well of Damon's love for Jubilee, she knew that had it fruited it wouldn't have been like his other liaisons (and one of her own). They would have parted. That Damon's love hadn't been reciprocated had naturally been gratifying to her. At the same time she'd been deeply sorry for his pain. Nothing was ever said between them, but she'd tried to nurse him by going out of her way to do small unostentatious things to please him, pretending they were normal occurrences. She knew by the way he nodded his head almost imperceptibly or made that audible indrawing of breath of his that her offerings were noted and accepted.

Liz thought regretfully they would have to leave the Château. When the book was accepted there would be some money - she thought that would have to be the moment. The girl no longer came to the room in the mornings but inevitably she was about the place - and the Addicots, as new members of the community, had even taken to sharing their evening meal in the kitchen sometimes. But a month had passed now and there was no move.

She came then to see that Damon, hand over hand, by a process of attrition of himself and, she hoped, perhaps a little from the silent balms she offered, would come back to her. It was the behaviour of a true philosopher, she thought. If any certainties of her own existed, they seemed inborn. Damon's came from the heroic application of his mind.

On this morning indicated, in an access of love she couldn't control, she leaned over him and warmly kissed his ear. He stirred. His eyes opened and encountered hers above him. 'What's this - fire?' he said.

She smirked at him, and lowered her eyes to observe the delicious curve of his humorous mouth. 'Raging,' she said. She pulled herself away from him and began to get up from the mattress. 'I have mushrooms for breakfast. A new find in the woods I've told no one about. We'll eat them here. They're much too good to share.'

Paul Beerbohmer woke and found his body diagonally across the emperor-size bed. He rose with unusual alacrity and went straight to the saxophone. He'd remembered this was the day his fellow Americans were arriving. Frederick had asked him to put on a jazz concert this evening.   He began to finger his way into the solo piece he'd written especially for the occasion.   It was entitled 'Château Lamartine - Nightingale Tones,' inspired by the song of one of these creatures, which sang regularly in the Château grounds.

June and Alfonso Aguas de Villanova were up at dawn and over in the tower. Alfonso, leaving things until the last moment as usual, had been labouring for two long days with a hired electric saw. He'd removed the temporary light metal capping of the tower and, beginning at the top, had stripped away the floorboards - and the cross beams on which they rested - of two and a half of the floors. As the steel bars of the telescope penetrated the flooring through holes he had bored, the boards had not only to be cut at the ends but, to be free from the sculpture, incisions had to be made from their sides inwards at all the points where they were the rods passed through.

Half of the planks of the first staging had still to be sawn, while held upwards by ropes attached to pulleys fastened to the walls of the tower.   Then, when freed at the ends and where necessary from the bars, they had to be twisted sideways, fed through one of the slits in the lower part of the tower, and pushed out. June was providing the essential balancing and steering of the planks for this operation.

After two hours of energetic labour there were only two cross beams left, on which the floorboards had rested.   Alfonso had been careful to construct his tower in such a way that no bars penetrated these beams, but they lay loose in recesses in the walls of the tower on either side and were heavy.   His plan was to cut them in two places, holding up the centre sections with the ropes and pulleys he'd used for the boards. This was both to prevent these sections from falling and to obviate the pinching or snapping of the saw blade.   While they were lowered to the ground, the four outer lengths would still be held horizontal in their deep sockets in the walls.   Finally, by roping up each of these in turn, it was a question of easing them out of their sockets in the wall by raising and lowering them on the pulley and, when they were wriggled free, again lowering them to the ground.

Finally, Alfonso was able to drag them out through the door.

A final job remained. Because of the flooring, it hadn't been possible to affix in advance the six large figures which were to adorn the inside of the sculpture. This was a comparatively easy task. The figures were purposely not heavy, being made of a steel much lighter and finer than that of the rest of the structure, and Alfonso had fixed ready a pulley at the top of the tower by means of which each figure could be brought to its correct position. He had made these sitings accessible from the spiral stone staircase which mounted the inside of the tower. From the staircase he bolted them in. The other larger figures - to be deployed on the ground at the foot of the tower and outside it - had already been temporarily shackled to the bottom regions of the structure.

The couple sat outside the tower on one of the lowered beams and wiped the sweat from their faces. '*Coño*,' said Alfonso, looking up. He used the Spanish word with some fervour. 'Joo old pig. Soon big flying pig, eh Juni?' He gave a raucous laugh, then remembering one of those English idioms which seemed to wedge in his mind more easily than other forms of speech, added 'Eef pigs had wings.'

Two further crucial events took place. Just before lunchtime Jan Topolski arrived by road with his assistant Miss Ann Flowers. Frederick, by this time having arrived back from Nice with his cargo of guests, received the two of them at the door with an appropriate flourish before taking them into the bar for drinks. An excess of courtesy then inspired him to address them as a married couple. It is worth noting *en passant* that this brought no correction or adverse reaction from either party, only an amused eye contact between the pair.

The second event, towards three, was the descent from the sky of the powerful helicopter. The guests had been alerted of this unusual arrival and of the reason for it. With the effects of a delicious lunch and accompanying wines still with them, and herded by Frederick, they gathered in a large excited knot on the gravelled terrace to watch its descent onto one of the lawns.

The two crew were taken inside for some fairly rapid refreshment, then the main drama commenced. Frederick, now at last completely in his element in his new-found profession and deploying his organisational skills with zest, steered his charges towards 'the launching tower' as he described it. In groups of six or so he took them inside to view the marvel and to watch Alfonso fussing over last details - he was half way up the spiral staircase at this moment attaching fenders made of sheeps' wool stuffed into leather bags to the walls to keep the lower and wider half of the telescope steady as it was withdrawn upwards. Then, when the engines of the aircraft started up on the other side of the Château, they were all outside, agog, and telling themselves it was scarcely possible that Frederick's explanation of what was to happen could turn out to be right.

The helicopter came in sight over the grey tiles of the Château's roof, its two blades twisting, and making a deafening roar. It steadied, stopped, and hovered. Three cables began to feed downwards into the open tower.

Inside, Alfonso was now assisted by Paul Beerbohmer and Damon Raspin. They'd mounted the tower by means of the spiral staircase then, clambering precariously into the structure along the struts, they shackled the cables to the waiting bolts about a third of the way down from the top. They all descended, and Paul and Damon left the building. At the last, Alfonso stood alone on the floor of the tower, earphoned and microphoned, sledgehammer in hand. He ordered the pilot to 'take slack,' the agreed signal. The helicopter rose fractionally so that the cables were almost but not completely taut.

'Ready to raise,' announced the second crewman from on high.

In its final position before the headquarters of the World Council, the modern Tower of Babel, in its secondary suggestive role as a telescope probing space, would be slightly leaning. In consequence the bottom rim of the structure would not be firmly on the ground but, as Alfonso had described it, balanced on one toe like a ballerina. It was this toe he now attended to. With a single well-aimed blow he knocked out the shackle which was the last physical link of this creative work of art with the Château Lamartine. 'E-shackle gone,' he reported.

Outside, the onlookers saw the cables strain as the full weight was taken. They saw the helicopter then almost imperceptibly rising further. The top of the telescope appeared, then metre by metre its entire length. They watched tensely, in awe at the spectacle, and aghast at the thought something might go wrong.

But nothing went wrong. The unsymmetrical base of the telescope broke free of its massive sheath, and the whole structure gave a small swing to either side as if in pleasure at its first tasting of a new-found freedom. There was further brief radio communication.

'The pig flies.'

'I read you. The pig flies, and we're ready to go.'

Alfonso emerged from the tower door just as the helicopter began to move away, and a spontaneous cheer went up. Included in the cheer were the voices, not only of the new guests, but of the entire staff of the hotel and the now eight members of the community. Liz and June, who happened to be standing next to each other, noticed simultaneously that their two most newly elected members, standing a little apart from the rest of them with their heads turned skywards, were holding hands. At the sight, they turned to each other and exchanged radiant smiles.

'A Healthy Contempt.' Maynard Temple, a worldly Cambridge don and successful TV historian lives with his talented wife, Rachel, a biographer. They have a young son. Their relationship is open, loving, rooted, until Rachel's sister, Rhoda, comes out of prison where she has served a sentence for an episode of violent idealism. Maynard contains his distaste for Rhoda's strident martyrdom to causes until he suspects her attitude to him goes beyond random dislike. To defend his marriage, against all his liberal principles, he is driven to an extreme act which tears his life apart. (Hard back. First published in 1993. UK price: £14.95. UK postage included).

'The Carthaginian Hoard.' Sir Alan Silverman, eminent archaeologist and discoverer of the legendary hoard in the Central Sahara in 1936, is buried in Westminster Abbey with full state pomp. But does he merit the international reputation he has won? Claudia Drake, his biographer, thinks so. But left-wing freelance journalist, Michael Strode, has another opinion. He guesses Silverman knew a lot more about the murder of one of his British assistants than ever came out. In an unlikely alliance, the two go out to Sahara, a vicious dictatorship, to find the truth. Amid unforeseen perils and hardship, they find their courage challenged and their view of each other changed. (Hard back. First published in 1997. UK price: £15.95 UK postage included).

'Second Time Round'. 'Rent a muscle . . . you must frighten him,' Jocelyn is told. 'Take out an injunction,' advises her daughter. Jocelyn thinks otherwise, for she knows the law will be ineffective against anyone like Leo, her ex-husband, who is pursuing her. She knows she must change her name, and disappear.

She takes a job in a large garden in Devon open to the public run by Henry Bordeaux, an ex-commando colonel. Henry is a kind and sympathetic employer and for a while she is happy at a job she finds she is good at. But she is threatened from two directions. Delia Bordeaux, afflicted with a terrible injury and bedridden, is jealous of her and willing as it turns out to go to any lengths to discomfort her. Then, when this problem seems resolved and a chance of real happiness dawns, Jocelyn is assaulted anew. Has Leo discovered her whereabouts and will he reappear? What will her feelings be if he does?

'In a second marriage there is always a locked room.' (Paperback. First published in 2000. UK price: £6.99, plus postage).

Collected Short Stories. Does a successful Midi butcher's wife know of her husband's fidelity, or is she really in the power of a famous and deceased French artist? A primary schoolmistress, en route for a holiday in Dubai with her sister, departs from the minute instructions given by a bossy brother in law. Will he discover what she did, and what will be his reaction if he does? Will the egotistic fictions of an ebullient tour guide be revealed when his shrewish wife unexpectedly joins one of his tours to Oxford? Such questions, and many others, yield quirky, often ironic answers. The author adds to his novels a collection of stories of colour and variety. (UK price: £7.99, plus postage).

Orders to:

Benchmark Press
Little Hatherden
Near Andover
Hampshire
SP11 OHY.
Fax: 01264/735205   Tel: 01264/735262